Nineteen Hundred and Ninety-Two

A Novel
by

Chiggers L. Stokes

Published by:

Flying *S* Press
2674 Dowans Creek Road
Forks, WA 98331
telephone: 360-374-2444
chiggers@olypen.com

Printed in the USA, July, 2006, by Lightning Source, Inc.

ISBN 0-9786941-0-4

Price - $12.95 USA

Cover © copyright 2006 by Carol Simons, a Pacific Northwest artist. Largely self taught Ms. Simons enjoys working in Acrylic, oil, watercolor, and colored pencil. Her favorite subjects include wildlife, seascapes, and landscapes. In the Forks' locality, her work can be seen in West Wind Gallery, The Inn Place, and The Smokehouse Restaurant. She can also be contacted at her studio at: 360-374-6545.

I would like to acknowledge...

...the hundreds of hours of painstaking review and corrections volunteered to this project by my editor and agent, Bogachiel Beth Rossow. Thank you, Bethy, for believing in me as a writer.

Apologia

Although woven on a framework of historical fact and eyewitness accounts to contemporary events, the basis of this story is a highly fictionalized confabulation, depending on imaginary characters. In hopes of capturing the reader's interest, I have accounted what little purchase of the facts surrounding Native America I possess, together with the entire sum of my imagination. To reach such a preposterous end, as is revealed in the conclusion of this story, I bankrupted my finite inventiveness and the pages are filled with names of characters that resemble real life equivalents. But, that being said, **this book is a work of fiction. People, places and events are the product of the author's imagination. Any resemblance to actual persons, either living or dead, or historical events, is purely coincidental.**

This story is dedicated ...

...to the elusive goals of peace and social justice. If within the pages occurs any affront to individual or organizations, I remain ready to change the text or personally burn your copy of this book. I am...

Chiggers L. Stokes

"It may be regarded as certain that not a foot of land will ever be taken from the Indians without their consent. The sacredness of their rights is felt by all thinking persons in America as much as in Europe."
- Thomas Jefferson
President of the United States

"Let it be signified to me through any channel that the possession of the Floridas would be desirable to the United States, and in sixty days it will be (taken from the Seminoles)."

- Andrew Jackson
President of the United States

"...you are instructed to pursue and engage (the Sioux) with vindictive earnestness, even to extermination."

- President Ulysses Grant
President of the United States
(Orders given to General George Armstrong Custer, Seventh Cavalry)

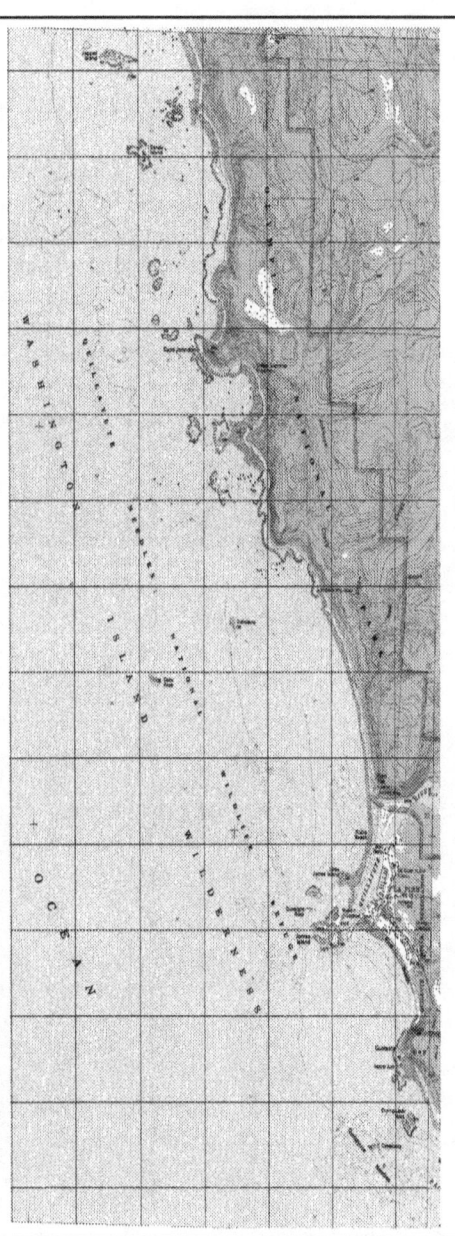

Prologue

At the far northwest corner of the northwestern United States, protrudes a thumb of land known as the Olympic Peninsula. Poised as if hitchhiking from the clenched fist of mainland Washington, the peninsula points to Asia, from whence came hominoids across the Bering Bridge in millennia long past. While a miniature species of horse exited to develop in size in Eurasia, perhaps passing the hominoids in their exodus, the American continents drifted on a sea of molten magma…until the horses returned as vehicles of conquest and war against the great, greater, greatest ancestors of the hominoid immigrants. The horse, the hominoids, and even the continents were pushed along on centrifugal sails to complete the hoop: The Sacred Hoop, that sees no end or beginning…like the cycle of water which falls as rain into the ocean from which it came…like a book bound by an endless spiral of words…

ONE

LaPush, Washington
Wednesday, November 4, 1992, 14:20 hours

*T*he Native American stooped over, holding onto the gunwales of the dugout as he stepped out of the boat onto the rocky and eroding jetty leading to James Island. A salty, wet wind whipped over the jetty lifting the man's rain hat. *The same agency that constructed this jetty had also given Native America the massacres of Sand Creek and Horseshoe Bend.* He clenched the middle fingertip of the right hand glove between his teeth and pulled the wool from his hand with a yank of his head. The glove flapped from his mouth like a windsock as he tied the chinstraps of the Nor'wester hat. Clarence shucked off the life jacket, and threw it into the canoe. He looked across the choppy tidewater to the small reservation village of LaPush. Even minutes before low tide, the furious ocean sent large swells up the Quileute River. A plains Indian by ancestry and experience, the coastal environment presented an antipodal realm from the Dakotas of his youth. He was a foreigner here, labeled "an outside agitator."

Clarence pulled the heavy cedar boat a few feet up on the rocks. He clambered up the steep leeward face of the jetty to stand in the full force of the ocean gale. He uncoiled the painter in the bow of his boat, and secured it to a large drift-log protruding from the jumble of half buried debris. Clarence buttoned his heavy rain slicker before restoring his glove to his right hand. He began the slow, lumbering 800 foot push into the southwest face of the storm which would lead him to the 300 steps climbing 200 feet to the top of the craggy cliffs of James Island. He skirted several charging waves as the rocky jetty gave way to the natural sandy causeway to the island complex. Clarence checked his watch. He would only be allowed a few minutes on top before the tide came in, reclaiming the brief access it had barely surrendered on this blustery day.

As he climbed the steps, the Coast Guard fog horn, at the top, grew louder. Clarence again pulled off his glove. He fished into pockets, underneath the rain pants, and retrieved two foam ear protectors which he balled up and pushed into each ear canal. If things went according to plan, reflected Clarence, by next week his ears would hear only infinity. The President of the United States, re-elected just yesterday for another four year term, would face challenges that would convulse his Administration, and bring the intolerable conditions of Native Americans to the forefront of world attention....still, the ear protection would help shelter his concentration from the blasts of the fog horn every twenty seconds.

On top of the island, he followed the little way-trail through salal and salmonberry to the unmanned Coast Guard installation. He overlooked the horseshoe bay, articulated by the u-shaped island. Twenty-foot swells invaded the small mouth of the bay and spread out as they rushed to crash onto the small, steeply curved beach below. The spent waves fell back into the spumy debacle. *The rolling roil collapsing into the boiling bowl of the bay...*

7

At the Coast Guard radio shack, the fog horn was deafening even through ear protectors. Clarence bent over and checked the pirate splice he and John Pinn had placed on the 110 volt line coming out of the ground before the line re-entered the shack. Tapping off the Coast Guard's power to the fog horn had been a bold and somewhat unnecessary move on Jeff Spark's part. Electricity for the mission, which would be carried out from this island outpost, could be provided by battery pack, but Sparks had argued that the Coast Guard came onto the island less than twice a year. He pointed out that deep brush and stinging nettle would conceal the pirate line and that, in these days of mega-volt transmission lines, the 110 volt supply line was too rare an opportunity to pass up. The regular power supply might give an edge to the high tech, but jury-rigged, ambush which would emanate from this island bastion. The splice was undisturbed, attesting that there had been no discovery of the new wires that ran through the tangle of foliage.

Clarence stood for a few moments looking west-northwest, out across the tumultuous Pacific Ocean. He saw the Navy's ship, the USS Alamo off in the distance, anchored near the large seastack known as Cake Island. Both the Alamo and Cake Island were dark hulks floating amidst a churning horizon.

As his gaze drifted southward a plume of water ejaculated from the frothy water between two swells. A gray whale sounded briefly, then re-submerged. Usually, the last of the gray whales were well on their way to Baja by this time of the year. Perhaps this individual had been cut off from the herd by storm, or disoriented by the sonar and other electrical noise of the Alamo. For a moment, Clarence reflected on the relationship between the whale and the Alamo LPH (landing platform for helicopters). The village of LaPush was here because the whales chose this bay between James Island and the Quateata headland to regroup on their annual peregrinations. Whatever the Navy said about training maneuvers, the Alamo was here because of the political unrest in LaPush.

Back along the way-trail on the palisades above the bay of James Island, Clarence stepped off the trail and fought his way through the dense underbrush to a point on the northern leg of the horseshoe. This offered an uninterrupted view of Rialto Beach. Below Clarence's vantage, a raven flew north towards the cliff/seastack known as Hole-in-the-Wall. Millennia of Quileute warriors had scanned the horizon from this point, looking for the dots on the sea which portended an attack from the Makah's. To this island had the citizenry of LaPush fled under attack. From its cliff walls and impenetrable brush, they had thrown rocks, spears and boiling water to repel the invaders. This island would again figure profoundly in forming the history of Native Americans.

Clarence again stooped to remove some cut salal revealing the terminal of the pirate wire: a large munitions storage container. He opened the ten latches which hermetically sealed the contents of the box from the watery insults of nature, and checked the red, *POWER ON* l.e.d. of the 12 volt converter. Attached to the converter was a laptop computer and a police issue, hand held traffic radar unit. The "MPH 55" radar unit was mounted onto the stock of one of two projectile ordinances laid out in the box. The two rockets were dubbed *Lightweight Armor Weapons* or

"LAWs" by the military who developed them. They were designed to take out tanks. A parallel connection to the 110 volt line went into a piece of computer hardware taken from a "Tank" arcade game. The "Tank" brain fed its data into the LP-2 serial port of the laptop. Clarence made brief system checks. He re-secured the lid on the box and carefully covered the cache with the cut salal once again.

As he came down the steps he was again looking out over LaPush. For four months LaPush had been a loom upon which Clarence had woven a ponderous blanket in an intricate design, tightening the yarns of traditional Native pride. That blanket, now finished, lay over LaPush. It cloaked the village concealing the true machinations of the loom. Clarence remembered his grandmother at her loom. She'd kept the past alive through her story-telling blankets. The symbols and patterns of woven blankets depicted memorable battles, won and lost, and other historical events of the People.

Clarence chuckled to himself, thinking his metaphoric blanket would make a good saddle for a Trojan Horse filled with warriors. All that was left for Clarence to do was to groom the blanket for loose threads. Such a loose thread was visible now in the form of a human figure passing the point where Clarence had moored the dugout. The stranger was proceeding along the jetty to James Island. Even at this distance Clarence was impressed with the incongruity of the intruder's costume. He was decked out in lightweight, colorful rain gear; the type worn by backpackers. He also wore a aluminum helmet which was standard issue to loggers. From under the "tin hat" blew a flag of long, brown hair. Clarence hurried along to head off the interloper.

Clarence pulled down his hat and pulled up his collar before making contact with the individual, who evidently was intent on a visit to scenic James Island on this stormy November afternoon. As the stranger approached, Clarence growled, "You're on reservation here and you need special permission. Beat it. The tide will cut you off anyway." The stranger said something, but Clarence couldn't make it out. Clarence realized he was still wearing the ear protection, but self consciousness prevailed and, at this juncture, he left them in. Clarence stole a look at the young man's face as they passed each other, and he said more softly, "The tide would cut you off anyway."

When Clarence got back to the dugout, he turned around to see if the trespasser had heeded his warning. In fact, the stranger was just fifty meters behind him. He looked again at the man's face, thinking *I know him from somewhere*. He took off his glove as before, untied the painter, took the ear protection out of his ears and pushed the dugout back into turbulent water. Again taken by self-consciousness, the Indian left the life jacket on the bottom of the canoe. He started up the 15 horsepower engine and powered out across the tidewater to the village. As Clarence looked over his shoulder at the man with long brown hair standing on the jetty, their eyes met and temporarily locked. Clarence then made the identity of the man. He was *Chiggers Stokes,* the choker-setter that John Pinn had roughed up in the Forks tavern the first day Clarence had arrived from Rosebud. They call him *"Hippie,"* remembered Clarence giving up eye contact and concentrating on his hazardous

9

crossing to the village. The name "Hippie" called up a wealth of associations from his college days at New York University in the '60s. "Hippie" was a term that no one in the new left liked much in those days of "yippies" and "freaks." Kind of like the word "Negro" to an Afro- American or "Indian" to a Native. *Still, what's in a name?* reflected Clarence Fourskins.

****

Alkee Creek, Olympic National Forest
November 4, 1992, 10:15 hours

Chiggers Stokes sat in the back of the steaming cab of the pick-up. He was sopping wet, even under his heavy raingear. The rain beat relentlessly on the roof of the "crummy." Stokes took off his tin hat, and pulled his wet, brown hair out from his rain slicker and left it drip drying on his shoulders with the hard hat on his lap. The truck was running, and the defroster was on. The smell of wet men, socks, boots and the flotsam of trash on the floor pervaded the close atmosphere of the truck. He began wiping the condensation from the side window and then rolled it down and back up, as he had seen the hook-tender in the driver's seat do a few minutes before. In the three seconds that the window was down, he could hear John Pinn's chainsaw revving up in the distance over the idle of the pick-up. At the edge of the cut-line, Stokes could see the huge cedars and Doug Fir dancing wildly to the rhythm of the wind.

"The crazy red bastard is going to kill himself for sure this time," one of the choker-setters grumbled from the front seat. "Have the Hippie jog over and fetch him out of there."

Falling trees in this kind of weather was more than a little dangerous. Though it had rained all night, winds were not significant when Soleduck River Logging had arrived for work on this landing. It overlooked several pockets of old growth forest. The fallers had trudged through the woods in the dark to find their cached saws. Before 7 a.m. they were trading chains on the saws, making carburetor adjustments, and studying the problem of falling trees over ten feet in diameter, up a steep hill, to avoid fracturing the valuable wood. Two of the fallers came back to get hydraulic jacks. John Pinn had come back to get a tow chain and a load binder clasp off of a log truck bunker. The saws began biting wood a little after 7 a.m. Since then had come the occasional crack and thunder of the tree giants severed from their stumps as they surrendered to gravity. The wind had arrived before 8 a.m. It had been in crescendo throughout the morning. At 9:15, the repeated tooting from the logging tower, and the message over the talkie-tooters which each logger carried on his suspenders, signaled the end of falling operations for the day. The other fallers had rolled out of there forty-five minutes ago in their own crummy. The four choker-setters, and their boss, were sitting unhappily in their crummy waiting for Pinn. They had gone off pay status 30 minutes earlier.

"Listen, Hippie," said the hook-tender, speaking above the wind-whipped rain drumming down on the shell of the pick-up. "How about if you take your afternoon jog over to the other side of the clear cut? You can get your exercise by dragging Pinn back by his pubic hairs."

Stokes cringed. He was not particularly intimidated by the weather; neither was he taciturn about the terrain between the shelter of the pick-up and Pinn. "There's bad blood between John and me. You know that. Keep calling him on the talkie, or send someone else."

"Stokes, you're a hard worker and good choker-setter. For a hippie you're all right. But if you don't get your ass out of this truck and bring back Pinn, you can jog back to Forks to file for unemployment."

Stokes put his tin hat back on and climbed out of the cab. "Take one of the talkie-tooters with you," said the hook-tender handing Stokes the loggers' mouthpiece to the outside world. "Give three toots if there is a *big* problem."

Across the deep ravine of the clear cut, Stokes could see the huge cedar that Pinn was working on. Pinn had been cutting on it, on and off for three hours, and it had to be ready to come down. In this wind, who knew which way it would fall? Pinn would be trying to fall it uphill and following the cut-line on the palisades above the ravine was the long way to get to Pinn. But going line of sight, down the hill from the landing, across the ravine and up the side of the clear cut beneath Pinn, presumed the tree would fall uphill and stay there. Getting in the way of a runaway tree in slash, would be like stumbling across the pavement of I-5 during rush hour wearing a blindfold. Still, the unease that Stokes felt was not fear of the cedar giant. One could avoid a run away log. Pinn was a different story. Pinn was certifiable and he was *HUGE*. He had almost killed that radio technician from Port Angeles. Viet Nam, or LaPush, or life, or all of the above, had pried open the armor of Pinn's cognitive thinking and gotten at the soft, gray stuff of his inner being. No doubt about it - Pinn was missing a clam shell.

Stokes opted for the high, indirect route and set off at a fast pace, which would not be described as a jog, through the tangle of slash and into the trees on the other side of the cut-line. The trees offered some shelter from the wind and rain. He was able to walk faster, occasionally stepping over or stooping under, haul-back lines, blow-down and timber felled earlier in the day. In less than twenty minutes, he was above Pinn's work site where the large chainsaw was still running. Now he had to find his way down to Pinn without being taken out by the cedar. He chose a diagonal path which allowed him to come in from the clear cut side of where Pinn was warring with the cedar. The top of the cedar swung wildly in the wind making wide arches. "Around and around she goes..." thought Stokes grimly. He came full into Pinn's view, and waved his arms while blowing the whistle attached to his suspenders. Pinn continued to work on the back-cut. The tree was over fifteen feet diameter at breast height. It was a formidable adversary even for Pinn, who was himself a red giant. A chain was wrapped around the trunk and cinched with a load binder. Four wedges were driven into the back cut and an axe was sticking out of the

11

toe of the tree. Pinn, ten feet above, sawed at the back cut with singular purpose. As much as anything, the tree looked like a heretic in the Spanish Inquisition. Stokes did not care to get any closer to Pinn as he worked. Surprising any logger at work was bad business, but tapping Pinn on the shoulder would be like using the horn on a slumbering rhinoceros for a boot dryer.

Stokes picked up a stick and threw it in Pinn's direction. The stick landed within a few feet of Pinn who startled and released his hold on the saw trigger. Hanging onto the brim of his tin hat, he looked up, yet again, at the pendulous cedar boughs above him for widow makers. Pinn looked at the alder stick lying on the ground, the trajectory of which he had seen out of the corner of his vision. Stokes hollered and waved again. Pinn finally looked fully at the choker-setter. Stokes drew his finger across his throat in the universal sign to shut down equipment and pointed to John and then across the ravine to the landing on the other side. His emphatic gestures clearly indicated that John should proceed there. John nodded and then went back to sawing. There was no getting him off the tree. Stokes would take his chances with unemployment.

Two

Alkee Creek, Olympic National Forest
November 4, 1992

*J*ohn Pinn had come out of the crummy this morning like a man sleep walking. His lack of bounce and verve might have been attributed to the incessant rain. However, Pinn's tin hat lay on the floor of the cab and he began walking into the dark woods with the rain spattering on his crew cut. Another logger named Rod had called him back and handed him the hard hat.

"You may need this in case you have to take a shit in it," he joshed. Most of John's co-workers enjoyed the quiet equanimity with which he faced his work world. It was hard to illicit more than a grunt on any given subject, even American Indian law, which had been in the news of late. Some enjoyed teasing this gentle giant.

John took the hard hat without comment and, disappeared into the woods along the cut-line on his way to the other side of the unit. In the pre-dawn, the woods would be quicker and safer than traversing the slash in the ravine. There was a big cedar tree just inside the cut-line which had caught his interest on his way out of the woods the day before.   He had pulled his steel measuring reel around its circumference at chest height on the uphill aspect and it measured 59.5 feet. John had retreated to a point where he could see both the base and top of the mighty cedar. He picked up a stick. Holding the stick vertically, he advanced until the stick was the same scale as the cedar, the bottom of the stick aligning with the toe of the cedar and the top of the stick marking the apical tip of the tree.   He then held the stick horizontally until he found a stump the same unit of distance from the toe of the tree. He paced off the distance between the cedar and stump and found it to be 240 feet. Judging from the canopy, it wouldn't be a record, but, all things considered, it was probably one of the ten biggest Western Red Cedars known in the world.   This morning he would harvest a tree that had shaded the ground since before Jesus Christ was born.

When he got to the tree half an hour later, he prodded in between the folds and ridges of the massive butt of the tree with the handle of his axe. He found a soft spot where the heartwood was superficial to the cambium of the tree and pushed through with the handle. He broke up the rot with several blows of the axe and pulled out the light, dry chunks with gloved hands, throwing the flammable tinder into the wet woods, away from his work area. Working with his flashlight held between his teeth, it took John about half an hour to ascertain that the rotten spot opened into a cavern inside the giant. He would be able to fall this tree with a 48" bar, but, for safety's sake, he would need to chain the trunk above his cut to keep the tree from barber-chairing. He turned off his flashlight on the trip through the woods back to the landing. His thoughts returned to the situation in LaPush involving all the trouble this guy Fourskins had stirred up.   John was overwhelmed by feelings of foreboding which combined with the trepidation and fear he still felt over his horrific experiences in Viet Nam. There in southeast Asia, the American command, in the face of combat, had suggested that there might be casualties for *the good guys*. But

13

here in LaPush, Fourskins had as much as promised annihilation. The attack strategized by Fourskins appeared to promise a crushing defeat for the Native insurgents...*the good guys.* Fourskins' plan called for John Pinn to spearhead the assault. In Viet Nam, he had only his own life and those of his comrades to worry about. In LaPush, his very home was the battleground and his family could be the collateral damage. He felt fury for the predicament of Native America and rage for a government that exported war and suffering, in the name of freedom, to every corner of the globe. But his dark anger did not ameliorate the gnawing in his guts. As he agonized, something inside of him was tearing away rotten heartwood and climbing inside his soul with a four-foot chainsaw.

He got back to the landing and fetched the two tow-chains and a load-binder out of the bed of the crummy. He wrapped the two chains around his chest like a bandoleer. He hung the binder, off its hook, at the X on his chest. He headed back to the tree, down into the clear cut and across the ravine. Back at the tree, he started up the saw. He cut steps into the base of the trunk so that he could place his cut above the ground swell of the mighty tree. He took out the one ear protector he carried, from the front pocket of his hickory shirt, and stuffed it into his good right ear. Viet Nam had left him with a Silver Star, Purple Heart, 10 point veteran preference, and significant impairment to the function of his left ear. He began the face-cut in the uphill side of the cedar which would guide its fall to the forest floor. 'For the greater good of Native America,' Fourskins had carved a face-cut into LaPush. Maybe the village of LaPush predated this tree. Within the week, the reservation town would also fall from its stump of tranquility, and crash devastatingly onto the floor of the United States of America.

A stream of red saw chips sprayed from the saw-cut above John's head. A rich incense of cedar was carried on the quickening wind. The heady smell of the wood, the vibration of the saw, the rain on his tin hat, and the rhythm of the work combined to set him free. He was momentarily aloof from his brooding thoughts. Though his concentration was upon the task of extracting a 250-pound perfectly shaped wedge of wood to make the face, John's spirit mingled with the saw chips and rain. It blew with the wind through the tree tops. His thoughts spun, cutting along the lubricated track of the four foot bar. John's spirit drifted through time and space, and converged with a UH-204 Huey, flying over Southeast Asia on November 30, 1967.

****

The four Hueys hovered above the clearing, next to the smoldering village of Quo Cien, twenty kilometers into the frontier north of DaNang. The targeted village had demonstrated consistently hostile behavior to the American and ARVN presence in the area about 30 kilometers south of the DeMilitarized Zone. There had been several occasions of isolated ARVN patrols coming under heavy attack. A Huey had been taken out ten days ago by a SAM (Surface to Air Missile.) This morning an air strike had been called in upon the target. This enemy entrenchment represented more than a casual threat to the American Command and the Republic of South Viet Nam. There was the usual complication of separating the civilian component from

14

the enemy target. In this war, it was becoming an increasingly fine line, but the presence of the ever-vigilant, sensational-seeking, atrocity-happy, U.S. media dictated at least the appearance of concern for the blurred distinction. Accordingly, the village had been "bombed" with leaflets the previous week. The leaflets had clearly warned of a retaliatory strike, and commanded citizens loyal to the Republic to leave the town and proceed south along patrolled Highway One, to the next village of Trin Byen. The propaganda explained to the villagers that they should leave everything. Assurance was given that all their needs would be provided by the program referred to as the "Vietamization" of refugees. There were cash incentives to anyone who could provide military information regarding enemy movement or strongholds. To date, zero citizens had made the fifteen-kilometer trip to Trin Byen nor had any refugees been spotted along the Highway.

This morning at 09:15 the target had been neutralized by incendiary high-drag bombs and later by artillery fire. At 11:30, ten minutes after the last artillery strike, two Hiller helicopters, and a crop duster, had sprayed the surviving rice paddies, vegetable gardens, and surrounding jungle with Agent Orange. Now, at 14:45, as the Hueys hovered beside the desolated village, there was no sign of life. The mission of the American platoon, and ARVN squad was to: establish control of access and egress to the ruins of the village; to make a systematic search of tunnels and bunkers in the area; and to process and evacuate whatever village survivors they found as Prisoners Of War. From the air it didn't look like there would be a whole lot to this mission. The village was a pile of char and rubble. If there were tunnels within 300 meters of the hamlet, the artillery craters didn't reveal it. A small hill overlooking the village showed fresh digging, but it looked more like an 11th hour attempt at foxholes than of any tunnel activity.

The chatter of 50-caliber machine-gun fire broke out as the gunners in all four helicopters opened fire on the jungle to suppress any enemy movement long enough for the Hueys to touch down, deliver their human cargo, and take off. The helo carrying Lieutenant Johnson landed first, discharging the Loot and eleven GI's. Then came Sergeant Pinn with his eleven-man squad. As the helicopters continued to lay out a din of suppressing fire, Pinn helped each of his men out of the bird and pushed them into the tall grass like a mother grouse settling her chicks. After counting to eleven, Pinn began pulling out cases of C-Rats two at a time: 2, 4, 6, 8...to 36: a case for each member of this U.S. platoon. The ARVN squad (South Vietnamese regulars) would eat their own cooking: dog chow mien, pussy ketchetorie, or gook de jour. With the third bird came the complement of the platoon with a dozen five-gallon cube containers of drinking water. Some of the more chicken shitted of disposition were complaining about drinking water laced with Agent Orange, and human excrement. The third squad, along with the ARVN detachment took the job of carrying the supplies through the tall wet grass, to the wall of jungle vegetation. Pinn, Johnson, and the other two squads made the initial assessment of the village. It had not rained today, but everyone was wet from Agent Orange. The taste and smell was pervasive.

Sizing up the village did not take long. No one could have survived this holocaust. With all the craters pocking the terrain, they would have seen evidence of tunnels had they existed. They saw none. "Where are the POW's we're supposed to process, Loot?. Where are all the bodies we're supposed to count?" asked Pinn of the C.O.

"There must have been an intelligence leak from the ARVN gook command. It looks like the whole village diddy mau-ed before we struck the first match here. My guess is that they went north and they'll be back, maybe with a detachment of regulars. They've got a strategic commitment here that goes beyond a few grass huts and feeble gook minds. We'll have to count on air and satellite surveillance to alert us to anything major coming down the highway. You take that hill over there, overlooking the village, and dig in with your squad. I'll secure the highway to the north with the other two squads. I'll send the gook squad south where they can't get in any trouble. They'll take one radio and the other comes with me. I suggest that you have your men dig in, in case of any mortar fire during the night. It kind of looked from the air like maybe some of the villagers had started the job for you. Shoot anything that moves during the night. If hell breaks loose, we'll come bail your asses out."

The small, bald hill into which Pinn's patrol dug, offered the easiest digging around. The site had been cleared by hand and there was fresh dirt spread around like the villagers were starting some more gook victory gardens. The first clue about what the digging really represented came from Private Harvey Simpson, as he dug his nest in the dirt accompanied by Private Randy Parts.

"Sarge! You better take a look at this!"

Sergeant John Pinn looked into Simpson and Parts' baby foxhole. A human arm projected into the middle of the little pit. "Shake hands with the enemy," said Pinn. "You're not planning on using it for an ashtray or anything are you?" asked Pinn pulling his bayonet from his webbing. Parts spoke for both, "These gooks don't have long enough arms for holding up a poncho or anything useful and this hand would be tapping our heads every time we sit up."

Pinn circumcised the arm from where it emanated from the earth. He took his entrenching tool and struck the exposed bone with a heavy blow, amputating the arm. He threw it into the jungle. "Aw, Sarge threw away a perfectly good arm," teased Parts. Simpson had a penchant for collecting ears and other appendages from the enemy dead. "Pass the word that if any more stiffs turn up to dig around them or through them."

Pinn returned to his own digging. Within a few minutes he had confronted a problem of his own. He struck something solid like a tree root and brushed away the dirt with his hand. He exposed the face of a young Asian casualty. Through the burns and torn skin, Pinn could see that the stiff was of pre-military age, even in this country of warriors in diapers. He preferred to believe that it was a young male. He moved over a couple of feet and began digging again. Before he had gotten down three feet, his shovel encountered another casualty. This one was an infant. He redirected his excavation around the new intrusion. He threw fresh dirt on the civilian casualties. By 18:10 the squad was hunkered down in their holes for the long night. Claymore mines were set, pointing out at the semicircle of the perimeter.

In the fading light the exhumed graves caused rats to visit the men in their places of repose. As light totally surrendered to the night, the ARVN squad began to take mortar fire. It only took a two man army to work a mortar, but it was unsettling to think that the enemy lurked to the south behind the buffer of the two American squads. The men ate their C-Rats in silence. They threw the empty cans at the wall of the jungle. Several U.S. 20-millimeter guns hammered randomly into the countryside. With no forward observer, the ARVN unit was calling, in the blind, for artillery.

At around 23:00 the mortar rounds stopped hammering around the ARVN position and the Army of the Republic came under heavy attack by ground forces. Pinn and his men listened to the ripping sound of the ARVN squad discharging the 20-round clips of their M-16's. After about 30 minutes, the automatic fire became more sporadic. There was the occasional pop of small arms. It sounded like the ARVN squad was being overrun and wiped out. Too bad for them.

"Set your weapons to single-shot fire!" Pinn called out in the darkness. "Fix your bayonets!" There was dead silence for two hours. Then came the dreaded pop of a mortar round being sent skyward. "Incoming!" yelled Pinn. The round landed inside their perimeter shaking the men in their holes and showering them with dirt. Pinn saw the flash from the ruined village a second before he heard the second pop. If he had a radio, he could end the attack by calling in one 20-millimeter round.

The second round almost joined Pinn in his foxhole. The ground vomited Pinn into the air where the concussion carried him horizontally five or six meters. He rolled another four meters before scrambling onto his feet and weaving back to his foxhole. When he jumped back into the hole he was not alone. He stood upon corpses of a naked infant, and the semi-clad body of the prepubescent. The prepubescent wore only a nightshirt and there was no pretending that the casualty was male. When the third pop signaled another incoming round, Pinn realized that he had lost hearing in his left ear. Sharp shrapnel protruded from his flack jacket. The third round landed, leaving a soldier screaming on the perimeter. Round followed round for two hellish hours. There was a brief respite. A Claymore mine was tripped followed by screaming and wailing in the jungle. "Holy shit! There's a million gooks out there!" yelled a soldier. Simultaneously, almost everyone opened up with automatic fire.

"Cease fire! Cease fire! Cease fire!" yelled Pinn, getting the attention of about half of the squad. "No automatic firing! Save your ammunition! No indiscriminate firing!" But the enemy was coming at them in the dark, and all the Claymores were going off. The men were spraying the jungle with their precious bullets. "I need more ammo!" came one cry. "Me, too!" called another soldier. By this time about half the squad had gone to semiautomatic fire and were shooting only identified targets.

There was no shortage of targets. It became evident that some of the foxholes had been overrun. Pinn could see the muzzle blasts of small-arm's fire directed at him from foxholes nearer the perimeter. In the flickering light of the fire fight, Pinn saw one soldier stand up to impale a charging figure with his bayoneted M-16. Before the soldier could retrieve his weapon from the victim, another figure was hacking on him with what looked like a meat cleaver. All three bodies fell into the foxhole.

Then Pinn saw a lone figure charging his position. He fired twice and the figure dropped. He stood up to see if there were any more coming at him in the dark. He was hit square in the chest with a round. Through the flack jacket it felt like he had been hit with a ball bearing, fired from a sling shot. He fell back into the foxhole and replayed the last 20 seconds in his mind. He realized that the shot that got him was fired by the figure that had gone down seven meters from his foxhole. He lay ready, waiting for a silhouette to appear over the lip of his foxhole. He could hear, out of his right ear, that automatic fire had again erupted near what was left of the perimeter. Pinn yelled, "Semiautomatic fire only! Semiautomatic fire only! Semiautomatic..."

A figure dressed in black pajamas jumped over his foxhole. Then another and a third jumped over him. Everyone inside the perimeter was screaming in Vietnamese. Most of the shooting was coming from Simpson's foxhole and from out in the jungle. Pinn knew that he was a dead man. Then he heard Lieutenant Johnson yelling, "Cease fire! Cease fire, you stupid bastards! CEASE FIRE, GOD DAMN IT, YOU STUPID FUCKS!" Pinn's squad was saved.

In the next few minutes it became evident that all that were left standing in Pinn's squad were, himself, and Private Simpson. Randy Parts and a few others were still alive, but they were cut and shot up pretty badly. They were being carried out by stretchers out to the meadow LZ. Things on this hill were too unstable to call for a dust off from here.

"Cool work, Pinn," congratulated Lt. Johnson as the growing light revealed a huge tangle of Vietnamese bodies. "We would have gotten to you sooner, but the ARVN guys got it first and we were on our way to their location. We skirted the village and mostly stayed off the road. By the time we got to the ARVN's, it was all over for them. We were on our way back to the village - which is where we figure the mortar that hit you was - when all this shit happened. When we came in behind them, we stampeded them right into you. It was like driving Bison off a cliff."

"By the time you got here, they had pretty much finished us off," said Pinn. "Most of them got away into the jungle. This was a whole village gone ape shit!" Pinn, Johnson, and Parts surveyed the carnage through bleary eyes. In the stark morning light, bodies lay everywhere. Added to the Vietnamese casualties of the previous night were an untold number that had been exhumed by the mortar fire. Less than five meters from Pinn's foxhole a young Asian boy lay dead in black pajamas. Clutched in the hand of his extended right arm was a .22 caliber single action revolver. Pinn kicked the weapon out of the hand and turned the body over.

The kid couldn't be over 13 years old. He picked up the .22 and opened the cylinder. There were only two cartridges in the weapon. One had been fired. Pinn thought a minute and checked his flack jacket. Shrapnel stuck out like porcupine quills. He pushed gingerly on a small hole in the middle of his flack jacket and extruded the .22 slug.

"Look at this, will ya," stammered Pinn incredulously. "He shot me as he died."

Lieutenant Johnson was impressed. "What could drive a people so crazy that they would send a kid into war with a cap gun with only two rounds in it. That's a .22 short for Christ's sake. The kid would have to stick the gun in someone's mouth to take him out. How are we supposed to respect gook life when they shit all over it themselves?" Lieutenant Johnson walked away in disgust.

Pinn put the slug and cartridges in his pocket. He put the .22 in his pack which was still in his foxhole with the two bodies. Private Simpson approached him. "Uh, Sarge, since you've already got your souvenir, do you mind if I take some trophies before they take the bodies to count them?"

Pinn felt his gorge rise. He wanted Simpson the hell out of his sight. "They're only gooks. Take what you want, Simpson."

"Thanks, Sarge," said Simpson, eagerly unfastening his bayonet from his rifle.

"But whatever you cut off these war dead, Private, I'm cutting the same part off of you."

Simpson walked quickly away from Pinn, who was now sitting in the foxhole with his finger inside the trigger guard of his M-16. Tears began rolling down Pinn's cheeks. His throat constricted in a sob as he swallowed the primordial sound that welled up from inside.

****

The stick landed beside Pinn. He was jerked back to an enormous cedar tree on November 4, 1992. He released the trigger on his saw. He looked up into the tree for widow makers. The stick was alder and it hadn't come out of the cedar. He looked around, and there was the Hippie, standing there, gesticulating that Pinn should shut down and go back to the landing. This tree was almost done and Pinn had no intention of quitting now. He went back to sawing. In ten minutes he shut off his saw. He drove each plastic wedge in a step further with the flat head of the single bit. The tree started to go. There was no point in hollering "timber!" for the Hippie's benefit. It sounded like the whole forest was coming down. John ran off to the side with his saw in one hand and holding onto the brim of his hard hat with the other. The tree groaned louder and cracked. The forest giant snapped branches and tree tops in its way, as it crashed to the forest floor. The earth rocked when it hit. Then there was silence. Trees were swaying in the wake of the fallen giant. Then John was aware of the rain pelting down on his tin hat. He stripped the chain off the trunk of the cedar. He gathered up the rest of his gear. He threw the saw over his shoulder and charged down the hill along the clear cut into the ravine. A Stihl 076 with a four-foot bar is a large saw, but it looked like a toy the way Pinn carried it. When he got to the ravine he un-shouldered the saw to carry it by its handle as he walked out over a log spanning the ravine. It was like a balance beam 30 feet over the little creek in the ravine. Pinn did not want to take a fall from the log with the saber-like dogs of the saw on the back of his neck. When he safely attained the other end of the log, Pinn again shouldered the saw. He charged up the other side of the ravine. He was back to the crummy before the Hippie got back. He threw the chain, the load-binder and his saw into the bed of the pick-up and got into the back of the crummy.

"What kind of logs were you sawing out there all that time, anyway?" asked the hook-tender, yawning.

****

I trudged back up the hill staying in the clear cut so that I could see the cedar coming if that crazy red ape tried to dropped it on my long brown hair. In ten minutes or so, I was back in the woods on the top of the hill and about five hundred feet from the cedar. Whatever Pinn did with the tree then, was none of my concern. But I heard Pinn stop the saw and begin driving his falling wedges. The tree began to fall and it seemed like the whole world was falling with it. Limbs and the tops of other trees were popping and the great cedar was groaning and cracking. The impact of the cedar with the hillside caused a thunderous crash that was as visceral as it was audible. I walked faster to keep distance from the lunatic, Pinn, because I assumed he would then be leaving his work site.

When I got back to the crummy 20 minutes later, Pinn was already there in the truck. He glaciated over to the middle of the back seat to make some room for me. I climbed into the steamy cab. Pinn was half squashing the red neck, Rod Hill, the other unfortunate in the backseat. Pinn's hulk occupied 50% of the entire backseat. Getting a seatbelt on would have required putting the clasp into Pinn's bellybutton, so forget that. No one else wore a seatbelt, anyway. Rod was unusually quiet and Pinn was his usual Cro-Magnon self. He ignored most of the babble coming from the front seat and responded to polite conversation with grunts and monosyllables.

"Say, Hippie," called the hook-tender from behind the wheel as the vehicle proceeded down the precipitous logging road through rutted mud tracks. "Had enough exercise today, or are you still going jogging...or swimming, I should say?"

"Actually, I thought I'd ride my bike down to Three Rivers and jog out to Rialto Beach to see that battleship that's anchored out there," I replied, half expecting some reaction from Pinn. Rialto Beach was contested territory. The tribe maintained that the popular beach incorporated into Olympic National Park in 1959, was guaranteed in perpetuity to Native America by the Treaty of Point No Point. There was enough legal substance in the Indian claim to trigger court action. The locals, who since before 1938 had ridiculed and criticized the Park Service for the agency's purest tendencies in land management, were now rallied behind a banner of "Save Our National Park."

"The beach ought to be green with sailor vomit on a day like today," piped up Rod.

"Better use Rialto Beach all you can before the KEEP OUT signs go up and the place is fenced in concertina wire. That Mora ranger disappeared last week and people say his body may turn up on First Beach," offered another from the front seat. Pinn sat like a huge cedar stump. I was wondering if maybe Pinn **ate** the Park Ranger.

"No shit!" called the hook-tender. Water was drenching the windshield. He piloted the crummy through a creek which was flooding the road from a backed up culvert. "You're going to ride your bike and jog in this piss?"

"Sure. I wear lightweight rain gear and it's no different than setting chokers in the rain. The brakes don't work so well on my ten speed, but if I have to stop, I just put my foot in the front spokes." In truth, I was just trying to be funny. I hadn't figured out what to do to stop the bike on a long downhill stretch in the rain. But it was flat to Three Rivers, anyway.

All of a sudden words came from the stump: "Try rubbing paraffin on the rims of your tires and on the shoes of your brakes. It's good for a couple of good stops. And stay off the reservation land south of the parking lot."

"OK." I said. Pinn's dissertation had shocked me into monosyllables. "Thanks."

The trip through the rain continued out to Highway 101 and stopped at Tillicum Park, just outside Forks. Pinn and the three other choker-setters got out to drive their personal vehicles home. Pinn addressed the hook-tender, "I already cleared this with the shop: I won't be coming into work tomorrow morning." He pulled his saw out of the bed of the crummy and walked across the lot to his little Datsun pick-up. He contorted himself to get into the small cab. In the truck he had to stoop, sitting down, to see out the window.

The hook-tender let me out at Calawah Way where I jogged in my Romeo slippers two blocks to my apartment. There, I changed clothes and traded foot and rain gear. I grabbed the bike and went out into the rain. I was anxious to get going, so the paraffin trick would wait for another rainy day.

Forty minutes later, I was chaining my bike to a tree at Leyendecker Park near Three Rivers, thirteen miles from Forks. Here, the Soleduck meets the confluence of the Bogachiel and Calawah Rivers and takes on the name Quillayute. It's about a five mile jog to Rialto Beach from here. I was already soaked from the bike ride and the weather was raining and blowing harder than ever. But I was warm from the physical exertion and the movement felt good as I jogged down the Mora Road, splashing through standing water on the pavement.

In another forty minutes, I was jogging by a turnout that offered a view of James Island and LaPush, looking across the little estuary of the Quillayute River. I could see a dugout canoe tethered to driftwood on the jetty across from the village. The river was too high for gill netting, so what was this guy up to? Looking out towards James Island, I could discern a figure coming down the steps of the island bastion. A whale was spouting in the tumultuous surf south of James Island. I jogged out to the parking lot. There was the USS Alamo. It was a couple of miles out and anchored like a rock. I headed out south on the beach, into the reservation. (*Screw you, John Pinn.*) I want to know what the guy is doing coming off of James Island. At a distance of a couple hundred feet, I recognized Clarence Fourskins, the troublemaker from the American Indian Movement. He had been there at Hang Ups Tavern when Pinn went nuts and strangled me. When I got within voice range of Fourskins, he grumbled a few un-welcomings and looked really uncomfortable. I followed him along, back to his canoe, and he shoved off into the river. Fourskins motored out about fifty feet. The surf was starting to toss his dugout about like a cork. He turned and stared back at me. It was like looking into two eyes of a hurricane. All around, the storm rages, but in the tranquility of those placid black eyes was the promise of a greater apocalypse to come.

There had been a lot of craziness coming out of LaPush. I mean no disrespect. After all, I'm part Indian myself. But, if you could smell craziness, the scent coming across the river from the reservation was pure low tide, rotten potato, shit your pants *CRAZY!*

I turned and began to walk back to the parking lot. I was enjoying the solitude of the beach in storm. Through the ground clouds and wind-whipped rain came a strange apparition. A phantom jogger swept noiselessly through the loop of the parking lot. There was no bounce to the stride and no sound emanated from the impact of his shoes with the wet pavement. My shock at the encounter of another jogger on the storm, gave way to recognition of the runner: It was James Crow from LaPush. He was just as crazy as Pinn and Fourskins, but his physical expression was clearly non-violent. He was at Third Beach Parking the night I met the Park Ranger whose mysterious disappearance remains unexplained. I waved and jogged to catch up with Crow to share a 'howdie do.' But the phantom runner glided silently up the road and out of sight. I poured on a burst of speed to catch up, and ran flat out for half a mile to the straight section of road approaching the Dickey River Bridge. James had vanished into the wind and rain. Strange bird...that Crow.

THREE

LaPush
Sunday, July 15, 1968, 07:45 hours

*N*ine-year-old, James Crow, pulled the deflated weather balloon out of the shed that was home to the broken shovels, empty wine bottles, spilled nails and lost car parts of his family's estate in the village of LaPush. The balloon was a trophy that he had found on Second Beach two days ago when he was beach combing for salmon plugs. It had been set loose sometime earlier in the week by the new weather station on the Quillayute Prairie across the river. It had drifted only slightly in the mild east winds of a warm, early summer. He dragged the balloon over to where he had set up the aluminum foil, sulfuric acid and 32 ounce Coke bottle. He would need ice to control the kilothermic reaction that would take place when he introduced the sulfuric acid to strips of aluminum foil in the Coke bottle.

He cut away the payload of weather equipment and a transmitter so that he could mail it back to the National Oceanic and Atmospheric Administration as requested on the package. The instructions were to dispose of the balloon in an appropriate place, so James was sending it back into the stratosphere. This would be his best experiment ever! If only his father could be here to see it!

James' father, Edward Crow, was a chemist by education, and a refrigeration technician by trade. In 1950 he left the Idaho country of his Nez Perce ancestors without a high school education, to enlist in the U.S. Army, which sent him to Korea. He worked in a field hospital as, what in times of peace, would be called a lab technician. His duties included cross typing patient and donor blood; disinfecting the emergency operating rooms; and preparing many of the elixirs dispensed by the U.S. Army to its shot-up, and land-mine mutilated troops. Crow developed a healthy cynicism for the alternative of war as a means of solving political strife.

Edward returned with the Army to Fort Lewis, where he was honorably discharged in 1952. He worked for a meat processing plant in Tacoma for four years, saving money for college, and learning some of the chemo/mecho machinations of modern refrigeration. He got his GED in 1956. He quit full time work to enroll in the University of Washington as a chemistry major. He had left the meat processing plant as a quasi-vegetarian. He was about six years older than most of his classmates, and from a totally different background. He made no friends. He began jogging to fill his time between studying and his part time job as an orderly at the hospital. On weekends, he drank wine and beer in his apartment, alone. He hungered for human contact.

On Memorial Day weekend in 1958, Edward hitchhiked out to the Olympic Peninsula and spent the night in a brand new A-Frame cabin at LaPush Ocean Park. On Sunday morning, he returned from walking on First Beach to find June Woodrift cleaning his room. He was too shy to engage her in much conversation, but decided to stay another night in the hope of a more romantic encounter on Monday morning. He never saw her Monday. He had to get back for school and work on Tuesday.

The following weekend he returned. He found June to invite her out for dinner. According to Crow's plan, one thing followed another, until romance glimmered like the green flash of the sun as it set on the summer calm Pacific. Hand holding and cheek pecking surrendered to gulping kisses and passionate embraces upon a blanket laid on the warm sand of Second Beach. Not according to plan, was: 1) the news that June was pregnant, 2) the hasty marriage, 3) quitting his job, and school, a year before graduation, and 4) moving to the Peninsula to live with June in the trailer that became the family estate. The Woodrift's had lived in LaPush from time immemorial and would not hear of their daughter moving to the big city of Tacoma.

Edward Crow planned to finish his schooling through correspondence courses, specializing in biochemistry. There was talk of expanding the Forks Clinic into a regular hospital. The possibility of heading up the lab of the new hospital seemed real and exciting. The logging industry was booming, carrying the economy with it. Opportunity was redolent on the wind for any young man to smell. But by the time James came along in March of 1959, things were changing in Edward's life. He worked sporadically. He was repairing and maintaining the refrigeration of Pay and Save Groceries and John Labell's meat lockers. The U of W did not offer distance learning in any chemistry courses. And a hands-on lab was a requirement to finish Edward's curriculum. After birthing James, June again took work at LaPush Ocean Park and claimed that her employment, and parenting, caused her daily exhaustion. Sex was forgotten in their relationship. Edward felt claustrophobic in the tin can of a trailer. He talked about building a real wooden structure in the spare time that he had between refrigeration jobs. He jogged on the dirt "Thunder Road" out to Smith Field every day. On weekends little James ran with him. Edward became a binge drinker. The volume potential of the wooden shed outside the trailer began to be displaced by empty wine bottles. June resented his drinking. She was jealous of the discretionary time that Edward wasted on his endless jogging. Though she enjoyed eating, she did not like cooking meatless dishes. She was annoyed that James was beginning to forsake meat in some misguided expression of humanitarianism. She was threatened by Edward's plans to replace the trailer with a house of his design and construction. Her postpartum figure continued to expand on a diet of macaroni and potatoes until she was, herself, the weight and breadth of a refrigerator.

By the time James was seven years old, his mother and father barely spoke to one another. Newer refrigeration units required less maintenance. His father had to travel to the Clearwater Honor Camp, Neah Bay Air Force Station and other outlands to keep in work. He spent weekends in the wooden shed with James and James' older friend, Jeff Sparks, and the empty wine bottles. They conducted chemistry experiments and built model rockets.

One Friday night Edward didn't come home. He came home on Saturday afternoon riding in a flatbed loaded up with lumber. Two tractor trailers followed the flatbed laden with cedar siding from the Rosemond Brothers and Doug Fir studs from Allen's Mill. June had come home for lunch from LaPush Ocean Park and tore out of the trailer to intercept the delivery. A domestic disturbance developed as the lumber was being offloaded. June could not forgive Edward the investment in the lumber. She would not permit him to begin building on Woodrift land. Neighbors began to "borrow" from the lumber stockpile. In a few months most of the steel banded pallets had been broken and sorted through. The week after James' ninth birthday, Edward left for a refrigeration job and never returned. About a month after he left, June received a cashier's check for $300 purchased from a Tacoma bank.. The check was signed by Edward, but there was no enclosed letter. Since April the checks had come about the same day every month. They were about $300, sometimes a little less, but usually a little more. James knew nothing of the checks. He was told only that his father had abandoned the family.

Filial devotion dies hard. For months James had mourned the absence of his father; but continued in the honor and respect he felt for the man. This experiment would be dedicated to the time they had spent together as father and son and to the knowledge of chemistry the father had imparted to the boy. The balloon would rise this morning with a hand-painted *HAPPY FATHER'S DAY* banner. It would carry a letter to his father stuffed into the Coke bottle once it had served its purpose as a beaker in a hydrogen generator. If the balloon came down in a city, it would attract some attention with its payload. Maybe they would publish the letter as a human interest story and his father would read it. James stuffed the aluminum strips into the Coke bottle and poured in four ounces of sulfuric acid. The acid immediately began to boil and the aluminum foil rolled around in the roil. He tied the mouth of the balloon around the throat of the Coke bottle and ran into the shed to get some ice from the freezer to slow down the reaction if it got too hot.

****

LaPush
Sunday, July 15, 1968, 08:45 hours

Jack Lowe caught the phone on the third ring, even though he had been asleep at the other end of his trailer. At this hour it would have to be his 28-year-old son calling from Seattle to wish him a happy Father's Day. It wasn't.

"Mr. Lowe, this is your next door neighbor, Jeff Sparks, calling about your cat. Look, he's over here again, and he's been caterwauling all night. The turkeys you keep are enough bother without your cat coming by to torment me. I didn't get any sleep." This 15-year-old kid talked like an old curmudgeon. "This morning I went out to chase him away and he had pissed all over my short wave antenna terminal. That cat piss is very caustic to electrical wiring, and it stinks. I have to get in there and clean it off with my hand. I don't want this to happen again."

Mr. Lowe was deeply disappointed by the call and was already going back to sleep standing up. The silence on the line made him realize that this little Professor Sparks dictator expected him to give assurances that he would lock his cat in the closet forever. "Look, Jeff, it's Father's Day. You should be cooking your dad breakfast in bed and not bothering me. Cats don't do well on a short leash. I moved to LaPush from Seattle so that my cat could run free." In truth, he had moved to LaPush so that he could collect tribal benefits entitled to him by his marriage, his second wife being a treaty Indian.

"Mr. Lowe, I'm doing a lot of experiments right now. You know what an EKG is? I made one out of amplifying a signal from a stethoscope, putting it through a graphic equalizer and playing the signal onto an oscilloscope. I'm looking for a live specimen to test the effects of high voltage on the heart muscle. What I do is put one electrode up the specimen's butt and the other..."

Lowe hung up on Jeff Sparks and headed back to his snoring wife. Jeff went outside. He lobbed a rock in the direction of the gobbling turkeys. He turned on the hose bib on the outside of his father's car body repair shop. He pointed the hose in the direction of the cat and chased it as far as the stream would allow. The cat ran away with his tail in the air. Then Jeff reconsidered and called, "Here kitty, kitty, kitty..." But the cat was getting on with his rounds. It was all done with Jeff and the terminal box for the time being. Jeff hosed down the terminal box. He took a screw driver out of his back pocket, opened the box and loosened the wires. He fetched some spray lubricant from his room and gave the wiring a generous douching. He replaced the cover and went back to his room.

The room was a labyrinth of screens and wires. On a shelf, a stethoscope was fed onto a wire mike which inputted a graphic equalizer/amp. While most of Jeff's young counterparts in the village experimented with their penises studying Playboy centerfolds, Jeff demonstrated the same intuition and manual dexterity manipulating the dials and leads of his multi-tester while studying technical manuals. He transmitted the message on his telegraph key and then spoke into the microphone of his short wave transceiver: "KB7 seven two zero, this is KB7 two one two."

Eighteen-year-old, John Pinn answered, "This is KB7 720. For gosh sake, Jeff, let a guy sleep!" John wasn't the most enthusiastic short wave partner. It was kind of a waste to entrust him with a base set that would broadcast halfway around the world when you could hear his mother calling him home for dinner from their trailer porch step. But John was long in patience. He left the unit turned on, which was a prerequisite of the loan of the station. Pinn would never pass the HAM licensing requirements, but representatives of the Federal Communication Commission were few and far between here in LaPush.

"That tomcat of Lowe's has been pissing on my wires again. How do you copy?"

"Loud and clear."

"After I take care of a few things here, I'm going over to the Crows' to get a formula from James." Since Edward Crows' departure, Jeff was a little self-conscious of visiting the nine-year-old boy. He felt better when he had a technical excuse. Jeff was more comfortable having older friends. Pinn, however, was joining the Army. Jeff would be looking for another home for the sister base station.

"I'll get up, I guess, and be over after breakfast."

"If you see that gray tomcat of the Lowe's see if you can catch him. I've got an experiment that he might help out with."

"See ya. KB7 720."

"KB7 212." Jeff also signed off with the key.

****

As Pinn and Sparks walked along through the village towards the Crow trailer, Jeff shared with Pinn the political insights of a fifteen-year-old prodigy.

"I can't believe that even you are stupid enough to join the Army. They'll send you to Viet Nam first thing after Basic Training."

"I don't mind fighting in Viet Nam. I would die for my country."

"See this village," the fifteen-year-old gesticulated waving his arm wildly. "This is your country. The US of A are the guys that stole our land and raped our grandmothers."

"I'm an American first and an Indian second."

"Whatever you are *second*, you're a dumb shit *first* if you kill yellow men in Asia for fat White dudes here in the U.S." It gave Sparks a sense of power to denigrate this gentle giant and his naive notions, "It's an idiot's war! Not only will you be fighting on the wrong side, but you'll come back all fucked up. I've talked to Viet Nam veterans and they're not right. The way my dad takes his teeth out at night and puts them in a glass jar...?"

"Yeah?"

"That's what you'll have to do with your brain so you can sleep. You may be a dumb shit, but you've got a conscience and it won't leave you alone if you go to Nam. You'll end up carrying your nuts around in your wallet the way most of us carry a rubber..." (Sparks had never even seen a prophylactic.) Holy shit, look what James is cooking up!"

The political diatribe ended as Pinn and Sparks saw the burgeoning weather balloon in the Crow's front yard. The balloon was pulling at tent-stake tethers from the ground and James was throwing ice into the basket hanging under the balloon trying to cool off the furious reaction happening inside a Coke bottle.

"Hi, Jeff. Hi, John," James called out with ebullience. "I'm sending a message to my dad!"

James had already prepared the banner by duct taping seventeen sheets of school notebook paper together, each with a capital letter or space:

HAPPY FATHERS DAY.

As the hydro-generator cooked, he was trying for a Father's Day verse that might catch the eye of the media and also appeal to his father:

> *The sulfuric acid came to a boil*
> *When I put in the aluminum foil.*
> *Hydrogen gas came from the roil*
> *And...*

James' was preoccupied in a search for a suitable word that would rhyme with his verse. He considered "toil" and "oil", but could not make it work. He was interrupted when Sparks and Pinn approached. "This is really cool!" exclaimed Jeff, speaking for John, as well.

"Hey, you're standing on the banner!" James reproved Jeff.

Jeff moved his foot, picked up the stack of paper and turned the pages of the banner without unfolding it. "HAPPY FATHER'S DAY," recited Jeff with a sneer. "You could at least give the world a message they might benefit from, like 'EXPLOSIVE GAS/NO SMOKING' or 'PINN HAS SHIT FOR BRAINS.' Hey, what's this!" Jeff's excitement grew as he picked up the weather instrumentation and transmitter.

"I'm sending that back to the weather guys like it says to do. You just drop it in the mail box or take it to the post office."

"Wait a minute," said Jeff, electrified with lightning flashes of a brain storm on the horizon. "The transmitter will still work; this thing just needs a new battery pack to work. I've got a great idea! Come on, John! Hold the launch until we get back," said Jeff hurrying off carrying the instrument package and the Crows' duct tape.

"Hey! We're supposed to mail that back!" chided James, though he knew that it was not in the cards for a nine-year-old to dissuade this rambunctious adolescent, particularly in the company of the reticent hulk. James went back to the business of his word search, but was interrupted by the business of shutting down the hydro-generator and securing the balloon's orifice. He wasn't getting anywhere with "coil" or "soil," either.

It took Jeff less than thirty minutes to ready his part of the project. He had replaced the battery cells of the transmitter with eight fresh mercury double A's. He had wired a sound-generating transceiver in parallel with the instrumentation so that the transmitter broadcast sound as well as data. John and Jeff had found some pantyhose somewhere. They had recruited a large gray tomcat for the experiment. The cat's front and rear legs were tied together with the tape and he was secured in a

28

screamer suit made out of pantyhose and duct tape. The duct tape all came up to form an eye over the cat's back. Pinn was carrying the cat by the eye like a suitcase. James heard the cat a full minute before Pinn and Sparks came into view.

"Almost ready for launch?" yelled Jeff jubilantly.

"No way!" countered James. "You'll kill that cat sending him up on my balloon. He'd run out of oxygen up there. It's cruelty to animals and I'm not letting you in on my experiment."

"Come on, James. Look, I rigged a transmitter so the cat can talk to the weather station out on the Quillayute Prairie. If the cat gets distressed, they can send out a helicopter or something. It's a great experiment! You can still fly your goofy banner."

"I'm going to send a message in the Coke bottle," protested James. "It's supposed to be a Father's Day surprise. I don't want a dead cat spoiling it."

Sparks moved in to tie the loose balloon shrouds to the cat and instrument package. James stepped forward to resist the hijacking but was restrained by Pinn. "It's my experiment. You're going to ruin everything!" lamented James.

Jeff had secured the payloads and bent over to pick up the banner. He cut one of the two ground tethers. He passed the running end through a duct tape grommet that James had devised earlier. He cut the other line loose and stood back.

The balloon lifted slowly with a cacophony of protests from James and the cat. A gentle morning sea breeze caught the balloon and it slowly drifted toward the top of a twenty-foot weeping cherry tree. Edward Crow had planted the tree almost ten years ago. Though the cat's legs were bound, it caught one of the tree's tendrils in its front claws and hung on. John let go of James, and took a twenty-foot 2" by 8" member off the remaining pieces of Edward's lumber pile. He pushed the cat loose of its purchase. The balloon sailed lazily into the air and eastward, up the Quillayute. James ran into the house. "God will punish you two for this!" he promised as he ran into the trailer crying.

In five minutes, he had changed into his Puma running shoes and come back outside. Several other laughing and drinking Indians had joined John and Jeff as they studied the speck in the sky which indicated the balloon's progress. Judging from the caterwauling, oxygen had not become a problem for the cat at this point in its voyage. To reach this decibel level, adequate ventilation was a prerequisite. Angry words streamed from James' brain. Unspoken, they bounced off the inside of his mouth, and ricocheted into his heart where they burned like white hot shrapnel. *God will punish you.*

James began running out of town. He ran by several residences with the occupants standing at the thresholds of their trailers looking and pointing up at the sky. His sorrow and sense of betrayal sought expression in the pumping of his legs;

the swinging of his arms; the cadence of his breath. He ran on past Second and Third Beach parking lots. He eventually passed Three Rivers Resort. Mile after mile, he ran along the LaPush Road, his heart a fiery furnace stoked on the injustice and suffering of the world...burning on the volatile fuel of rage and despair. He ran on. He had run fifteen miles in a little over two hours, when he came to the intersection of Highway 101. He turned around and began running home. Half way home, James' muscles arrived at the a point of glycogen depletion known to runners as "the wall." He began walking tiredly the seven miles back to LaPush, but things inside him had been set straight. There would always be injustice and suffering in the world. He would always oppose these forces for whatever good it would do. Without Edward to father him, he would pray regularly for spiritual guidance, so that he would never be given to such acts of cruelty and betrayal as Pinn and Sparks had committed today. James resolved to keep a daily journal; and to run five days a week through the rest of the summer.

****

As James was walking home in a spiritual funk, that Sunday afternoon, the northwest regional NOAA director received a telephone call at home from one of his subordinates. "Mr. Wells, this is Jerry Lammers out on the Quillayute Prairie. I'm sorry to bother you at home, but we're picking up a very strange signal from one of our balloons. I thought you'd want to know about it. This afternoon we started getting a signal from one of our balloons that should have gone down three days ago. You know that the batteries on board only last for 24 hours? Anyway, there was some noise interference coming in with the digitized signal from the instrumentation. We put the signal over our oscilloscope and it looked like something from outer space. So I dialed up our frequency on a little short wave radio receiver I keep on my desk. I'm going to hold the phone to the radio now so you can hear it."

Jack Wells could not believe what he was hearing. It was not a language that he could recognize, nor did the voice sound human. But there were definitely mewling pleas followed by an agonized wail followed by more piteous begging.

"Mr. Wells, it sounds like a baby going through a buzz saw or a rhesus monkey being vivisected. That's not just some technical electrical problem we're listening to."

Jack Wells scratched his head. "It's probably some kind of joke...some kids fooling around in their basement with one of our transmitters or something."

"We thought of that, Mr. Wells. We triple checked all our vectors and the signal is coming from over our heads, about half a mile east of here. We'd hear a helicopter and it's been in about the same position for half an hour, climbing very slowly. I turned off the radio and went outside. God help me, I could hear one of those wails coming from six thousand feet above us. This is really weird! Mr. Wells, do you want me to call the media? Sometimes they help us track down the cause of these inexplicable events."

30

The headlines on the tabloid exploded in Well's imagination. "I don't know what's going on or which space alien has hitched a ride on what balloon. But if you breathe a word to the press, Lammers, you're fired!"

****

LaPush, Washington, 20:45 hours

Jack Lowe caught the telephone on the second ring. This would be his son for sure.

"Mr. Lowe, this is Jeff Sparks calling back. I wanted to apologize for what I said this morning and tell you that I won't be bothering you about your cat again."

"That's OK, Jeff." The genius runt had a conscience, after all. There was a pause on the other end of the line. "Listen, Jeff, I'm expecting an important call."

"Also, I thought you'd be proud to know that your cat is making important observations for the Weather Bureau. His presence may be missed by some, but, in light of the importance of the work he's doing, we will endure the sacrifice."

What was the little shit talking about now? Where was the cat, anyway? "Jeff, have you done something to Fur Ball?"

"I just told you, your cat has joined the ranks of the Weather Service. *Hair Ball* is miles from our location and I'm not talking about a horizontal plane."

"Listen, Sparks, I want to talk to your father. If you've touched a hair on my cat, I'll tear down your antenna mast and piss on the terminal myself."

"My dad is enjoying Father's Day which is what you should be doing, Mr. Lowe. Good evening," Jeff said sweetly hanging up the transceiver. *If that phone call was part of God's punishment,* reflected Jeff, *let His wrath rain down on me.*

****

After a long bath and dinner with his mother, James Crow had rummaged around in his parents' room. He found an old 4" by 5" six-ringed, loose-leaf binder that his father had used for college notes. He removed the pages used by his father. He placed them in the top drawer of his bureau, wrapping them in plastic and securing them with a rubber band. He began transcribing the events of the day in a neat, minuscule hand. He would persist in this format for the rest of his life, narrating the events and spiritual concrescence that would combine to push him into his future failed roles in tribal leadership and world-class running competition.

31

FOUR

University of Miami, Florida
October 14, 1968

*F*red Prue sat amidst his fraternity brothers and political compatriots in the meeting room of the student union. Looking around at the attendees of the third meeting of the U of M chapter of the Young Republicans, he was impressed with the significant representation of Sigma Alpha Epsilon in this organization. Several freshman in the audience, like himself, had survived the fall "rush," where incoming students chose and were, in turn, chosen by the different fraternities, that fringed the campus. The social sifting of this process to some degree followed a cast system, but even the liberal and Cuban infested fraternities left alone the hippie/freak component of the student body. The Students for a Democratic Society had become active on the campus and, as usual, their activity portended a threat to the peace and American way, which the Young Republicans were dedicated to preserving.

General Lemay, a decorated veteran of the Viet Nam War, was coming to Miami in support of Richard Nixon. The school radio station had covered the last SDS meeting and reported on the reception for General Lemay planned by the long-haired hippie scum. They intended to purchase a dog from the County Humane Society and bathe the dog in a gel of Ivory flakes and gasoline. When the eye of the media fell on the disheveled insurgents, they intended to ignite the pooch. Somehow, explained the speaker, in the dim light that burns under all that hair, the hippies calculated that this act of brutal sadism would call attention to the horrors befalling the villagers of the Viet Nam theater. The point was made that the bad press generated by the canine immolation would hang on the SDS organization like lice on a Cuban toupee. Another speaker felt that allowing the SDS to proceed with this bit of inhumanity would be tantamount to accessory to the act. A vote was taken to determine the Young Republicans' stance, and it was decided that the igniting of the dog would not be permitted. Enforcement of the decision would rest with a volunteer posse who would convene after the conclusion of the official meeting. Fred was a young man of average stature, but he had been a high school wrestler in Darien, Georgia. He knew that he could wrest a napalm soaked dog from a mob of SDS faggot freaks, and maybe stick a few long-haired heads in the gas bucket while he was at it.

About a dozen Young Republicans stayed in their chairs after the adjournment of the meeting to join the vigilante posse. Fred noticed with some satisfaction, that five of the posse were his fraternity brothers. A stranger in a three-piece suit was there to instruct them in self-defense and pain compliance techniques. He demonstrated methods of controlling an insurgent with a "chicken wing" wrist cock. By using the tension and release, used on a plow horse, the subject could be led compliantly past press cameras, to the fringe of the crowd, where the wrist could be inconspicuously snapped like a dry twig. He showed different methods of taking a person down to the ground by hair holds. He explained that, "by providence, most insurrectionists come with the convenient, extra-long handles." The unidentified man asked if the group would like to get together Saturday morning in gym clothes to

33

learn a few more techniques, and practice what they had learned. All of the dozen students were excited to learn more. They agreed to convene at the Sigma Alpha Epsilon fraternity hall for the instruction.

On Saturday, October 19th, the stranger met the group at the fraternity house just off campus. He was wearing sweats. He had brought six wigs with chinstraps to drill the students on hair hold techniques. During the practice, Fred enjoyed the sense of power when he executed the controls and take downs. When it was his turn to wear the hair, he was obdurate in resisting all force applied to achieve his compliance. He frustrated even his fraternity brothers by not following his wig to the ground. At one point, he twisted out of a "come-along-hold" applied by one of his fraternity brothers and reversed the hold. The reversal was so sudden, and applied with such commitment, that the brother went up on his tip toes to relax the tension on his arm and there was a popping sound from his wrist. The young man screamed and went over in pain, clutching his wrist. The guy lay on the ground nursing his injury and began sobbing. Fred tried to help him up, but the brother ignored him and was lifted to his feet by two other frats. They examined the swelling and discoloration of the young man's wrist and announced that they would be taking him to the University infirmary for x-rays. The stranger said that the group had achieved a level of expertise sufficient to accomplish their mission. He began packing up his wigs, ninja sticks, and other props. As the other participants faded into the Saturday morning activity, the stranger asked Fred to follow him out to his car.

In the parking lot, the stranger offered Fred his hand and introduced himself. "My name is Gary Shortbrand, and, as you probably figured out, I'm a Special Agent for the Federal Bureau of Investigations."

"I'm Fred Prue."

"I know who you are. I've got a file on you. You could have really hurt that guy in there. You've got to learn to save that kind of energy for the freaks and shitheads who need it."

"Yes, sir."

"But I also want to tell you, that we need a few young men like yourself, whose allegiance to the United States is beyond reproach; and who aren't afraid to stand up and be counted as Americans."

"I'm proud to be an American, sir."

"I know you are, Prue. That's why I'd like to tell you about a recruitment program we have for young Americans like yourself. If you pass certain criteria, the Agency will enroll you in a six-year program giving you a BA degree in Criminal Justice. All your tuition and living expenses are paid by the Bureau. You are also paid a salary which is placed in a high-interest trust. In six years, when you're through with the program, it's a nice little nest egg. Also, if you succeed in staying

34

with the program for the whole six years, there's a job, like mine, as a Special Agent waiting for you. You can retire with full benefits before you're 40 years old.."

"Why does it take six years to get a four year degree?"

"You have to be willing to move from school to school. You may have to pretend to drop out a time or two. We stay on top of the accreditation. As long as you keep up the grade average, you'll get the degree from a reputable institution."

"It sounds too good to be true. What's the catch, sir?"

"You belong to us for six years. You'll need to grow your hair long. We tell you who to associate with. You have to live like a hippie."

"Could I keep on with Sigma Alpha Epsilon?"

The stranger snorted as he climbed into the driver seat of his Ford convertible, which was backed into a parking spot. "Did you hear what I said? You'd be a long-haired freak! Those guys in there would toss you out on your ear for wearing the wrong deodorant."

"Excuse me, sir, those are my brothers. We're family. I'd really like to be a Special Agent, but I'm not going to pretend to be something I'm not. My fraternity is my family."

"OK. I'm glad everything is working out so well for you here. I'll give you my card just in case you change your mind. Good luck with protecting General Lemay, and the pooch, from all those hippie degenerates." Special Agent Shortbrand started the engine and drove out of the parking lot.

****

Fred Prue kept thinking about the offer he had turned down and the change it would bring to his life. He was trying to study his World Civilization text in the lobby of the fraternity house when his three brothers returned from the infirmary. The one wore a plaster cast from his elbow down to his hand. The injured brother went up to his room escorted by one, while the other broke away to talk to Fred.

"You broke Clyde's wrist."

"I feel really bad about it. I'll go up and apologize."

"Yeah, you do that. And while you're up there, get your stuff and clear out of here. It has to be by vote, but you're here on probation and you don't fit in with this fraternity. I'll give it to you officially tomorrow, but you might as well make arrangements to move back into the school dormitory."

"Yeah? Well fuck you. And fuck Clyde, too." Twenty minutes later, Fred was talking to Special Agent Shortbrand from a pay phone on campus.

December 16, 1968, 09:00 hours

Fred stood on *Sewer Beach*, with a motley group of about twenty young men. About a dozen of the group had long hair and appeared to Fred to be a genuine representation of the species, Hippie Americani. Even with his own hair growing down over his ears and below his collar, and the knowledge that these young men were like himself, Federal Agents, it seemed difficult to relate to them on a personal basis. There were no long hairs in Darien. Fred's only exposure to this social anomaly, previous to Miami, was from seeing the misfits parade across the television screen on the Six o'clock News.

Special Agent Shortbrand was on hand to supervise the morning's activities. Sewer Beach had been his choice of training sites. Though the east coast of Florida, particularly within a few hours of Miami, was teeming with tourists, fishermen, beach combers, and dope runners; the large pipe discharging effluent within site of this beach, afforded some shelter from the madding crowd.

"We're going to be following up on some of the officer survival training we started last Saturday, so we'll be pointing these sanctioned weapons at one another and pulling triggers. Am I correct that no one brought any real weapons or ammunition to this training?"

Shortbrand looked out over his charges. Surveying their appearances, it was hard to swell with pride, but these were good recruits. He anticipated real results in infiltrating and debilitating the new left political scene. They had received enough indoctrination to make them plenty paranoid. He hoped that none of them were concealing any weapons in their underwear. Shortbrand's own hardware was locked securely in the trunk of the Ford convertible. "OK, sanctioned weapons and ammunition only on this beach. My own weapon is modified to produce a loud beep when I pull the trigger."

With his hands in his pockets, Shortbrand sauntered over to one of the students, who stood with a sanctioned revolver modified to accept only starter pistol rounds. "OK, cover me with your loaded weapon and I'll blow you away." The cadet pointed his weapon at Shortbrand's head. "Now be ready..."

Shortbrand interrupted himself to jerk his head left, out of the line of fire. A loud beep brought attention to the snub nose, five shooter in his hand. "Where did that come from?" marveled the cadet, who had not gotten off a round.

Shortbrand squared off on another cadet, who likewise, put his aim into the special agent's face. "You jerk-offs are slow learners..." began Shortbrand again interrupting himself to pull his head out of range and, with a rattlesnake strike from his pocket, the Chief's Special claimed its second victim.

36

"OK, Killer, you're next." Shortbrand approached Prue, who immediately began backing away, pointing his dummy gun into Shortbrand's center of mass. "Where are you going?" Shortbrand's attempt to distract, duck and retrieve his pocketed weapon were punctuated by two cracks of Prue's starter rounds. A third crack came as Shortbrand tried to find Prue in his sights. "That's it, Killer! You got the picture! What this illustrates is the deadly potential of a suspect with his hands in his pockets. Don't be pointing at the man's face. That's the easiest thing to move out of your line of fire. Do like Killer here: cover down on the kill zone - the five ring between the chest and belly button. If you give yourself space, you can take the advantage away from the suspect because he will lose time trying to find you in his sights instead of instinct shooting. Good officer-survival, Killer! Let's show you how you can use the element of surprise to your advantage in a hostage situation."

Shortbrand broke the group into groups of three. From each group he selected a "bad guy." He had them wait 100 yards off, by a grove of palm trees, while he explained the survival technique to the hostage and fellow officer. "All the time cops, judges, and other innocents are taken hostage by well meaning, but misdirected, agents of new left politics. Understand, that as soon as the scumbag points a gun - or what looks like a gun - at anyone besides himself, the green light is on for you to take him out. On the other hand, you can imagine what it feels like to have a gun stuck in your face by some trigger-happy maniac while your compatriots play shoot/don't shoot with your life. Well, us good guys in the criminal justice system have a universal language we use to co-ordinate the neutralization of hostage takers. It works on the principle that it takes a half second for human beings to react to anything. I showed you that, by pulling my weapon from my pocket and shooting you. If you're taken hostage, and the gun is at your head, keep talking to distract the scum-sucking maggot. Talk to your partner who should be covering down on the suspect. Offer small resistance to increase the distraction. When you're ready to play your hand, say, 'Don't let him shoot me, Johnson,' and dive for the ground. Next January, you would say, 'Don't let him shoot me, Nixon,' and dive for the ground. Get it? When you call your fellow officer by the name of the President, he drops the hammer and you're on the way to the ground. If the puke gets off a round, it will probably glance off your skull and you'll survive it. We'll practice it. I'll give the bad guy my beeping Chief's Special so we don't get any powder burns to the face."

One by one, bad guys were brought over to try their luck as hostage takers. The first two hostages hit the ground without a beep from the snub nose. The third bad guy got off a beep almost simultaneous with the starter round, but the covering officer got in two more shots to neutralize him. Then Prue was brought over from the palm trees for his turn as bad guy. "Better put two cops on Killer Boy," said Shortbrand.

Fred put his hostage's neck into the crook of his left arm and began to force the snub nose into the cadet's mouth. "Hold on, guy," said Shortbrand. "You'll knock out his teeth. This is just an exercise." Prue pulled the back of the cadet's long hair with his left hand and put the gun under his exposed chin with his right hand. He moved backward and started talking, "Stay back or I'll blow his brains out. I'm a crazy son of a bitch! Stay back now!"

The cadet tried to talk over Prue's growling. "He's going to shoot me. Don't let him shoot me! Don't let him shoot me, John..." Prue's right wrist snapped forward. The beep signaled the death of the first cop covering him. "...son," finished the hostage cadet. As he dropped to the sand, Prue dropped with him, and the second beep indicated the neutralizing of the second covering officer. As the hostage and Fred hit the sand, the third beep announced the execution of the hostage and Prue rolled out from under the cadet covering the group with the Chief's Special.

Special Agent Shortbrand was delighted. "You *ARE* one, mean, nasty, crazy son of a bitch!"

FIVE

Seattle, Washington
September, 1973

The highway to the glittering Adult city from the parochial village of Childhood is fraught with accidents, road hazards and devious, demented hitchhikers. You might stop to pick up such a respectable looking hitchhiker along the roadway. Maybe it's Alcohol, Drugs or Tobacco. Somewhere approaching the city limits of Adulthood, the hitchhiker asks if you want him to drive, and you say, "Sure, why not." Once in the city you refer to your road map looking for the sectors of "Success" and "Meaningful Relationships;" but the hitchhiker keeps turning off on the side roads to "Ruin." And he drives so damn fast! Before you know it, he's driven you through the city of Adulthood, too fast for you to see anything, and, bingo, he's taken you into the suburban ghetto of Geriatrics. And just as the hitchhiker drags your dying body from the wreckage of your life, to devour your vital organs: your lungs, liver, brain and heart; you start to think, "Maybe picking up this hitchhiker and letting him drive wasn't such a hot idea!"

There is no clear posting of the city limits, as you approach Adulthood from Childhood, and many of the structures of Adolescence bear false fronts and affect an Adult facade. One minute, on the thirteen year mile mark of the highway, you're well within the limits of Adulthood, standing with your contemporaries in front of the middle school. You are all smoking cigarettes, except for one citizen of Adulthood, who prefers chew, and talking about getting laid. You evidently are the only virgin in this quorum of distinguished citizens. But you talk convincingly of technique, come on lines and how to obtain a contraceptive five pack from an exam glove. A teacher comes out of the building to make trouble for the assembled precocious constituents. Everyone skies.

You run like any Adult fugitive and feel the cigarettes beginning to bounce out of your front shirt pocket where they are displayed like a flag of your Adulthood. As you look down to reposition the cigarettes, you miss your footing and go down face first into the moat of mud that surrounds the institution. You come up with a coat of mud from where your nose rudders into the quagmire, to where your toes dug in applying brakes to the skid. Your new shirt and your good pants are screwed, man. How are you going to get this shit off! How are you going to go to class? Your contemporaries have stopped running to point and laugh at you. You look down at your feet and you see the corner of your cigarette package protruding from under your left foot in the mud. The teacher seizes the opportunity to advance on your position. The Adults fade into the rainy morning leaving you muddy, wet and humiliated, to explain to the teacher, with sobs on your cigarette breath and tears on your manly cheeks...to call your mommy for clean clothes so you can go to class. You never know when you reach Adulthood, but the best indication is that you begin to fiercely reminisce about, and wildly misremember Childhood.

****

39

LaPush   September, 1973

James Crow had a long road of it, though, run like a man, he did. He lacked fantasy and conviviality as a child. He was short on humor and social skills as an adult. James manifested two ancestral vulnerabilities of his Native blood: gullibility and earnestness. It delighted other school children when he went home with a small *KICK ME* sign taped to his jacket one afternoon and reappeared the next morning still wearing the sign. When he sat on thumb tacks left point up by his classmates on his desk chair, he would jump up, oblivious to the snickering all around him, pull the point out of his bottom and reapply it to the undersurface of his desk. He evidently assumed the tack was vibrating loose from this mooring and positioning itself on his seat. The same tack was used over and over, until James routinely checked the seat before applying his fanny. Then other torments were conjured up for the quiet and long-suffering youth. His teachers felt that the lack of a father figure in his life contributed to his unwillingness to take a stand with his tormentors. The knot securing most youths to their mothers had been frayed by his father's departure and James shared little interest with June. His mother never owned a car or learned to drive. She passed on this enigma to her son. Preoccupation and introversion stunted his social development. He used the notebook journal he'd started when he was nine, as his *confidant.*

Chemistry and running remained James' consuming interests. When James was twelve he enrolled in two different correspondence courses which shared one prerequisite of a monthly tithe. He took odd jobs to support these courses and to purchase supplies for experimentation. When he was sixteen, he took the remnant lumber supply, left by his father seven years before, and built a shack a little bigger than the utility shed, that housed the wine bottles his father had left, to conduct his experiments. He moved his bed from the trailer and took up residence amid the beakers, Bunsen burners, test tubes, and drying tube socks which characterized his existence.

There was no Middle School in Forks when James was growing up. He had to wait until he was fourteen to join the high school track team. After participating in his own rigorous training program for four years, he competed easily with boys three years older than himself. In that there was no school bus service to LaPush for after-school activities, he would jog to Tillicum Park, where he would ride home with loggers, getting off work, or other commuters. Occasionally, he ran fourteen miles home, after his team's training. He achieved school records in every running event in which he participated, except hurdles. Over the years, athletic event records had been commemorated by the entering of names, times and dates on a big brass plaque in the gym. James hardly paid attention to the quiet racism that kept the plaque from being edited to reflect his accomplishments. In his sophomore year, he set a new national high school record for the mile, with a time of 4:12. He was a full fifteen seconds ahead of the next runner, who happened to be a White student who had set the previous Forks record for the mile. The somber crowd applauded wildly when the second place crossed the finish. By the request of the other boy's family, James was taken off the mile event for the rest of the year. James noticed these things, and referenced them in his journal; but they did not have a profound impact upon him.

40

His hunger was for running itself - not for the notoriety that competition yielded. In his junior year he joined the cross-country team. He led the Forks team to victory at the State championships in 1976 and 1977. A talent scout from the University of Oregon attended both these championships. In April of 1977, James received a scholarship offer from the U of O.

James had virtually no social life. He began attending the LaPush Pentecostal Church on Sundays when he was thirteen. Like other fundamental churches, the LaPush Assembly preached sexual abstinence except within a marriage. James developed a fear of the opposite sex. He committed his energy and interest to his vocations of running and chemistry. He drifted in conversation of such innocent topics as weather, into dialogue of God's will. Even his fellow church-goers found his didactic dialogues tiresome.

****

Seattle September, 1977

My mother delivers me to the front door of the dormitory of the University of Washington. I feel surely I have arrived at the citadel of Adulthood. Unquestionably, the village of Childhood is in the past, right? I will only see my parents on holidays, summer break, and weekends of my choosing, so their impact on my emotional development is over...right? I wave off my mother, who is getting out of the car to give me a hug, for Christ's sake, *right in front of the whole dormitory.* She is half Creek Indian, explaining the totem of *Chiggers* she hung on me when I was but a fetus. Now she doesn't come up to my armpits. I would have to bend over to hug her. Fat chance of that! I bend over and pick up my two bags and retreat into the Adult halls from the maternal assault. Once inside, I apply the new tobacco pipe to my hirsute cheeks and proceed up the stairs to find my assigned room. Though I am unquestionably an Adult, with my long brown hair, my Algerian briar pipe, and my independence from my parents...certain insecurities sneak into my realm of calm. What if my roommate is a dork? How far will I have to go at night to pee? Will I be able to eat the food? Will I lose my virginity in this Adult world or go to my grave in a white suit? Where is the nearest phone and how will I cope with the overwhelming homesickness, and need for my mommy and daddy, which is already infiltrating my Adult bastion?

****

Eugene, Oregon
September, 1977

As he gets off the Greyhound Bus, at this moment, James Crow is experiencing his own culture shock. He pulls his bags from the luggage compartment and walks towards the dormitory. He wears some Adult raiment, though he is in emotional diapers. Over the years he has run over 25,000 miles in all kinds of weather. Rain, wind, and sunshine are his friends. These friends were his only companions on weekend outings exploring the jungle of Teahiwit Head, camping out with only a warming fire for shelter. James had learned to navigate

41

through the walls of vegetation that surrounded LaPush. He never keened for a place to urinate or sleep out of public view. He had discovered that he could go days without food while he still trained. One time he stopped running and eating for two weeks. Though he did not eat meat and avoided junk, he was not preoccupied with the taste or immediate availability of the fuel he put in his body. James was secure in the workings and protections of his human body. He was aloof from the socio/sexual dilemmas preoccupying most of us babes washing up on the foreign and faraway island beach of Adulthood.

However, an exploration of James' journal would reveal much insecurity. He was totally ill prepared for the un-cloistered, Adult world that presented itself as he walked the three blocks to his dormitory. Like an aborigine, James' felt absurdly transplanted in this strange environment. It lacked thick vegetation and untrammeled dirt roads that had always provided for James' privacy. Unlike Forks, this city sprawled beyond the immediate horizon. He experienced agoraphobia. James passed a group of several youths his own age sharing marijuana in front of the dormitory. As he searched for his assigned room, he passed an open door where a student was kissing and embracing a girl. He had one hand on her breast and the other on her buttocks. James' trembled over the indecency of it all. His roommate reeked of marijuana. His eyes were glazed. He overshot James' proffered hand, connecting thumb to thumb, fingers over the dorsal surface of the hand. "Name's Burt," said the stranger. A minute later, James realized his roommate had identified himself and was waiting for James to speak. Words would not come. In the awkward silence, James picked up his pacifier: a pair of well-worn running shoes. He stripped off his pants to reveal his running shorts, which he had worn all the way from LaPush. He sat on a bed to kick off his street shoes. He laced his Pumas; Burt wondered at James' gall, to use the made bed that Burt had obviously chosen for himself. Burt stared, in stoned awe, as James threw his leather shoes into the middle of the floor and ran from the room without a word of greeting or acknowledgement. James ran for two hours through the strange city of Eugene, Oregon, fighting sometimes for breath through a throat that was nearly choking with sobs. In all his life, the farthest he had been from his home in LaPush was a Bible Camp outside of Seattle. He already missed the smell of the ocean, the sound of the fog horn, the green tangle of rain forest. The only jungle in Eugene was spiritual.

****

College is a lions' den of predators for young people crossing the threshold to a world of adult privileges and responsibilities. Drug dealers, prostitutes, and fraternity houses, along with army and corporate recruiters, growl and prowl the campuses. Young lives can be irreversibly changed with a flash of ivory and a few snappy remarks from such powerful jaws. In loneliness and insecurity, the freshman lambs often seek protection and comfort by sleeping with the lions. Bones in loose sacks of skin, litter the methadone and v.d. clinics of the local communities. There are hostile grounds where the lambs are drug off to be consumed by the ever ravenous predator of the young - war.

For James Crow, the insecurities and awkwardness of the first 24 hours of college were unbearable. On the second day, he registered for classes. He met his guidance counselor, Steven Holloway. Steven, a 26-year-old alumni of the U of O with a masters in education, seemed from the start to demonstrate a personal interest in James.

"I like to see the students I work with fully deployed in their curriculum," explained Steven. "If you think you can handle 21 credit hours of courses, plus your running, I'd like to see you give it a try." James felt like a hungry waif in a candy store looking at all the chemistry courses offered. He signed up for three courses plus the English, world history and calculus prerequisites. His schedule left 3:00 to 5:30 p.m. free every afternoon for training and dinner. "If you get bogged down in all the work, let your least important class go and concentrate on the others. You can make up the one you drop and it won't go against your grade average."

After James had registered for his classes, Steven took James across campus in his personal red Porsche to meet the track coach. Jack Burns, the coach, had been forewarned of James' prowess as a runner. He was obviously happy to be adding him to the team. He shook James' hand and said, "As a representative of the U of O team, several expectations are placed upon you. We don't tolerate drugs of any kind. You can drink only in moderation. We expect you to put in at least 50 miles a week, and most of that will be at our afternoon training. Last of all, it's always the team first, and the individual second. We're not looking for any hot-dog loners. We're a team."

"I run because I like to, not to show off. I don't go near drugs; this last summer I was running about 90 miles a week; I drink about five liters a day."

"You drink more than a gallon a day, of beer, or what?" exclaimed the coach, anxiety bringing up his voice in decibels and octave.

"Water. H2O. I've never drunk beer. I don't drink pop, or milk, or coffee, or anything besides water."

Jack Burns grunted. This Crow was a strange bird, all right, but all reports were that he could run like the wind.

After finishing up with Burns, James and Steven returned to the Porsche and it was 11:45. "Why don't we go back to my place for a quick lunch?" suggested Steven with an illuminating smile. "I've got some chicken salad in the fridge I want to get rid of. I can bring in a garden hose for your refreshment."

"I don't think I could do that."

"I'm not gay or anything James, and it's no trouble, really." intoned Steve, persisting in his smile.

James had only a vague notion about what heterosexual sex was about. He didn't understand the word 'gay' as it applied to sexual preference. "I don't eat chicken. I'm vegetarian is the problem."

"That's no problem, Jim. I have plenty of vegetables that aren't so moldy." Steven was already driving off campus towards his apartment.

"Thanks, then, Steven. I prefer you call me 'James.' "

"Home, then, James. I prefer you call me 'Steve.' "

At Steven's posh apartment, James ate zucchini and sprout sandwiches. He listened as Steven pontificated techniques of time management, organization and concentration.

"I like to see the students I work with fully invested in their studies," Steven repeated the theme he had touched on earlier in the day. "It's better to be overworked than under worked. The stress will force you to be creative and productive, which are two qualities that will help you immensely when you leave these hallowed halls. If you feel yourself drowning in the work, let me know. I'll throw you a rope. I take a personal interest in all the students I counsel. Your success means everything to me. It's no secret to the faculty that a lot of our students use drugs. I want to keep my students on the right road. A little speed once in a while to help a guy study is one thing, but there are hard drugs available to anybody on campus. Some drugs will swallow you whole and spit out the bones. Again, I'm not naive about pot, and the other recreational substance abuse that goes on here at the U of O. Sometimes drugs are OK, like with a prescription or something. Just don't let anyone convince you to trade your future for a minute's worth of pleasure."

James didn't know smack from his crack. "OK," he said, thinking that he had never seen a smile so big on a White man

SIX

*S*teve Holloway's gleaming smile became a familiar backdrop for the socio/emotional problems, and academic crisis that swarmed like angry bees around the head of James Crow in his first semester of college. Steve called James at his dorm before dinner, the first day of classes, to see how things had gone for James. He called again a week later to remind James that any time he had a problem, day or night, he could call on him. Besides chemistry classes, and track, James had nothing but problems. His roommate smoked pot right in the shared room. The food in the cafeteria lacked nutritional value. There was a no substitution policy, making it hard for a vegetarian to maintain sufficient caloric intake in heavy training. He was losing weight. His mother had written him letters reflecting a deep depression caused by his absence. He was not doing well with world history, English, or calculus and found it hard to study at night after classes and a 15 mile work out. He worried about losing his scholarship.

He called Steve on a Friday evening, three weeks into his college experience, asking for advice on these problems. The first battery of tests had left James insecure about his survival in all subjects except the four relating to chemistry. Steve suggested that James come over again for lunch. James jogged over to the apartment at 11 a.m. Steve had a way of making James feel special. It was obvious to James that Steve was helping a lot of other students with their problems because three different students interrupted their lunch and conversation by ringing the bell to the apartment. Steve greeted them cheerfully. He excused himself from James to minister privately to their needs for a few minutes. In the course of their discourse on James' problems, Steve made it clear that his field of expertise was in academic, rather than social matters. He indicated that he could find expert help for James in the sociology and psychology departments, but James said just talking to Steve about it helped a lot. Steve told James that it was normal for mothers to experience acute anxiety and depression when their only child left for college. He said that it usually passed as the mothers came to appreciate the extra time, and the freedom from the demands of their children. Steve obviously was more tolerant of substance abuse than James and explained that marijuana was everywhere on campus. Steve said that he knew plenty of professors who smoked dope. He said that James' fears of being ensnared in the legal repercussions of Burt's indiscretions were unfounded. Steve indicated that he would talk to a friend of his who supervised the cafeteria operation to make sure that James' diet and appetite were accommodated. On the subject of James' academic fears, Steve stressed time management. There was no substitute for study and no shortcuts to learning. Most students borrowed time from their social lives or from their sleep when they were in academic trouble. That's why amphetamines were so popular among students. In James' case, he had no social life from which to borrow. The extra time would have to come from cutting back on training or sleep.

"I have an obligation to myself to run 90 miles a week. I run 15 miles a day, six days a week. I rest and stretch on Sunday. It's what I have to do. I can't take away from it."

"Then borrow from your sleep. Late-night study offers less distraction and can provide greater retention value. Make up for the sleep on weekends and when you're ahead on studying. You told me about how you went without food for two weeks. Learn the same discipline on your sleep management."

"But, if I don't get at least seven hours I fall asleep in class."

"That's why amphetamines are so popular and widely available on college campuses."

****

A full smile from incisor to incisor is eight teeth. That's what James saw three weekends later as he looked up from the table at the proffered solution to his study problems. "It's a prescription drug, James, just like antibiotics if you're sick. But I'm not a doctor, so there's the technicality of the prescription. It's best to keep this matter of the amphetamines strictly between you and me. Like doctor/patient confidentiality..."

The smile, Lord, that smile. Eight top teeth. Each tooth holding a letter placard: E*A*T*-*S*P*E*E*D. "Speed" is what they called amphetamines on campus. Steve was correct: Most of the students seemed to use speed to cram for tests and term papers. The only drugs that had found their way into James' body in his eighteen years of life were 21 tablets of antimyacin, which June Crow made James take when he was seven years old for an ear infection. He drank half of one of his mom's Pepsi's when he was five and threw up for two hours. He never went near caffeine or carbonated sugar beverages again. He remembered his father's alcoholic binges, and the impact they'd made on his life. James avoided alcohol when all the other young bucks in LaPush attacked every known keg party like mud wasps upon a rivulet.

James had lived the pure, drug-free life. Still, in his second month of college experience, James came again to Steve for consultation on the problems he was having studying English, calculus and world civilization. His scholarship would be threatened if he couldn't keep up his G.P.A. If he couldn't stay awake of an evening to study, all would be lost. He trusted Steve. He felt certain that Steve wouldn't be recommending anything that would jeopardize his health or discredit his academic integrity. Still, every week, Jack Burns warned his track team of the dangers of drugs. The coach had mentioned amphetamines specifically as an illicit substance that would not be tolerated on the team.

Steve discussed James' intolerance and prohibitions. He explained that by taking the vial of 30 pills with him, he was under no obligation to ingest them. Sometimes just knowing they were there helped a student to keep awake. Steve showed James how the capsules could be broken in half. He told James he could cut the halves into quarters for a minute dose. "Amphetamines are like medicine. It's not like drug abuse where people ingest some unknown, untested substance for recreational use. This stuff is made by students here at the U. It's as safe as the drugs made by the pharmaceutical giants."

The smile. James left Steve's apartment with the amphetamine in his fanny pack. As he opened the door to leave, another student was just about to knock on Steve's door. He recognized the student from his world civilization class. "That world civ's a real head nodder, isn't it?" said the student. James wondered if narcolepsy was rampant through the whole class.

On Monday evening, 54 hours after leaving Steve Holloway's apartment with a vial of amphetamine, James Crow became a speed freak.

****

University of Washington
October, 1977

I stare at my reflection in the rain-spattered window of the U of W dormitory as the lights in the room overtake waning daylight. I draw on the hash pipe and hold the smoke in my lungs while it burns and tickles at the same time. I start coughing and the smoke explodes from my lungs. It eclipses my reflection in the window and leaves a film of condensation on the glass. It's just as well. I don't enjoy my reflection as much as I did a couple of months ago. I've put on about ten pounds eating all this cafeteria cuisine. I've become a hermit, hanging out in the room, smoking dope while my roommate goes out scoring coeds like he was shooting hoops. I'm not even hungry, though it's almost chow time and I know I will shovel in another 3,500 calories. I am possessed with a sense of restlessness; a sensation of self-reproach; a free floating and bloated feeling of helplessness and lack of self-determination.

"That's it," I say to myself. I break the hash pipe in half and flush what's left of the gram down the toilet. "Screw dinner!" I put on sweats and jogging shoes, which are almost new though they are a year old. I pull on a light rain jacket and go out to war with my fat by jogging 16 laps around the track in the rain. After the cold rain, the hot shower feels great. Then I go over to the student union where I find my roommate trying to work two coeds simultaneously. One I recognize as a student in my basic computer science class, and she is a *babe*! I get talking to her about how computers are the future of everything; about couples I know, who met through computer dating services; about how I skipped dinner to run tonight; and my mouth runs on, un-muzzled of its customary shyness. It's 10 o'clock, and they are closing the student union. My roommate has disappeared with the other coed, and I walk Sally Singleton back to her dormitory. At the door to her room she says she has noticed me in class and really enjoyed getting to know me better. I say that I hope I can see her again, and she gives me her telephone number and says call anytime. She kisses me, good night, on the lips. I am lightheaded and high as I run down the stairs. "Fuck drugs forever!" I yell as I run back to my dormitory.

47

I stop at the door to my room just before I insert the key. From the noise on the other side of the door, I know that I don't want to go in right now. I jog back to the track and go another four times around the track. I get back to my room just as my roommate and the coed are leaving. She looks at the sweat and rain pouring off my face and my hair plastered to my head. She rolls her eyes and asks, "Is Sally in the same condition you're in?"

"She didn't stay as dry as me," I say with a wink. "She was on top." Fuck drugs forever!

****

The failing light and rain, that gave Chiggers a reflection of himself in the dorm window, found James Crow entering the 80th lap of his afternoon run on the University of Oregon playing field. Drug abuse had settled like the night on this Native American. He was just coming down from a speed high that began after lunch when he popped a pill to keep him awake through the two-hour world civilization class. He had gotten so agitated sitting in his chair that he had left class 45 minutes early to take this extended jog. He had been late to his Introduction to Chemical Analysis class at 9 o'clock because he'd run 16 miles in the morning after taking a pill for breakfast. He had run 36 miles on this Friday. That made over 140 miles since Sunday. He was planning on running Saturday, too. His weight was down from 165 to 143 pounds. The coach was after him to eat more, and workout less. James couldn't sit still.

A few minutes later, in the locker room, James stood under the hot shower. The cold rain that had fallen on his nearly naked body for the last two hours had chilled him to the point of near hypothermia. James felt the hot water strike his head and neck. It cooled as it washed down his body. By the time it reached his legs, the water was cold. The warm water dilated the arterioles and veinlets of his skin. This allowed his blood to circulate through the chilled environment of his body's outer envelope. James shivered under the hot water. His hands felt numb as he turned up the hot and turned down the cold.

James began to think about his big Friday night. He would stop by the cafeteria on his way back to the dorm and eat a grilled vegetable sandwich, tomato soup and green salad. The eating had become a nuisance, but he had to do it. He would take a pill so that he could study. It was the last of the second bottle of 30 that Steve Holloway had given him. He would go to Steve tomorrow and get some more. With all the studying he was doing at night, he still was barely holding his own on the academic line. He missed so much in classes when he felt drowsy. The pills made his running increase, and that felt great. But he needed more pills to stay awake in class. James continued to shiver under the hot water.

"I'll just get more pills and everything will be great," he thought, putting out of his mind the warning he had gotten yesterday from Coach Burns. "I told you from the start, James, that this is a team show. You're missing our team workouts because you're working out on your own. There are no lone wolves on this team,

48

James. Come in with the pack or get off the team." James had studied his toes while he received this admonition from Burns. "You're losing too much weight," Burns dismissed James with this advice. Maybe James could force down some of the sugary junk they peddled for dessert in the cafeteria. He would have to remember to always take the pills after eating.

The next day, James had coughed down breakfast at 6:30 a.m. He was at the cafeteria when it first opened . He wanted a pill before his morning workout. He was knocking on Steve Holloway's door at 7:04.

"Do you know what time it is?" exclaimed Steven as he looked blearily at James through the crack in the door allowed by the night chain.

James looked at his watch and said, "Four minutes past seven. Am I disturbing you?"

"No. That's all right, I guess. Come on in. I'll get us some coffee."

"I don't drink coffee," reminded James. "Listen, Steve, I need some more amphetamine. I can pay so it's not a burden to you."

"How much would you like to pay?" asked Steve Holloway, as he rustled around with a coffee grinder and tea kettle.

"I can afford to pay you five dollars a bottle, but if you can take less that would be fine."

Steven laughed and looked up from the electric coffee grinder to beam a smile at James. "Actually, my costs for 30 tablets is about $25. I know you can't afford that kind of price on your scholarship stipend. So maybe we can work something out that would be mutually beneficial. Today might be a good day to take you over to the lab and show you around. Since you are a chem major, I should have known that you would take an immediate interest in pharmacology."

In fact, the life-sucking, poison-fanged, predacious, and honey-tongued, guidance counselor had anticipated this vulnerability of James' to drug addiction. He'd been given the personal profile and family history, which were part of James' application for his scholarship. Steven needed a cook in the lab who could be paid with product. Someone who would keep his mouth shut. From their first meeting, Steven Holloway's cleaver-like eyes had cut through the flesh of James' health , and spiritual purity, to reveal the bones, and DNA, of a potential addict.

****

Steven and James were alone in the lab, which was off campus. It was on the outskirts of town, north toward Springfield. In the time that James would work in this lab, he would never meet another person in it; and this would be the only time that Steven Holloway would be there with him.

49

Though synthesizing methamphetamines from the array of chemicals in the lab was a complicated and delicate process, James already understood the molecular relationships of the reagents involved. There was not much that Steven Holloway had to tell him. James examined the reflex tubes, the gallon beakers, the trays, the blenders for chopping aluminum foil, and the industrial ice maker for cooling down the kilothermic reaction. He studied the exhaust system, the fire extinguishers, the breathing masks, face shields, the eye wash station, and rubber gloves.

"I used to do experiments when I was a kid that were something like this. I never did anything with Benzedrine. You end up with some nasty byproducts with this kind of thing. The aluminum forms a toxic sludge that's hard to get out of the bottles. Where are the sinks to wash out the beakers? What do you do with the sludge?"

"You won't have to worry about that a bit," Steven was all ivory. "You just leave the sludge in the beakers in that locker over there. A guy comes around twice a week. His only job is to get rid of it. We just throw the beakers away."

"Those beakers cost $50 a piece at the surgical supply store in Eugene! What do you mean you throw them out? And the sludge is really toxic, so you don't just drop a beaker into a dumpster! Where do you keep the ether? Just a half pint of that stuff would blow this lab sky high!"

Steven's smile clouded for a minute. "Listen, James. The sludge and the used beakers are taken far away from here. You don't have to worry about where they go, but they're gone and that's the end of it. We buy new beakers every week through the U's Chemistry Department. One of your professors is in with us, but I'm not at liberty to say which one." The cloud passed, irradiating Steven's face with full smile light. "The ether is kept in a safe place. One of your duties will be to bring as much ether, acetone and methanol as you need to do one job. You can see that we have given some consideration to health and safety in this operation."

"Steve, I know about these chemicals and their reaction to one another. There is no health or safety to be found anywhere near it." James thought about the offer of $200 a job, which he could send to his mother, and all the product he wanted. "But I'll do it. For a while, anyway."

50

SEVEN

Normality is a mirage in the life of a drug addict. Stumbling across the desert of their addiction, the substance abuser sees normalcy shimmering on the horizon, like the oasis that sustains life. It is real, yet so ephemeral. The addict attempts to drive a car while stoned, and puts himself in the hospital; and some innocent in the graveyard. The addict goes to work stoned, and is the first to be laid off in a reduction in force. The addict tries to have sex with his wife, and finds that he cannot. The addict tries to lean his weary soul against the pillar of normalcy, and falls, crashing to the ground. For the addict, normality has no substance, no buffers, no water of life...it is only the absurd, glimmering reflection of reality.

So James Crow drug himself through the first semester of college believing that he only used amphetamines to study, and run harder; believing that his part time job was a way to send money home while pursuing his academic goals; and believing that he would put aside the use of the drug when it was no longer incidental to the achievement of his objectives. He did not see his body being physically consumed by the drug as he continued to cannibalize his body weight. He became obdurate in believing that his precautions in the clandestine lab were adequate to protect his health. He somehow believed that his use of amphetamine would go undetected by Coach Burns, even though the Collegiate Track Association of America threatened drug testing by urinalysis as a prerequisite to competition in all the spring events. In the distorted dimension, that James thought of as reality, his life was still on track. He had encountered no major challenges to his principles. He somehow held the line on his studies, kept out of trouble with the coach, ate food that disgusted him, and ran more than 80 miles a week, on top of the 35 miles he did with team practice.

When Christmas break arrived, James had plenty of money to get a bus back to LaPush. He had thought he would leave all his amphetamines behind, but at the last minute he packed a supply of 100 tablets for a 10 day trip. He rationalized that just packing them did not necessitate ingesting them. He would enjoy running his old courses out of LaPush. His mother hardly recognized him when he got off the Greyhound Bus in Port Angeles. She immediately started to cry when she did make him out. He had changed so, she remarked between sobs. It was an hour and a half trip back to LaPush. They were driven by John Pinn, who had been married now for six years and now had a five-year-old daughter. He had married a counselor at the Forks Outreach Services while he was receiving therapy for post traumatic stress syndrome, growing out of his participation in the Viet Nam conflict. Most of the trip out of Port Angeles was in silence beyond the snuffling of June Crow which went on for the first ten minutes.

John Pinn broke the silence to make small talk as the cramped vehicle crested Govan's Hill, and they came into the National Park around Lake Crescent. "I was telling June on the way over that my little Dorothy is hanging around with your nephew Wally Woodrift. They're a real terror together. Wally's a little Houdini and can get into anything. I keep an empty .22 pistol locked in the nightstand next to my bed. The other day they came running by playing Indians and cowboys, and Wally was dry firing the pistol at Dorothy. I got madder than hell. I sent him home, and told Dorothy to go to her room. I came in later to check on her, and she was asleep under the covers...that's what I thought. When I went to the sink in the kitchen to get a drink of water I could see them both running around outside still playing Indians and cowboys. The little snot had come through the window. They made a dummy out of stuffed clothing to take a nap for Dorothy and out the window they both went. This kid is only six years old, but he's more wily and persistent than a case of the clap. Um...excuse me, June. I don't think I want Dorothy playing with a kid like that." More snuffles from Mrs. Crow were the only answer to Pinn's bid for conversation.

John Pinn followed James to the door of his shack/bedroom as Mrs. Crow ducked into the trailer to start supper for her son. "One thing my wife has helped me with is dealing with guilt. For a while that Viet Nam thing was driving me nuts and every time I saw a helicopter, a rat, a rifle, a bowl of rice...anything at all remotely related...I'd be back in the jungle, hunkered down in an open grave, shooting at women, and kids, and God knows what...I know I killed people for a cause I don't believe in. I didn't believe it, even then. Whatever was righteous and enduring in that war...maybe the little yellow people were closer than we were because it's their flag that flies over the jungle now. Anyway, for a while, the grief and guilt...became too much for me and I started to flip out. My wife, Julie, she helped save my life by getting me to talk about it. God knows what would have happened to me if I left it all bottled up inside. I can deal with it now."

"I want you to know that I feel bad for what Jeff and I did with that weather balloon. You were just a kid having a fun experiment, and we ruined it for you. It's been ten years, but I want to say I'm sorry." John held out his hand. James studied him for a while, wondering if shaking his hand would shut him up so that he could take a couple of pills, and go out for a run before dinner. James took John's hand and shook it. He took his bag from John's left hand, and entered his shed.

"It's OK," James said over his shoulder. "The whole Father's Day thing was a dumb idea, anyway." James shut the door on Pinn and began unpacking his jogging ruck. He popped two amphetamines into his mouth, and swallowed them with his saliva. He heard Pinn start up his small pick-up and drive off toward his new home up at the Second Beach housing project.

The day after his return, James got a telephone call from Timothy Clark Gable. Tim Gable was not a friend to James as they grew up together in LaPush. As children, Tim had frequently made fun of James' religious beliefs and, as young adults, he criticized James for having no political inclinations. For James part, he found Tim Gable spiritually bankrupt. Quileute spiritual leadership is conveyed from one generation to another by heredity and family lines. There is no bureaucratic machinery for impeaching a spiritual leader run amok. As a child, James found Tim to be brash, and rude. As a young adult, he equated Tim's interest in beer, illicit drugs, and fast women to moral depravity. It was a surprise to get a telephone call from him. He was asking James, if he could come over to discuss an item of mutual interest.

When Tim Gable arrived at the Crow residence he got straight to the point. "I hear you're dealing speed. I'd like to get some from you."

"Who told you I was selling amphetamines?"

"I have friends in Oregon. Word gets around who's supplying what. How much are you asking for a hundred tabs?"

"Listen, Tim, I have never, never sold drugs, and I never will. Whoever told you I was dealing speed told you *wrong*."

"Do you, or do you not, cook speed for Steven Holloway in a lab just north of Eugene, Oregon?"

"Uh...maybe." James had always thought of himself as a laboratory technician rather than a cook in a clandestine lab. Tim Gable's questions were hemming him in, and making him feel claustrophobic.

"Well, do you have speed or not?"

"Uh...maybe." He needed to get out and run off the feeling of being trapped.

"Well, fuck you, Crow. If you ever need any help yourself on some spiritual quest don't come around looking for Tim Clark Gable." Tim stormed out the door in self-righteous fury.

The confrontation with Tim hung around James over the Christmas vacation like a fart cloud. He tried running minus the preliminary ingestion of amphetamine, but ended up cutting his training short without the drug's influence. It scared him to realize how dependent he had become on a substance.

On the third day of his vacation, his mom called him into the trailer to take a phone call. "It's your old friend, Jeff Sparks," announced June Crow. Like hemorrhoids, or an impacted toenail, are old friends, thought James.

"Hello, this is James Crow."

"James this is Jeff Sparks. I'm calling from outside Washington D. C. and I'm using a government satellite - part of the Defense Early Warning system, to talk to you. It doesn't cost me a penny." Sparks paused to let the message sink in. He got no reaction so he plodded on. "Say, I'm staying in touch with what's happening there in LaPush, even though I've been gone for eight years, and I understand you're going to the University of Oregon." Sparks paused for what he expected to be a torrential collegiate report of challenging classes, pretty coeds, sports achievements, inedible institutional food and the usual sundry details pertinent to young academics. There was only the faint hum of radar searching the horizon for incoming nuclear missiles or enemy bombers. Evidently Crow was still pissed about that God damn weather balloon. Jeeze! What a sorehead! "Look, James, if you're still mad about that weather balloon, I'm really sorry. We were just kids having fun, all right? I need you to get a message to an old friend of mine who is coming to the University of Oregon to give a speech. I'd contact him myself, but the FBI is all over him, because of some shit at Wounded Knee back in 1973. Will you give him a message for me?"

"I don't think so."

"Come on, James, hear the message, and then decide if you'll give it. You won't go to the Feds with this will you?"

"No."

"Here's what I want you to tell my friend, whose name is Clarence Fourskins..." Sparks related a message that would cause a Secretary of Defense to defecate in his underwear; a message that would cause Abraham Lincoln to roll over in his grave. When he was through with the message, Sparks asked, "Will you please give that message to Fourskins?"

"Maybe, but I don't think so."

"Jesus Christ! You stupid, skinny, shit eating..." James Crow hung up on the _D_efense _E_arly _W_arning system.

****

Nothing felt right to James on this trip. He was shy of the fellowship that used to envelope him at the LaPush Assembly. There was nothing exciting or compelling in his experimentation with the chemistry equipment, and bottled potions that filled all the voids in his bedroom shed. The gulf that separated him from his mother had become deeper and more vast. It was with some relief that New Year's of 1979 came and went, and he was again on the Greyhound, on his way back to Eugene. As the trees, and dense foliage of the Olympic Peninsula, surrendered to the naked openness of the I-5 corridor, James ran a mental inventory of the few dear possessions he had needed to remember for his return to academia. His three pairs of running shoes, two pairs of shorts, school texts, money, amphetamine...*THE AMPHETAMINE!*: he had left the unfinished supply of speed on the night table by his bed. He would be without the drug until he made more in the lab, and his mother might discover his drug dependence.

A chill ran down James' spine and the air inside the bus turned rank as the coach passed into the atmosphere of the Chehalis stockyards. No feces smells good, reflected James. But somehow, the smell from animals on their way to the death of the slaughter house smells the worst. *PEANUTS: THE ONLY THING TO COME OUT OF GEORGIA THAT MAKES SENSE* read the billboard with Uncle Sam's likeness. The billboard owner referred to his disgruntlement with the Jimmy Carter administration. Politics were the last thing on James' mind. But James turned his head to read the message on the south facing aspect of the sign. *AMERICA: LOVE*

54

IT, OR GIVE IT BACK TO THE INDIANS. James wondered that the author saw the two as mutually exclusive.

****

June Crow was left with a great restlessness from her son's visit. She felt a deep foreboding. June sensed the barrier that separated her from her son. It had existed since Edward had walked out of their lives a decade ago. To this wall had been added a new bulwark that cut off all meaningful communication and the light of all emotion. June understood that the college experience had implanted something upon her son besides a higher education, and she entered James' shed room in search of clues. When she found the bottle on the night stand, her world closed in on her. Her son, the drug abuser. It was too much! All his life he had been a paragon of virtue and now he was abusing drugs! She had lost Edward, and now she had lost James. What was there left to live for? Making beds and cleaning toilet bowls at LaPush Ocean Park? Sweeping out her mobile home, or reading *People* magazine drinking Pepsi? A monthly check from a husband who was unseen now for ten years? Nothing seemed worth the pain of living in a vacuum of love. She lifted the vial to her lips, and upended the bottle. She swallowed a dozen amphetamines. She went inside the trailer to sit in the Lazy Boy, and wait for the end. In five minutes she was sweeping, and cleaning the glass of the trailer, while she waited. She felt like she had drunk a hundred Pepsi's except her mouth was dry, and she didn't have to pee. She dusted; she stacked the *People* magazines chronologically; she cleaned out the refrigerator and the oven; she went over the entire trailer looking for a speck of dirt or item out of place. When the trailer was immaculate, and she realized that death had eluded her; she searched her environment for stronger medicine.

EIGHT

*I*t was the meaty knuckled hand of politics that first slapped James into an awareness of where he was going with his abuse of amphetamines. When he arrived back at his room on Saturday evening, Burt was in the room with the ubiquitous cloud of marijuana smoke. "Well, are you going to hear 'Two Dogs Fucking' talk to the Native American Caucus tomorrow night?"

"No." James neither knew nor cared about what the dead head was talking about.

"Since I got back three hours ago, there's been four calls from your red brethren on campus that want you to be there..." Burt is interrupted by the phone ringing. "It's for you," announces Burt without moving from his supine position on the bed.

"Hullo," James said into the mouthpiece, with a sense of foreboding.

"Hello, James, this is Ellen Rainwater, with the AmerInd Caucus. We haven't had the opportunity to meet, but I've heard about your achievements with the track team, and it's an honor to get to speak with you." Ellen Rainwater waited for an acknowledgement of her compliment, which was not forthcoming. She went on with her pitch. "Tomorrow night, Clarence Fourskins of AIM will be at the Student Union Hall to discuss issues relating to our activities here on campus." She again paused to allow James to acquiesce to the imperative. Silence. "So, James, it's important for us to have a good turn out. This guy Fourskins is coming all the way from the Rosebud Reservation in South Dakota, and he's going to address issues that affect you and me. I'm asking you to be there at 7 p.m.." Again, only silence. "Hello, James, are you there?"

"Yes, Ellen."

"Will you be there tomorrow night?"

"Uh, I don't think so."

"I want you to be there, James. What can I say or do that will change your mind?" Ellen Rainwater waited out the silence this time. She had spent her persuasive arsenal, and could now only wait to assess the impact she had made.

James recoiled with discomfort. He had never been to be a political rally in his life. He had no interest in what Clarence Fourskins had to say to the assemblage. But saying 'no' had always been a little tough for James, and Ellen was so sincere. With the free-floating anxiety he felt from his trip to LaPush, he felt like he was drowning in loneliness and self-doubt. He momentarily thought of asking Ellen to join him for lunch, but knew the suggestion would not issue from his lips. "OK, I'll be there."

PROPERTY OF KVUO, 103.7 FM
TRANSCRIPT OF SPEECH GIVEN BY CLARENCE FOURSKINS AT THE
UNIVERSITY OF OREGON ON SUNDAY, JANUARY 7, 1979.
     Transcript made by Russell Jordan, student reporter.　47 people in
attendance.　Pro tempore president of the U of O's AmerInd Caucus introduces
Fourskins at 19:10.

Rainwater speaking: "A lot of us find ourselves butting our heads against the wall of authority.　Anyone who is in the position of challenging authority will agree that it always seems like our heads will break before the wall comes tumbling down.　In the five centuries that Native America has come under the influence of European colonization, and settlement, we have experienced a history of conflict and repression.　How to use this university as a theater for civil rights issues; how to become ourselves instruments of social justice; how to regain a perspective and relationship with our ancestral heritage, and ethnic culture; and how to use conflict and confrontation as tools towards the advancement of Native America, rather than as the excuse for her repression and extirpation.　These will be the topics we address tonight.

"With us tonight is Clarence Fourskins, himself an Oglalla Sioux, but a spokesperson for all of us in his secretariat position with the American Indian Movement.　Clarence knows the headaches that come from confronting authority. He knows the sting of betrayal and is familiar with the oppression meted out to those who dare to oppose the authoritarian elements of White America.　(That's 'Amerika' with a 'k' for that young White man in back recording this for the school's radio station.)

"Clarence spent two years in a Federal prison.　It was an attempt to silence a voice that would not be quieted.　Instead of abiding in silence, Clarence Fourskins has spent most of the seven years since his release from the penitentiary crying out for social justice; for an end to repression for Native America; for BIA reform; and for Red-man sovereignty in Indian Country.　Our collective cry will not be silenced. Sisters and brothers, it is my pleasure to introduce to you, Clarence Fourskins of AIM."

(Enthusiastic applause lasts for 25 seconds.　Mr. Fourskins smiles and waves and drinks from a glass of water on the lectern.　He arranges a few pages of notes and begins speaking, apparently from memory:)

"The Great Chief in Washington sends word that he wishes to buy our land.　How can you buy or sell the sky, the warmth of the land?　The idea is strange to us.　If we do not own the freshness of the air and the sparkle of the water, how can you buy them?　There is no quiet in the White man's cities.　No place to hear the unfurling of leaves in the spring or the rustle of the insect's wings.　The clatter only seems to insult the ears.　And what is there to life if a man cannot hear the lonely cry of the whippoorwill or the arguments of the frogs around a pool at night?　The Indian

prefers the soft sound of the wind darting over the face of a pond, and the smell of the wind itself, cleansed by the midday rain, or scented with piñon pine. So if we sell you our land, love it as we've loved it. Care for it as we've cared for it. Hold in your mind the memory of the land as it is when you take it. And with all your strength, with all your mind, with all your heart, preserve it for your children, and love it...as God loves us all."

"These words were spoken by Chief Sealth, during treaty negotiations near the present-day city that would be named for him, Seattle...Negotiations that ultimately separated the Suquamish Indians from the land base and resources which had sustained them for millennia. I feel that any discussion of Native America is properly introduced by the perspective of our forefathers. But any wisdom or insights that I can share with groups like this kind of pale, and seem banal in comparison with their wisdom. Did you know that the United States Constitution, heralded as one of the greatest literary pillars of human rights, was plagiarized from the Iroquois Confederacy? Do you doubt that every underlying principle of the modern environmental movement was articulated by American Indians a century ago? Most of us can't even communicate in the language of our forefathers. Our reservations are bizarre, and horrible, intercultural mutations where broken beer bottles, and gutted, overturned vehicles landscape every yard. The warriors and great orators of our forefathers have become the street punks, and beggars of this nation's cities. We have become cut off from the power and spiritualism of our culture.

"I want to thank the red sisters and brothers in the audience for coming here tonight to ponder our dilemma. To the sprinkling of White faces I see in the audience, I say, welcome, and may you leave here with an understanding that we aspire only for peace and equality in a system that has stripped us of our land, our resources and our dignity. To the traitor in the audience, for I have learned over time that every audience has a pair of treacherous ears that report my so-called sedition to authority which perpetuates the repression of my people...**(Mr. Fourskins pauses and drinks again from the glass of water.)** To you, traitor, I say go in peace tonight. In peace from us, but not in peace from your conscience, which I hope torments your sleep, and attacks your appetite, and softens your penis **(nervous laughter)** until you see that we are your planetary brothers, your equals in this wonderful creation...until you desist in your slavery to White authority, and join us in a quest for an America that serves the interest of the red-man as it has long served the interests of Whites. **(Sporadic applause).** Thank you.

"My name is Clarence Fourskins. It was the name given me in consideration for four wolf skins that my maternal grandfather offered as a dowry for his impregnated daughter...my mother. My people lived off the reservation because they wanted to live in the old way and they saw the reservation as challenging the culture they wanted to hang onto so desperately. In that tradition, each generation carried its own unique name given to us out of events surrounding our parents' courtship or our conception. When I was six years old, mandatory education required that I attend school . Rather than move to the reservation, my parents sent me to school with the poor, ignorant Whites that filled up the space between the reservations, and the few thriving cities of North Dakota. *'Clarence Pecker Hat'*

59

some kid called me in third grade and I didn't know what he was talking about, but it was a good enough excuse to fight at the time. You've all been exposed to the joke about the young Indian who goes to his father to ask about his name. His father tells him about the events that led to the naming of his sister, *'Full Moon Rising'* and his brother, *'Three Swans Flying.'* The young boy's name was *'Two Dogs Fucking'* and that's a funny joke if you're White and as stupid and ignorant as the kids I grew up with. Well, some of them called me *'Two Dogs Fucking'*. I didn't care what they called me. Anything, besides *'Clarence Fourskins'* was answered with a punch in the whatever. I'll admit that, win or lose, I enjoyed fighting my tormentors and though my instincts are far more pacific these days, I don't think it hurt me to learn, at an early age, to rage against racism on a personal level. The teacher in this two-room schoolhouse I attended, was not happy with the methods by which we settled our political differences, so rather than going to the parents of these darling little racists and saying, "This little Fourskins is getting real touchy about his name, so tell your kid to lay off," he went to my parents and had them legally change my name to *'Foskins'*. Fat lot of good that did, because I was still *'Glans Foreskin'* to my classmates. I had to wait 13 years until I was 21 to legally change my name back to *'Fourskins'*. I did that in a Federal penitentiary.

"Some of you may have heard that I became a parent myself three years ago. My wife was pregnant, and it was kind of hard on her. To keep her mind off the distress of what was happening inside her, we spent time poring over ideas for names. Of course, I searched my memory and could remember the night of conception. But try as I might, I couldn't place two dogs in coitus in the picture...**(pauses for laughter)**, so my childhood name was out. Four wolf skins, back when I was conceived, was a pretty big deal. By 1976, there were no more wolves at all in North Dakota, so I figured four wolf skins ought to still convey a certain premium. Incidentally, it wasn't Indians that extirpated the wolves in the Dakotas and the skins that gave me my namesake were older than my grandfather. Anyway, it came as a little bit of a shock to me when I got a post card from my grandfather, who never said boo to me when I was in the jug... **(pulls out a U.S. Mail postcard from his papers and displays it)** a post card which says only: *"It is my desire for my great grandson not to be a Fourskins."* I was hurt, I can tell you, because it seemed like a betrayal of all my family's intentions to live, as much as possible, within our cultural heritage. Felicia, my wife, had been teased some about her name in school **(Mr. Fourskins talks through some isolated laughter)** and she wanted to get clear of any names that would visit trouble on her kid. We looked over traditional Sioux names. I was fond of a unisexual name, *'Nauto'*, which is like an angel or manifestation of nature. It's the wind, or rain, or frogs arguing around a pool. We both agreed that this was a pretty name. But then there were twins, boy and girl, so what to do about that? I brooded over this shitty post card my grandfather had sent. Then the inspiration came to me...Two cowboys with one arrow so to speak. In every question of uprearing since the naming of the children I have deferred to Felicia, but, God help me, I named them *'Nauto B.'* and *'Toobe A. Fourskins'*. For the first year I was asking *'Toobe or Nauto B.?'* for real. **(Laughter begins to break out and grows in intensity as Mr. Fourskins talks.)** You think my two kids won't turn out to be warriors by the time they are through school? I expect my daughter to get through law school and be a go-for-the-jugular civil rights attorney. I expect her to bail my tired, and gray, ass out of the slammer. **(Laughter and some applause.)** Anyway, they can always go by their middle names and be Brian and Ann Foskins if the going gets too tough. **(Drains glass of water and another glass of water is brought to him by Ms. Rainwater.)** Thank you.

"A little historic perspective here: In late November of 1864, Colonel Chivington of the U.S. Cavalry mounted a campaign against the friendly and peace loving Cheyenne tribe under Chief Black Kettle at Sand Creek. Though he was a brave and resourceful warrior, Black Kettle had been persuaded by President Lincoln himself, that sanctuary from hostility existed under the large American flag which the President gave the chief. The braves of the Sand Creek tribe were off hunting, so Colonel Chivington led his 700 men against 35 Indian men and 600 women and children who huddled under the American and white truce flags peacefully in their own village. It was easy to find troops willing to fight the poorly armed and hungry Indians, as the alternative was fighting troops of the Confederate States of America on the southern front. These Indian women and children were slaughtered and mutilated begging for peace. Babies were pulled from the arms of mothers and killed. The mothers were in turn slaughtered. A pregnant woman was cut open, and her fetus drug out of her womb; women's breasts and genitalia cut off; every head of the deceased scalped. The soldiers used the collected scrotums for tobacco pouches and used the women's genitalia for saddle-bows and to decorate their uniform hats...your government at work. This is history. It represents a pattern in the treatment of Native America by the United States.

"How were our forefathers to defend themselves against such atrocity with only stone arrowheads and single-shot rifles? Two winters after Sand Creek found the Sioux, Crows, Arrapahos, and Cheyennes in alliance with one another in an effort to avenge such brutality and to drive the Bluecoats from their illegal occupation of Powder River country. The great minds of Red Cloud, Crazy Horse, Dull Knife, and Man-Afraid-Of-His-Horses combined to strategize a defense. A decoy war party was sent out against a wood cutting party within sight of Fort Kearny. Artillery was fired on the war party and a company of soldiers dispatched to chase the Indians away from the fort. The soldiers had orders not to pursue out of sight of the fort, but placing confidence in their numbers, their repeating rifles, and the power of modern artillery, they chased the war party into a draw of Peno Creek where more than two thousand confederated, and angry Indians popped up to wipe out the eighty-one soldiers in hand to hand fighting. The history books of the White man tell of the poor, broken and mutilated bodies of the Bluecoats. The White military command composed essays philosophizing on the red savages 'paganistic brutality' that were circulated to inflame White America, and justify a campaign of genocide against our ancestors.

"Ellen mentioned that I would be talking some about confrontational politics and the use of force to achieve political objectives. Believe me, I'm no coward when it comes to throwing punches, but look at the history of Native America, and look at where we are now. For many Indian tribes and nations, conflict was a game of 'got-you-last,' and stealing ponies back and forth. It proved our manhood, but it did little to secure our security. Here in the Northwest, some of the coastal Indians fought more conventional wars with villages in siege by naval assaults. Again, intertribal warfare did little to prepare us for the European onslaught. Red Cloud, Sitting Bull, Chief Joseph and countless others of the most brilliant and courageous warriors in the history of mankind...did their armed resistance save us our land, or preserve the bison herds? Did riding into a shower of bullets from repeating rifles brandishing stone arrowheads save our women from being raped, or our young braves from becoming alcoholics? Did fighting to the last man keep the iron horse from coming over the horizon or stay the wave of gold-hungry settlers that washed like an ever-waxing tide over our continent? Look at...''

(Change cassette to side 'b' of tape number #1. Mr. Fourskins is speaking:)

"... Roman Nose of the Cheyennes, who rode within easy-firing range of two hundred stirred-up cavalrymen with repeating rifles to demonstrate the potency of Indian medicine. Look at Sitting Bull, who crushed the forces of the United States government at Little Big Horn. General Custer had repeatedly promised he would not harass the Sioux. The squaws that scoured the battlefield pierced the General's ears with their sewing awls so that he could hear his own words when he spoke in the afterlife. Look at Joseph, of the Nez Perce. Faced with fight or die, he fought with such ingenuity and cunning that it took three horse-soldiers for every man, woman and child in Joseph's ward to round up and arrest the refugees. Did Chief Joseph leave us with the message, "Pick up a gun and go for it, dude," or did he say "I will fight no more, forever." Well, the fight is a long way from being gone out of me. But I am asking you all to consider how much protection our brave and resourceful forefathers afforded Native America by resisting with bow, and contraband carbine, the onslaught of White military technology.

"Before any one of you ambushes the National Guard with a .22, and a case of dynamite; or takes on the Secret Service, and the Park Police, around the White House, with an assault rifle... stop for a minute and reflect on this: The pen is mightier than the sword. A picture is worth a thousand words. How significant is a spot on the seven o'clock news depicting the plight of the American Indian? I've sipped cocktails with television news personalities at restaurants, where I couldn't afford the ketchup, and I've tried serving up Molitov cocktails to a university computer. In the former case we had the press eating out of our hand. They carried our message to about half a million viewers. In the latter case, I got thrown in jail to rot for two years. I'm thirty years old. I've been raising a fuss, demonstrating openly for the liberation of Native America. Drawing attention to the oppression endured by our people has been the goal of my entire adult life. I've had my skull fractured twice by cops that thought the best way to preserve law and order was to fracture the heads of the American Indians who were peacefully assembled outside a government building, exercising their first amendment rights. Then, in 1968, I got smart and went to the *New York Times* news desk. I asked if they would print some close-up pictures of police brutality... photocopy of cops with their sticks up high, thumping on coeds and kicking them onto the pavement. They would *pay good money* for these kind of pictures. So, I gave my head a vacation at our next demonstration in front of the Federal Building. I went across the way with a thousand millimeter lens and ten rolls of film. We got two pictures, and a feature story, on the front page of the *New York*

Times. I got an interview and a lot more pictures published in the Sunday edition and we got $5,500 for our war chest back at our N.Y.U. AmerInd Caucus. Could I have done this well getting a stick away from a policeman, and busting a cop's head? Three NYCPD cops were fired because of my pictures. I'm sure if you interviewed these outstanding officers, they would have preferred the stick , to the camera.

"Not everything I did for the two years I was in college was so smart. I was demonstration happy...we all were. The war in Viet Nam; the treatment of Hispanic fruit workers who were trying to unionize; the breakdown of process in the Democratic convention party in Chicago; the unrest of our Black brothers; the tendency of cops to break heads any time more than two citizens came together to post a grievance...well, we had plenty of issues keeping us out on the street mixing it up with the police. Four students were killed in an antiwar/anti-ROTC demonstration at Kent State, by an insufficiently trained, and scared detachment of the Ohio National Guard. We all went ape shit. I forgot about all my classes and obligations, and hitchhiked out to Kent State to co-ordinate a retaliatory strike against the military complex that had shot-up the students. When I got there, three days after the shooting incident, there were *NO TRESPASSING/STUDENTS ONLY* signs everywhere. My presence there, as a big-time agitator, was grossly illegal. Goodbye Bill of Rights. The students were terrified and all hunkered down. All they wanted to talk about was how much they would miss their four friends, and what great people they were. Every time I came around with plans to tear up the ROTC building again, or take out the motherfucker CO - excuse me, Ellen - the misguided commanding officer that ordered his men to open fire on an unarmed crowd of students. Let's get one thing straight: the crowd was chucking rocks. But I did my own investigation. Like always, the craziest most dangerous and radical demonstrators that day were two spooks. Trust me on this. The FBI infiltrates all so-called '*seditious*' student groups with long-haired, rabble-rousing agents of their own. In the demonstrations they're the ones out front, nose to nose with the cops, throwing back the tear gas grenades and screaming, "You fucking pigs!" That's how it was that April day in 1970 at Kent State. And two FBI agents almost got shot. Instead, a kid out in front, trying to stop the agent from throwing rocks, got it through the chest. I had plans for the FBI as well as the CO, and ROTC building; but these students were extremely unmotivated. About all they were up for was staggering around from funeral to funeral, all weepy eyed with black arm bands on their left arms. I got disgusted and left. But before I left Kent State, I bought an old rattle-trap Ford convertible from one of the students. The three hundred and fifty dollars represented my life's savings, but I was tired of hitchhiking, and too cheap to take the bus.

"The rig was a gas hog, but had a good a.m. radio. It kept me entertained as I drove back to Manhattan Island. The news was that colleges had erupted all over the country, everywhere but Kent State, in reaction to the shooting. The car got towed from in front of my dormitory within a few hours of my return. The politics so absorbed me, that I never got a chance to get my car back from the impound yard. In ten days I got thrown into the impound yard myself, so the cops got to keep the car *and* the operator. When I got back, NYU had cancelled all classes and was shut down like many other universities. But the students were still around demonstrating against the war and mixing it up with the cops every day. We formed 'cells,' which is a unit of three to five people you can trust, to establish one strategic objective, and to operate without support or a lot of communication with the infrastructure of whatever political body you owe allegiance. It worked for the French underground in World War Two, so we thought it was tried-and-true. I picked two partners for my cell. One guy was an American Indian from this part of the country. He was an electronics whiz kid. I knew him through our AmerInd Caucus, and I trusted him with my life. I'll call him 'Johnny Ohm' to protect him from the FBI ears in this audience. It was his name during our clandestine operation. The other was a White kid from Georgia. He was kind of a hanger on, always asking questions about the politics of being an Indian. Where did I stand on the use of force and how did I feel about the Constitution of the United States? His questions should have tipped me off. He seemed a little crazier than me, but I suppose I respected that about him. He talked in a soft voice with that Georgia accent and was always showing that southern gentility to girls I was hanging out with. I liked the guy. I wanted a White face in our cell because this was a thing about Viet Nam and not strictly an AmerInd issue. He went by the name of *Ron Gibbs*, but I had time in the slammer to put my ear to the ground. Special Agent Fred Prue of the Federal Bureau of Investigations, was my so-called *partner* in the NYU computer hostage thing.

"It was Gibbs that came up with the plan of taking the University's computer hostage, and holding it ransom for the $30,000 it would take to spring three Black Panthers that were being held in a New York City jail. Taking the computer was as easy as walking into the room with some gasoline and traffic flares. We had a time-bomb arrangement to light up the computer without incinerating ourselves, if NYU refused to cough up the thirty large. Of course, they did refuse. Then it was a question of blowing up the computer just to keep our part of the deal, or bailing out the fire escape and probably getting away scott-free. We were up there for five days and the cops got tired of waiting for us to make our move. We went out a few times to stretch our legs and get some food. When we got it through our heads that NYU wasn't going to cave in on account of their beloved computer, Johnny Ohm and I were for bailing out and forgetting the whole scheme. But Gibbs made a big deal about how we would discredit future threats from the New Left, and did I want to be like the ball-less wonders I had seen back at Kent State. Gibbs knew how to operate this computer. He showed us how it had information relating to ROTC recruitment, and military contracts relating to the medical campus downtown. So it was a coin toss for me and I said, "If it will make you happy to blow this puppy up, Ron, you go ahead and do it." Then Gibbs came up with some song and dance about how he had already been popped, down at the University of Miami, for some similar show-boating with incendiaries; and how he was out on probation, and they would lock him up and throw away the key if he got caught lighting the fuse on another gasoline bomb. So I said I would do it. Gibbs almost kissed me, then he was at the door. "Don't fuck up," he said real sweetly in that southern accent as he went out the door..."

(change tape to side 'a' tape #2.)

(Mr. Fourskins is talking:)

"...Johnny Ohm and I had a minute while I set things up. I could see that he had a clear shot down the outside fire escape so out he went before I engaged the five-minute electronic ignition. I set it, and went down the inside fire escape. When I opened the door to the first floor to affect my exit, there were seven FBI spooks, and about ten city cops to say hello. Ron Gibbs, as I said, was Special Agent Fred Prue. They'd had a bug in the room, but let Johnny Ohm get away so they could have me, hot-handed, in the act of blowing up the computer. Fred Prue led a five-man charge up the steps to pull the plug on the detonator and save the computer. I went up for two years on something that any legal intern could have spotted as entrapment. They went after Johnny Ohm, too, but he disappeared from campus and there are limits to how far even the FBI will follow you on an accessory charge. They didn't even know the guy's real name. If there is not a Special Agent in the audience tonight, there is an informant reporting back to one. Please get word back to Special Agent Prue that, though his betrayal makes an interesting story, and makes a good point for student political activists, I'm not prepared to forgive him, just yet. We will meet again. I will be avenged for the two years that was stolen from my life.

"Not that I dwell in vengeance. There's a verse in the Old Testament about vengeance belonging to Jehovah, and I'll go along with that. Ellen asked me to address spiritualism, and I have to say that I am impressed with Christianity. That is, I am impressed with the doctrines of Jesus Christ, and the common sense tenets of Mosaic Law. I've got no fight with any true Christian, because they will have no fight with me. They are prohibited from killing me or doing unto me in any manner that they would not like done unto themselves. How many true Christians are there in all of Christendom? Not but a few, I fear. In general, Christianity has been a catalyst in the rape of Native America's spiritualism. As the tide of White settlement left only islands of Native America, the settlers used their Bibles to assuage their consciences from the disease, starvation, genocide, and the cultural annihilation they visited upon the original landlords of this continent. They thought of themselves as the chosen people, and red Americans as savages. They corrupted our innocence with rape, and the scalping of adversaries. Then they attributed such atrocities to Indian customs when we were finally debauched. I had a young Christian theologian explain to me that all races, except White men, were the seed of Cain, who murderously slew Abel, invoking the ever spiteful curse of Jehovah. Look in the stained glass of the churches here in Eugene, and you will see a Caucasian Christ crucified. My understanding is that history has somehow bleached the complexion of Jesus from one darker than any in this room, to the lily-white face we see uplifted to heaven in the stained glass. If Jehovah God sent Jesus to round up the good and salvageable human elements of this world - and I'm not saying He didn't - I can't believe that He would have chosen White men to the exclusion of the American Indian. Nowhere in the history of civilization have a people shown a reverence or love for the Creation that blazed brighter than that of the American Indian. Somehow a spiritually solid, and morally correct message, was twisted to kill and oppress our people. But I don't recommend anyone outright reject Christianity without giving a close examination.

65

"Especially since most of us have drifted so far from our ancestral spirituality. I'm not recommending any one of you drive bone fragments through your chest and hang from rawhide while suspended from the light fixtures in your dormitory. I'm not recommending that you blow out your brain cells on Peyote buttons, or dehydrate in a sweat lodge. But I am challenging each one of you to reflect on the spirituality of your ancestors, and walk as far as you can on their path. Each of us, born of Indian blood, should be on some quest...some search, to find our way back to the spiritual refinement of our cultural past. Whatever you call the God you worship, be sure that it is the true God, and that His face is not masked by tinsel and golden icons. Deliver us from the greed and lust for power that characterize the White man's worship. You must love and respect this planet, as did our forefathers. You must work tirelessly to save it from the destruction of technology...as did our forefathers.

"Spiritualism goes hand in glove with Indian mentality. You may remember how I said earlier in the evening that the U.S. Constitution was a rehashing of American Indian political ideology. Let's look at that claim for a minute. The five nations of Iroquois were the Mohawk, the Onedeis, the Senecas, the Cayugas and the Onondagas, who were cannibals. They shared a belief that creation was the product of the Jehovah God, who they referred to as Master of Life, or 'Teharonhiawagon.' He was opposed on earth by an evil brother that promoted the intertribal fighting born out of eye for eye, murder for murder blood revenge. Promised to the Iroquois, was a 'prince of peace,' who would lead the five nations to a glorious time when peace would spread like a snow-white carpet across the forest floor of the northeast portion of this continent. The story goes that Deganwidah, which means "He, the thinker," was born to a young, virgin Huron. The Hurons were the enemy of the Iroquois. Young Deganwidah had a speech impediment. At an early age he had a vision of a tree of justice and prosperity growing from the aforementioned carpet of peace from an anchor of five great roots, which young Deganwidah interpreted to be the five nations of Iroquois. Even without the handicap of a speech impediment he would have had a hard time selling the Iroquois' "chosen people" idea to the Hurons. A hole was cut in the ice of a frozen lake. The young prophet was tossed in and the ice plug returned to its hole. Deganwidah escaped the icy waters and returned to camp to continue the business of his stuttering soothsaying to the unhappy Hurons who continually persisted in their unwilling audience to the young omnipotent.

"Meanwhile, in the cannibal camp of the Onondongas, another young visionary was having troubles. Among a people that believed in loving your enemy like you loved a good rump roast, he extolled the virtues of the peace of the Master of Life. His name was 'Hiawatha.' He organized peace rallies and was opposed by an influential elder statesman named Atotarho. Atotarho was a warrior. He derived his power from war mongering. He took prisoners as slaves and comestibles. He was not enthusiastic about the prospect of peace. He attacked Hiawatha at his point of vulnerability, which was his love of his daughters. One by one, Hiawatha lost his precious daughters to the assassins. Accidents were arranged by the cunning and evil statesman. After losing daughter number five, Hiawatha began to think that maybe peace wasn't such a great thing after all. He went out on a little war party of his own.

"Now American Indian mythology, like so-called 'history,' is a skeleton of truth supporting a flesh of social vindication. If you don't believe the twist this story is about to take, that's fine, but I'm not making it up, and Teharonhiawagon strike me down from this lectern if I'm not giving you the story straight out of the book, which in this case was written by J.N.B. Hewitt in 1918 and entitled A Constitutional League of Peace in the Stone Age America. So here's young Hiawatha, returned from kicking some ass and in the tradition of his clansmen, cooking up the casualties of his ire in a big stone kettle. The stuttering peacenik, Deganwidah climbs up on Hiawatha's roof, and peers at the proceedings through the smoke hole. Hiawatha saw the charismatic face of Deganwidah reflected in the face of his gumbo. He thought for a moment that someone had fetched-in the head of his enemy from where it was reposing on the end of his spear outside Hiawatha's lodge. Then, as the face smiled in friendship, he was overcome with disgust and shame for the strange appetite of his nation. He went to empty the concoction from his kettle in the babbling brook that ran before his lodge, and there he met Deganwidah who congratulated Hiawatha for his repudiation of cannibalism. Together they formed a peace party, Hiawatha being the orator, and Deganwidah being the big thinker. It's funny how history remembers, and eulogizes the mouth pieces and forgets the brains and soul of any movement. Peace blanketed the land of the divergent Iroquois like snow, freezing active hostility, and blanketing old hostilities. Hiawatha and Deganwidah established a formal federal government with parliamentary procedures, and a bill of rights to ensure the rights of every individual. The sanctions and guarantees of freedom were written into the wampum currency with far more clarity and detail of purpose than the "In God We Trust," you see on the currency of the United States. I'm not suggesting that Thomas Jefferson and Benjamin Franklin stole the language of 'When in the course of human events..." or "We the people of the United States...' from wampum beads, but both these men studied the Iroquois government and borrowed heavily from the Indian political infrastructure. If you have trouble believing that Deganwidah survived being sealed up in a frozen lake, or that Hiawatha smoked the peace pipe with the man responsible for the killing of his five daughters, try throwing a silver dollar across the Potomac or cutting down your old man's prize cherry tree sometime and see how your throwing arm or bottom feel the next day. **(Sporadic laughter from up front.)** For that matter, what has more dignity: suing for peace, even when it means calling it even with the murderer of your family, or violating an understood truce by crossing the Delaware River by darkness, on Christmas Eve, to round up a bunch of drunken Hessians? Clearly the history books were not written by Red Americans.

"Some of the fliers I saw passed out, promised that I would talk about the American Indian Movement and how it could support political activity on campus. AIM, I regret to tell you, is a dying organization. I'm here to offer you the full support and resources of AIM. Check your shoelaces, because that's the most you'll ever get from our war chest. They paid my ticket here tonight, but - for real - I've got no money for a motel, so if someone can put me up for the night, I won't be out on the street. **(A few hands go up - mostly women. Mr. Fourskins ignores this.)** I brought my sleeping bag. Anyway, it's important that you Red Americans carry the objectives and aspirations of AIM in your heart, because, I can tell you, the social discrimination, and political injustice which AIM was developed to combat, will survive the organization, and our most passionate efforts..

"AIM isn't going to tell you how to take over an admin building or throw picket lines around an art gallery for not displaying AmerInd art. For that, you are on your own. If I give you any advice at all it's: go slow, plan things through, avoid violence, respect property, know your compatriots, involve the media, and avoid jail. Jail is a waste of time. Going to jail does nothing for our cause. Nor, contrary to popular opinion is a dead Indian a good Indian. Protect yourselves. Young people so often ignore the possible consequences of the risks they take. In even their most dangerous actions, they feel invincible. Don't be arrogant. Don't tear down anything, be it a flag or institution, without a vision for its replacement.

"Let's close our eyes and explore a little fantasy together. In the wilderness a campfire is burning down into ash. My forefathers kindled their warming fires with Buffalo dung, but for this illustration we will use the sweet smelling incense cedar of the nearby Siskiyous. It is a time when this continent is virginal, and not bleeding acid and oil from wounds inflicted by the mineral explorations of the Whites. A pure and fresh wind blows on the slumbering fire, exciting a few flames from the embers. Sisters and brothers, the campfire is the soul and collective spirit of our Native consciousness. Feel it smoldering in your hearts.

"The intruder enters the camp and covets the warmth of the little smoldering fire. He lays upon you and defiles you. You smell the stale, whiskey breath on your face. You know the pain of every private thing of you being violated. Let the fire burn hot in your chest. Let the fire singe the naked, and hairy chest of the intruder. Burn hotter and drive the intruder away.

"As the fire flickers cheerfully in the night, again the intruder returns. He covers our little flame with a heavy, suffocating blanket. As the flame sputters, and chokes in smoke, you see the colors of the blanket and they are red, white, and blue. These are the colors of strangulation. The fire starves for air. You must share every breath with the struggling embers. Even a few sparks might be enough to scorch the blanket, weaken the fibers, and finally burn a hole, through which fresh air might return to revive this flame that can sustain your soul.

"Brothers and sisters, let your hearts burn hot. Fuel your fire with justice. Ventilate it with the clean wind of purity in your lives. Forsake alcohol, and drugs, for they are the White man's piss on the fire of your soul. Keep your minds and bodies from licentious liaison, and blow on the fire of your heart with a breath uncontaminated with the corruption that the intruder has brought to the campsite. Let this fire be the conflagration that drives every intruder away.

"Please open your eyes." **(Mr. Fourskins turns to face the American flag which furnishes the meeting hall of the student union.)** "I spit upon the symbol of our oppression." **(Mr. Fourskins does spit, but the spittle falls just short of the target. Two members of the audience in the front row leave their seats and pick up the flag. One pulls out a lighter.)** "Brothers, brothers, remember what I said

68

about tearing something down without a replacement. You may find me on my hands and knees after this meeting cleaning up that spit, but will you buy the university another American flag?

(Pause, as the two students consider the challenge of Mr. Fourskins. One of the student answers:) "I'll replace the flag with a condom. If the White man must fuck us with what's on this pole, I prefer it to be with a rubber." **(Laughter from audience. Mr. Fourskins laughs, as well. Students replace flag and return to their seats.)**

"There are different ways to demonstrate the intensity of our collective soul. I want to commend a young man in the audience who radiates the energy of our forefathers' tireless footsteps...a young man who obviously has gotten to where he is without drugs or the other crutches imparted to us by White society. My understanding is that we have among us a student who will represent Native America at the U.S. Olympic try outs here in Eugene this spring. Jim Crow, please stand up so that we can recognize you as a model in our emotional growth...

(Audience begins to applaud. Long pause with no one standing up to be recognized. Ms. Rainwater crosses the room to talk with a student sitting in an aisle seat. Applause increases as student stands. Mr. Fourskins:) "I would be shy, too, if I had a name like '*Jim Crow.*'" **(Laughter.)**

(James Crow speaks after long hesitation:) "My name is James. I was told to give you a message from Johnny Ohm..."

(Mr. Fourskins attempts to interrupt:) "Excuse me...hold on a minute...wait!..."

(Mr. Crow continues oblivious to the protests:) "...He says that he is in position to control the DEW system. He has been working with the high-tech defense contractor, TRW, for the last three years. He says..."**(Mr. Crow is shouted down by Mr. Fourskins who is yelling into the microphone:)**

"Hold it! Shut up! For Christ's sake, hold on! This meeting is adjourned. I need a private minute with Mr. Crow. To the White people in this audience, thank you for coming; please leave now. Ellen see that the cub reporter shuts off his recorder and erase the last two minutes on the tape..."

(Russell Jordon exits with recorder before Ms. Rainwater can get to him.)
(End of recording.)

NINE

*J*ames got back to his room late that night after a lengthy round-table discussion with Clarence Fourskins, Ellen Rainwater, and a few other students that cared to trade a few hours sleep to save the world. Though James had said little, he had heard plenty and, just as Clarence had planned, a fire had sputtered to life in James' chest. He went to his morning training in a daze.

He was met by coach Jack Burns who had a small bottle for him, into which James was to urinate. "James, I've been meaning to tell you. You've been selected for the mile, and the marathon, for the Olympic tryouts in three months. We may use you for other events depending on our team's strength in spring. Congratulations. We might as well get the drug screening done now." James peed into the bottle with the coach standing next to the urinal. He ran through the morning training like a zombie. It was becoming very evident that he would have to quit taking amphetamines.

****

Five days later, James was in his room after dinner, six days away from his last amphetamine. The room was filled with the smoke of Burt's pot and James was on the nod for want of a pill to stimulate his interest in the studies at hand. The phone rang. As always, Burt picked it up to answer it.

"It's your coach," said Burt offering the phone to James like it was a hash pipe.

"James, this is Coach Burns. The results from the urinalysis came in a few hours ago, and you're off the team. I guess I don't have to tell you what we found. It's a mandatory six- month suspension, so the Olympics are out, but, if you clean up your act, we want you back next year. I'm sorry about what this does to your scholarship, but you certainly should have seen this coming. If I can help in any way to get you off speed, and keep you off, you can call me 24 hours a day. I want you to clear out your locker tomorrow. I'm sorry, James, but you brought it on yourself. Goodbye."

"Good news, I hope," offered Burt as James hung up, and sat down at his desk with a sigh. He sat for ten minutes just looking straight ahead into the light of the fluorescent desk lamp. The phone rang and Burt answered it. "Your guidance counselor, now."

Hello, James, it's Steve. Did you get my Christmas card? How was your vacation? How's your mom doing?"

"OK, I guess."

"Say, James, one reason I'm calling, besides that I'm really interested in how you're getting along, and how your mom's doing, is that you missed a job two nights ago. I'm just wondering if anything is wrong."

"Maybe. I don't know."

"Listen James, if there's a problem you'd better come by my apartment at nine Saturday morning, so we can talk about it. Otherwise I expect you to make your appointments. A lot of people depend upon you. Will I see you Saturday morning, or will you be going back to the lab to make up the work you lost? I can't have..."

"I'll think about it. Goodbye." James hung up on Steve Holloway.

"Wisdom from on high?" asked Burt, as James returned to his desk chair to resume his study of the fluorescent fixture. In two minutes the phone rang again. Burt talked for a moment, and handed the phone to James. "It's Edward Crow for you," announced Burt.

"Hello... father?" The word "father" felt strange coming from James' mouth.

"James, it's wonderful to finally talk to you. I have so much I want to say to you and so much I want to hear..."

"I know, Dad, me too." Something was on the wind. Something catastrophic about to unfold...

"Your mother died at Olympic Memorial Hospital this morning. She died of pneumonia, but it was from a self-inflicted condition. James, she found out you were involved in drugs, and it was too much for her. I know I'm mostly to blame, abandoning you two when you were so young..."

"Oh, Papa..." James began sobbing.

"...but it's time for me to explain why I left."

"What did my... mother... do to herself?"

"I don't want to get into that right now. James, I can't expect you to believe that I left for your good, but it really was something like that. Your mom and I weren't getting along too well and that's no secret. But I would have toughed it out to be with you. Except that I was no good as a father. I was weak. Your mom was domineering, and I was too weak to take a stand. All my luck was going bad. I thought of myself as a loser. I was drinking wine to escape, you know. I really worried about what kind of role model you were getting for a dad."

"I was always proud of you...you shouldn't have left us."

"I've always been proud of you, James. And it's true, I shouldn't have left. I was running away from my problems, and they followed me. I had to confront my problems. I remarried, you know..."

"No, I didn't know..."

"...and that marriage was no better than my relationship with June. I thought opportunity was passing me by, there in LaPush, but for a good while it passed me by in Tacoma. I quit drinking, I went to counseling with my wife. I read a few books on self analysis. I spent a lot of time with myself hiking, and working outside in our little garden. I still have a long ways to go, but I'm no longer ashamed of who, or what, I am. I win some; I lose some. You will do the same. Sometimes, through no fault of mine or your own, you will lose. That's life. Don't dwell on what you can't change.

"But, now you're on some kind of drug thing. Jeez, James, that must stop. Your mom told me about the pills she found..."

"About mom's death: Why did they call you instead of me, Dad? How did they find you?"

"My telephone number has always been in the Tacoma directory. I kind of expected a phone call from June or you. About five years ago I started sending my checks *with* my address and phone number on them, so it's been no secret..."

"What checks?"

"I was wondering if June had kept that from you. Since the month I left ten years ago, I've sent about 25 per cent of my take-home pay - whatever that's been - to June. She's been rat-holing it in a savings account in custody for you. BIA paid most of her medical expenses, but there will be a funeral, and I went into the bank today to try to keep her assets out of probate. They showed me the account June set up for you. She must not have spent a penny of the money I sent. There's almost $80,000 in there. I understand you're on a full scholarship there at Eugene, but this money may open up some doors when you need it."

"I just want my parents back."

"Well, we've lost June. Blame me or accept part of the blame yourself, but she's gone. I'm sorry. Let's not get mired down in things we can't change. You taking drugs is something we *can* change. When want you to desist this minute. Never again. I understand that your scholarship is based on your performance as a runner. James, they will test you for drugs and if you come up dirty, they'll throw you out on your ear. Quit drugs today. Now! OK?"

"All right, Papa." James was drained and the tears had begun to dry into tiny crystals of Sodium Chloride on his cheeks.

"Your mom's funeral is Monday, in three days. I'm at your home, here in LaPush, if you need to call me for anything. Just check directory assistance for Tacoma whenever you need me after the funeral. I know that you were just up here for Christmas break, but I would sure like you here for the funeral in three days. Do you need me to wire you money for bus or plane fare?"

"No, Father."

"Then just call and let me know when and where I should pick you up. Don't forget what I'm telling you about facing things, and quitting drugs, OK?"

"Yes."

"Goodbye for now."

"Goodbye, Dad."

James returned the phone to cradle, and turned to find Burt staring at him.

"Heavy conversation, huh?" offered Burt.

James ignored the query and put on his jogging shoes. He was thinking about a recipe that he had to cook.

****

You have to try pretty hard not to blow up a Methamphetamine Hydrochloride lab. Many of the *precursors*, which are the vital ingredients of the reaction, are incompatible compounds that can cause fire, explosion or poisonous fume generation when they are incorrectly introduced to one another. The *reagents*, which act as catalysts in the process, are typically strong acids, bases or oxidizers and can result in apocalypse if they are spilled on anything. The *solvents*, which are used to separate the product from its highly toxic environment, are invariably explosive of themselves. The result is that you have unstable compounds, releasing poisonous and flammable vapor which do not invite the close management required to avoid an explosive environment. The lab in South Springfield, where James worked, produced Phenyl-2-Propanone as a precursor for the manufacturing of methamphetamine. The highly poisonous reagent, Thallium Nitrate, was used to produce the P-2-P.

When James arrived at the lab, on the night of January 15, 1979, he was not behaving like a chemist who wanted badly to avoid an explosion. He had brought with him two liters of ether, well beyond the 100 milliliters called for to wash out the meth crystal from the secondary product. He set up the five liter flask, mixing the reagents: Thallium Nitrate in with Freon, Sulfuric Acid, Sodium Hydroxide and shredded aluminum. To this he added 50 grams of yellow phosphorous. He poured in the two liters of ether, and checked the safe. He found most of December's product still in tact. He put the product next to the beaker which had begun to boil, much like the Coke bottle he'd used to fill the weather balloon a decade earlier. This recipe was not found in any of the drug cook books on the shelves above the tile counters. This was a recipe from hell. James turned off the light, and shut the heavy steel door. He checked to make sure that it latched and locked. He ran dead out to the nearest pay phone which was 1.4 mile from the concrete block structure of the lab. He did not have a dime so he dialed "0."

"Operator. May I help you?"

"This is a police emergency, operator. Please give me the Springfield police department."

"Hold on a minute, sir."

"Springfield Police Department, Sergeant Siel."

"Hello. I have reason to believe that there is a clandestine methamphetamine lab at risk of explosion in South Springfield."

"Give us the exact location of the lab."

"If I give you the address, you'll go running out there and someone will get hurt. It's really going to blow and I don't want anyone around when it does. Notify the Fire Department. Have them geared up in haz-mat suits because it's going to be a dirty explosion. There shouldn't be any secondary fire."

"We'll stay back, but please give me the address."

"It should be the only meth lab blowing up in South Springfield in the next hour or so. You don't need the exact address, believe me."

"Please give me your name, and the phone number you're calling from."

"All you need from me is that there is going to be a big explosion in a rural area of Springfield. Tell the fire department, and your investigators, that Thallium Nitrate was a reagent. The flash you see in the sky will be a phosphorous agent. Believe me, you'll see the flash. Don't go in until then, and everyone should be wearing haz-mat suits."

"Please give me the phone number you're calling from, so the Fire Marshall can call..." Sergeant Siel was talking to a dead line.

James dialed "0" again. "This is the operator. May I help you?"

"This is James, and I would like to make a collect call to the following number..."

Steve Holloway was a little annoyed at James for calling him collect at 40 minutes to midnight on a Friday night. He excused himself from the coed he was entangled with on the couch, and left the phone off the hook in the living room to take the line in the bedroom. "Please hang up the line, Barbara....What's up?" asked Holloway, after he heard the line in the living room click dead.

"I thought you'd want to know there is a problem over at the lab, Steve."

"Please don't use my name," said Holloway in almost a whisper. "I thought I told you not to bother me about business here at my apartment."

"Suit yourself, Steve, but there's going to be an explosion."

"An explosion! Turn off the heat or cool the reaction with ice! Where are you? Get back there and stand by with a fire extinguisher!" Holloway's voice was quite loud now. James held the receiver away from his ear.

"It's too late for that now, Mr. Holloway, and a fire extinguisher would just go up with the explosion. There's two liters of ether in there."

"Two liters of ether! Have you gone mad! And don't use my name in connection with this business, Goddamnit!" Holloway was shrieking now. He tried to calm himself. "Did you get the product out of the safe as per our protocol?" Holloway's breathing was labored, and he was talking unevenly.

"I took all the product out of the safe, but it's at the epicenter of the impending explosion."

"Are you trying to fuck me up here!" Holloway screamed. "You get back to the lab right away and get that product! Put ice on the beaker! Turn on all the exhaust fans and stand by with a fire extinguisher! I'll be right there! Now move," Holloway hissed the last two words.

"Steve, believe me, it's too late. The lab's going to blow in less than fifteen minutes. I quit. You've got no control on me..." James was talking to a dead line. He began the jog back to his dorm room. He wanted to write some notes, get his cash, and leave town. He did not want to talk with Steve Holloway anymore, especially not tonight.

****

"An emergency has come up. Please be sure the door's locked when you leave," cried out Steve to the pretty coed as he ran out of the apartment. He didn't have time to tuck in his shirt tails or put on a coat. Holloway jumped into the Porsche and streaked off to the lab like a fire engine. He checked his watch just after running his first traffic light: 11:41 on his Rolex. He could make it to the lab in 12 minutes going flat out. He hadn't brought a flashlight, so if that crazy-red-asshole, Crow-shit, dumb-fuck hadn't left the lights on, or minded him and gone back to help, he would

76

have to take the chance, and throw the electric light switch. That might be a problem. But Holloway sure as hell wasn't going to leave a month's worth of stuff next to an out of control cook. If there were any complications getting the lab back on line, he would need all the product he could lay hold of. STUPID DUMB FUCK, INDIAN SHIT! I'M GONNA KILL THAT RED MANIAC! GODDAMNIT TO HELL...

****

James was within two miles of his dorm room, and running hard when the lab blew. He checked his watch which read 11:53. He had expected the explosion about the time he reached the dorm. The white brilliance of the flash told James that all the phosphorous and solvents in the lab had gone at once. Four seconds after the flash came the thunder of the concussion. There shouldn't be much physical evidence left to investigate, thought James. His problems would be with his guidance counselor, not the law.

By the time James got to his room, fire engines and cop cars were rolling north on I-99, code three, hammer down. Burt was kneeling on his bed in his underwear, watching the commotion. "Hey, Red Bro. That was some kind of explosion! It looks like it came from Springfield. Someone at the Kessey dairy probably dropped a reefer in a pile of cow shit and set off an ammonium nitrate blast. Maybe it will rain cow shit for a month, and we'll have psilocybe mushrooms growing on every lawn in Springfield."

"Listen, uh Burt. I'm leaving campus for a while. I'm giving up on my classes. I'm leaving all my stuff here in the room. I'll be back later to pick it up."

"No shit! Where are you going?"

"You're better off not knowing. I don't really know where I'm going myself. If anyone comes around asking where I went, you don't know anything. I'm leaving a note for you to give to my coach, and a note to Ellen Rainwater. If Edward Crow calls, tell him I'm trying my best to make the funeral. If anyone comes around asking questions - my guidance counselor or anyone - don't let them in. Don't tell them anything."

"Heavy, dude!" Another fire engine rolled by competing for Burt's attention. James scribbled his two notes and packed away: a small flashlight, a space blanket, lightweight rain jacket, three $50 traveler checks, a small vial of phosphorous, and powdered aluminum (for fire starter), a condensed version of the New Testament, and extra socks in a fanny pack. If James had known that he would be running, sleeping, eating and living in his sweat clothes for the next 16 days, he might have taken two pairs of socks, and a change of underwear. He went to his desk and pulled out the little loose-leaf notebook that had been his journal since he was nine years old. He put this in a plastic bag, and zipped up his fanny pack. James went for the door. "Hey! Where are you going?" called Burt.

"Goodbye," said James. Whatever secrets rested with Burt would sleep soundly on the mushy mattress of his brain.

****

James did not want to run to the bus station. That would be the first place Steve would check if he were looking for James, and, certainly, he would be looking. James had no experience with hitchhiking, but figured he could give it a try once he was on the other side of Springfield. He began running at a moderate pace dodging lights of vehicles as he worked his way north on I-99. The road came within half a mile of the lab site and, as he ran by at about 1:00 a.m., he could see the glare of emergency lighting, but no flickering to suggest fire. Like James had predicted, it had been a big, dirty bang with no secondary fire. Most of the toxic aftermath had gone into the stratosphere.

By three o'clock, James was pulsing along on a runners' high, and had taken off his sweatshirt to tie it around his waist. He realized he was probably far enough along to risk hitchhiking. But only eleven vehicles came by in the next two hours, and none of them were motivated by what they saw attached to James' extended thumb to stop. A sweaty, half-naked Indian carrying God-knows-what in an ass pack, barely inspired a flicker of consideration in the early morning minds of these motorists. James ran along at an easy pace, breaking to a fast walk for ten minutes every hour. By 6:30 a.m., there were more cars on the road.. James had gotten into the rhythm of the march and realized that he could make Corvallis on his own power. He could catch the bus there. By 9:35 on Saturday morning, he had come to the Greenberry Store/ Tavern, six miles from the city limits. He went in to refuel.

He picked up several items of fruit from the refrigerated compartment. He selected some hard rolls, and went back to get a block of cheese. Since leaving his dorm after his father's phone call, he had come 68 miles including the running back and forth from the lab to the dormitory. He was really hungry! He picked up a quart of whole milk. He craved the fat. He had been drinking from drainage ditches, but he was still thirsty. He took his armful of purchases to the counter and reached into his fanny pack to fetch his travelers' checks. The headlines to the *Corvallis Gazette*, by the cash register froze James like a statue. The older woman proprietor studied James and saw a young man on the edge of an abyss. She wondered what was wrong with this sweaty, young Indian buck that stared at the newspaper like he was reading his own obituary. "Is there something wrong, sonny?"

There *was* something wrong. Everything wrong, and nothing right. James had killed someone. If the police weren't looking for him now, they probably would be soon. His name was on the travelers' checks. He couldn't use them. He had no cash to pay for his purchases. He wouldn't be able to eat. "I...I just remembered." James stammered. "I forgot my money."

James returned the rolls to the shelf. Carefully, he replaced the fruit, milk and cheese to the refrigerated compartment. The proprietor smelled the hunger and despair on this young man. "Do you live around here?" she asked sympathetically. If he said yes, maybe she could trust him to pay her back later.

"No ma'm, I'm not from these parts." He walked by her to go to the door and she saw his ribs through the sweat-soaked T-shirt. The poor bastard was probably on drugs, though he was polite enough. Being a barkeep in the back for twelve years had given her the ability to read body language. This young man had come through the door a lion, and was skulking out a coyote. Could forgetting his money and not getting a few lousy grocery items have done this to him?

"You can take the rolls. They're a day old, anyway. And you can take the fruit because it's ripe today and will be rotten tomorrow. I can't give you the milk and cheese."

"God bless you," whispered the coyote.

****

University of Washington, Seattle
Sunday, January 17, 1979

Sally's strokes my hair as her head rests on my shoulder. I am reading the front page of the Sunday *Seattle Times*. We're both naked in my dorm bed and we assume our roommates are similarly reposed in Sally's room across campus. On the lower right corner of the page I am reading an article I find amusing:

DENTIST IDENTIFIES MAN KILLED IN METH LAB EXPLOSION

AP-Eugene, OR- A Eugene dentist has positively identified the skeletal remains of a man killed in the explosion of a clandestine methamphetamine lab in the small rural town of Springfield, Oregon. The explosion, which rocked the neighboring town of Eugene sometime after 11:30, Friday night, completely leveled a 1,000 square foot concrete and cinder-block warehouse, throwing debris more than a quarter mile from the site of the explosion. A vehicle found near the explosion was so severely deformed by the blast that police were required to make identification by the serial number on the frame of the car. The vehicle was found to belong to Steven Holloway, a faculty member of the University of Oregon. Dental casts were sent to Mr. Holloway's dentist.

Dr. Benjamin Gasmen, D.D.S., identified the remains as belonging to his patient. "I'd recognize those teeth anywhere. You don't have to be a dentist to do it. Anyone who has seen Steve smile would recognize medial spectra of the mandible and maxilla.."Though no official report has been released, police sources who wish to remain anonymous speculate that Mr. Holloway's death may have been suicide. A phone call was received by the police department to tip them off on the impending explosion of the clandestine lab. The caller advised the police to use extreme caution in dealing with the toxic fallout from the explosion. Police theorize that the caller was Mr. Holloway himself and that his suicide was drug related.

Police are asking anyone who knows anything about the laboratory or explosion to call Springfield Police Department at 503-929-4354. All information received will be confidential.

"Fuck drugs forever," I say out loud and throw the paper down on the floor.

"Fuck me forever," says Sally demurely and I try.

TEN

*J*ames Crow took the fruit, and sourdough rolls outside. He bit into a pear. The juice squirted and splashed down his cheek. He ravenously tore into the flesh of the fruit, gulping it down, core, stem, and all. He pushed a roll into his face, and found that this required more mastication to ingest. He drank water from a drainage ditch, then walked along the road eating the rolls and fruit. He finished eating about a mile north of the Greenberry store. Then he realized he would have to find shelter to rest. He could not risk using his travelers' checks, so there would be no bus ride back to the Olympic Peninsula, and hitchhiking seemed dangerous now that he perceived himself a fugitive. He figured that it would be best to rest during the warmth of the day, and travel at night when his exertion would inure him from the cold. James found a cow barn. He slogged in ankle deep mud, through the barn, to a ladder that led up. He climbed the ladder to the hayloft and found an opened bale of alfalfa. He put on his rain gear and dry socks and pulled the hay over himself. In three minutes James was asleep.

He slept for nine hours and woke up in the dark. He used his small flashlight to find his way out into the cold, clear, dark night. He was hungry again, but food would be a long time coming. The next meal was 57 miles in James' future. It was after 10 p.m. when James arrived in Corvallis. On a Saturday night, there was a fair mount of activity, but James did not have a vagrant's instinct to home in on free food. He knew there were soup kitchens in Salem, and pushed on through the darkness at the pace he had established the previous night, punctuating an hour's run with a ten minute walk. He approached the outskirts of Salem by 6 am. He had spent much of the night thinking about what he would tell his father on the phone. He hungered for his father's voice. But having traveled well over 120 miles on six hard rolls and a few pieces of fruit, James' body was in an accelerated state of starvation. Now, he knew that finding food was a priority. He needed fuel to clear his thinking. He would call his father after eating. He found the shelter on Mission Street. At 8 am on a Sunday morning there was only a short line for the scrambled powdered eggs, frozen hash browns, and week old toast which was the primary morning cuisine of Salem's homeless community. James took his plate to one of the unoccupied tables, and folded his hands in prayer. The odor of the fuel competed for his thoughts in his prayer: for consideration of his deceased mother; for the gift of his father's voice; for forgiveness for James' complicity in the death of Steve Holloway...Saliva drooled from James' lips, precipitating upon his folded hands. He gave up on his prayers with a preclusive 'amen,' and turned onto his food which he ingested in 97 seconds. He bussed his plate, and glass, and went through the line again. He returned to the table, and again prayed over his second breakfast. He took more time with this meal. After a few bites he realized that ketchup might be required, if not for taste, at least for lubrication. He finished this meal, bussed the dishes and went back for a third. He was intercepted by the management before he got his third serving.

"Most of our clients come in for breakfast sometime after nine o'clock. We wouldn't want them to come into an empty kitchen. Why don't you digest what you've already eaten. If you're hungry in an hour, you can go through the line again."

James returned to the table. He cradled his head on his arms, upon the table. In 30 seconds, he was asleep. It seemed like he had just closed his eyes when a gentle arm on his shoulder awakened him. "There's plenty of food left over from breakfast, if you're still hungry." The same man who had stopped him before, was now giving him the green light. There was no line at 9:30, and James was given a substantial portion of reconstituted eggs and potatoes, and six slices of desiccated toast. He prayed over this, and went back for more, which he also prayed over. When he finished with his fourth serving, he felt dizzy. He again put his head down, and was drifting off when the same hand was placed on his shoulder. "Would you like to lie down in a bed for awhile?"

"God bless you."

James slept for ten hours. He was awakened by a strong urge to defecate. After taking care of this business, he attended the shelter's dinner, which was hot dogs, beans, and fruit cocktail. James asked the server for the bun, sans hot dog. James went through the line a second time, unchallenged and then left the shelter in search of a phone. He found a pay phone two blocks away and called the operator to place his collect call. There was no answer. James began the walk towards the northern outskirts of Salem while digesting his dinner. He tried to call his father an hour later from Keizer, north of Salem; but there was still no voice from his father to accept the call. As suburbs yielded to countryside, evening yielded to night, and James yielded to the inertia that pulled him along the road, mile after mile, town after town. He believed that he would be able to reach his father first thing in the morning from a pay phone in Portland.

****

Edward Crow had expected James to call sometime Saturday with news about when he would be home. With the funeral only two days away, it seemed reasonable to assume that James would be coming home straight away. There was no call all day Saturday. On Sunday the phone rang at 4 p.m., and Edward ran to catch it on the second ring. It was John Pinn inviting him over for dinner with his family. John had found June Crow a week ago, following her suicide attempt, and had called the ambulance. He knew that Edward was alone, waiting for James' return. He wanted to extend the support and hospitality of the Pinn family. "Thanks, John, but I'm waiting for a call from James."

"Dinner will only take an hour or so, Mr. Crow. If James calls while you're with us, he'll just try calling back."

Edward had declined, but John Pinn had persisted. In the end, Edward had agreed to come over for dinner at six. He tried calling James in Eugene before going to the Pinns'. He learned from Burt that James had left under mysterious circumstances. Burt said that James was not returning to the dormitory.

Edward was lonely. It felt comfortable to be in the bosom of the Pinn family. His ex-family had lost its bosom and his current wife was in Tacoma minding her own bosom there. He was still with the Pinns at 8:40 p.m. when James was trying to call from Salem. He got home at 8:45 and slept fitfully, waiting for a phone call that never came. At 6:30 a.m. he got up, showered and got dressed for the funeral scheduled for 9:30. At 8:10 he went over to the LaPush Assembly building to sit an hour with his deceased ex-wife. It disappointed him immensely that James would not be with him for the service.

The turnout for June Crow's funeral was sadly scant. A few employees from LaPush Ocean Park, the Pinns, the Woodrift clan, and Edward. It seemed so pathetic to Edward, and he kept brooding about the absence of his son. The Pinns brought some food over to the Crow trailer. For a couple hours, Edward passed the time making small talk with the Woodrifts. They still seemed to resent him. Watching young Dorothy Pinn scamper around the trailer reminded him of how much, and for how long he had missed his own son. Then the company left, and he sat in silence, and in total loneliness, waiting. He had told his wife in Tacoma that he would be gone for two weeks, while he settled the funeral of his former wife, and reconciliation with his son. Had Edward antagonized James on the phone by being so firm about the drug thing? Had Edward driven James away? Had he blown it again? There was no joy in Edward's heart as he sat all day Sunday, waiting for a phone call that still didn't come. At 6:30 p.m., Edward gave up waiting, and went into Forks for groceries. The phone rang eight times, on three different occasions in Edward's absence. When Edward got back to the trailer a little after nine, the phone had stopped ringing. Included in Edward's groceries were two gallon jugs of red wine.

****

When James got to Portland on Monday morning, he too was possessed with a feeling of loneliness and depression that he would not be at his father's side for the funeral of his mother. He found a pay phone before he got to the downtown shelter, and tried calling Edward at 8:30, but there was no answer. The food at the Portland shelter was identical to what had been served in Salem, except that there were blobs of processed cheese and SPAM mixed in with the powdered eggs. James picked out the SPAM. Another diner, seated across the table, asked James if he could have it. James gave it to him and watched the man carefully wrap the pieces of meat in his handkerchief, and put it inside his coat pocket. James was denied a second serving. He returned to the table to sleep until lunch. Grief intruded into his rest as he woke up from time to time, realizing that his mother was being buried, as other indigents burped, farted and picked SPAM from their teeth with dirty fingernails. He ate lunch, slept at the table, and then ate dinner. By eating early and then napping, he was able to go through the line twice. He departed the shelter at 7:45 p.m. and went straight back to the phone. He stood by the phone for an hour and had the operator dial his home phone three times. Then he became too cold to stand around. He continued his march north. At about midnight he found a phone and tried again to reach his father. As the phone rang its eighth ring, and the operator said, "I'm sorry sir, there doesn't seem to be anyone home to take the call," Edward was tripping over chairs, and stumbling into walls, trying to get to the phone, drunk in the dark. In the morning he would clutch his head from the hangover and stare at the bruises on his shins, but he would not remember the race for the phone. He would open the second gallon of wine; and when that was gone, he would buy more from LaPush Grocery. He would answer the phone several times, and field several phone calls with slurred speech: a woman from Forks wanting to invite June to a Tupperware party; his wife wanting to know what day he was coming home to Tacoma and *was Edward drinking again*; John Pinn wanting to know if everything was all right. An awkward silence grew as John realized that Edward was drunk.

Fate and alcohol conspired to keep James from reaching his father on the phone. James pushed north making 40 to 60 miles a day. He found no more shelters. A Native American woman picked James up near Chehalis, Washington. She took him home for a meal, and nine hours of sleep on her couch. She couldn't believe his capacity for food and sleep, nor could she believe that he had come by foot from Eugene, Oregon in five and a half days. Thursday morning she took him back to the point where she had picked him up the previous day. She let him out of her car, glad to be done with his lies. Good riddance to his voracious appetite for food, and sleep; and goodbye to his total lack of appetite for the one thing for which she hungered.

James was glad to be in Washington. He reached Aberdeen after midnight. It was Friday morning now. He had left Eugene six days ago. He was literally starving. He knew there was a mission in town, but the one he remembered had recently burned down. He couldn't find the new, temporary location. The YMCA offered shelter for a price, but no food. In desperation, James began progging through a dumpster behind a McDonalds. He pulled out styrofoam cartons and placed them in a big cardboard box. The weather was below freezing and he would need to make a nest to survive. When he found leftover food, he ingested it eagerly. He was gobbling down cold, limp french fries, stumps of fruit pastries and pickles. He was dipping pieces of hamburger bun in a ketchup fondue. He found two thirds of a Big Mac and thought about it a moment before ingesting the two-story burger, meat and all. He realized that he absolutely required the fuel to run the final 120 miles between him, and home. At first he was happy that he had found, and eaten the hamburger, but five minutes later he was doubled over vomiting out the meal for which he had worked so hard. Weakly, he carried his nesting material down the road. A police cruiser slowed down and gave him a close inspection as he proceeded north along Highway 101. James concealed himself in the shadows and waited fifteen minutes before the cold drove him on again. He stopped behind the Kentucky Fried Chicken in Hoquiam where he was able to make a buffet of the coleslaw, potato salad, and white biscuits he'd found in the stinky dumpster. He collected newspaper, and another cardboard box. He drug this bedding across the railroad tracks just south of the dumpster. He made his nest under a bridge trestle.

Thirty six hours later, James had closed the distance to LaPush by 105 miles. He was running flat out towards LaPush from Forks. He had just crossed the Calawah bridge, and was less than a mile from the fifteen mile LaPush Road, when a vehicle reduced speed and followed him slowly. James feared it was the police and did not dare to look over his shoulder. The vehicle tooted its horn, and pulled over. James turned around to see a middle aged Native getting out of a compact pick-up. The Native's eyes were bloodshot like he had been crying, but something about the man's countenance made James' heart go out to him. James stopped and stared at the man, trying to understand the sense of familiarity he felt for this stranger. "Are you James Crow?" the stranger asked.

"Yes. Who are you."

"James, it's me, your father."

"Oh, Papa, sobbed James, embracing his father. Both men clung to each other, crying.

ELEVEN

*T*he years washed over James Crow like tides over a beach, picking up something here, and leaving something there; but leaving the beach fundamentally unchanged. Crow continued with his running. He took some classes through the University of Washington Distance Learning. The courses were easy and bored him. He never obtained a degree. He took on construction jobs and, later on, carpentry work to derive income. He became convinced that in the cultural impact of the two civilizations, Native America had been vilified and denigrated to the point of showing major psychological debilitation. The poverty, alcohol abuse and dinginess of the reservations testified to a gaping moral abyss. Life is a tiny beach-like interface between the infinite here-before and the eternal here-after. Men such as James' father spent their whole lives tripping in the kelp, and slipping on the slick rocks on that beach. Before the intrusion of White culture, Native America was keenly acclimated to the present moment. In August of 1986, Edward Crow was taken to the hospital with a liver disorder, and, in October, James stepped onto the beach without a family. First his mother, then his father: both carried away on the outgoing tide of life.

James talked frequently to his church congregation about the need to instill a sense of personal worth, and cultural pride, in the ghetto-like reservations across the continent. He began discussing the problem of self-mage with the young people in the village. He spent time with his cousin, Wally Woodrift, who was breaking into cars, spray painting signs, and expressing the same social behavior that came from rebellious young Natives as one voice. Their angst and anger needed a constructive venting. James began working on a project that would offer the young people of LaPush the ultimate physical expression of their pent up disillusionment: a walk from the Pacific Ocean to Washington, D.C., where the young Natives would tell Congress and a hungry media of their frustrations in being Native flotsam tossed around by the capricious waves of a White ocean.

The logistics, funding and other organizational details of the event, took a year out of James' life. In May of 1988, it was with immense pride that he and twenty-two other young members of the Quileute Nation walked under banners and through the fanfare of fawning family and amused media, to begin the 2,955 *"Longest March,"* to the Nation's capitol. The southern route drawn out on the map, added about 200 miles to the distance, but allowed for the march to continue through the winter. The party was scheduled to arrive at the Capitol steps in 365 days. Several school-age teenagers, including Wally Woodrift, would continue their education through a home-tudy package while on the trip. Much of the food and equipment had been purchased by local churches. The food caches were mailed ahead to different post offices, while equipment was carried in a support van driven by volunteers from reservations across the country.

Wally Woodrift ran over to hug his friend, Dorothy Pinn. Dorothy had tears in her eyes, and after ending the embrace Wally shook hands solemnly with her father, the red giant. Tim Gable, the 28-year-old ancestral spiritual leader of the Quileutes, came out of his trailer drinking a 16 ounce Malt Liquor at 9:15 in the morning. "Carry

87

only hard liquor!" he exhorted the retreating column of hikers. "Beer weighs too much and makes you piss! And take a lot of drugs or you'll just be back tomorrow." Of all the advice dispensed that morning by doting parents and all the timetable predictions made by the media, Gable's proved to be the most prophetic.

****

It had been seven months since I quit my secure and well-paying computer software job in Seattle and pushed the reset button on my life. In the five years since college I've yearned for something different; something with greater physical expression than the nine to five routine of selling business software packages. I was seeking relief from the endless commuting to and from work on the traffic choked Seattle thoroughfares. The rustling feathers of the spotted owl, in the news I read in the *Seattle Times*, signaled the fall and winter of the timber industry...like the dry leaves that fluttered in the crisp October weather outside my office window...or the withered relationship with the girl I loved in college. *I quit*, I thought. I walked into my supervisor's swank office. "I quit," I said, and did.

Moving to Forks, I had found a job setting chokers with Soleduck River Timber in one of the many mini-booms that were preceding the inevitable bust. The other loggers had laughed and called me a city-slicking hippie because of my striking natural head piece. Tolerance, in a timber community, is born largely out of physical performance, not spiritual intonations or physical appearances. In a town where the men were happy with horses for wives, and a jackass for President, it hadn't taken me long to hump my way into acceptance.

****

In a school bus crummy, coming back from Hunger Mountain, several of the other loggers are petitioning the driver to stop at the Loop Tavern so they can pick up a case of beer. Twenty-four beers will last ten thirsty loggers a little less than ten minutes which is how long it will take the school bus to drive from milepost 200, on Highway 101, to Forks where they can purchase a proper supply of beer for the evening's campaign. Now, the driver, Jimmy Shamuck, myself, and the other eight passengers are in varying stages of finishing their first bottle. We pass a beleaguered column of twenty or so Indians carrying a banner reading *The Longest March*. My certifiably crazy co-worker, Rod, in the seat in front of me starts bouncing around. He swills his beer and pulls down his window to throw the empty bottle at the Native demonstrators. I put my hand on his shoulder and say, "Don't."

"My brother's with that outfit," calls the driver.

"They already have half the fish, half the game and a quarter million acres on the Peninsula, says Rod in strained voice. "I swear, I'm tired of all their whining."

"Yeah, but I hate litter," I say hoping to defuse the man's anger.

It works. Rod drops his empty bottle on the floor and walks forward to get a full one. "I get it! Let's turn around and offer them a ride! I heard about these red jokesters and they think they're going to walk all the way to Washington, D.C. Shit! This will really fuck them up! Turn around, Jim, I mean it!"

"Turn around! Turn this shit heap around!" the loggers are all hollering over the belching and farting the beer has set off inside the bus. "Yeah, let's rap with the fuckers!"

The bus pulled over and made a wide U-turn. The driver pulled into a turnout just a few hundred feet beyond the eastbound hikers. He opened the folded bus doors and Rod bounded down the steps, beer in hand. He charged out to meet the demonstrators like a Chicago cop in front of a Daily convention hall. I watched apprehensively from my bus seat as Rod held up his opened right hand and addressed the group of Natives. "How!" he exclaimed.

The vanguard of the group attempted to ignore the heckler and moved around him with their banner. "Hey, how far are you going tonight? Chicago? Denver, that's about half way. No shit, how far are you featherheads pushing tonight? We'd like to help out and give you a ride!"

Most of the party was limping. From the stragglers a quarter mile down the road, a Native abandoned the rear of the column and began running toward the confrontation like a runaway log truck. In about a minute he arrived. Rod was discussing his offer of assistance with the tired Natives.

"We've got beer and plenty of chew aboard. We can stop at Beaver grocery if you guys need anything for your feet - Moleskin, Second Skin, extra toes - and we can get cigarettes and more beer. Do you guys drink beer..."

"Excuse me!" the thin Native interrupted so everyone could hear him. He wasn't even breathing hard having sprinted more than 400 yards in about a minute. "We're contained and self-sufficient."

Rod considered this challenge. "What's that supposed to mean? You drink your own piss and shit your pants? These boys are tired. Look at 'em limp, chief. They can get infected blisters and lose their feet! You want that on your conscience? Do you even have a conscience?"

"Because I have a conscience I am walking - **we** are walking. You may walk with us. We will welcome your company. Otherwise, please leave these young people alone."

As the stragglers came into the knot of the conversation, they all began to support the idea of a rescue in the school bus. They appealed to their leader. "You said that if there were any injuries we could use the van for an ambulance. Most of us have blisters. Tumbling Rapids was too far for one day. Let's, just this once, take the offer of help."

"Please leave us to our quest," said the thin Native. Rod snorted at the word 'quest.' He stared incredulously at the Native, at the bedraggled party, and then shrugged.

Rod swilled the rest of his beer, burped, and poured out the backwash from the bottle at the feet of the group's leader. He then dropped the empty bottle, and crossed the road to return to the bus. He came up the steps and picked up his third beer from the depleted case. He announced, "Chief Runs-Like-Shit no want'um beer from paleface. Good thing, too. We're almost out."

****

On the following evening, the crew bus came on the vanguard of the demonstrators at milepost 211. They were spread out over a mile, but at three o'clock in the afternoon, the party was at a crawling speed from where they had camped the night before at milepost 203. That evening, Sappho Cafe was chosen as the emergency beer supply by the loggers. After the purchase of three half racks, Rod was adamant that the bus return to the head of the column of demonstrators. Back at milepost 212, Rod was Mr. Ambassador, passing out beer and cigarettes to the thirsty and tobacco hungry Natives. He invited them into the bus with the promise of a ride to Klahowya Campground, their destination for the night. The loggers pulled their tired legs off the double-wide seats to accommodate the refugees from the march. Fragments of conversation, in disgruntled tones, passed by the loggers as the Natives of the fractured group climbed onto the bus. "James is fucking crazy, man. He's pushing way too hard... We were only supposed to go ten miles a day, max, and yesterday we went twenty-seven miles! He doesn't let us buy cigarettes...James went through my pack looking for pot, man...He confiscated my condoms."

This guy, James, is a regular demagogue. By the time he showed up on the horizon, a dozen of his party were in the bus guzzling beer and smoking. He told them to put down the beers, extinguish the smokes and exit the bus. They ignored him. The stragglers got on the bus. They, too, were greeted with cold beers.

Rod said to the leader, "Come on, Chief. Be reasonable. These young bucks are all tuckered. Get your ass on the bus, have a cold beer and we'll go collect the rest of your party."

"We are here to walk and talk. Not to drink beer and smoke tobacco."

"Have it your way then. Jim, turn this shit heap around and let's go get the rest of these braves. Tonto, here, will just hoof it alone."

The bus U-turned and left James standing by the crumpled *Longest March* banner. It proceeded slowly down the road picking up the balance of the party. For a while, James was running like the wind, behind the bus, trying to intercept the stragglers the bus was stopping to collect. The last two members of the march, which represented the female contingent, were picked up in the bus and delivered to the Sappho Cafe. They went in to buy smokes, while Rod negotiated another two cases of

90

beer. A young Native by the name of Wally, shoplifted enough snoose to flood the bus in tobacco spit. The troupe re-boarded the bus, minus several loggers and one Native, who had tired of the sortie and opted to catch the County Bus back to Forks and LaPush. The crew bus passed the leader named James who had picked up the discarded banner and was jogging out toward the Klahowya campground alone. The young Natives called out cheerfully, "See you at camp, James!" and Rod yelled out, "We got enough beer for everyone!" Looking back at James' face, it was hard to read his expression, but his face was wet from the eyes down, and his vision seemed focussed a hundred miles down the road.

****

Monday, May 9, 1988, James Crow, wrote the date in his journal. He then detailed the violations of his trust and the abuses against his authority, which caused him to surrender *THE LONGEST MARCH* a few days earlier. When he had gotten to Klahowya campground, it appeared that all of the members of the walking delegation were in various states of inebriation. The support van had arrived, and the driver, Peter Shamuck, was smoking pot with three of the juvenile marchers. One of the two young women of the delegation met Crow and complained that her sister was in a tent with the van driver's brother, Jimmy. She told James that the reclusive couple might be making it and that her sister was only fourteen. Before James could get to the only tent that was set up in the campground, a fight developed between three Natives, about who would get the last two beers. Someone broke an empty bottle to use as a weapon. Then there was blood. James broke up the fight and got a dressing and bandage on the laceration of the young man's forearm. Before he got to the tent, he was stopped by a delegation of the demonstration who informed him that a vote had been taken and tomorrow was established as a day of rest. The group would remain there regardless of agenda or order. James got within ear shot of the tent, and it became evident that either Jimmy Shamuck or his fourteen-year-old partner was a screamer. James unzipped the tent to censure the couple, but the fourteen-year-old, unabashed by her nakedness, rolled onto her back and sat up with fury in her eyes. She came at James like a junkyard dog. She told him to take 'a flying fuck, and get off my back,' which was the pursuit and position of Jimmy a moment before.

Something snapped inside of James. There was something base and evil about this whole thing. Nothing that was happening was consistent with his purpose in leading the march. He had no authority or responsibility here. These reprobates were an embarrassment to him and to all the values he hoped to display in this demonstration. He would wash his hands of the whole lot. He began the 36-mile jog back to LaPush. Wally called out to him with his mouth swimming in tobacco and spit, "Hey, James, where are you going?" But James had that far away focus in his eyes. Wally thought to look at his watch - 4:35 - and thought that if James wasn't back in an hour, he would get Peter to drive him back to LaPush. He missed Dorothy already and maybe a year was too long away from home, even for a big fifteen-year-old juvenile delinquent.

James was not back in an hour. He was already approaching the Sappho Cafe running as if in a trance. It was 6:30 when James turned off Highway 101 and

91

began this fifteen miles at a full sprint. The weather was cool and overcast but sweat and steam poured off the Native as he sprinted, totally immersed in his running. *I am not of flesh and blood. I feel no pain. I have no sorrow. I am a well oiled machine. My arms are pistons. My lungs are bellows and my heart is only a pump with no feelings. My legs are on a track and I roll west toward the ocean...*

Tim Gable was coming back from Forks. For company, he had a partially consumed case of beer in the front of the pick-up. He was so surprised to see James running alone down the LaPush Road, after so much fanfare yesterday, that he spilled the beer nestled between his legs. He rolled down his window and threw out the mostly empty can. "Hey, Crow!" he yelled, but the runner was tripping on some kind of runners' high. Gable wished they bottled endorphines and marketed them in a twelve-ounce bottle.

As the train runs west it pushes the buffalo...and a crow flies on the wind...there is no pain, no feelings, no sense of humiliation...just the wind under the bird's wings...

"Hey, Crow, you crazy son of a bitch. I'm talking to you!" The runner's only reply was the staccato breaking of wind of a charging Indian war pony.

The Native ran faster and faster. He passed Three Rivers Resort as a Park Ranger walked out of the small restaurant, wiping the remnants of a Quilburger from his face with his handkerchief. "Hey, Crow, Washington, D.C. is the other way!"

I am the wind under the bird's wings. I cannot feel myself. I have no substance. I am movement with no body...anesthetic...I am wind...

The first van load of march refugees passed James Crow at Second Beach Parking. From the front passenger's seat, Wally Woodrift checked his watch. It was 7:25. He checked the mileage records for the trip, and came up with the road distance from Klahowya to LaPush. "Can he have run 35 miles in under three hours?" Woodrift marveled out loud.

The distance of 35 miles is not a sanctioned event in any foot race or register book. There were no banners, cameras or trophies to commemorate the establishment of this human record as James Crow raced into LaPush, and walked to his shack with his hands on his head. The one passing remark made by fifteen-year-old, Woodrift, was the only ripple in the collective human consciousness caused by this event.

James Crow had lost more than two quarts of water to sweat, and respiratory vapor, in the run. For the past three hours his body had been motion itself, burning every molecule of fat, and then muscle fiber, in a fiery anaerobic furnace. Thick and acidotic blood serum coursed through his arteries and his muscles began to cramp violently. He turned on the spigot outside his parents' old mobile home, and tried to drink the cold water. After his third gulp, he vomited it out. The water was as cold coming out of his stomach as it had been from the spigot. He collapsed with intense cramping. More than being overcome with the physical agony of his exertions, he was suddenly overcome by the shame, embarrassment and sense of failure that had chased him for 35 miles. *A whole year of my life for nothing...ended in disgrace!* And as James Crow sat trembling in the puddle of water that pooled under the running spigot, as his body temperature collapsed into the cool May evening, his muscles turning hard and rigid, a strange perspective overwhelmed his vision. As he looked out towards the sun setting behind James Island, the sky began to shift color, and shapes began to melt and metamorphose.

The big island began to pitch and shift, losing its articulation with land. In Crow's vision, lesser James Island became a battleship swarming with soldiers like ants on a floating leaf. Some of the soldiers dove from the battleship of the lesser island and began to swim towards the bastion of James Island, which crawled with Native defenders who set fire to the top of the island. The warriors poured fire and boiling water upon the attacking soldiers. Boulders crashed down from the cliffs, bombarding the soldiers. Drift logs pitched around in the rolling surf inflicting further casualties. The ocean waves broke red on the rocky beach of the jetty. Stars moved around in the heavens. There was a flash as two collided. James Island escaped the moorings of the jetty, and miraculously floated off, burning, into the ocean with the soldiers swimming in pursuit.

On his way up to tell Dorothy Pinn about the failed march, Wally Woodrift found James Crow, cold, still and lifeless in the puddle of water. He turned off the spigot, and went inside the unlocked trailer to call an ambulance. He told the hospital that the patient appeared to be dead. James Crow also appeared to be dead to the ambulance attendants. As one attendant pulled out the semi-automatic defibrillator, and began setting up for the first 200-joule shock, the other attendant tapped James Crow's shoulder and yelled, "Hello! Are you OK?" As the second attendant held his fingers on the pulseless throat of the patient, his ear poised over the breathless mouth, sighting down a still chest and abdomen...a cold breath of acidotic wind blew into his ear. The patient, James Crow, whispered, "No. I am not OK. No."

****

The following day at the hospital, an IV running into each arm, James Crow called the University of Oregon. He asked to talk with the program director of the college radio station. The extension was picked up by a man who introduced himself as 'Jordan.' Crow explained that he was trying to get in touch with a man by the name of Clarence Fourskins. He said that nine years ago, the man had spoken at the U of O, and the college's radio station had covered the event. "I was there!" responded Russell Jordan. "I taped the whole thing."

"I need to get in touch with Mr. Fourskins," explained Crow. Jordan said that he would see what he could dig up. He asked if Crow would like cassette copies of the speech given nine years ago. James agreed to send $10 to the U of M to cover the cost of the tapes and Jordan said that he would call him back at Forks Hospital with Fourskins' number - if he could find it. It took about an hour.

93

The young girl answered the phone, "Nauto Fourskins." Then James Crow was talking to Clarence Fourskins, who was at his home just outside the Rosebud Reservation. Crow told of how he had endeavored to call national attention to the plight of Native America; how his efforts had been frustrated by the young Native hooligans; and ended by describing the strange vision he had experienced in the altered state resulting from his dramatic run.

"Look, James, next time don't depend on your leadership of kids to make your point. I'm not saying that kids aren't great vectors for reaching the media, but it's a delicate business. It requires some social savvy. No offense, but I remember you from nine years ago - you're the runner. I don't recall people management as being your strong suit. Next time, go it alone. Dream up some athletic stunt and use the media.

"I'm interested in LaPush. As you remember from that message you tried to blurt out in front of the University of Oregon, I've got another friend from your part of the country who is currently employed in the aerospace defense industry..."

"You mean Jeff Sp..."

"Don't say the name! Listen, Crow, you need to learn a little discretion in how you shoot off your mouth! You need to get realistic in how you manage your public campaigns. As I said, I'm interested in LaPush and may make it out there someday. Things can be done with the issues that are surfacing there, and I'd like to provide some leadership if there's a confrontation."

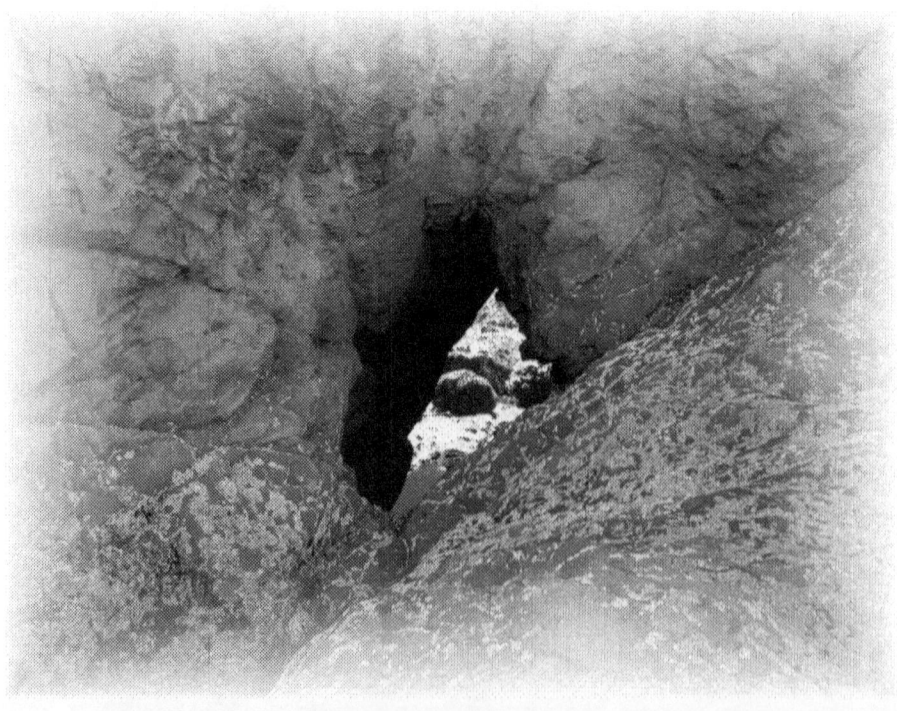

TWELVE

*T*he pyramids of Egypt are a startling manifestation of mankind's domination over his environment. Erupting from the flat desert floor they can be viewed from a greater distance than the concrete skyline of most great North American cities. Though the technology of early Egypt is still not understood, there are some romantics that hold onto the notion that the mighty pyramidal structures are constructed to depend on one central block. If that one small block is moved, gigatons of rock fall down from the sky.

****

Los Angeles, California
October 16, 1991

John E. Ohms climbed back into his underwear and collected the rest of his clothes from a basket that was pushed through a small swinging door. The doctor pulled off the latex exam glove, and threw it into the stainless steel trash can. When one resigned unexpectedly from the high-tech aerospace defense contractor of TRW, a free proctological exam was thrown into the retirement package, and the outgoing employee's clothes were searched meticulously for smuggled software secrets. Almost as invasive as the anal exam, were the questions asked earlier in the morning by the panel of TRW executives, and Federal agents, who debriefed Ohms. He finished dressing and came out into the lobby. He walked over to the security desk where he had checked his briefcase. The contents and structure of the briefcase would be searched completely by high-tech security before it would be delivered to him in person at his residence, by one of the security guards. The rest of Ohm's office would stay with TRW. Naked, had he come into their employ; naked would he return forthwith.

"I understand why the briefcase has to be quarantined. Security has to go over the laptop in the briefcase and sterilize the hard drive. I've already taken an oath that I'm not smuggling out any secrets or software. What I need is my tea cup. I was always losing and breaking my cups, and my girlfriend made one for me on the kiln at UCLA. I told her I'd never let go of it."

"Sorry, Mr. Ohms you know the rules." The security man's eye contact with John Ohms was broken as he glanced at a pretty Hispanic woman approaching the desk. She did not have a visitor's pass. She would be required to stop at the desk.

"Can't you just look it over now and let me have it? It's just a tea cup. X-ray it, ultra sound it, autoclave it...do whatever you do, but I need to take it with me."

"Hi, John," the ravishing young women, in the low-cut peasant blouse chirped to Ohms. The security guard could smell the perfume and the sweet reek of shampoo from her long black hair. Ohms put his arms around her, and kissed her cheek. "Almost done, hon?" she asked cheerfully. She looked at the guard and said, "We're going to Yosemite to hike for a whole week! John never had time to take a

95

walk around the block when he worked with this stuffy outfit, and now we're going for a whole week!"

The guard envied Ohms, and would have gladly quit his security job to hole-up in a tent for a week with this specimen of Hispanic womanhood. The guard thought longingly that he would quit his wife, his kids, his home, and his soul for a week with this woman. She looked the guard square in the face and said, "Ready to go?" For a second the security man allowed himself to believe she had asked him the question.

Ohms answered for the guard. "We've got a problem, Maria. I need a certain piece of personal property before I can leave this office. Officer, isn't there something you can do to help me out here?"

The guard went to the briefcase which was already sealed with orange security tape. He broke the tape against all policy, and pulled out the small tea cup. He tapped it with his pen and examined it from all angles. Etched on the bottom was a small heart with the inscription *Maria & John*. The guard passed the cup over to Ohm and said, "Enjoy your new life, sir. I know I would."

Ohms and the young woman walked with their arms around each other across the lobby and out into the October morning. She laughed gaily at something Sparks said. As the security man replaced the seal on the briefcase with fresh tape, Ohms turned to face the pretty Hispanic in the big parking lot. "You were really good in there, Camille. I'll be sure to tell your agency how pleased I was with your service. Can I drop you off in Hollywood?"

****

That afternoon, alone in his apartment, Sparks took the cover off a desktop hard-drive which connected to his AT-486 computer. He removed the ceramic element from this 240-megabyte hard-drive. He replaced the element with the homemade teacup. When he booted up the computer, he was able to call up the secrets of the United States' Defense Early Warning System and Strategic Air Command. Into the hand of a loose cannon were nestled both high-tech testicles of a modern superpower.

****

Special Agent Fred Prue specialized in Native American activities. 'Activities' was too all embracing a word to describe his field of interest. The ceremonial drum, and intricately woven baskets, which adorned his office in Quantico, Virginia were for show. The only Native activity that concerned him personally or professionally was insurrection or espionage. Routinely, across his desk came the background checks for security clearances, and up to date intelligence reports on Native felons such as Clarence Fourskins, a.k.a. 'Two Dogs Fucking.' The folders bulged with documents. On the front of this particular jacket was a cross reference, in Prue's handwritten scrawl, 'Known accomplice: alias 'Johnny Ohm.'

Besides a few notes, and some photos dating back to 1968, the file was empty. When he picked up the dossier, on a routine resignation from defense contractor, TRW, he was astounded to be looking at the face of Johnny Ohm plus 23 years. Noticing in the documents that the subject, Ohm, John E., had been recruited in 1981, the FBI man was relieved. From 1979 to 1982, Fred Prue had been on special assignment in Minnesota, developing Federal indictments against the known Native participants of an armed insurrection on the Red Lake Reservation. The hostilities had held 50 tribal, and BIA police pinned down by gunfire in a stinking mobile home for days. The search for the guilty had led him to, but not through, the door of his old friend, Clarence Fourskins. Prue was relieved that he had not been sitting at this desk when Ohms' recruitment papers came across it in September of 1981. The shit was going to hit the fan on this one! Prue went into his supervisor's office.

Supervisory Agent Gary Shortbrand had been with the FBI since 1960, and with 31 years of government service, he thought he had seen the entire rainbow of bureaucratic fuck-ups, but *this* was an entirely new color on the spectra. "Are you sure that this Star Wars guy is your Johnny Ohm?" he asked again in disbelief.

"I'm ninety-eight per cent positive. Check out the blown-up picture from his company I.D. We have photos of Johnny Ohm coming out of that NYU, computer hostage incident. We prosecuted his partner, - remember Two Dogs Fucking?"

Shortbrand felt beads of perspiration breaking out on his forehead. He felt the bile rising as his ulcers kicked in. *An insurgent working in a sensitive position of this nation's critical defense with a top secret clearance!* Somehow the Bureau would have to shift the blame for the background investigation back to the private sector. "Call our L.A. office right away. Have them pick up a couple of security dicks from the TRW plant, and go to this guy Ohms' apartment with a fishing-license search warrant and kick down his door. Get a Federal arrest warrant for sedition, also. Move on it now! If the suspect slips through the cracks you'll be tied up for months with damage control."

****

When the two Special Agents arrived at Ohms' apartment, with the two TRW rent-a-cops, they were tired of hearing from the one about how Sparks was leaving with Miss Hot Tamale on a backpacking trip. They could hear the TV playing through the door - so much for the trip to Yosemite. The two agents drew their forty-caliber semi-autos, and pressed their backs against the wall, while the unarmed guards knocked on the door and shouted. Several doors opened with disgruntled neighbors yelling to 'keep it down, for-Christ's-sake!' but Ohms' door remained closed.

Eventually, a voice answered from within. "Who's there?" came the muffled voice through the thick door.

The senior spook asked the TRW dicks in a whisper, "Is that Ohms?"

97

"Yeah, it sounds like him," answered the dick who had believed that Ohms was en route to Yosemite. "He must not have left on his trip yet."

"Police!" announced the spook. Best not to announce 'FBI' to this brand of convict. Let him think it's something about a parking ticket. "Open up! We want to talk!"

"How many of you are there?" came Ohms' voice from behind the door.

"Four! There's four of us!"

"Then that's how many I.D.'s I need to see before you come in. Slide them under the door. Do it now!"

So much for the parking-ticket scam. The FBI returned their weapons to their shoulder holsters, and fumbled for their shield wallets. They opened them flat to get them under the door, the dicks did the same. They put them on the floor and slid them through the crack and over the threshold. Whirring machinery started on the other side of the door, and the I.D.s were pulled like credit cards into a cash machine. The spooks pulled their weapons, and put their backs against the wall again.

"Is that all of your I.D.s?" inquired Sparks' voice from behind the door.

"Four officers. Four I.D.s. Now open up! We're disturbing your neighbors!"

"Thank you for the identification, officers. This is a recording. Johnny Ohms no longer lives here. Have a pleasant day!"

Then the Special Agents took turns with the security cops trying to kick the door down. One-by-one, they bounced off the fortress of a door. They were comedic in their failed attempts and panted with the exertion. Finally, one of the Special Agents excused himself, and came back with the apartment supervisor. The manager asked to see the warrant; examined the date, seal and wet smudged ink. He unlocked the door. Just inside the door was a large vacuum cleaner connected to a wide vent and heating duct. Into the bowels of the *Shop Vac*, Sparks had installed the garbage disposal removed from under the sink. The blades of the disposal pinged, whacked and ground as jagged pieces of badge shrapnel ricocheted around inside. A microphone was pointed at the door, and a pressure sensitive mat was set under the heating duct which had swallowed the cops' I.D.s.

"Who's there?" the portable tape player began again. "How many of you are there? Then that's how many I.D.s..." The senior FBI man kicked the portable recorder across the room forgetting its evidentiary value. He had a sinking feeling.

"This guy is loose in the world. He has had access to top-secret defense documents! Jesus Christ!"

****

Jeff Sparks at that moment was driving north on I-5 with $126,000 in cash in the trunk of the rattletrap he was driving. Over his decade of employment in the high paying think tank, it had been easy to rat hole away a fair grubstake. Earlier in the afternoon he had traded in his red BMW convertible on this 1962 Valiant sedan. He had not returned to LaPush in 22 years and there was nothing to trace him to his home. In the glove box of the Valiant was an empty ceramic tea cup. From this empty cup would dribble such secrets as to short circuit the entire high-tech infrastructure of defense, constructed by a rich nation preoccupied with warfare. Jeff recalled the smell of cat piss, sizzling on a transformer, in his youthful experiments. It would not be a cat sent into the stratosphere this time. He would knock the United States ass over teacups.

****

The next morning Special Agent Prue conducted an inquiry at the TRW headquarters into vectors of possible intelligence leaks associated with the Sparks a.k.a. Ohms retirement. The business about the teacup surfaced, and by noon, the guard who had wished for a vacation was permanently in that status. It was not the paradise he had envisioned. In the weeks that followed, he found that TRW had done a thorough job of besmirching his name among the various security employers of this city of fallen angels. As weeks became months, and he began to wear out his welcome at the state unemployment office, he surrendered his pride and joined the ranks of the armed thugs, drug addicts and overworld criminals that calls itself "the LAPD."

THIRTEEN

Forks, Washington
Wednesday, June 3, 1992

*T*he black steam engine had been donated to the town of Forks by the timber company Rayonier, subsidiary of the mega-conglomerate, ITT. It was enthusiastically received by the children of the town, who explored every secret compartment, and climbed to every high place of the lumbering machine. A percentage of broken bones attended this exploration and discovery, and in the late 1970's a fence was erected to protect the juvenile populace from a gift that was deemed too terrible and dangerous for their stewardship.

James Crow stood in front of the black engine in the parking lot of Tillicum Park waiting for the arrival of a special visitor. Waiting with Crow were Jeff Sparks and Wally Woodrift. It was Jeff Sparks who had prevailed upon Clarence Fourskins to come to LaPush to lay the framework for a gala demonstration to commemorate the 500th anniversary of White intrusion onto this continent; and to push for recognition of Native claims on the Olympic Peninsula. James couldn't wait to see what strategies would be revealed to him by the politically erudite, and historically adroit Fourskins.

Wally Woodrift was selected by Sparks to attend the greeting delegation. In the three years since Crow's 'Longest March' Woodrift had gone through the metamorphosis of character and sweetening of disposition that accompanied many adolescents' voyage into young adulthood. He had reformed his delinquent ways, and had become a reserve officer with the Quileute Tribal Police. Upon high school graduation, Wally had joined the National Guard. He'd participated in armed artillery practice at Fort Lewis. He represented a window into the minds and will of the youth of LaPush.

John Pinn had been invited to attend the welcoming by Sparks. For whatever purpose Sparks had invited Pinn to meet Fourskins upon his arrival in the Northwest, Pinn's intellectual prowess, or political acumen were not among the reasons. John had indicated that he would be there if he got off work on time. The arrival of the Soleduck River Timber crummy in the parking lot heralded Pinn's timely appearance. He got out of the six-pack crummy with his cork boots dangling by the laces over one shoulder, as a woman might carry a purse. He pulled his Stihl 076, with its 48-inch bar, out of the bed of the crummy. He walked over to his little Datsun pick-up to stow it. He took off his hard hat, and brushed saw chips out of his butch haircut with his hand. He tossed the tin hat and boots into the bed along with the saw , patted more saw chips off his clothes and lumbered like a steam engine over to the three men. Visible around Pinn's bulk was the arrival of the Clallam County Bus, which connected Forks with Port Angeles, which connected, by Greyhound, to South Dakota and the rest of the continent. The four men went to meet the legendary Fourskins.

The front door swung open and the passengers filed out one by one until the bus was empty. "What the hell! He's not on the bus!" Sparks was incredulous.

"Maybe he's still in Port Angeles," said Pinn.

"He had forty-five minutes to make the connection. The Greyhound came into the same station that The Bus left from. How could he miss that?"

"Maybe he's not coming at all. It was too good to be true," James was crestfallen.

"Never trust an Indian," said a voice behind the four, and the men turned to face Clarence Fourskins who grinned, and extended his hand in greeting. "I'm sorry guys, but I love to hear what people say behind my back." He shook hands with the three. He embraced Jeff Sparks. "It's been a long time, brother," Fourskins spoke softly to Sparks. "Is there some place where we can sit down together and have a beer."

"I don't drink," offered James Crow.

"Me neither," enthused Pinn.

"I'm not twenty-one," said Woodrift.

"You want privacy?" asked Sparks, ignoring the feedback.

"No. It's best that we show from the beginning that we have nothing to hide. We *want* to be seen together."

The party retrieved Fourskins' bags from the Greyhound and secured them in Sparks' Valiant. They walked the quarter mile to the Hang Ups Tavern, where Fourskins and Sparks ordered a pitcher of draft; Woodrift and Pinn ordered Cokes and Crow ordered a glass of water with no ice. The bartender tolerated the presence of the Native minor. Besides the proprietor and Natives; the establishment was empty at 4 p.m.

Fourskins drained his first glass of beer, and wiped his mouth with a bandanna. As he poured a second glass he addressed Sparks, "I can't tell you how pleased I am with how much you've accomplished since we parted company back at NYU. I've just been instilling foment in young minds and cluttering up jail cells, but you've reached out and grabbed the establishment by the nuts."

James Crow cringed at the coarse expression. He withdrew a little from the conversation to watch the news bulletin, which interrupted the ball game on the TV. United States naval forces in the Persian Gulf had shot down a second Iranian commercial airline with 226 civilian casualties. Fanatical elements in Teheran, who had held 16 American hostages for 20 months, were threatening to execute the Americans, in retribution.

102

"I understand, Wally, that you're with the National Guard. There's certain...uh, equipment, that you encounter on a regular basis during the course of your Guard duty, that would prove useful in the kind of demonstration I have in mind. I wonder if you would be able to procure some of these items?"

"Sure," said Wally. "What do you need?"

Fourskins lowered his voice. The voice of the President of the United States almost covered his words as he said to Woodrift, "We could use a few LAW rockets; maybe ten pounds of C-4 explosive; four or five M-16 carbines; and all the ammunition you can lay hold of..."

"Those are weapons!" exclaimed James Crow. "This is supposed to be a nonviolent movement."

"Lower your voice, James," Fourskins hissed. "We don't need to bring the world in on this."

The party fell silent. President Shrub continued his speech on the television, "The United States has always been first at peace, and has exerted a kind and gentle influence upon the unstable politics of the Middle East. Our military presence in this region is a peace-keeping force..."

Wally spoke sideways to Clarence Fourskins, "No prob. Can do."

"Thanks," answered Clarence.

The President was saying, "...We hold the leaders of Iran responsible for this tragic loss of human life. It was no accident that put this civilian aircraft directly over the air space of a United States battleship. To the leaders of Iran who sacrificed these innocent civilians in a vain attempt to disgrace our peace keeping force I say: the blood of your people is on your hands; you are accountable to the court of world opinion. To those who imprison American hostages, and who threaten retaliation, I remind you that it was the Iranian government which put the air bus over United States Naval airspace. Read my lips when I say, we will never negotiate with terrorists..."

"Read my lips, George," said Wally in a loud voice and pointed his rear end at the image of the President, breaking wind violently. Fourskins looked uncomfortable. "Sorry," said Wally. "Coke gives me the farts."

"Listen," said Fourskins intensely. "I don't think you clowns understand what we're going up against. In the Rosebud Reservation, Tripp County Water and Housing Authority is responsible for hooking up sewage and water to new homes. White households pay $1,500 for the hookup, while Natives are assessed a $9,400 charge for the same service. A friend of mine was organizing a deal where all the reservation families were going to flush crank case oil down their shitters to protest.

Believe me, it would really mess up the treatment plants. He called me up to say that he was getting threats on his life. I met him the next day, outside the County Building to talk it over with one of the government water men. Three thugs came out of the building and pulled guns on us, for Christ's sake. They said that we were going on an inspection trip to the sewage lagoons which were eight-miles away. They put my friend and I in handcuffs. They pushed me into the back seat of a county sedan and told my friend that there was no room for him to ride, so he would have to run along behind. They tied the handcuffs to about ten feet of rope and took off at about ten miles an hour for the lagoons. They drove through town like that with no one stopping them. Then they went faster and faster, until my friend fell down. They dragged him about seven miles on the pavement. He stopped screaming about half way. He was dead when we got there. His lower body was abraded down to the bone. They were going to throw me in the sewage lagoon, but the County Sheriff showed up. He treated them like good old boys. He told the driver he was under arrest, but didn't put him in handcuffs. He took me and the driver back to town, and didn't even bother with the accomplices. The driver copped an assault plea, bargained down from manslaughter, and never even served time in jail. The other two were never charged. It still costs $9,400 for a Native household to hookup on a reservation where the average per capita income is about $100 a month. Can you imagine the pain of being abraded to death?"

The five Natives fell silent. John Pinn brooded deeply, his anger focussing somewhere between the sewage lagoons of Tripp County, and the rice paddies of Southeast Asia. The men turned as the door banged open, and one of John Pinn's co-workers entered the nearly empty tavern. "Hey, howdie, you featherheads!" the long-haired Hoquat greeted the Natives.

****

All my life I've had the ability to say the wrong thing at critical times. My intentions have been misunderstood for as long as I can remember having intentions. I brush off the woods detritus from my clothing and walk into my apartment. The phone begins ringing. I answer, "Good afternoon; Chiggers Stokes speaking."

"Hello there, lumberjack!" It's the only woman in my life, since Sally: my mother. She tells me some small news about the homefront in Seattle: a bulletin about my father's impending retirement; more problems with the neighbor's cat and then, in international news, "Did you hear that another Iranian jet got shot down flying into American airspace? Another air-bus with two hundred and twenty-six civilians aboard..."

"Where did this happen?"

"In the Persian Gulf, of course."

"Since when does the United States have air space over the Persian Gulf?"

"We have a peace-keeping force there and the crazy leaders of Iran had the commercial airliner fly right over one of our battleships so the Americans thought it was an F-14..."

"Mom, those American ships over there have the most sophisticated intelligence systems in the world. They must have known that it wasn't an F-14."

"Whatever. Anyway, the President is on TV right now explaining our position. You ought to watch it if you have any questions."

"I've got plenty of questions. It's the TV I lack."

"Well, go over to a friend's, or listen to a radio. Your dad called a few minutes ago to tell me, and he was at a bar..."

"That's it! Thanks, mom. I'll call you back later."

****

I walk into the bar still wearing my tin hat. A quick check of the TV screen tells me that I'm too late to catch the President whitewashing the murder of 226 civilians in a corner of the world to which atrocity is as common as Wednesday afternoon baseball. But a beer might taste OK right now, anyway. The big gentle giant, John Pinn, is sitting at the bar drinking with some chums. If I turn around and walk away, they'll think I don't like Indians.

"Hey howdy, you featherheads!" I call out to josh these guys. (I've never had a chance to tell John Pinn that I'm a quarter Indian myself. Over a glass of beer might be the best way...)

I sit down at the bar beside John Pinn and feel a wave of hostility and suspicion like heat from a blast furnace. I reach across Pinn, and take the half-empty pitcher. I pour beer into the three glasses nearest me which finishes the pitcher and call out to the proprietor, "Another glass and a pitcher of suds, please, barkeep."

"You're not welcome here," grumbles Pinn and I wonder if I heard him right.

The bartender comes over with a fresh pitcher of beer and another glass. He leans over and tells me, "The three guys you poured for aren't drinking beer. These guys are having some kind of private conversation." He takes my five dollar bill and goes off to make change, leaving me to figure out what to do next.

"You guys aren't drinking beer? What'll you have - my treat. Wine coolers?"

"Scram!" rumbles Pinn and it's like thunder from a building squall.

105

The bartender comes back with change and, without taking the change, I tell him, "Three more of whatever it is they're drinking." The proprietor withdraws and I try to break the ice with these stony Natives. "Did I ever mention to you that I'm a quarter Native myself?," I say holding the pitcher. I feel like I'm sitting next to an electrical storm with a lightning rod in my hand. But in my nervousness, I am trying to show familiarity. "You red monkeys on the reservations aren't the only Americans with aboriginal blood..."

Pinn comes off his barstool in a blur, striking like a snake for my throat. His big, meaty paws catch me under the jaw and the thrust carries me up off the stool. I try to stand up, to keep my head from flying off. I'm six foot two inches, but I'm hanging from my neck trying to touch the ground with my tiptoes, looking into the crazy eyes of a rabid Native. I hear my tin hat clattering down behind the bar along with the broken pitcher. I am making gurgling sounds as my brain sends the message, "Put me down! I can't breath." In the reflection from the mirror opposite the bar, I see a giant holding up a dangling doll. The doll's legs kick and the hands pull at the iron bands around the throat. Behind the bar, the bartender drops the two Cokes he is holding which shatter on the floor with the fallen beer.

As the lights go dim and the curtain of my consciousness is pulled down on the show, I hear the audience applauding with my brain, "He can't breath! Put him down! God-damn-it, put him down or I'm calling the cops!" My ass comes down on the bar and I gulp the sweet, delicious, stale air of the tavern in the encore of awareness. "I did...n't mean...any harm," I stutter out.

The bartender presses a five dollar bill into my hand and puts the tin hat back on my head. "Do you want me to call the cops?" he asks, "Or do you just want to get out of here?" I opt for the latter and, without saying anything more, I shuffle for the door. As the door closes behind me, my breath catches in a sob and my eyes burn. A tear runs down my cheek. Christ, I'm thirty-three years old and crying like I did that time twenty years ago when I fell down in the mud running away from the teacher! *Get a hold of yourself!*

****

"I've got to take a piss," grumbled Fourskins inside the tavern. "Let me confer with you a minute, Jeff." Sparks and Fourskins left the three other Natives sitting at their barstools staring at glasses of beer. "Just sit there. Down, boy!" Fourskins voice conveys disappointment.

In the men's room, Fourskins micturated into the toilet, in the stall while Sparks used the urinal. "I'm not happy with what I'm seeing so far, Jeff. You told me that you would put together a team I could count on, and what I see is junk. Pinn is a big, trip-wire time bomb; Crow is some kind of love-peace-flowers-born-again loser; and Woodrift is just some kid with a shiny new badge who thinks the wind blowing out his ass is as funny as Saturday morning cartoons. I don't know if we can expect much from this gang." Fourskins pulled the handle on the flushometer. "What about the ancestral leader we talked about...Gable? You told me there was some kind of book written about him. He's got some kind of alcohol and chemical dependency problems, you said..."

Sparks flushed his toilet. "Forget about Gable. He's a big beer boozer and he pops downers like candy. The book was written by Ruth Kirk, and deals with him as a kid. It doesn't help us. These three guys are OK. They're very loyal and dedicated. Just give it a chance."

"One more incident like Pinn roughing up that redneck hippie and you guys are on your own and I'm outta here." Fourskins pushed out of the door. Sparks followed him out of the restroom back into the tavern. "I want to go over to the library for a minute," Fourskins said. "I might need to check out some books so one of you better come with me. I'll meet the rest of you back at the car. Try to stay out of any fights."

****

Fourskins walked into the Forks Memorial Library with James Crow. Behind the check out desk, four librarians knelt beside two manikins, supervised by two ambulance attendants in blue coveralls. As the two Natives approached the desk, one of the EMT's was counseling the librarians, "Before you kneel down beside anyone to start CPR, you want to make sure that you're not putting your knees into a bunch of broken glass with the patient's blood. We already talked about the chimney masks and how they protect you from the patient's saliva. Why worry about a little spit if you're going to become blood brothers with the patient..." The attendant recognized a former client.. "Hi, James. How's the marathon man?"

"Hello," said James.

The senior librarian, Francis Morganstern, excused herself from the party and came to the desk. "Good afternoon, gentlemen. How can I help you."

Fourskins spoke, "We're interested in local Native history. In particular, I'd like to see a book by Ruth Kirk about a Quileute named Tim Gable."

"That book is on the shelf with other books that might interest you on that last shelf on the right, starting with 941. on the Dewey system. Let me know if you don't find something you need." The librarian returned to assist in the resuscitation of the lifeless manikins.

Fourskins and Crow walked to the section on Native America and pulled a few books. Fourskins opened a small book called A Quileute Chief, by Ruth Kirk to the last page which showed a young boy in ceremonial dress dancing around an auditorium. He read the last two sentences: *That the burden of spiritual leadership should fall on a boy, is of Quileute tradition, and, in keeping with the practice of much of Native America in conferring hereditary roles. For after all, what hope and despair lie in the future for the Natives of this tiny coastal village, are encapsulated in its youth.*

"How old is this guy today?" asked Fourskins, skimming over to the middle of the book.

"He's about my age or a year older. I'm thirty-three now."

Fourskins found a section on Quileute mysticism and mythology. He glanced at references to whale hunting and of how the harpooner, who commanded the expeditions, would surrender the carcass to the village. After the butchering, the harpooner retired with his portion and fasted for three days while he sang, danced and performed skits for the amusement of the whale spirit which presumably resided in this portion of the carcass.

Fourskins read briefly about James Island and how it had served as a bastion for the defense of LaPush. Down from the cliff walls and crumbling steep slopes had come landslide, fire, and boiling water, upon the heads of the attackers. That at one time hostilities between the Quileutes and the Clallams - their neighbors and enemies to the east - resulted in armed conflict with the area around Lake Crescent being chosen for a battleground. The fighting raged for three days, whereupon Mount Storm King, tiring of all the commotion, hurled down rocks to bury both delegations of warriors. Geologists confirm that the land bridge separating Lake Crescent from Lake Sutherland was from an apocalyptic landslide. The momentous event instilled the Quileutes with an aversion to land war - much like the taste of Viet Nam on the palate of the U.S. military - and naval confrontations were again the only approved arenas for their truculence.

"This is interesting," said Fourskins, reading from the book. *"Quileute legend promises a messiah to the Natives of LaPush. Ancient tribal song and story refer to a sachem - or medicine man - who will be brought up in troubled times when many of his brothers are being corrupted and poisoned by a great demon that lurks inland. The sachem confronts this demon and appears to be subjugated by it. The Quileute Medicine Man is executed by the demon, but flies from his grave and a great battle ensues in the water and out into the heavens. The demon is badly injured and retreats from the coast to far away beyond the mountains. All the coastal nations put down their weapons, and a great period of peace follows..."* Fourskins lowered his voice and went on excitedly, "Don't you see the parallel? This guy Gable is caught up by the White man's demon of alcohol and substance abuse. If he can break the hold on that demon, and we can push the demon and White government back away from the reservations, and end the fighting and jealousies among ourselves. We could realize a similar victory. Let's check out these books, and get to LaPush. We need to talk to Timothy Gable."

The two men went to check out the books with James' library card, which was his face. The librarian, Ms. Morganstern, pulled herself up from where she offered mouth to mouth resuscitations to the manikin. Her partner desisted in the chest compressions she administered to the dummy. "Will those four books be all for you, James? Are there any books I can special order for you?"

"Thank you, no," answered the svelte Native.

The EMT who supervised Ms. Morganstern's resuscitation of the manikin spoke to Fourskins, "We heard you reading that mythology mumbo jumbo a minute ago about the medicine man flying out of his grave. I hope I'm not violating patient privacy to tell you that the guy beside you was as close to dead as anyone can get. We were all set to zap him with 200 joules when he started talking to us. Get him to go fight the demon."

"We'll all fight the demon. Thank you." The two Natives left the library.

FOURTEEN

LaPush Village
Friday, June 5, 1992

*J*ames Crow counted the metal chairs he had unfolded and placed in rows in the meeting hall of the Quileute Tribal Council, for the audience of Clarence Fourskins. There were ten rows of eight chairs. It seemed unlikely that President George Shrub, or Sitting Bull, or even Pee Wee Herman would draw a larger audience from the young adult population of LaPush. Jeff Sparks had argued with Fourskins that Friday of commencement week was the wrong time for a political rally. Better to catch the young adults on a Sunday, when they were partied out and repentant of their ways. Fourskins had remained obdurate. Posters and word of mouth advertisement had proclaimed Friday at 6 p.m. as the time for the community of LaPush to consider the impact of 500 years of White oppression. John Pinn walked through the door with his pretty daughter, Dorothy. Wally Woodrift followed them into the room. Wally was wearing his tribal police uniform.

The first miracle of the night began about 5:45 as a constant stream of youths paraded into the meeting hall. At 6 p.m., when Fourskins went up to the lectern to address the assemblage every seat was taken. Crow, Pinn, Woodrift and Sparks were setting up the rest of the folding chairs; and raiding the tribal offices for movable furniture. A reservation village with a total population of less than 200, had turned out an audience of over 100. Even more people came in as Fourskins began speaking. A few attendees were turned away by Woodrift and Pinn because they were not recognized as familiar faces. Fourskins had insisted on this aspect of security along with a ban on recorders and cameras.

Fourskins began his address. As was Crow's habit, James made notations in his personal journal about the speaker's points. *"Tell General Howard I know his heart. I am tired of fighting. Our chiefs are killed. Looking Glass is dead. It is the young men who say yes and no. He who led the young men is dead. Toohoolhoolzote is dead. The old men are all dead. It is cold and we have no blankets. The little children are freezing to death. My people, some of them, have run away to the hills and have no blankets, no food; no one knows where they are - perhaps freezing to death. I want to have time to look for my children and see how many I can find. Maybe I shall find them among the dead. Hear me, my chiefs. I am tired; my heart is sick and sad. From where the sun now stands, I will fight no more forever.*

"These were the words of a man baptized as 'Ephraim,' born of Nez Perce parents who had been converted to Christianity by a missionary named Henry Spalding. As the Natives of the northwest considered the impact of White civilization upon their society, some nations panicked at the threat of annihilation from introduced disease and from the corrupting effects of alcohol, which spilled across all interracial transactions like a bottle with no cork.

111

"In the late 1840's, the missionaries of the Whitman mission were massacred by Cayuse Natives, and the clergy fled the Northwest. Young Ephraim joined the U.S. Cavalry, as a guide and interpreter, to suppress the violent undercurrents of the Yakimas and Cayuse.

A large reservation was ceded to the Nez Perce in 1855; five years later, gold was found in the Wallowas. The White man again conspired to take away the land of the Natives. In 1863 a corrupt chief - whose name happened to be 'Lawyer' - signed a treaty which reduced the reservation to 25% of its previous size. Old Chief Joseph's band was not represented at these treaty negotiations, though their land was among that which was sacrificed to appease the Whites. The Chief tore up his Bible in anger. Before he died, he directed young Ephraim, thusly: *'When I am gone, think of your country. You are Chief of these people. They look to you to guide them. Always remember your father never sold the country. You must stop your ears whenever you are asked to sign a treaty selling your home. A few years more, and the White man will be all around you. They have their eyes on this land. My son, never forget my dying words. This country holds your father's body. Never sell the bones of your father and mother.'*

"By 1873 the Wallowas swarmed with White miners and homesteaders. They were intruding onto the tiny reservation left to the Nez Perce. President Grant ordered Whites to get out; but Governor Grover forced the Administration to reverse its proclamation. The young warriors hungered to throw out the White interlopers by force. A man called 'Thunder Travelling to Loftier Heights' - Heinmot Tooyalakekt - urged the young Chief, who inherited his father's name - to keep the peace.

"In April of 1877, a commission of the Military of the Columbia led by General O. O. Howard, found that, quote: *non-treaty Nez Perce cannot in law be regarded as bound by the treaty of 1863,* unquote. He was missing an arm, but at first, his mind was fully in tact.

"Nonetheless, the Nez Perce were ordered to round up their cattle and contain themselves within the boundaries of the tiny, postage stamp of a reservation which had been generously set aside for them while the Whites ransacked the sacred Wallowas in their never ending quest for gold. On June 13, 1877, this tribe of Nez Perce was poised at the reservation boundary for one final hunt before being forever denied their nomadic, peripatetic existence. They would sacrifice the lifestyle, and freedom that they had enjoyed from the beginning of time, to avoid war with the Whites.

"A young brave named Wahlitus, whose father had been killed by a White man, was taunted by an old warrior. While Joseph was away from the tribe butchering cattle in preparation for the move; Wahlitus stole away from his people, and killed four Whites along the Salmon River.

"Captain David Perry responded with eleven civilians, twelve treaty Nez Perce, ninety troopers, and four officers to the White Bird, to negotiate the tribe's surrender. The Nez Perce sent out a truce party to ascertain the desire of the military column. A civilian fired on the mounted Natives. From the Nez Perce side a warrior lobbed a rifle round at the Corp's bugler, and he dropped dead with the lucky shot. The brave regiment considered the marksmanship demonstrated by their quarry. They threw down their weapons and ran like hell. Less than fifty marginally armed Nez Perce took sixty-three of the soldiers' carbines, and as many sidearms.

"General Howard, and Captain Stephen Whipple, committed themselves to the vindictive campaign against the Nez Perce. They rallied their troops across the Salmon River. Here, the soldiers received a rumor that Chief Looking Glass, from the treaty tribe within the reservation, was planning an exodus to join Joseph. The troops raided the reservation. They destroyed the peaceful encampment that had violated no article of White law. The rumor was fulfilled because Looking Glass had no choice but to seek the protection of Chief Joseph's band for himself and the 550 women and children that had survived the soldiers' attack. Howard pursued the combined bands; crossing the Salmon on rafts and boats. Rumor that the Nez Perce had cut the supply lines disrupted the pursuit. But on July 18, 1877, the 400 soldiers with another 200 scouts, packers, and teamsters moved in on the 100 or so braves of the Nez Perce. Toohoolhoolzote was the war chief making major decisions, while it fell on Joseph to protect the woman and children. The Nez Perce cunning and marksmanship again pushed the soldiers back in humiliation.

"As the Natives made their retreat across the Bitteroot Mountains, on the Lolo Trail, the U.S. government telegraphed ahead to the Seventh Infantry to stop the hostiles. Thirty-five soldiers, and a couple hundred citizens, built a log fort to defend the eastern terminus of the trail. Just a week after repulsing the soldiers on the Clearwater, the Nez Perce arrived at the log fortification. They sent Joseph and two other chiefs to parley. The Nez Perce explained their peaceful propositions. They promised to inflict no violence upon the settlers. This was good enough for the militia. They quit the campaign but Captain Charles Rawn remained loyal to orders. The Natives were not allowed to pass. The Nez Perce withdrew; they seemed to be preparing for a mighty battle as the handful of soldiers dug in. They combed their hair for what they suspected might be the last time.

"Later in the day a handful of warriors came whooping down for the fight. After much commotion, and hacking and sawing on the logs of the fort, they surrendered the attack and fled eastward. The confused soldiers waited several hours before venturing from their fortification. The column of some thousand Natives had circumnavigated the fort and were marching toward Stevensville. The town was undefended. When they arrived, the Nez Perce bought supplies with gold dust, made friends with the citizens and repaired to the Big Hole Valley to camp and rest a few days.

"As General Howard foundered along the Lolo Trail, with his heavy supply train, Colonel John Gibbon was dispatched from Fort Shaw. He led his troops to Stevensville, and hurried to attack the peaceful camp of the Nez Perce. It was August 8th. The soldiers concentrated on a vindictive push into the main column of noncombatant woman and children. Chief Joseph's wife was shot down as she fled with the chief's young baby in her arms. The Natives counter-attacked with grave

113

determination. They eventually routed the soldiers. Almost a hundred Nez Perce lay dead, including the chiefs, Rainbow and Five Wounds. Lean Elk emerged as the supreme war chief. Howard arrived at the scene of the carnage two days later.

"The remaining band of the Nez Perce Nation resumed the retreat to Canada through Targhee Pass. They crossed the Great Divide and entered Yellowstone National Park unmolested. That was in the days before entrance fees and flat-hatted dime snatchers. A sneak party of Nez Perce doubled back and stampeded Howard's entire pack string. While in the Park, the Nez Perce took two groups of tourists away from their sightseeing and held them as hostages. General William Tecumseh Sherman was also enjoying a recreational outing in Yellowstone, but remained oblivious to the Indians' activities. The Natives soon took pity on the frightened and troublesome Whites and allowed them to escape. The Seventh Cavalry, under the command of Colonel Samuel Sturgis, laid an ambush at the eastern boundary of the Park on the upper Yellowstone, but the Nez Perce, again alluded a fight by skirting the soldiers, and emerging on the Clark's Fork River. Outside of Billings, Montana, the Nez Perce took over a stage coach, turned out the passengers and driver, and took turns piloting this strange land craft across the rocky and rutted road. The diversion cost them time, and they were overtaken by the detachment of 300 soldiers of the Seventh Cavalry. This was the resurrected unit from General Custer's debacle. They pushed the Nez Perce into a narrow canyon where they were blocked by brush and boulders. In the bloody battle, three more Nez Perce were killed and twelve wounded before the soldiers were pushed back. By then, the Appaloosa horses of the Nez Perce were going lame. The energy of the people was exhausted after the thousand-mile flight through the wilderness. Their vitality was low after the incessant fighting inflicted upon them by the U.S. soldiers. They needed a place to recover from the recent onslaught, undisturbed.

"The Nez Perce enlisted their old allies of the Crow Nation to act as their guides crossing the Musselshell River to the Missouri. On Cow Island they took over an army commissary, and allowed the supply sergeant and dozen enlisted men to escape unharmed. As they proceeded across the Badlands, the Nez Perce defeated an attack from Fort Benton at Bear Paw.

"In 1877, there were no big signs 'Welcome to Canada' on the international border on the Prairie. With no good maps, towns or large topographic features, the Nez Perce relaxed, believing that they might have reached Grandmother's Country. They were certain that they had outdistanced their pursuers. They desired from the start of their exodus only to surrender their ancestral land, which the White man coveted. They wanted only to proceed unmolested into Canada with merely the clothes on their backs. Here at their camp on Snake Creek, in the early winter of September 30th, they were discovered by Cheyenne Scouts who betrayed their position to General Miles of Fort Keogh. Six hundred soldiers from the Second, and Seventh Cavalries converged on the Nez Perce. The women and children fled the fight, onto the freezing plains. Most of them starved or succumbed to hypothermia. Colonel Miles fought a savage battle of extermination, worrying that General Howard might arrive and take title to the victory. Chief Joseph came forward under a flag of truce, having repelled the soldiers in bloody hand to hand fighting, and was taken hostage. The Nez Perce pressed forward and captured one of Miles' officers. Chief Joseph was released in exchange for the soldier. The Army pulled back and let their howitzers and snipers slowly annihilate the Nez Perce. On October 4, General Howard arrived; his troops mercilessly picked away at the remaining braves. Chief Joseph learned of Howard's arrival. He rode up the hill on his limping horse, and crossed the kill zone with his rifle slung over his back. He reached the soldiers, surrendered his carbine, adjusted his blanket and uttered the surrender speech that I related to you in the opening of this narrative. For their restraint and heroism in battle, Joseph and the handful of survivors were removed to an arid and hot desert where they starved and languished. U.S history text books call this the last military campaign against Native America; discounting the massacre of unarmed Natives at Wounded Knee, South Dakota, later in 1879.

"Native American history is chapter after chapter of genocide. I don't think that most White people are deliberately cruel. It's just...what can you do with a Native population after you've stolen their land and other natural resources? The presence of Natives embarrasses White Americans, because they have this illusion of moral righteousness. The Third Reich used gas chambers and ovens. Manifest Destiny used howitzers, starvation, and disease. The results were the same. Only the Maker of Life can balance the hearts of Nazis and the Indian Agents to see which is more shriveled and less worthy of redemption. It is for us, the survivors, to arrange a more amenable relationship with the government which has inflicted itself upon this continent. I believe that the Quileute Nation can be a door, through which all Native America may pass, to find the green pastures and free-roaming bison that were envisioned by the Ghost Dancers massacred at Wounded Knee.

"First, I'll lay it on the line that the organization that is being born on your reservation has no room for substance abuse. That's a given. No one who abuses drugs or alcohol will be involved in any capacity with this movement. Our Confederation of Non-White Americans proposes autonomy, compensation, and a brighter future for Natives and Afro-Americans across the United States. There will be sacrifices of immense proportion, and...suffering. You are not required by anyone to join us; but you will not be allowed to betray us.

"Before we get down to brass tacks, let's involve ourselves with a little imagery. Most of you have grown up here in LaPush and have lived next to the ocean all your lives...Listen, you can hear the ocean now. The same ocean that has been drumming in the ears of your forefathers for century, after century, after century...Some of the elders here are old enough to remember before the Coast Guard installed the fog horn..."(the fog horn blew its mournful two-second note, as if on cue; Clarence Fourskins interrupted himself)"...Excuse me. Uh, Mr. Crow! Would you mind not taking notes at this juncture. We already prohibited cameras and recorders and your note taking is in about the same class. Do you take notes like that in church?" asked Fourskins jokingly.

"Yes," answered James Crow, shutting his notebook and thusly pulling curtains across our only window into the organic Congress of the Confederation of Non-White America.

FIFTEEN

Forks, Washington
Monday June 22, 1992, 06:15 hours

*T*he owner of the only saw shop in Forks, Jerry LaBell, was furious with the Forks cop. "What do you mean you're not going to collect the evidence?" bellowed LaBell in the officer's face. "It's your job to make a thorough investigation of this kind of thing. How can you pretend to be investigating if you don't take the evidence with you? Send it to the FBI lab and find out what the environmentalist scum ate before breaking into my shop!"

"You don't know that this was the act of environmentalists," reasoned the policeman. "It looks more like a stunt that a disgruntled employee might pull. Whoever did it had to get by all the infrared alarm system you've got hung on this place. It *had* to be an employee, and I'm not equipped to collect evidence like this."

The evidence in this investigation, was a large human bowel movement, which had miraculously appeared inside the cash register of LaBell's Small Engine Repair. The perpetrator had evidently wiped his anus with two different dollar bills and, left them with the feces, in the otherwise empty register.

"Only some granola-bar-eating, yogurt-sucking environmental extremist would pull a stunt like this," offered Jack LaBell, Jerry's father, who had turned out to participate in the excitement of the investigation. In addition to a flower shop; commercial meat locker; dairy distributorship; and ice cream bar; Jim owned a small video arcade across from the high school. He had seen enough vandalism in his establishments to consider himself an authority on this aspect of social aberration. "Those dollar bills are covered with fingerprints, and they've got serial numbers you can trace."

"The serial numbers don't give you anything except the mint where they were printed. The fingerprints don't mean anything unless you have a suspect to match them to. We don't exactly have a file back at the station of cash box defecaters...Look give me a list of who works here, and everyone who has worked here in the last three years."

Jerry LaBell wouldn't let the Green Peace'rs out of the investigation. "It's the Sierra Club! They take someone in the community who is out of work, and pay them two thousand dollars to do this to me! They're mad about the reader board I keep outside my shop."

Officer John Rice had seen the message-of-the-week, minutes before, as he parked outside to initiate this investigation. It read:

Loggers cut trees. College kids cut class. Preservationists cut cocaine. Cut Forks a break! "You've been running messages like that for four years, Jerry. Why would it all of the sudden annoy the crap out of anyone?"

Jack LaBell didn't like police officers using words like 'crap.' He made for the door. "Well, I better go check my registers to make sure no one's gone potty in them. Don't fumble this investigation, John."

Jerry was still arguing with Officer Rice about disposal of the corpus delicti of this crime when the phone rang. "Jerry's," said the proprietor into the mouth piece. "Yeah, dad, he sure is...You want to talk to him?...Ok, I'll tell him." Jerry hung up the phone. He snapped at Officer Rice with growing agitation, "You better get over to dad's arcade right away. Someone stole the brain out of his 'Tank' game. Probably the same nut who shit in my register."

"OK, I'll be back," said the cop, leaving the saw shop. He unlocked his cruiser, and started the rig up. He picked up the microphone to announce this latest turn of events to his dispatcher, and noticed that something inside his vehicle was different. His radar unit was missing!

****

"You should have seen the distraction tactics I pulled to get this stuff!" Wally Woodrift brought back the trophies of his diabolical binge to the body shop, turned laboratory, of the Sparks family. He laid the traffic radar and 'Tank' brain on a stainless steel table, amidst a wild array of clutter. On one end of the table Jeff was yoking together what looked like six satellite de-scramblers. On the other end of the table two young men worked on connecting what looked like a commercial telephone screening device to an AT 386 computer. A technician was taking out the guts of a microwave oven, and mounting them on a walnut stock like a death-ray gun. Clarence Fourskins had appointed Jeff Sparks as chief engineer and head of counter-intelligence for the Confederation. Jeff was obviously taking the mission seriously. The men were engrossed in their tasks. They hardly looked up from what they were doing as Wally spoke, "I should have known you wouldn't be chipping away at arrowheads in here. What is this stuff, anyway?"

From behind the pile of components, Jeff gave Wally a privileged introduction to the high-tech insurgence that was being cooked up in this laboratory. "That man is putting together a strong, portable, radio-jam device that'll also knock out a vehicle's alternator. The other partners are putting together an outgoing telephone screening device from some commercial incoming screening devices. We just patch in a line from the Peninsula Telcom digitizer over by the Coast Guard station. With it, we can be alerted to any outgoing calls from LaPush to the Federal government. When I left the employ of TRW I brought with me a classified government directory with me. There are always some finks in an operation like this. We need to keep a lid on what's going on here until we're ready to tell the world.

"*I'm* working on a super descrambler, said Sparks expansively. "It's a critical component in the whole scheme we're developing. If we wanted to, we could use it to patch into the Strategic Air Command, or the Defense Early Warning systems, and call the President in the middle of the night on the hot line to his bedroom. We'll be putting in an uplink station up by Second Beach Housing. We need more room, so I'm moving the main central intelligence up there."

"What we developed in the six years that I was associated with the Strategic Defense Initiative was basically a new radio-jam system. What do you know about radio waves, Wally?"

"Uh, you can listen to a wave on the ocean; but you can't surf a wave on the radio."

"It began with Samuel Morse developing telegraph. In 1896, Guglielmo Marconi sent Morse Code 9 miles away on the radio waves discovered by Heinrich Hertz. By the turn of the century, an American by the name of Fessenden, was transmitting voice messages. In 1904, a German, Arthur Korn, sent the first wire photos over a telephone line and twenty years later, an American by the name of Richard Ranger sent the first trans-Atlantic still photographs by radio wave. The cathode ray and image orthocon tube were developed. At the 1939 New York World's Fair, television was introduced. The public was unaware of its hunger for this kind of recreational media, but found an immediate and insatiable appetite.

"Until 1934, radio and television were confined to the amplitude modulation band of the wave spectrum, which is from five hundred thousand to one million cycles per second. On A.M. frequency, a constant impulse is distorted by amplification of the waves to impose the signal on the carrier wave. In 1935, Edwin Armstrong introduced the method of modulating the frequency of a much shorter carrier wave and opened up the spectrum all the way to fifty billion cycles per second for radio communication. Radar is in the F.M. band. Visible light is about four, to eight hundred, trillion cycles per second and gamma rays start at a zillion c.p.s. on the spectrum. Sound is below one and a half kilohertz.

"The Soviet Union launched Sputnik in 1957. On January 1, 1958 the United States put Explorer I into orbit. Normal F.M. is 'line of sight' from the antenna, the curve of the earth placing a limit on its range. It didn't take long to realize that man-made satellites offered more telecommunication potential than bouncing A.M. radio waves off of the moon and, in the 35 years since Sputnik, space has become cluttered with F.M. satellite relays. The whole technological explosion took well under a century. Do you understand how orbit is achieved, Wally?"

"The satellite travels linearly, at the same rate it falls?"

"Yeah, that's good enough. Well, you put a satellite twenty-two thousand, three hundred miles above the earth, and you can make it geosynchronous, which means it hangs above a fixed position over the earth. Gravitational effects of the sun and moon, the squat shape of the planet, solar wind, and a few other things, create drift in the satellites, so they are equipped with hydrazine jets to keep them over their targets. Commercial telecommunications satellites are mostly positioned over the equator to conserve on the low-pull band of zero latitude. This saves on hydrazine gas. When boosters run low on gas, or the photovoltaic cells run below seventy per

119

cent efficiency from being chewed up by space dust, the satellite is retired to a 'zero pull' graveyard over the International Date Line. The batteries and communication equipment aboard that fleet of scuttled satellites are all operational. They offer a tremendous communication power to anybody capable of pirating their capabilities.

"The SAC and DEW uplink antennas on earth have to be precisely aimed at their satellites in space to successfully transmit the messages at about fifteen megahertz which are, in turn, down-linked on a lower, scrambled frequency back to an antenna and Earth Station Receiver at seven megahertz. When I left TRW, I brought with me the codes to the frequencies which activate the hydrazine boosters on all the government satellites. The satellite dish outside my place is being converted into an uplink station with some old F.M. transmission gear I got two months ago from the commercial radio station in Forks. We can resurrect eighty percent of that junked fleet from the space graveyard, and position them anywhere we want . We can use them as cross links or we can set them on collision courses with the DEW and SAC satellites."

"Even if you can pull off the 'Night of the Living Dead' part, I thought you said the junk satellites were running on empty. How do you move a whole fleet six to ten thousand miles and then ram a bunch of new satellites hard enough to knock them out of space?"

"All we have to do is push a junked satellite slightly west of the dateline and it begins to drift to the east. Nudge the satellite east of the dateline and it begins a slide to the west. Raise it's orbit and the satellite's orbit is slower than the earth's rotation; lower it and it's faster. It's just a fart's breath of energy and you initiate a externally powered peregrination that will carry the ship anywhere. When satellites collide in space, believe me, you don't need thrusters blazing full throttle. It go boom!

"Anyway, I've got the codes to activate the boosters on the junked satellites...you can get that at Radio Shack; but I'm working on the codes for the DOD ships. If I get that, we could push one button, and collapse the orbits of the entire DEW/SAC system. It would rain satellites on Cheyenne Mountain. Either way, we'll have the U.S. of A. by the short hairs."

"Are you going to go through with it?" asked Wally in awe of the power of this electrical buccaneer.

"I don't think we'll have to. It's like nuclear war - just the threat is good enough. Besides, we'll be using the government communication systems to our own advantage. Remember what I said about the SDI plan? Believe me, there is no way to shoot down five thousand guided missiles coming at you from all over the world. The point of offensive vulnerability is in the guidance system. Attack that and you can turn offensive weapons back at the enemy. Well, we took eight years, and ten billion dollars to find out the obvious...it can't be done. Each missile has it's own scrambled frequency across the whole F.M. band from ten million to ten billion c.p.s. You can't search and descramble that wide a spectra, five thousand times, in the time allowed between launch and nuclear holocaust. But we did find out how to isolate, and pirate, any given frequency of the F.M. band. That's all I need to put the big squeeze on the government..." Sparks did not interrupt his own tinkerings or disturb the work of his co-workers as he explained to Woodrift the chain of high-tech components, interfaced with military secrets and ordinary commercial equipment, that would be combined to place a strangle hold on the government of the United States of America. Against this backdrop, shitting in the cash drawer of Jerry's Small Engine Repair seemed somewhat less of a coup.

SIXTEEN

Smith Field, Olympic National Park
June 10, 1992

*T*he herd of nine feral horses ran through the mist, and tall grass, of the 300 acre meadow known as Smith Field. Former pets of the village, the horses now ran wild, forgotten by their owners. Like Ranger Ed Whitman, they were spooked by what they saw in the large, grassy meadow. The ranger lurked amid the alders, and vine maple along the river. He marveled at what he observed 700 feet within the territorial/maritime exclusive jurisdiction of Olympic National Park. Whitman counted 37 Indians, and 14 dogs sitting peacefully in the wet grass surrounding a tall Native standing next to a flip chart. The Indians with dogs had been drilling the canines, while the couple dozen dogless contingent had looked on with interest. An exercise in dog obedience so close to LaPush ranked among the strangest, most unlikely sights that Ranger Whitman had ever encountered in his decade of prowling the perimeters of the reservation. A ranger from Lake Crescent had taken a dog to the County pound outside Port Angeles, and come back with the curious information that someone in LaPush was bailing out all the dogs from the death-row kennel. The suspicion was that the dogs were going into some "authentic Indian Tacos" hawked by the Natives at local events. Ranger Whitman retreated to the Quillayute River, with this strange intelligence, and found his seventeen-foot aluminum canoe. He paddled across the water, to the government residences, campground, maintenance buildings, search and rescue cache, and ranger station which made up the Park Service installation of Mora.

Having received several obedience training modules since their rescue, the canine recruits sat easier than the Native Americans who faunched, sitting on the cool wet grass in the foggy mists of the meadow. The dogs and several Natives watched as the horses ran with their tails up, out *Thunder Road,* and back toward the village. "Before we get going again with the dogs, we need to go over some more of our so-called 'dirty tricks,'" Fourskins spoke from beside a flip chart. "Last week I explained the chain-letter scheme we want to use to recruit more warriors. By now, each of you should have sent out three letters inviting new recruits to LaPush. What Colonel Sparks and I will be covering in the next few minutes are guerilla tactics to share with sympathetic agents who won't be able to physically attend the events unfolding here. We're going to publish these techniques in the same chain-letter fashion by which we are recruiting for new participants to become warriors in our campaign. In the chain communiqué, which we are going to set up, there will be a specific time for these techniques. We will stress that all targets should be Federal government. Colonel Sparks, why don't you present the first ten techniques."

Jeff Sparks brushed off the crumbled leaves and dried grass that clung to the seat of his jeans as he approached the flip chart and turned over the cover leaf which read *Nuisance Guerilla Tactics Upon Federal Targets.* The first diagram depicted a shot-gun cartridge with fins attached to the outside of the casing.

123

"From now on I'll use the term 'Confederate' to mean 'one of us.' This technique is very simple to put together, but depends on the Confederate being able to access Federal building tops, or other high vantage points controlling government worker access.

"You just tape a BB or small ball bearing to the center fire primer of the shell. If you don't have time to glue on the fins - which work the best - just tape on flagging. Use a twelve gauge shell, since a sixteen gauge is less devastating and you need the full weight of the twelve to avoid misfire. Use bird shot and you achieve maximum exposure to the nuisance, but trade seriousness of the injury caused by larger pellets. Questions?"

There were none. Sparks flipped the chart. "Colonel Crow taught me this trick when I was nine years old..."

"My name is 'James,'" Crow interrupted. "And someone could get hurt with that shotgun shell trick!"

"Yeah, well...," continued Sparks. "They used to advertise this hairgoo for men that was supposed to make you sexually irresistible to women. You take HDH - that's crystallized chlorine used in swimming pools - put it in one side of an envelope, and put some of this Score goo in the other side of the envelope. A little dab will do you. You instruct the recipients of our chain letter to fold over the envelope to separate the components, and go to a U.S. mailbox on Columbus Day. Unfold the envelope and hold it up like this, allowing the HDH to run down, like an hour glass, onto the Score. Mush it together like this, and drop it into the mailbox." Sparks threw the envelope onto the grass. "Walk away. You might mention in the chain letter, for the benefit of our less intellectually nimble brothers, *not* to use envelopes with their names and addresses in case there is incomplete combustion." The envelope burst into flames on the grass. "We'll be using this technique on just about every Federal Building and mailbox in the United States. If components become a problem for mailbox targets, we can always just dump in lighter fluid, or diesel fuel, and toss in a traffic flare. But not gasoline, OK Einsteins?"

Sparks turned over the flip chart to the next leaf which was entitled **POISONOUS GASES.** "You can use this HDH stuff for a lot of different recipes. Take kitchen ammonia, and half fill a quart jar like this in the picture. Then take a closed half-pint jar of HDH and put it in the jar with the ammonia. Put the lid on the quart jar. Now you've got a grenade that's a lot more potent than the tear gas the government is throwing at you. Another advantage is that you lob just one of these babies at the troops, and right away, the government dons gas masks. Then they can't see for shit. Get them a little agitated and they start shooting each other and poking themselves with bayonets." He flipped the chart.

The next leaf read **EXPLOSIVE HDH GRENADE,** depicting a quart and half pint jar. "The funny thing about HDH is that it's made to be introduced to water. But introduce water to it, and it explodes. Put water in the half-pint, and the HDH crystals in the quart jar, and it makes a hell of a mess when it hits pavement. Don't try it in your home."

James Crow was on his feet. "Wait a minute, Jeff. These techniques are really dangerous. People will get hurt. We've agreed on a course of passive resistance, and this threatens real violence!"

Clarence Fourskins spoke from a seated position. "Thank you for your concern, Colonel Crow. We are advocating resistance here. I told you and everyone else that violence could be counterproductive. However, we need these techniques as a smoke screen to mask the larger, and more potent aspects of our campaign. Nothing is ever won without conflict. Please go ahead, Colonel Sparks." James Crow sat down with an audible sigh.

Sparks flipped the chart to **SHORT RANGE EXPLOSIVE PROJECTILES**. A lot of you crazy fuckers probably played around with filling CO_2 cartridges with match heads." Sparks held up a contraption of five pieces of one inch galvanized pipe, welded to a piece of angle iron. "This isn't any more dangerous to launch and it's a lot more fun. We give the expended CO_2 cartridges a warhead of lead azide, which also improves their ballistics. Instead of match heads, we use a formula of powdered charcoal, potassium chlorate, and sulfur for propellant. We use Estes Rocket igniters on a circuit trigger. The five barrels are designed to spread out across a twenty-foot roadway and make a hell of a noise. A direct hit to the engine block would stop a troop carrier; but wouldn't dent an M-1 tank. We're working on some oxygen-bottle missiles with larger warheads for the M-1's. The CO_2 cartridges are packed into these wooden speed-loader strips. You can fire the thing from a tripod or the crazier among you can shoot from the shoulder. But it burns off your eyebrows and you need eye protection. These things will really make the National Guard jumpy."

Sparks flipped the chart to **EXPLOSIVES FROM FERTILIZER**. "You can make shit explode big time. The loggers use an explosive called 'ANFO' in the quarries around here. It stands for Ammonium Nitrate with Fuel Oil. Fertilizer trucks blow up all the time. Just take the composting horse flop you find in this field; put it in a contained environment; add diesel; and hit it with a fast primer like potassium percolate, or fulminated mercury...you can take out bridges and roads. As a matter of fact, we'll be collecting horse shit from this meadow for just that purpose. Twenty-four years ago, Colonel Crow and I peppered the campground across the river with shrapnel and rock fly from a horse shit bomb..."

James Crow was back on his feet. "I told you then that it was dangerous and I'm telling you again, now. Someone is going to get hurt here!"

Clarence Fourskins stood up. "Colonel Crow, we acknowledge the risk of casualty in these techniques and we will accept the consequences of our actions. We are not children playing with horse manure. We are an army in quest of freedom and sovereignty. These come only at a price." Fourskins walked over to the flip chart and shuffled to a leaf entitled **SHUTZHUND**.

125

"Thank you, Colonel Sparks, we'll come back to these techniques later. It's time to get back to the dogs. I thought I'd better get the spelling of this word on the board, since I've been hearing some funny pronunciations of it. Shutzhund is the method of protection training we're applying to these dogs. As you will see, it will instill confusion and panic in our adversaries while promoting good public relations through media coverage. A lot of these pups come from environments where they have been abused and beaten. So far we've been using rag-play to build confidence and work on their bite development. These pooches need a lot of positive reinforcement, so always, always, *always* praise your dog; unless it's actively screwing up. We have been working on our dogs' defensive drive so that they react to pressure with aggression rather than avoidance. So what we will be doing now is giving the dogs controlled threats, and rewarding them for reacting to the threats with aggressive behavior. Colonel Sparks and I will demonstrate."

Fourskins held a dog on the end of a leash, while Jeff Sparks approached in a strange, crouched manner making eye contact with the dog. The dog began to growl and Fourskins said, "Good boy! Get him! Good dog!" The dog pulled on the leash to get at Sparks. Fourskins held the dog back while praising him, as Sparks was running away. "When your dogs get comfortable with this, we'll give out the padded arms, and allow them to repel the threat with a bite. This builds confidence and establishes behavioral imprinting. We will carry this through to pursuit training later on this week."

The horses had ventured back into the meadow; but the sight of the dogs lined up in a row, growling and snarling at the human assailants, sent them stampeding back down Thunder Road, again, with their tails held high in the air. This time the attention of the Natives remained in the meadow.

SEVENTEEN

LaPush Village
June 18, 1992

*J*eff Sparks couldn't believe that his cousin, Mark Wright, would be so deceitful. As he sat beside the stainless steel table in the high-tech laboratory of his shop, he listened to Clarence Fourskins. The tall Plains Indian paced the room. "The call went out at twelve minutes past midnight, this morning. It was one of the new telephone numbers you plugged into the computer last night that keyed the call. After all these years, Agent Prue is still on our tail. I guess he's never heard of the Statute of Limitations for arson."

"He's probably got a bone on for me because I laid a little trap for the cops in my apartment back in L.A. I figured the FBI would be involved in damage control."

Fourskins pushed the play button.

"Mr. Prue, this is Mark Wright, in LaPush..."

"I told you not to say our names over the phone!"

"You really think my cousin could have the phone lines tapped?"

"Sure. That monkey genius learned all kinds of tricks working for TRW. Just tell me the latest developments and get off the phone."

"I'm still working at the cannery and Fourskins is having me steal about fifty pounds of minced fish a day for the dogs. I still can't figure out what he intends to do with the mutts, but it's some kind of attack thing. Fuck, I don't understand how he plans to overrun the Army with these mangy hounds, but that's what he's planning..."

"He said that the dogs would be used to attack an Army facility?"

"No. No one's saying nothing about what's going to get attacked. We talked about a bunch of dirty tricks, burning up mailboxes, and screwing around with Federal buildings. That sort of shit. Oh, they're putting out this chain letter thing that goes out to reservations all over the country to bring them into it. You want I should send you a copy?"

"If you can do it without being detected. It's critical that you not tip off these nuts. You're our only window into this subversive activity, and God only knows what Fourskins would do if he found out you were supplying the government with information. Listen, call back this weekend on your days off from the cannery. Call back from Forks. Don't risk using the phones there in the reservation!"

"You want that I should start poisoning the mutts!"

"Hell, no! Just keep your eyes and ears open, go along with their program and call back next weekend."

"You'll be hearing from me...Oh, and, uh Fred. I'm a little low on weed down here and no one in the reservation is doing the stuff anymore. Can you send an agent from Seattle to help me out?"

"We sent you two ounces in June! Are you feeding that to the dogs!"

Fourskins pushed the stop/eject button and handed the tape to Sparks. "Can you beat that? The FBI running dope from Seattle to LaPush to the one pot head we didn't cure...why don't they just say, 'no.' Listen, your cousin has to be dealt with severely. He's already compromised our position. The success of our movement depends on strict security."

"I know," said Jeff Sparks. It was sad. He had played with Mark when they were kids.

****

Jeff found James Crow by himself in the old Shaker Church. The congregation had gone home to their Sunday dinners. Crow needed time to think about the avalanche of events that had been set in motion with the arrival of Clarence Fourskins in LaPush.

Jeff sat beside James and spoke quietly. "Do you have a second to answer a question for an old playmate?"

"Sure. What do you want to know?"

"If you were interested in setting up an electromechanical trigger...say that you wanted a pin to fail at an exact moment... how would you go about it?"

"What's this pertain to. Who's going to get hurt?"

"It's just a trick I want to play on an old friend. It's nothing I wouldn't do to my own family...I swear it."

"You can accelerate the oxidizing effect of acid on steel by running electricity across its surface. Rust is just an electrical process caused by water moving over steel. Or, if you want a pin failure simultaneous to triggering, use magnesium. It's really strong so you can use a finer filament. It will ignite under heavy amperage. A lot of jet parts are made out of magnesium."

"Where could I get some magnesium?"

"I've had some magnesium cores around for fifteen years or so. I can give them to you."

"Can you work it on a lathe, and dye it like old steel rod?"

"Sure."

"Can we go get it now? I'm anxious to get going on this project."

****

Mark Wright could never get used to the stink. Even growing up next to the cannery had not prepared him for the olfactory insult that belched from the machinery every time it caught the hollow organs of the large tuna and halibut carcasses in the macerators.

He had to lean on the machine as he wrestled the large fish skeletons into the bone-crunching blades, always careful to keep his arms, hands and fingers on the safety zone prescribed by a red rectangle above the jaws. To minimize vibration to the worker who pushed heads, and skeletons, into the bloody chipper; the machine depended on four coiled springs, held in tension by four heavy half-inch pins. The ten horse power engine to drive the blades were turned on at eight in the morning, when Mark arrived. They stayed on until four thirty in the evening when he shut off the machine to go home to shower, and get shit faced.

Mark checked his Timex. 9:46 a.m.: late enough for his ten o'clock smoke break. He pulled off his bloody latex gloves, and pulled down the spattered surgical mask from his mouth. "These hands: I could have been a doctor," muttered Mark pulling out a pre-rolled reefer from the shirt pocket under his rubber apron. The joint in his lips, he struck a kitchen match on the machine; lit his smoke; and stepped over to the open doorway of the cannery to enjoy his break away from the smell of the offal.

He lingered by the open door with a cup of coffee, and a second joint until 10:10. He returned to the carnage with reluctance. Pushing down a particularly recalcitrant carcass, that seemed to yet possess a will of its own, Mark picked up a wooden staff reserved for this situation. He kept on pushing within an inch of the whirling swords. Whether this old tuna, minus his meat, would go into fertilizer, pet food, or Gordy's Fish Sticks, would depend purely on the appetite of the respective industries. It seemed odd that the only job that *wasn't* done here at the cannery was the product labeling.

Mark's sense of sight gave him the first niggling impression that something was really wrong. As he was pushing an entire dog shark into the jaws, the whole machine seemed to jump up toward him. He jumped back and both his hands had gone the way of the shark. He looked dumbly at two jagged stumps six inches proximal to where his wrists should be. His mind flew into fast denial. *No! This is not happening!* Fighting dizziness and nausea he staggered to the phone to call 9-1-1. *This is just a dream...or, I'm watching a movie...*He reached for the phone with a spurting stump. *Shit!* he thought. "SHIT!" he yelled. Then, he ran out the open door of the cannery screaming for help.

"He'll have a little trouble reaching out and touching the FBI from here on out," said his cousin, who, with Clarence Fourskins, watched through binoculars as the wounded Native collapsed on the ground. Fourskins called for an ambulance while Jeff Sparks ran out to his cousin with compresses and elastic bandages.

****

The two EMT's stood outside the ambulance bay, waiting for the third team member to show up. The first looked at his watch.

"OK, that's five minutes since the call came in. I think we'd better call second out for another person or see if we can grab a nurse," said Greg Banter, who happened to be the President of the local fraternity known as the Ray Ellis Memorial Volunteer Ambulance Corps.

The second EMT, Bob Stork, was less impressed with the emergent nature of the situation. "Two of us can handle whatever there is in LaPush. I haven't had a serious run down there in thirteen years. Not since that Crow woman - whatever her name was - tried to end it all by drinking toilet bowl cleaner."

"She did end it all. The toilet bowl cleaner killed her. It just took a couple of days. The citizen who called this in said it was a serious injury over at the old cannery."

"Probably a cat with a bone caught in its throat and the cat owner wanting a ride to Hang Ups on the way to the vet. What was that Crow woman's name, anyway. April?"

"Some kind of month. I think her name was 'May.' Anyway, I'm going to look for a loose nurse."

"Don't find one that's too loose. Remember, we have a run. Hey, I'll do it. I have to take a piss, anyway. And that patient's name was *June*. June Crow."

"Use the bedpan if you have to, here comes Pat. We're outta here."

****

Twenty minutes later the EMT's were at the scene of the injured cannery worker. The patient was in profound shock. He was attended by a man who introduced himself as the patient's cousin; and a Petty Officer from the Coast Guard who had responded when he heard something about an injury at the cannery over the station's scanner. The Coastie, and the cousin, held blood drenched compresses on the stumps.

"You guys sure took your time," observed the patient's cousin.

The EMT, who introduced himself as Greg, spoke; as the one named Bob relieved the Coastie of his purchase on the bloody compress. The EMT's all wore rubber gloves and surgical masks. "No one said that this was a bilateral traumatic amputation. That might have hurried us along a little. Pat, get me one of those instant heat packs so we can try to bring out a vein. Bring the Ringer's Lactate, and two sixteen-gauge needles. Dump out that bed pan, while you're at it. We don't need that getting kicked over while we're jumping around in back."

Mark Wright still wore the surgical mask which had protected his mouth and nose from splattering fish entrails. Greg cut it away to put in a nasal cannula to give the man oxygen. "Who put the mask on this guy, anyway? You can't catch AIDS from your own blood!" Pat laid out the intravenous therapy supplies. "Thanks, Pat, and, hey, go into the cannery and bring back whatever is left of the patient's hands in the machinery."

Two minutes later, Pat was back, white faced and empty handed. She spoke quietly and intently in the senior EMT's ear so the patient would not hear her report. "You want what's left of his hands, you go get it yourself. There's metacarpalphylangeal extensor tendons mixed up with dog-fish intestines. It would take a high school biology class just to identify the cut up worms in that pile of gore. His hands are cat food!"

****

As a cat lover, lonely spinster, and high school biology teacher, Clara Ball knew that the feline appetite was capricious, and frequently intense. Still, 'Purr Purr' had never behaved like this! Nor had any cat, in the three feline generations of Purr Purr's ancestors known to Ms. Ball.

'Tres Meow' (a.k.a. *Fur Ball)*, the great grand-puss, now he was a strange cat! And he had a right to be. It was 24 years now since Clara Ball came from Maryland to Port Angeles, Washington to teach young minds the wonders of dissecting frogs and fetal pigs. It was in that first summer that she was awakened one night by the strange, mournful caterwauling from the lone cottonwood tree in her small backyard. It went on all night, and into the next morning. As she left her front door, she heard three small mewling pleas from under the porch. She shone a flashlight under her new house. She saw the two reflective orbs of the cat's eyes, but Tres Meow was not quite ready for human society. Ms. Ball left a saucer of milk, and some ham slices, near the front steps and it was gone when she returned home. That evening, she was able to coax the cat she called 'Tres Meow,' from under the house with the smell of bacon fat and tuna oil. To her horror she saw that the poor creature was ambulating on three legs. There was a chewed off stump where his front left leg should have been. Tres Meow had not wanted to go to the veterinarian's office that night. He lashed out with his three paws like a weed whacker. It was only by the straight jacket of a pillowcase, and duct tape, that the cat was persuaded to make the visit.

It was on the return home that evening, that Clara noticed the deflating weather balloon stuck in the top of the cottonwood. Tres Meow had been a fine pet for the lonely teacher. He had adapted to his handicap without major complaint. In 1979, Tres Meow was dead, and in the ground for two years, when the cottonwood blew over in the same windstorm that blew away the Hood Canal Bridge. Examining the shreds of the balloon, which had hung like a ghost over her backyard for eleven years, Clara was horrified to see, tied to a piece of flat nylon webbing, what she recognized from her training and experience as a biology teacher, as the skeletal remains of a cat's foot.

But one paw completed the list of missing appendages. Tres Meow left LaPush an un-neutered male, and arrived in Port Angeles in the same condition. Clara's neighbors had observed Tres Meow in copulation with their un-spayed house cat and offered Ms. Ball the fruit of that union on their way to the Humane Society with the whole brood, sans one kitten. Clara had picked out a female, 'Frisky Whisker,' who, in turn, was impregnated by her brother, who resided with the neighbors. Tres Meow begat Frisky Whisker who begat Purr Purr.

On this June day in 1992, she opened the can of "Feline Feasts: Tasty Ocean Tidbits," and hoped that Purr Purr would like it. He was a moody cat and sometimes expressed his culinary disappointments in destructive behavior. Purr Purr really liked it!

As Purr Purr bit into the saucy chunks, microscopic watch fragments and processed flesh of the Tidbits, a light was turned on in the dimly illuminated office of a cat's consciousness. As he tried to make some connection between the orgasmic pleasure reaching the cortex of his brain, and his experiential consciousness, a furry paw rifled through the clutter of files representing the diversions of a cat's life. The paw pushed aside files with such labels as: *Shit on Carpet, Shred Curtains,* and stopped at a folder labeled *Sex. "Nope, no entries in this file since the old bitch had me neutered."* Anyway, there was something here in this food loftier than serenading the neighborhood on some love quest. The paw went to the obscure cabinet on genetic memory and leafed through the files therein. In front was a file labeled *Balance: Land on Feet* and toward the back, *Water: Fear of Baths.* Right behind a dusty file labeled *Saber Tooth Tiger* was **the file**. It read *Savory Vengeance. "This is it, all right. There's something primordial in the hearty eye for eye, hand for paw flavor of this chow!"*

Purr Purr laid back his ears and hissed at Frisky Whisker when she came to sup beside her spawn. He finished with his portion, ignoring the remonstrations of his mistress, while he ate the mother's share, as well. A different can of the same brand of Ocean Tidbits, lacking one ingredient, was served for breakfast the following day. This produced an entirely different reaction from Purr Purr. Perhaps it is expecting too much from the gentile, patient, reader to believe that such associations, and thought processes are articulated inside a cat's cranium. But a cat can articulate a turd on the living room carpet, which Purr Purr did so explicate after inspection of his breakfast. Purr Purr also chose the medium of expensive silk curtains, upon which he raked his claws, annunciating his disappointment with the turn in menu. Later in the morning, Purr Purr beat up his mother, and repaired under the bed to sulk. At their worst, cats behave not unlike their human counterparts.

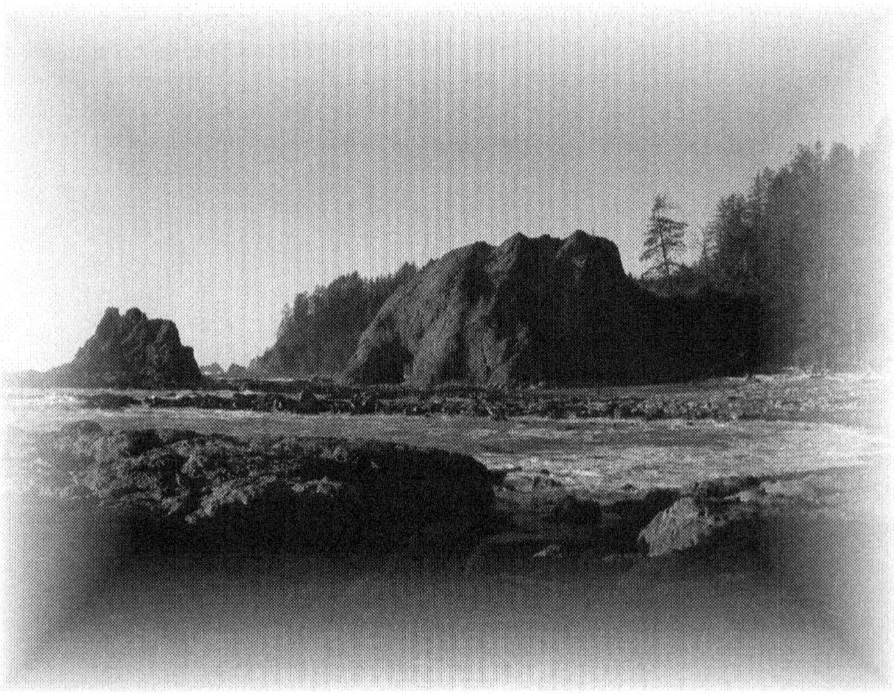

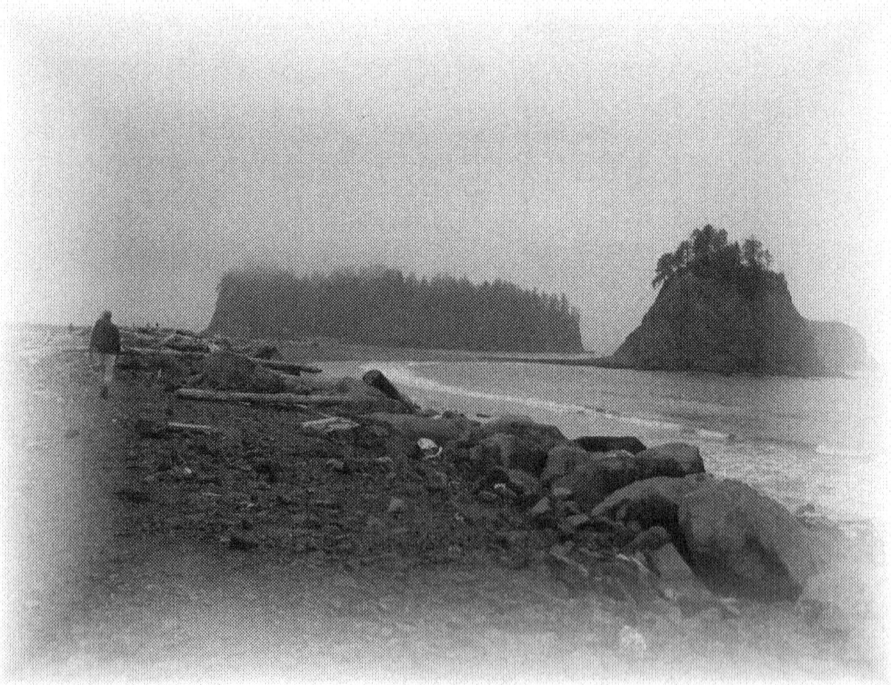

EIGHTEEN

LaPush Road
Friday, June 26, 1992

*I*t's hard to get up the energy to jog when you've been busting butt, setting chokers on steep, slash-strewn slopes all day. But I pledged to myself that I would run 40 miles a week, on top of the exercise I get humping chokers. So here I am on the LaPush Road at eight o'clock at night, running from Three Rivers to LaPush village and back. Summer usually comes late to the Pacific Northwest, but this June heralds an early heat wave. I seek refuge in the deep hours of daylight for the exertion necessitated by my promise. I run across the Bogachiel Bridge, which spans the confluence of two of the Three Rivers. On the left side of my face I feel a cooling, down-valley wind beginning to blow to Rialto Beach five miles below. It's curious, as a half hour later, I approach Third Beach on the short straight-a-way of road, and, now, the ocean is only a mile distant and to my left. How did Balboa ever find the Pacific when it insists on following the chicken across the road?

As I run by the trailhead parking lot, trying not to slap my feet on the still warm, soft blacktop, I hear a creature moving through the trees behind the parked cars. I glance over, expecting to see a deer, but through a matrix of salal, salmonberry, and young alder, a Park Ranger is stealing from a spruce tree to the concealment of a large hemlock root mass.

"Howdy!" I call out to the uniformed ranger who disappears silently behind the hemlock. I feel a little bit like Brer Rabbit, spurned by da Tar Baby. What's this pine pig doing lurking furtively about the parking lot, anyway? Whatever happened to the friendly dudes in flat hats that greeted you at the park entrance with a visitor map and directions to the nearest comfort station? It is a momentary annoyance and soon the rhythm of the running and the tranquility of the advancing evening preoccupy me with thoughts of practically nothing.

As I jog down the hill toward the village from Second Beach Parking, the jagged ramparts of James Island come into view. It silhouettes a sky rampant with color. The big red beach ball of a sun is settling slowly, down into the pastel pillow of the horizon. I lose my view of the ocean as I plod the last thousand paces toward the village. Rumor of deep tribal unrest and conspiracy seem as ephemeral and far flung as the wispy, pink cirrus clouds that strew the stratosphere. A new, red, Japanese four-wheel-drive pick-up passes me driving towards the village. Inside the cab are four Natives crowded onto the bench seat. A payload of three more young Indians is carried in the bed of the pick-up. "Hey, you're running the wrong way, longhair!" calls one of the young braves, whose hair is longer than mine.

At once, I remember the bald aggression and hate of that crazy son of a bitch, John Pinn, and from the wispy clouds of tribal unrest begin to sprinkle droplets of paranoia. What if I jog right into that big red ape down here in this enclave of White hatred? My 25% Native ancestry wouldn't keep these savages from burning the other 75% at the stake. I decide to cross the road, and U-turn before the road to

135

First Beach Parking. I turn tail, and run with my back to the red glow on the horizon, the susurrant surf waving me *adieu*.

As I come back to Third Beach Parking, my quiet thoughts are again intruded upon, this time with the message: **Urinate now!** I run behind the parked cars and, to guarantee my privacy, I push into the woods to the private stall provided by the hemlock bole and extruded root where the ranger had been skulking about. I pull down my jogging shorts, and jock, and a moment later, am splashing happily upon the tree.

"HOWDY YOURSELF!" says the voice directly behind me. I jump almost out of my jock and abort the piss, mid-mission. My pecker burns. I feel myself blushing as I turn around to face the Park Ranger who has re-materialized five feet behind me.

"Is this some kind of a bust?" My embarrassment is turning into anger.

"Not at all. Go on with what you were doing. I just won't be using that spot to hide for a little while." The Park Ranger unzips and takes a piss so I go ahead and finish my job.

"What are you doing hiding back here anyway?" I ask the ranger.

"Last weekend we had several car clouts at this trailhead. I'm going to try to catch the thugs who are doing it."

"What's a car clout?"

"Breaking and entering of vehicles. In the incident last week, the operative word was "breaking." All the glass was smashed out of three of the five vehicles that were parked here."

"Do you have any idea who did it?"

"My guess is that the perps weren't White. The two cars that weren't hit were a party of Indians from the Quinault Reservation."

"So you think they did it?"

"Not really. I think this was some kind of political statement and that the person responsible had access to the D.O.L. computer."

"I thought only cops had..."

"Quiet! Shhhh...." hisses the ranger.

I hear a car approaching from LaPush, and realize that it is slowing down as if to turn into the trailhead. "Get down," orders the ranger, assuming a crouched position behind a root mound, himself.

The vehicle turns in and I see a light bar on top of a sedan. I recognize the presence of fellow law enforcement and begin to stand up. "Stay down," growls the Park Ranger. A car door opens and shuts and, over the idling engine, I hear approaching footsteps through the spongy forest floor. It feels like a game of hide and seek. A young tribal officer jumps up on the root mass directly above the Park Ranger and takes off his cop hat to run the palm of his right hand over his almost clean-shaven head.

"Good evening, Wilbur. I thought I'd find you here." Then, the young cop looks over at me crouching behind the hemlock. "Hello there," he says to me amicably. "Listen, Wilbur, I'm going off to Guard duty in two weeks, so I won't be around to help you keep these parked cars safe from the criminal contingent. I'll be on duty all night in case you need me." The Park Ranger merely stares at the tribal officer who hops off the roots and heads back to his black and white. He calls over his shoulder, "Incidentally, Wilbur, you may want to shower when you get back to the ranger station. A lot of people piss where you're lying." The cop drives off.

I realize that I am the reason for the wet ground from which I have become a sponge. The ranger is apparently making the same realization. "Fuck me," he mutters and stands up brushing off his uniform. "The little shit knew exactly where I was."

"Were you trying to hide from him?" I ask incredulously.

"That young buck is bad news, whatever uniform he has on. He used to prey on cars at this trailhead, himself. I know he did, but I could never catch him or prove it. The young punk was always pulling my chain. One time I came out here, at almost midnight to investigate the theft of four tires off of a Chevy Suburban. The complainant's rig was left sitting on the naked drums in the dirt. The poor son of a bitch made a big deal about how valuable the chrome rims were. We couldn't remember the lug configuration on the rim, so we went over to the government Suburban to check. The stolen tires, and rims, had been put on my Suburban. The government tires washed up on Rialto Beach the next week."

"How do you know it was him that did it?"

"He was always pulling shit like that. He featured himself as some kind of juvenile Robin Hood. He'd brag to his friends.

He'd leave notes and make telephone calls. I recognized his phony hand writing, and disguised voice. I just could never prove anything in court."

"So he's a suspect in this car bashing last weekend?" I ask.

"I never said that my fellow officer, Walter Woodrift, was suspected in these recent car clouts. Just because whomever did it was probably an Indian with police access to D.O.L., and nothing was stolen from the vehicles, which fits a long time pattern of behavior demonstrated by this certain person...that's no reason to jump to conclusions, and think that a commissioned officer with the tribal police could have anything to do with blind acts of vandalism."

I was experiencing a certain sense of intimacy with this Park Ranger. We had just laid down in piss together and now he had bared his soul and told me a secret. "I see what you're saying, Wilbur. My name is Chiggers Stokes," I say extending my hand.

"*Ed* is my name. Woodrift just calls me 'Wilbur' to get my goat." Ranger Ed shakes my hand, "Ed Whitman."

As twilight pulls a blanket of dusk over the bed of the forest and begins to turn on night lights in the sky, I realize the need to get jogging back to Three Rivers before lights out. Somehow there is a temptation to linger and bullshit this affable warden. "So how long have you worked here, Ed?"

"Too long. I got here in 1979 and I've been trying to get out of here ever since."

"You don't like Forks? The Olympic Peninsula? What?"

"I love the Peninsula. I love the Northwest. I'm from North Carolina originally, but I'd like to settle out here. It's LaPush I don't get along with."

"Lately, I'm having some problems, myself. There's something scary on the wind down in that village."

"My problems are not recent or short lived. When I learned that I was getting transferred from Cape Hatteras, to Mora just across from LaPush, I started reading up on Native American history. I read **Bury My Heart At Wounded Knee**. I believed Ruth Kirk in a book she wrote about LaPush back in the early 60's. I had a picture in my mind's eye of Natives plying the waters of the Quillayute in dugouts, wearing grass skirts. I saw them throwing flowers across the river to me. Within the first week of my transfer out here, I drifted the river in the park's Zodiac inflatable from Three Rivers out to James Island. I passed a lot of unfriendly Indians tending their gill nets on the river. I had a beer with the Mora maintenance man that evening and told him how I had been received. He said that the Quileute word for friend was "Hoquat." He said that it was synonymous with 'Kemosabe.'

"So, I drifted the river a few days later and to every red face I met I uttered, 'Howdy, Hoquat!' It didn't melt the ice, in fact, the Natives seemed provoked. I conferred with my supervisor, the District Ranger, a few days later. He explained that 'Hoquat' was the original diminutive given to describe Whites in the Chinook dialect and translates something between 'honkey, mother fuck' and 'shit, floating on water.' The maintenance man had set me up for a fall.

"In the thirteen years since then, not a whole lot has gone right with the reservation and myself. Now the tribe is using language from the Point No Point Treaty to confer title to Rialto Beach. Just before I got transferred out here, the Park gave back First Beach, and LaPush Ocean Park, to the tribe. You give an inch and they take a mile of beach."

"Do they have a legal claim to Rialto Beach?" I ask trying to apply basic jurisprudence to the presented case.

"Who knows. That's not for me to worry about. I just do what the park tells me to do; and the park does what the judges tell them to do; and the judges just try to figure out what Congress meant when they said what they wanted done."

"If the treaty bequeaths title of Rialto to the Quileutes, I don't blame them for making noise to get it back."

"It's not as simple as all that. The Stevens Treaty, which is the basis for the Bolt Decision, is cloaked with language guaranteeing the northwest tribes fishing and hunting rights 'for as long as the sun shall hang in the sky and for as long as fish shall swim in the sea.' But it still takes a judge to say, 'OK, that means a fish for you, a fish for me, a fish for you and a fish for me.' Then the judge has to invoke protections like conservation closures and creel census to assure the distribution and protect the fish populations from annihilation."

"That sounds fair to me," I say.

"Well, it doesn't seem fair to me. The Bolt Decision gives half the fish in this state to the Indians. If I spend all my time and money cultivating a trout pond, a Native can come onto my property and take away half my fish. An anadromous stream runs through your property and no-way can you tell Natives to pick up their beer cans and get their gill nets off your property. The implications are scary and, to me, infer second class citizenship to Whites."

The ranger sighs and pauses to reflect. "I shouldn't talk about politics while I'm wearing uniform and on duty, but the politics of my job follow me on my time off. I go to town with my wife and two kids and some young Indian punk in a new four-wheel-drive pick-up that I arrested for D.U.I. the week before is cat calling and scaring my children. These young Indian bucks wreck a pick-up driving drunk, without insurance, and BIA picks up the medical bills for all the Indians hurt in the accident. The tribal police investigate it and there's not going to be any prosecution. The young drunk gets over his hangover and goes out the next morning with money allocated him from the Quinault timber trust. The next night he's driving drunk again with a brand new pick-up.

"That's another thing: the resource management that goes along with giving land back to the Indians. Have you looked at the Quinault Reservation? It's 200,000 acres of clear cut. Would you want Rialto Beach to look like that?"

I think for a minute. "I'm getting kind of used to clear cuts. And what you just said: 'give the land back to the Indians.' How do you figure that we ever owned it if the treaty does not extinguish the Indians' claim to the land? What they do with it is their business."

The ranger takes off his ball cap and runs a handkerchief over the top of his head. "What's your line of work, Chiggers, anyway? Do you work for the tribe?"

"No, I set chokers. I sold software in Seattle, but the city finally made me claustrophobic and I set out for the life of a lumberjack in the twilight of the timber industry."

"You don't much talk or think like a logger, Chiggers."

"Yeah, well actually I'd like to be a writer. It's just that I'm kind of stumped for subject matter. I don't really feel like writing glowing reports of my day at work, extolling the virtues of the timber industry."

"I see what you mean. Anyway, my political philosophy in a nutshell is that I'm for equality across the board. As far as I'm concerned the Indians lost any special privileges of their indigenous nativity when they signed on as American citizens. It's un-American to put one man higher on the pecking order than another.

"If I sound racist, let me tell you my background. I've always spoken out for civil rights. I told you I came from North Carolina. There were elements in my home town that didn't enjoy what I had to say about all men being equal. My family belonged to the Society of Friends – Quakers. We were always crashing heads with the racists. In August of 1963 I went on a bus trip to Washington, D.C. with about twenty other members of our fellowship. I marched on Washington as a 13-year-old kid to call on the Federal government to pass legislation guaranteeing the fair treatment of all its citizens. It was there that Dr. King made his famous '*I Have a Dream*' speech. I've always advocated equality. But now I'm an embarrassment to the Friends because basically I advocate abrogation of all treaties with Native America. The only fair way to cut the pie is an equal sized piece for every citizen. In the case of fish, Indians get half the pie, and then you and I fight over the rest."

I eye the ranger's side arm with a little suspicion. "I thought Quakers didn't believe in guns."

"It's war that they won't abide. The use of force, to maintain the peace, is endorsed by most pacific religions. But it's been about fifteen years since I've been to Friends Meeting. Forks isn't a real haven for Quakers."

"Good thing for you," I say. "With your views of treaty abrogation you'd probably get run out of..."

"Shhh. Quiet..." the ranger hunkered down again, this time avoiding the wet ground.

I saw the Indian running by the parking area heading northeast towards Three Rivers. He glided by without making a sound at a speed that made my pace look like Old Black Joe coming in from the cotton fields. Twilight gleamed like a halo on his shoulders and face from a slight gleaning of sweat from the exertion of his pace. In less than half a minute he had disappeared from sight without a whisper of sound.

"That guy runs like a ghost," I whisper.

The ranger waits about 15 seconds before replying in a whisper barely audible above the quickening evening breeze. "He runs like the wind. 'Crow' is his name. He's run all his life. He's tied his running into some kind of political thing. He tried to lead a group from LaPush on a walk from the village to Washington, D.C. to protest federal manipulation of treaty Indians. He left on a Sunday with the group and he was back that Wednesday. They didn't even make it to Port Angeles. I saw him running home on the LaPush Road and it was like the devil was chasing him. I guess the kids he was leading were swilling beer, smoking pot and making love. Crow is some kind of holy-roller with the LaPush Assembly. He couldn't handle it."

"I remember that! The guys I work with bought those kids beer. It screwed up the whole march!"

"Last summer, he hatched some plan to drum up some publicity about the plight of the poor, deprived, Native Americans by running from Chief Seattle's grave to LaPush. Chief Seattle is buried out by Poulsbo some place. It's maybe 150 miles from here. He was planning on running it nonstop. It was going to go in the Guiness Book of Records. There was press all along the way for the first half of the trip to record the event and commentate on whatever it was that Crow was trying to get across. They had live coverage on the eleven o'clock news. They set up light banks and had some reporter in a jogging outfit, trying to run along beside him...asking him questions about how he felt and what he had eaten for his last meal and all this trivia stuff. Crow proselytized about the strong hope that the U.S. would honor its promises to Native Americans. He did not expound upon his recent menu. The reporter pressed him about diet and Crow said that he had been feeding himself on high-carbohydrate beverages for the last week.

"I already told you, I'm not a champion of Indian rights, but for my own reasons, I decided to be on hand for Crow's triumphant finish in LaPush about 36 hours after his departure. I expected there to be wall to wall press. The only people on hand were a small band of Quakers from Port Angeles, and a few of Crow's cronies. The Friends had been manning aid stations for Crow. I asked them where was the press. They told me that Crow had been caught short and had to defecate.

He did it in the bushes at night in between aid stations. No one would have known except he wiped his ass with his shirt and asked someone at the next aid station to go back to collect his shirt. The press got disgusted and left. One minute, they were pumping him about what kind of socks he wore and what he ate last; the poor guy pulls off the road for a two minute bowel movement, and the press no longer cares if he dies. When that poor Crow son of a bitch came across the finish line and hit the yellow flagging they had stretched across the little driveway to his residence, there were only a few Indians and Quakers to cheer his accomplishment. I guess the guy was on a liquid diet for a day before the event, just to avoid what happened."

In a cedar swamp between the parking lot and the ocean, the frogs begin to argue in the ensuing darkness. I search my memory bank for a relevant comment. "Shit happens," I say.

"Shhh..." hisses the ranger and I think he is about to offer some further editorial about the subject at hand, but as he dives behind the root wad, I am again remanded to furtiveness. A new red, four-wheel-drive pick-up was pulling into the trailhead parking area.

NINETEEN

LaPush Road

*T*imothy Clark Gable was driving his new, blue Ford four-wheel-drive pick-up while under the influence of alcohol and barbiturates. The newness of his pick-up was based on events paralleling the scenario outlined by Ranger Whitman. Two weeks ago, Tim had wrecked a four-by Datsun pick-up. Though the incident had occurred in the reservation, he had been taken by ambulance to Forks Community Hospital for observation because his unrestrained head had bashed into the windshield as the car rolled over the bank below Second Beach Parking. A Clallam County Deputy had busted him right in the emergency room for Driving Under the Influence. The following day he had called a BIA lawyer. While the issues of exclusive, and concurrent, jurisdictions were being settled out of court, his drivers license had been returned to him.

He had agreed to meet with James Crow, and Wally Woodrift, at the Third Beach parking lot at 10:00 p.m. this evening for business 'concerning the spiritual welfare of the tribe.' Gable could not ignore this appeal to his ancestral title as Spiritual Leader of the Quileute People. But, the Second Beach parking lot was within sight of where fate had conspired to trade his trusty Datsun pick-up for a big bump on his forehead. He told Wally that he would only agree to meet at the Third Beach Parking. Then Wally had insisted that he come alone, and foreswear alcohol and drugs before the rendezvous. Who the fuck did Wally think he was, his mother? Tim had been drinking beer with three friends on a logging road just southeast of Second Beach parking. Along with his old time friend Peter Shamuck, Tim had been drinking with two 17-year-old sisters who were visiting their cousin in LaPush. They had drunk most of the case of Budweisers, so before disposing of the empties, Tim took a couple of soapers to mellow him out for his meeting and washed them down with the last of his beer. He threw out his can, but his friend Peter and the two bitches still clung onto unfinished beers as he started up the new Ford pick-up to roll to his meeting on spiritual matters. He could leave his company to finish their beers in the pick-up, if Wally and James the Saint needed to talk with him alone. And he was more sober than usual for a couple hours until midnight. He didn't see either Wally, or the Saint in the Third Beach Parking Lot as he pulled in. Peter belched and rolled down the window to get rid of his empty beer can.

"I've got to pee," said Doris or Delores or whatever her name was. Neither of these two bitches were too modest or, for that matter, much to look at. Still, seventeen-year-old cunt was pretty sweet, and Timothy reflected on the spiritual side of things: beauty was *not* just skin deep. Peter got out and Doris or Delores exited the Ford to stumble off into the bushes.

****

Upon Clarence Fourskins instructions, James had approached Tim Gable to set up a meeting to bring him into the Confederacy along with his ancestral title. James had mentioned Second Beach Parking as the logical rendezvous. For some

143

reason Tim had resisted the suggestion. He offered Third Beach Parking, in Olympic National Park, as the alternative. James had reluctantly agreed to Third, but had stressed to Tim that he come alone and that he foreswear alcohol and drugs before the meeting. Though it was too early to be meeting with Fourskins himself, the need for long-standing sobriety is better discussed with a sober person.

Wally Woodrift had checked out Third Beach trailhead for heat as a precaution. The worst case scenario proved to be reality with Ranger Whitman lurking off in the bushes. The meeting site would have to be changed. Wally had returned to the village to warn James who in turn ran up the road to intercept Tim if he approached from Three Rivers in his truck. Wally meanwhile took up a vigil at Second Beach Parking where he could stop Tim if he came from either the village or the housing project. For sure, Tim would not be walking to the site and no one in LaPush was crazy enough to loan him a vehicle. So he would be in the new Ford pick-up. Wally was still waiting at the trailhead at 22:10 when he heard the bust come down over his scanner. He hit the hammer, and scooted down the road to observe the melee. Fourskins would be furious that James and himself had exercised so little influence upon Gable. Wally would make the point to Fourskins that Tim was uncontrollable, and a risk to their clandestine organization. He would also mention that Ranger Whitman was a liability and would require close supervision.

****

The empty Budweiser can thrown from the pick-up window arches through the dark and clatters to the gravel parking lot, revealing a violation to Ranger Whitman. The ranger tenses, like a coiled snake and hisses, "God, I hate litter bugs."

The pick-up door opens and, in the dome light I can see a medium-sized Native exit the passenger's side. He unzips next to the pick-up and begins to relieve himself. At the same time, a young female Native clambers out of the pick-up and begins to trudge into the brush where the ranger and I are secreted. She holds one hand out from her side like a trapeze artist to maintain balance, while the other hand clutches a beer can. About 10 feet from me, the young Native finishes the contents of the can, and throws it into the woods in front of her. The can barely misses Ranger Whitman, crouched behind the root wad. She pulls down her pants, and squats to pee, whereupon Ranger Whitman illuminates a powerful Keolite flashlight and points it at the young woman's face. She goes over on her side, still conducting her business like a half full beer bottle knocked over on the bar.

Ranger Whitman charges out from behind the root wad, crashing through the woods. He lands in the parking lot waving his torch beam around like Luke Skywalker. He's collecting ID's like an Immigrations Officer grabbing green cards. He's chattering on his portable radio like an auctioneer at an estate sale, running the license plate of the pick-up. James Crow appears out of the dark as the driver is reciting the alphabet to the ranger, who is right in the man's face. James Crow asks if he can be of some service in this situation and is told to 'get the hell out of here' by the friendly Park Ranger. The driver is now trying to balance on one foot and the two

144

girls are crying with the realization that this prick of a Park Ranger is going to give them tickets for Minor In Possession. Ranger Whitman promises to notify their parents of their little indiscretion. Now the driver is being asked to focus his eyes on a small penlight which is drawn horizontally across his field of vision. For his cooperation and performance in this battery of tests he is rewarded with news from the Park Ranger, "Mr. Gable, you're under arrest for driving under the influence of alcohol and/or drugs. I'm taking you to Forks Police Department where you'll be required by Federal law to give me a breath test. If you don't cooperate with the breath test, that's a separate violation, and we'll go over to the hospital where I'll get a blood sample."

Red and blue flashing lights signal the arrival of Tribal Police Officer Wally Woodrift. He confers briefly with James Crow, who is abiding in the fringe of the parking lot. He approaches the Park Ranger who is putting handcuffs on Tim Gable. The Native is professing his innocence, "You stupid fuck, Whitman! I only drank a couple of beers! These two sniveling cunts scarfed them all!"

"Can I be of assistance here, Ranger?" Officer Woodrift's voice is polite and respectful.

The ranger huffs, "Get lost, Woodrift. This doesn't involve the tribe. Chiggers, take these keys and bring up the Suburban which is parked 300 feet down the trail." Ranger Whitman is trying to pass me some keys.

"I'm not real sure I should get involved..." I start to protest.

"I can supervise your prisoner, and detainees, while you get the vehicle," Officer Woodrift is still offering assistance.

The ranger puffs, "That's OK Woodrift, my deputy will get the rig. Chiggers, take the keys." I take the keys and walk into the darkness along the trail where I wait for my eyes to adjust to the dark. I find the soft gleaming body of the Park Service rig in the moon glow and drive it back along the old logging road, turned trail, to the parking lot. When I get out, Ranger Whitman is nose to nose with Officer Woodrift and they are yelling at one another.

Ranger Whitman is yelling for Officer Woodrift to keep his nose out of Park Service business. Officer Woodrift is hollering that events involving tribal members as defendants involve tribal law enforcement. Ranger Whitman is yelling, "Who knows where these young tribal pukes will break the law? Keep your nose out of the park." And Officer Woodrift is responding in like decibels, "One of these young tribal pukes may haul off and poke *you* in the nose, you White racist pig! We better not catch you on the reservation." And Whitman is yelling, "Yeah? Are you going to chase me away with the pound-puppy squad?." And Woodrift is collecting Crow, slamming doors on his patrol vehicle and driving off with the blues still flashing. "Keep your nose out of the reservation," Woodrift yells out of the window as he leaves. It would occur to me later that this was the only occasion in which I encountered Ranger Whitman's nose..

145

TWENTY

Sparks Auto Body Shop, LaPush Village
Sunday, June 28, 1992

*W*ally Woodrift watched Jeff Sparks work. Sparks looked like a mad scientist with the clutter that was strewn over the table. Sparks pushed away an open can of tuna fish; a woman's negligee; several flowering heads of pussy willow; and vials containing various potent and volatile chemicals including lead azide, fulminate of mercury and various phosphorous compounds. To the glycerin, Sparks would add the oil from the tuna fish can before combining it with the powdered nitrogen fertilizer. Now he was occupied with the art work of the project. He was tracing a naked woman holding a lit firecracker from a cartoon Woodrift had found in a *Penthouse* magazine. As usual, someone had made a mess, and Sparks' scientific talent was being invoked to clean it up. Like back at TRW: A President promises the people of the United States a Strategic Defense Initiative which totally contradicts the laws of gravity or of economic plausibility. Sparks, and a room full of other high powered electronic and ballistic wizards were called in to clean up the mess. The result was that the system was still impossible. However, the obvious crinkles and blisters were buffed away, and the lie was whitewashed to stand the gaze of a gullible citizenry.

In this case, Crow and Woodrift had fucked up. Ranger Whitman was becoming an increasing pain in the ass, but they had provoked him into confrontation. Now the ranger's nosiness was driven by a sense of anger which would make him more persistent. Gable, the stupid fuck, was in jail. Fourskins had about popped a blood vessel in his head about that. Sparks had watched Woodrift cower under the contained rage of the Plains Indian. Fourskins had barely spoken above a whisper, and what-the-hell authority did he have over the Quileutes, anyway? But, when Fourskins told Crow and Woodrift that they would have to 'terminate, with prejudice, Whitman's interference' at least Wally understood what was required. Chemistry wasn't Sparks' thing and, getting a formula for a letter bomb, from Crow, had been like getting a recipe for meat loaf from Mahatma Ghandi.

"I don't want anyone hurt with this," Crow had cautioned.

"No one's going to feel anything," promised Woodrift, confident that Ranger Whitman's would be a painless end.

"We just want to scare a few people," Sparks had lied. In the end Sparks had gotten a formula, and chemicals, to make a percussion sensitive device; but Jeff knew enough about it to adjust the phosphorous to make a friction trigger.

Woodrift tried his hand at calligraphy. He dipped the special pen into the fulminated mercury and wrote: *This Fourth of July....* He set this aside, and cut out a piece of the negligee. "What if Whitman doesn't activate the igniter?" Woodrift asked Sparks as the latter poured a few drops of tuna oil into the glycerin. Into this, Sparks dipped a pussy willow flower which he had cut in half.

147

"He will," assured Sparks. He dipped the glistening pussy willow into the powdered nitrogen. He then sprinkled the phosphorous onto the flower. "We'll just put instructions on the card on how to blow his head off. Any pussy will tell you: Curiosity is a lethal weapon. Whitman's nose is a big bulls-eye."

Wally took the tracing Sparks had prepared of the naked woman, pictured standing next to a bed. He again dipped the stylus in fulminated mercury and scrawled: *I hope you get a bang out of me.* At the bottom of the card he drew in small, ornate handwriting: *Another 'Snatch and Scriff' Production.* "I really hate to do this, you know. I've been pimping on Whitman most of my life. Frankly, I'm going to miss him."

"Don't kick over a bucket of shit and then complain about the stink."

****

Wednesday July 1, 1992

Subdistrict Ranger Whitman walked from the mailbox to the Mora Ranger Station. He walked through the unlocked door, and grunted hello to his subordinate, Sid Divine, the Area Ranger. Ranger Divine had recently received his annual appraisal from the Subdistrict Ranger. He was still a little sore about criticism relating to his low marks when it came to evaluation of uniform dress code. It was hard to stay looking crisp after a day of moving outhouses around on the beach.

Whitman threw two items of personal correspondence in front of Ranger Divine. Whitman retreated to his office, a room on the east side of the "Mission 66" ranger station. He carried the large envelope of personal mail that had arrived for him, and some incoming government mail, including the seasonal NO FIREWORKS posters. The Tacoma postmark on the personal mail meant only that it had been mailed from somewhere in northwestern Washington...not from his wife or kids who had left two days ago for a family visit back in North Carolina. Who would be sending him a card, anyway? He set the mail on his desk. He sat down heavily in the swivel chair.

He hadn't gotten much sleep the last four nights. There had been that business arresting Tim Gable. There was no sleep that night. His wife Carol had left the next day. Whitman found it hard to sleep worrying about his family travelling. Last night, he had to participate in biannual weapons qualification. He had missed the regular qualification earlier in summer, and had to attend the remedial shoot last night with the seasonal rangers who were having trouble with their night shooting. They hadn't left the Kalaloch range until almost 1 A.M. He pulled his service revolver out of the holster and dumped the six live rounds into his hand. These he in turn dropped into the top drawer of his desk to prevent any chance of a bullet inadvertently being introduced to the chamber of his weapon as he cleaned it. When he returned from qualification at 02:00, he sure hadn't wanted to bathe the weapon in banana oil. He set his service revolver down on the desk, cylinder open, and went across the room to get the cleaning kit. In the next room, Sid was laughing over

148

something he was reading in his mail. Whitman felt tired and depressed. He was so lonely without his family.

He sat back down. He pushed the thirty-eight caliber brush into the banana oil solvent. He pushed the brush through all six cylinders of his .357 Smith and Wesson, and sighed. Sid was laughing again at his mail. Maybe there was something in this card to brighten Whitman's day. He laid the weapon cylinder down on the table, and opened the envelope of the card with his pocket knife. The face of the card was the silhouette of a negligee over a naked female character. Bold letters read, **This Fourth of July**... Ed Whitman could look through the scant negligee and see a bulging mons veneris on the underlying card. He lifted the face of the card and revealed the totally naked character. She stood next to a bed grinning with a firecracker in her hand, which had been hidden by the front of the card. The caption at the bottom of the card read...*I hope you get a bang out of me!* The bottom line said *A Snatch and Scriff Production.* The damn card almost looked homemade. The character's pubis looked like it had been made out of a pussy willow. Who would send him something like this? He turned the card over and looked at the back. Whitman read:

You look like you could use some cheering up. How about a whiff of something that will really spark your interest? Scratch the you-know-what of the you-know-who, with your nose where it can sniff the quiff, and you may get a real Fourth of July surprise!

Whitman returned to the naked character and put his nose to the pussy willow. There was an aroma there that encouraged further exploration. He scratched the crusty fur of the pussy willow with his trigger finger. His nose was pressed onto the card between the pussy willow and the negligee. This was Ranger Whitman's last excursion into the world of olfactory.

To Ranger Divine, the explosion from the next room was deafening. "What the living fuck..." he was saying as he ran into his boss's office to find Ed Whitman, face down on the desk in a puddle of blood that was spreading across the desk.. "Oh, Jesus, no!" uttered Divine. Without disturbing the recumbent head, he pushed his hand into Whitman's throat, sliding his fingers off to the groove beside the trachea, to check for a carotid pulse. There was a pulse! He heard slurping sounds as Whitman began to aspirate blood from the desk. Ranger Divine grasped Whitman's hair and lifted his face off the desk a few inches. He saw the bloody .357 on the desk and threw it across the room in case his lunatic boss revived and tried to finish the job. Holding Whitman's face a few inches off the table, he called 9-1-1 and asked the Forks dispatcher for an ambulance, Code III. He hung up and called the West District Office to notify the bureaucracy that his boss had flipped out. When he heard the District Ranger's voice he said, "Howard, Ed just shot himself with his service revolver...No he's not dead...Yes, of course I called the ambulance...Damn right I moved the gun, I don't want him shooting me!...I'm with him right now and I can hear him breathing...I don't know. He's been depressed since his wife left two days ago...OK, I'll see you when you get here."

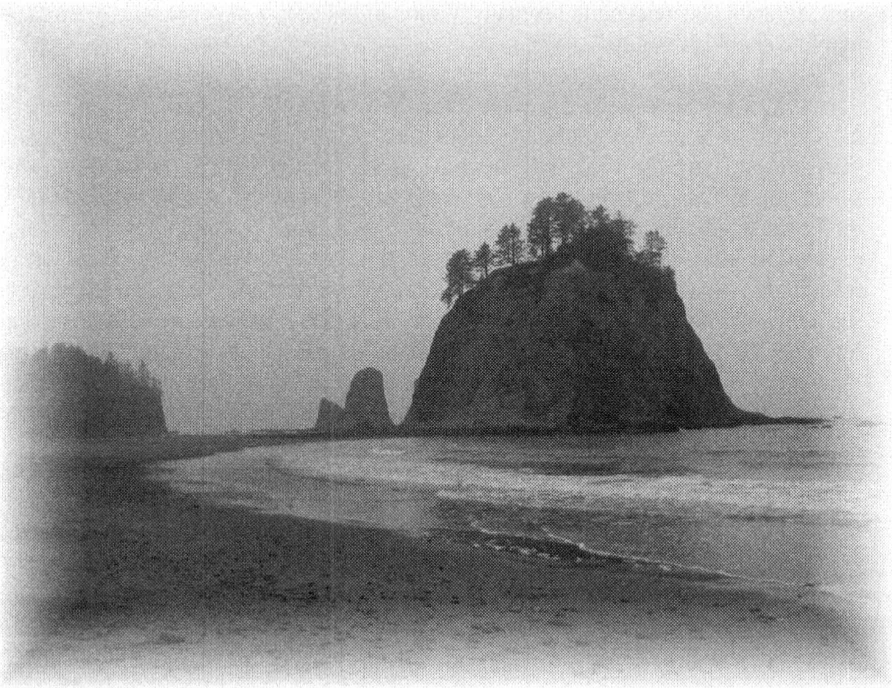

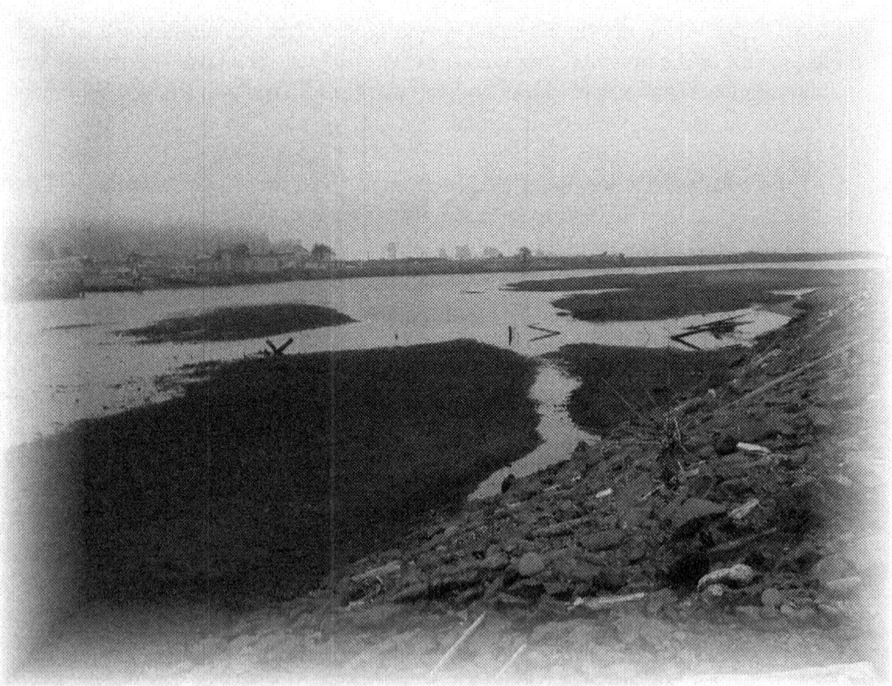

TWENTY-ONE

Friday, July 3, 1992

*T*im Gable drove his Ford pick-up carefully through the streets of Port Angeles. Riding as passengers were his friends Peter and Jimmy Shamuck, and in the bed of the truck was Freddie Jackson. Gable had to drive carefully. His drivers' license had been revoked. When Ranger Wilbur had dragged his ass into the Forks Police Department last week he had blown a .04 on the Blood Alcohol Verifier, which *proved* that Tim wasn't drunk. But then Ranger Wilbur had drug him over to Forks Hospital where he had ordered a blood sample. The sample had revealed the barbiturates and the hold on Gable's license was upheld. Gable had just learned that Ranger Whitman's nose had been blown off by some kind of a letter bomb. Gable and his three friends were heeding the call to celebrate. Besides, tomorrow was the Fourth of July. It was every Americans duty to party be they red, white, or turning blue.

Tim realized, as he parked along Front Street, that a full-on beer drunk would have to wait until he got back to LaPush. If he so much as got stopped tonight, sober or not, they would probably haul his ass back to jail. Then he would spend the Fourth, slamming the ham in the slammer; instead of drinking beer and porking Doris (or was her name 'Delores?') To help him mellow out, and go easy on the beer in the beer hall, Gable took out a couple more soapers. He popped them down his throat as he and his three friends jaywalked across the street to The Salty Dawg Tavern. Christ, he was thirsty, but he would just drink enough to quell his blistering thirst and flush the downers the rest of the way down his throat.

The Salty Dawg was really crowded this Friday night before the Fourth of July. By luck, three loggers got up to leave, vacating a table near the door as the four Native Americans came in. The Indians took the table, and stole a chair from a customer who'd left a small table to go to the restroom. They were soon greeted by a young barmaid who cleared away two empty pitchers left by the loggers.

"Three pitchers of Bud, my good wench," ordered Gable cheerfully. The young woman glared at Gable without comment and left to fill his order. "We'd better order all we're going to drink now, 'cause it's so crowded," explained Gable. She came back with three large pitchers, and four ice rimed glasses, bumping through the crowded room to access their table. "That's twelve dollars," said the barmaid.

Gable gave her three five dollar bills. "Keep the change, sugar." The barmaid said 'thank you' and left. It was immediately obvious that his three partners were as thirsty as Gable. In less that fifteen minutes, the group was quaffing down the contents of the last pitcher. Peter Shamuck said that he would get the next round. Gable felt the beginnings of a drunk. He realized that he had better slow down. He popped a couple more soapers to take the edge off and allow him to relax without drinking so much brewski. The barmaid noticed the empty pitchers on the table and fought her way back, through the crowd. She thirsted for another tip with or without an attending insult. "Another pitcher, guys?"

151

"Bring three, while you're at it, bar bitch," Peter yelled to be heard over the din of the crowd. The barmaid pushed and shoved her way through the crowd, and pushed and shoved her way back with the pitchers and three freshly rimed glasses. "That'll be twelve dollars, sir," she chirped to Gable. Tim pointed to Peter who took out his billfold and pulled out a twenty. "Keep the change, cunt." The barmaid took the money and left without comment. Everyone seemed to be filling Tim's glass, though a couple times he filled it himself. Gable was getting shit faced. As they swilled down the last of six pitchers, Tim reminded himself to put on the brakes and took two more soapers to reinforce his resolution. Jimmy saw him popping the downers and told some kind of joke about a lion eating a barmaid. "It must have been the bar bitch you ate," finished Jimmy. "Get it?"

Tim didn't get it. Things were getting confusing. The barmaid appeared and Jimmy was retelling the joke for her benefit; she interrupted Jimmy saying, "Do you guys need a refill, or not?"

"Refill, bitch!" demanded Freddie. "One more pitcher," confirmed the barmaid. "Three, God-damn-it!" yelled back Freddie, who evidently was ordering more beer. Three fresh pitchers appeared and Freddie, by drunken accident, sent the barmaid away with $25. "I just tipped the bitch thirteen dollars!" Freddie was screaming, but Tim couldn't make much sense of it. *No more beer for me*, thought Gable and popped one last soaper to put the lid on things.

Now, he really had to piss! Everyone at the table had to piss. The problem was, if they got up, someone might steal their chairs, and it was a long crowded way to the men's room. Jimmy was announcing to all that would listen, " 'Micturate.' That's the real word. 'Urinate' is when you pass piss from your Kidneys to your bladder."

"I've got to micturate this second," said Peter taking an empty pitcher off the table and holding it between his legs He said something about "Warm, pissweiser on tap." The pitcher was passed around under the table until it came to Gable. Tim was made to understand that he was to piss in it. He pulled out his penis and attempted the feat, but the room was starting to go around and everything was running together. He put the pitcher on the table.

"Christ! It's only half full," yelled Freddie. "It was three quarters full when I passed it to Tim."

"He must have siphoned some off with his hose," ventured Jimmy.

"Shit, look at Tim's leg! He's got piss all over himself." Tim thought he might have to throw up. He put his head down on the table. He could barely hear the activity at his table as he began drifting off...a dark cloud swallowing him alive.

The barmaid had reappeared at the table, hungry for another tip. "Refill, gentlemen?" she asked. Peter was pointing to Gable. "No more for him. He's driving. And this pitcher was totally flat. Send it back to the bar and bring back one with fizz."

"Our beer is never flat, sir," said the barmaid with confidence. "Nor are our waitresses," leveling her bosom at the Indian.

"God-damn-it, the pitcher's flat! Flat *and* warm!" persevered Peter. "Have the bartender taste it. Get it off the table. Flat beer disgusts us!" The barmaid took the two empty pitchers and the half full one and repaired to the bar, where the manager poured out a glass of the warm, amber liquid and lifted it to his lips.

****

Something profound was happening to Tim Gable physiologically, as he passed from consciousness into a great dark cloud, face down at the table. Let's explore the impact of the synergistic effect of alcohol and barbiturates upon the human body. We'll take an ordinary healthy adult male, but, for our protection we'll pick one of slight stature and pacific disposition. This male will think of sex on an average of once every four minutes. Take away this man's sustenance and starve him for calories and his fixation turns to food. He can easily survive for eight weeks. Deprive him of water and he soon forgets his hunger and focuses on his thirst. He can only live a week without drink. Here, I'll hold him and you kick him in the nuts. Go on and do it! This is a scientific experiment we're doing. Good kick, right in the old crotcheroo! As the man goes down, another layer of discomfort temporarily eclipses his thirst, hunger and loneliness. Now that he's down, I'll hold his head and you put on these thick leather gloves and pinch his nose and hold your hand over his mouth. It's OK, we're not going to kill him. [1]That's good, now we're cutting off his air and he forgets all other insults and woes and focuses on the threat to his supply of life giving oxygen. See how he struggles now. It's instinctive. Every creature struggles to return to a breathing environment just like a fish on land. With whatever disdain mankind treats the air on this planet, his hunger for oxygen clearly surpasses all other appetites. He twists and turns trying to hold onto his life of hungry, thirsty, nut-aching loneliness, but within 180 seconds his eye lids flutter and he falls into the realm of unconsciousness. This gets to what I wanted to show you, so hold your hands there a little longer. He can survive at least four more minutes.

Using the powerful and magical lens of imagination, we explore the physio-dynamics of hypoxia upon the man's body. It appeared to be the lack of air that caused our subject to engage in that brief combative episode. Yet here in the man's bloodstream, the body shows no immediate concern for the lack of oxygen. In the medulla oblongata, a message is being received by the nerves of a build up in carbon dioxide. There, the alarm bells are ringing off the wall. The heart is slowing down and the body is making its last frantic efforts to ventilate. Now, as the carbon dioxide continues to build up, the bicarbonate buffer is overloaded and the blood becomes acidotic sending the strongest and most basic distress signal the body knows. It is at

---

[1] Trust me, I'm the author of this book. If you don't like it, get the hell out of this paragraph. Here my editor abandons ship.

this level that the synergistic effect of alcohol and barbiturates attack the human body's efforts to survive. The blood's capacity to move oxygen, it's ability to deliver oxygenated blood and it's facility for balancing the narrow acid/base spectrum necessary to maintain life, are defeated by the logarithmic, combined power of sedatives and alcohol.

The arterioles and veinules of the capillary beds, at which point oxygen and waste products are exchanged are smaller than the blood cell itself. It's like a barmaid squeezing her way to the table of the tissue cells with three pitchers of oxygen on her tray of hemoglobin. She picks up the empties, which are usually CO_2, but occasionally contain uric acid, salts and other byproducts of metabolism. The heart, like the man behind the bar, is the overall motivator in dispatching the barmaids with oxygen and receiving the carbon dioxide, but the tissue can give special incentives to the blood based on chemical messages sent to the entire cardiovascular system. Barbiturates, combined with alcohol, render a profound and potent insult at the most basic level of life support. The bartender slows way down in pouring pitchers, the barmaids are sluggish and overwhelmed by the oxygen thirsty crowd. The empty pitchers pile up on the tables. The crowd can go fuck itself as far as management is concerned. The human body can cope with celibacy, hunger, thirst, pain and even hypoxia, but the insult of a barbiturate/alcohol overdose is too much.

The addict believes that he is choosing this challenge to his bodily systems for recreational reasons, but it is a disease just like <u>AIDS</u> - and just as deadly. In most cases, the disease - which the addict considers his best friend and ally in life - interferes with the victim's sex life. The addict is most usually poorly nourished and dehydrated. He stumbles and falls, inflicting localized injury to his extremities. Still, he clings to his addiction until it suffocates the life out of him and the disease moves on to prey on his children.

Here now, take your hand off that poor man's mouth! You weren't supposed to leave your hand there, you stupid dolt! You've killed that poor innocent man! Don't try to blame it on me, I was just trying to make the point that Tim Gable is in trouble. You were the one who occluded the airway until this other poor son of a bitch died, never to return on the pages of this story. Next time, don't do something you know is wrong, no matter who tells you to do it.

Next time someone puts a repeating rifle in your hands and tells you to take a continent away from its rightful owners in the name of Christianity or manifest destiny, look into your heart. Look into your bag of trading stock - the baubles, glass beads, technology, mandatory education, meaningless treaties, small pox, venereal disease, alcoholism and drug addiction. Ask God Almighty if you have anything in that bag that justifies taking the land base away from an indigenous population that shrivels like a tree removed from its soil and water. Look at Native America this minute and you see the white hand in the leathered glove, suffocating the life from so many nations.

TWENTY-TWO

The Salty Dawg Tavern, Port Angeles, Washington
Friday, June 26, 1992, 21:45 hours

*T*im Gable is floating in the dark, cold, timeless cloud. A light is coming. The light is coming for him...or is it that *he is the light*? The light illuminates a strange and bizarre apparition. An Indian who looks just like Tim is lying on the bottom of some kind of boat. It could be a dugout, or it could be a Boston Whaler - there is no definition of the vessel. Two men huddle over the supine Native. They are dressed in the same kind of uniform that Ranger Whitman wears, except one wears a life jacket. This man leans over the Native's face and - oh, gross! He's kissing the Native that looks like Tim! Gable can taste the breath, and it is beer puke and death. Oh Christ! The ranger's are homos! The other one is tearing off the Native's shirt and feeling up his chest. Gable can feel the pressure of the palm of the ranger's hand on the chest and it hurts. God Almighty! Ranger homos! The light fades and Tim is left floating in the dark, cold void.

****

The bartender must not have enjoyed the taste of piss. He was right in Peter's face. "That's it, you punks are out of here right now! Take your passed-out, fart-breath friend, and get the **FUCK OUT OF HERE RIGHT NOW!**" Peter and Jimmy pick him up from out of his chair and drag him to the door which Fred is holding open. From the place where Tim was sitting, to the door that was swinging shut, is a line of the bartender's recent beverage.

As the door swung shut behind them, cutting off the noise of the crowded tavern, Jimmy observed, "Timmy's pissed all over himself. He's not riding in front with me!" Peter and Jimmy loaded Tim into the bed of his Ford pick-up like he was a sack of potatoes. The three got into the cab with Peter assuming wheel-watch. "Get out of the truck. Get the keys from Timmy, would you Freddie?" Fred was grumbling as he climbed into the bed of the pick-up and had to prog around in urine soaked pockets for the keys.

He climbed back into the cab and gave the keys to Peter. "Let's stop off and get a case of brewskis for the return voyage, *Capitan*."

"Ya Voul!" agreed Jimmy. The first stop was to get beer. Thus, re-supplied, the Ford progressed up Lincoln street. Peter pulled open the sliding glass window behind his head. "Throw your empties in back with Timmy or you'll bring down the litterbug Gestapo on us. I don't need to lose my license because of you drunks. Shit! We're almost out of gas!"

Peter pulled into the Texaco Station. "We better get full service," announced Peter. "You drunken fuck ups would probably put gas in the tires, water in the tank, and air in the radiator."

The bell rang and the attendant came to the driver's side of the pick-up. "Help you gentlemen?" asked the pump jockey.

"Fill it with premium," ordered Peter.

"Which tank do you want filled?" asked the attendant, considering the two fuel ports.

"The one that's empty, asshole," offered Fred. The pump jockey got lucky and got the thirsty tank on his first try. As he was filling the tank, he wondered at the prone body in the bed of the pick-up. A beer bottle sailed out of the rear window. It hit the body full in the head with a thud. The man down didn't even grunt. He didn't appear to be breathing. Was this guy alive? The young attendant resolved to call the police.

The pump cut off and the gas jock rounded it to $22. He came over to the driver and said, "That will be twenty-two bucks, please."

Peter started to dig into his rear pocket and then announced, "This truck belongs to the guy in back and he's paying for the gas. Get the money from him."

"I don't even think he's alive. I'm calling 9-1-1."

"Wait!" ordered Peter. "Freddie, get out and help Timmy to pay the nice attendant."

Fred stepped out of the cab. He climbed into the bed of the pick-up and turned Tim on his side to get at this pocket. He found the wallet, opened it, and looked inside. There were only $20 bills. He took out two bills and gave them to the young attendant. "Here. Keep the change."

Fred got back into the cab, taking the wallet with him. The pump jockey looked in awe at the two $20 bills. "An $18 tip! Those guys are all right!" He forgot about calling the police.

✳✳✳✳✳✳✳✳✳✳✳✳✳✳✳✳✳✳✳✳✳✳✳✳✳✳✳✳✳

Ted Cox was having vehicle problems trying to limp from Port Angeles to Forks on the power of his battery. He would be entering this old beater of a Cadillac in the Forks, Fourth of July Demolition Derby. It was lacking a working alternator. A battery was all the electricity he needed to power this old, yellow bulge-mobile around the track destroying every vehicle that dared to get in his way. An alternator, like the power steering still attached, was just another thing to go wrong in a front-end collision. But, as he crested Govan's Hill, between Lake Sutherland and Lake Crescent, and came into a thick wall of fog, he needed the extra illumination afforded by a working alternator. He had meant to leave the battery charging when he left for work that Friday morning. He had forgotten it. The battery was drained from his last drive in the Caddy. He might have made it to Forks if he had never had to use his brakes and headlights. He had turned on the headlights when he came into a fog pocket in the Elwha at about 9:30 P.M.. Now he was in even denser fog coming down the steep hill toward Lake Crescent going a little faster than he wanted to be going. He could hardly see the road. He was just passing Govan's Falls when he felt his bald tires slip a little on the damp, greasy and fractured pavement near the hanging waterfall. He tapped his brakes and the brake lights came on dragging down the voltage enough so the coil missed a few sparks. The engine died. It took a few seconds for Ted to realize the engine had quit and he barely missed a turnout 200 yards west and downhill of the falls. Without power steering, he was having trouble controlling this battleship of an automobile. He stopped just on the downhill side of the turnout and tried to start the Cadillac. The starter growled; but there was no fire. He considered his situation. Without an alternator to excite a spark, the hill was no advantage for starting the rig. He couldn't remember where the next turnout was, downhill from here, but he wasn't going to risk running out of gravity on a blind corner in the fog. Besides, there was an advantage to being right in the middle of the road. Most anyone would recognize the hazard he presented and help him with a jump start. He left the rig in neutral and pushed the emergency brake to the floor. He got the jumper cables out to attach the alligator clips to the posts of the discharged battery. As he popped the hood to access the battery, he was hoping for uphill traffic. This fog was thick as piss-green soup! Ted wished to Christ he had a traffic flare...or a screw driver to pull off the license plates and let the Caddy go down the hill by itself. He would hitchhike or walk home.

Murphy's Law! The emergency brake wasn't holding and the Caddy was starting to go down the hill on its own. Ted had the positive cable on the battery post and as the car pushed him he dropped the other positive cable against the fire wall and there was a shower of sparks, further depleting the battery. He put his full weight into the front of the Caddy. He was committed as a human brake until a motorist would happen by to help him out. He could hear a vehicle coming, but, in the fog, he couldn't guess its direction. Christ, the rig was coming too fast, which ever way it was going! What a blow job! What a...

****

Peter felt exhilarated, accelerating over the crest of Govan's Hill in Tim Gable's new pick-up. This rig had guts! And how it handled curves! He was rocketing down the hill in the fog with a beer between his legs when his brother said, "Better rein in some horses, Pete. This fog is thicker than flies on a Chinaman's ass." Pete tapped the brakes as he passed Govan's Falls, and the rear end broke away a little. He took his foot off the brakes and was going to tap them again when, out of the fog sprung a vehicle directly in his path. He locked up the brakes. In the ensuing skid he tried to avoid rear ending the car by steering to the right, into a turnout. The Ford's rear end broke away and the Ford drifted sideways slamming into the back of the Cadillac at 59 miles per hour. The blue Ford began to turn over in the air, but a millisecond later, impacted the guard rail. The body of Tim Gable was catapulted out of the bed in a remarkable trajectory. Gravitational and inertial forces argued over authority of the falling body. It articulated a lazy arc as it plummeted all the way to the surface of the lake, a hundred vertical feet below the surface of the highway.

Meanwhile, the Ford overtopped the guard rail and began a crashing, grinding, descent to the lake. The vehicle and its three mutilated, and unconscious occupants, were swallowed by the dark water eighteen seconds after the Ford had collided with the Cadillac.

****

The two Park Rangers leaned over Ted Cox who was bleeding and unconscious. "He's got bilateral femur fractures, John. We'll have to put on the Sager splint before we put him on the backboard. I'll get the stiff collar and call Olympic Ambulance." Ranger Art Saddison went back to the patrol vehicle, leaving John Word with the bleeding patient.

"Get some of those Bloodstopper or multitrauma pads to throw over these open wounds. Yikes! Bring back some rubber gloves. Lucky for us it's just a one car, single-injury accident. Call Elwha Ranger Station for backup traffic control..."

Ranger Word was shocked to see the patient open his eyes. "You're going to be OK, guy," Ranger Word said without much confidence. The prognosis for two femur fractures wasn't that rosy. "Do you remember what happened?"

"Some crazy fucker rear-ended me going a hundred miles per hour," mumbled the patient.

"What's your name?" asked the ranger.

"Cox," murmured the patient.

"Pardon me?" queried the ranger.

"My name is Ted Cox."

"Have you had anything to drink tonight, Mr. Cox?"

"No. How is the son of a bitch that drove into me?"

"There's no other vehicle here, Mr. Cox. Either this was a hit and run, or you're mistaken about someone rear-ending your Cadillac."

"Whatever hit me, couldn't have driven away. They were going a hundred miles an..." The patient was losing consciousness again. Ranger Word could smell the acidosis of trauma on Cox's breath, but he could smell no alcohol. Ranger Word went running over to the patrol rig to grab the gloves, dressings and oxygen unit.

"He says there was another vehicle involved!" Word yells to Saddison who is using the radio mike while standing next to the ranger vehicle. "Check out that guard rail!"

Ranger Saddison finished on the radio. He came running over to where Word was working on the patient. He dropped off a rolled blanket and Sager splint. "Dispatch couldn't get anyone from the Elwha. Both of the Olympic Ambulance rigs are out, so I had the dispatcher call Forks Hospital for an ambulance. Sid Divine is at the hospital guarding Ed Whitman's room, so I told the dispatcher to get him on the ambulance to help out here. They can get someone from Forks P.D. to guard Whitman while Divine's gone."

"Good work, Art. The Cadillac *does* look like it was rear-ended. Now, check out that guard rail by the turnout. From here it looks caved in. Look for signs of another vehicle."

Saddison went over and studied the caved in railing for a minute with his Keolite. "There's blue paint all over the rail. There's pieces of headlight all over the pavement. Are the headlights still in tact on the Cad."

"Yeah," calls Word who is setting up the Sager. "Check over the guard rail and come over and give a hand here."

Saddison looked over the veritable cliff with the powerful beam. Through the fog he could barely see the surface of Lake Crescent, but what he saw caused a knot to form in his stomach. He could see a pocket of total calm on the lake. At the edge of the placid water, he could see the sheen of petroleum. There was a funny red glow. Saddison turned of his flashlight, and after a second his eyes adjusted. Somehow one of the rear running lights had survived the crashing descent and the red lens was holding water off the bulb. The battery was still illuminating an incandescent bulb from a point of rest on the moonscape bottom of the lake - maybe 100 feet under water. "There's a rig all the way down in the lake!" called Saddison.

"We'll have to clean up this mess before going out in the boat," called back Word. "There's no emergency down there, anyway, besides a gas spill." Saddison understood that there would be no survivors in this kind of apocalypse.

****

It was past midnight when the three rangers got to the placid water. Sadison and Word required only five more minutes to access the Ford pick-up which lay submerged on the floor of the lake 110 feet below the boat. The necks of the three occupants had been broken on the descent and they were goners. Saddison and Word left them in the cab to be retrieved with the vehicle. They began the ascent which would require 20 minutes to prevent the divers from developing an air embolism or the bends. Word was back in the boat when Sid Divine saw another shape floating face down in the water. Art Saddison swam over to bring it to the boat where Word and Divine pulled it aboard. The neck of this patient was in tact.

Ranger Divine blew two gusts from his own lungs into the patient on the floor of the boat and said, "Dear God, that tastes terrible! He's been throwing up beer. I don't have a chimney mask."

"No wallet in his back pockets to tell who he is," Ranger Saddison was saying. "He's been dead for a couple hours, Sid. Don't get us into a CPR show with a stiff."

"No one's dead in water, until they're *warm* and dead," said Ranger Divine. Two hours ago Divine had been reading from the new Brady EMT to pass the time guarding Ed Whitman. He ventilated the patient with another gust from his lungs, gagging on the smell of the breath that was blown back on his cheek ... the tendril of mucousy vomit that connected him to the patient. "Begin CPR!" he croaked.

"Here we go!" muttered Saddison tearing away the wet shirt from the patient's chest and pushing his middle finger into the patient's sternum to find the landmark for his hand placement. "He's cold, all right."

The Boston Whaler streaked across the dark lake. From the entrance to Pirates' Cove, Ranger Word navigated toward the lights they left on at Storm King Ranger Station. He called for another ambulance on the boats radio. Then he shown his flashlight behind him on the floor of the boat, temporarily illuminating the scene of the emergency operation.

"Good Lord," exclaimed Ranger Divine in the flash of light, "This is the same character Ed busted last week for D.U.I. there at Third Beach."

"If you resuscitate him, you can arrest him." said Saddison. "This time he was Diving Under the Influence." Ranger Divine started to laugh and then lost his dinner from the Forks Pay and Save coffee shop. He continued to kneel in the vomit, breathing for the unconscious Native, as the boat careened across the dark, cold lake.

TWENTY-THREE

Second Beach Housing
Monday, June 29, 1992

Clarence Fourskins quaked with quiet rage at the news that Tim Gable had been lost. He never should have trusted a reformed juvenile delinquent and a born again bozo to execute the task of bringing Gable into the Confederacy. The headlines in the *Daily News* had read **Three Local Indian Youths Die in Plunge Into Lake Crescent**. The Park Service was holding names pending notification of families, the article said. Then there was some bullshit about the Native legend that the lake did not surrender its dead. In this case it had required a big magnet being lowered down into the lake's depths to drag the demolished Ford pick-up to a level that ranger divers could access it and remove the bodies. Almost drowned in the watery bullshit of the story was the one bit of news that cried out to Fourskins' attention: *"A fourth Native youth nearly drowned in the incident, but was resuscitated by Park Rangers and is in critical condition at Forks Community Hospital. Rangers speculate that the victim may have been in the water for two hours and, if the patient survives, the case may represent the longest manifestation of reversed clinical death in the annals of medical history...*It was too much for Clarence Fourskins to hope that the one survivor might be Gable and that he might yet be brought into the plan. Nonetheless, it was this hope that drove Fourskins to take the county bus into Forks, a trip that he had not frequently made since his arrival to LaPush some months ago.

Clarence got off across from Tillicum Park, though he knew the bus would drive on and stop by the hospital, he preferred not to be seen getting off at that destination, in case fickle fate returned to him that which had been taken away. He used the concealment of a grove of trees just west of the hospital and pulled out a pair of blue coveralls and a carpenter's utility belt from the duffel he carried. After donning these, he put up his long black hair under a blue ball cap upon which was a large patch reading *ASCON GLASS SERVICE.*

Thus attired, Fourskins began a survey of the windows on the west facing aspect of the hospital. Two windows of the rooms on the southwest corner of the building were protected by heavy wire screen. Figuring these to be the detoxification units of the hospital, Clarence started there. He inspected the screening which was a six-gauge mesh of eighth-inch steel, pinned into the mortar and concrete of the building. He looked through the steel mesh at the metal framing and glass of the window. It was composed of several large frames, but only one small window which opened. How did they go about cleaning the outside of this window, anyway, Clarence marveled. Lastly, Fourskins allowed his gaze to invade the privacy of the room. He then peered in at the patient. He observed the activity inside the room. Bandages were being removed from the face of a patient. Was it Gable? A doctor and nurse were cutting away multitudinous layers of gauze and kling while making cooing conversation, of which Clarence could only catch pieces: *"...two or three procedures a week...grafting tissue from your thigh and buttocks...prevent sinus infection with antibiotics..."*

All but the last of the bandages fell away. Clarence was looking at what might have been a White man or a Native. Through the burns, facial scarring and suturing it was hard to tell. The beginnings of facial hair supported Fourskins' growing suspicion that this patient was a White man. The gauze pad fell from the patient's nose, or where a nose should have been, and Fourskins realized this was the mutilated face of Ranger Ed Whitman. Well, at least Sparks and Woodrift had fixed it so that the ranger wouldn't be interfering in tribal affairs for some time to come.

Fourskins walked over to the other screened window. After an abbreviated survey, he gazed into the darkened room. He had to cup his hands to shield his vision from the July glare. Inside the room was a patient who was the focus of extreme medical intervention. Two tubes ran out of his mouth and an I.V. came out of each arm. The ventilator and I.V. monitors took up most of the room around the bed. The small porthole of glass was open and Clarence could hear the chirping and clacking of the medical apparatus.

Through the tubing and apparatus it was hard to make the identity of the patient, but for sure he was Native. The longer he looked, the more Fourskins allowed himself to believe that he had found his target. A nurse came into the room. She checked the plastic bag of urine hanging on the side of the bed below the patient. She then took a syringe out of the pocket of her white coat and removed the cap. She spoke to the patient with words that filled Fourskins with joy. She said, "Tim, I don't know if you can hear me or not, but I'm increasing your medication so you'll be more comfortable. I'm giving you ten more c.c.'s of Valium in your I.V. We don't want you convulsing. While you're staying with us you're going to get sober. We want to make you as comfortable as possible, Tim, but you are going to get sober. And then the Park Service has some questions for you; but, right now, just rest."

****

Clarence Fourskins had worked at acquiring intelligence from the hospital. A young Native woman, working in records at Forks Community, gave Fourskins some of what he needed. Both Gable and Whitman were under the guard of one officer 24 hours a day. The duty officer was either a ranger, or Forks cop, who sat out in the hall. Checking the duplicate patient chart before filing it, the informant was able to tell Fourskins that Gable was being sedated by Valium. The I.V. delivery was set to a higher drip rate from 18:00 to 06:00 to allow the patient to sleep. The Valium had some effect in diminishing the combative behavior Gable was beginning to demonstrate. The patient's lungs were clear and miraculously unimpaired by the near drowning episode. He had been taken off the ventilator. Now he was demonstrating bellicose, and loud behavior. The guarding officer was usually requested by the nurses on their missions to help Gable to the bathroom or bring him food, which he didn't eat. During the day, he was presenting full-blown delirium tremens. The Valium helped with the D.T.'s and the combative behavior. It was unclear to Fourskins upon whose authority Gable was being detoxified.

Tim's father told anyone that asked, that his son had been taken from him by white man's demons many years ago when Tim had begun his chemical dependency. The Park Service had come to visit Gable, senior. Maybe he told the rangers they could do whatever they wanted with his son. Perhaps he refused to believe that Tim's body, and soul, had survived fifteen years of alcoholism and drug abuse, not to mention a two hour breathless swim in Lake Crescent. Maybe the Park Service told the old man that his son was a suspect in a man slaughter case involving the death of three other Natives. Maybe it was more convenient for the father to think of his son resting in the long house in the sky, rather than the big house in Walla Walla, Washington.

Things were coming back into reach for Clarence Fourskins. As he rode along the LaPush Road with a dozen long-stemmed roses, and a box of chocolates on the lap of his blue coveralls, he dared to believe that everything might turn out OK. Jeff Sparks was driving him in the old Plymouth Valiant. James Crow and John Pinn were crowded into the back seat. John would have been crowded sitting by himself. Their objective, this July evening, was to retrieve the spiritual leader of LaPush: To find a *sachem* for the Confederacy.

James had provided a chemical formula for dealing with the steel screen. James would manage a diversion which would be necessary to accomplish the rescue. James had also filled Clarence's own prescription for Tim Gable. Several vials which appeared to contain Valium, varied in strength from pharmaceutical formula to total placebo. John could provide the muscle necessary to move the patient, and he could move cops if it came to that. Jeff was just the get away driver. The scanners, radar detectors, and high-tech communication and radio jamming components built onto the old Valiant might prove useful in the get away. But Sparks and Woodrift had been principles in the Whitman thing. Clarence didn't want Jeff getting out of the car.

Arriving at the hospital, Sparks parked the Valiant at the far west end of the lot, behind the ambulance shed. Crow and Fourskins fetched a bottle of hydrochloric acid; a large dry-cell battery; a plastic bucket; some window cleaner; and glass cutting tools. They walked boldly over to the screen on the southwest corner of the building. Crow put on heavy rubber gloves. He poured the acid into the plastic bucket. He took out a bulb syringe and aspirated several ounces of the acid into the syringe. He squirted it along the perimeter of the screen. He attached an alligator clip, from a lead on the dry cell to the outermost perimeter. The other lead he attached to the center of the screen. He took off his gloves and handed them to Fourskins. "The screen should give, in about 10 minutes. Just give a squirt every two minutes or so and don't step in the bucket," advised James without smiling.

James left his political mentor. He walked over to the vehicle. He sat in the Valiant for about eight minutes until he got a nod from Fourskins who was pulling on the screen. Crow exited the vehicle with the chocolates and flowers. He walked slowly around the north side of the hospital to the general entrance of the hospital on the north east side. He checked his watch before entering the hospital. He went right by the receptionist, and continued past the nurses' station unchallenged. He came to the entrance of Whitman's room, and knocked on the open door. He checked his watch. Things were moving a little too fast. From his bed, Ranger Whitman looked like a mummy. His hands and face were entirely wrapped in gauze bandaging. James Crow had heard rumors that a letter bomb had done this to the Park Servant. He had no idea from what address such a letter might have originated. Crow made no connection between the injury inflicted upon Whitman, and the formula he provided Sparks for a percussion-sensitive trigger.

The soft knock on the door bestirred Wilbur E. Whitman. Crow could see the surprise in the man's recognition of his visitor. Crow saw the patient hit the call button and heard footsteps coming from down the hall. "Hello, Ranger Whitman," said James starting to walk into the room. "I'm bringing get well wishes from La..." someone pulled backwards on Crow's shirt collar so hard that he popped his two top buttons. He dropped the flowers, as he was plucked from Ranger Whitman's company. In the hall he was spun around and he was in the company of another ranger, who was right in his face.

"What do you mean coming around here!" the ranger, fairly screamed. The ranger grabbed the chocolates and get well card out of Crows grasp and slid them along the tile floor, away from the doorway. The nurse passed the two and ran into Whitman's room making some comforting remarks. She retrieved the flowers which she placed on the floor by the chocolates and card.

"Hey, I just came to say 'get well' to my old buddy Wilbur Whitman," protested Crow. He dropped his eyes and found the ranger's name plate which read **Sid Divine.**

"Do you know this guy, Ed?" Ranger Divine called into the patient's room.

"Ya. It'sh Jamezz Cw...Cwow. He'zz da runner. He wazz der da nyight Aye bush...ded Gable."

This news excited Ranger Divine even more and he began an aggressive pat down of Crow. "What do you want here, Mr. Curo?" asked the young warden.

"It's *Crow*. James Crow. I told you: I'm here to give the tribe's regards to your injured...Hey, please give that back!" The ranger had found and removed Crow's private journal from the holster case on his nylon belt. "It's personal."

"I'm putting it right here, Mr. Crow. You can take it all with you when you leave." The minion of the law placed Crow's journal carefully by the gifts. "Ranger Whitman isn't receiving presents from anyone right now. Tell you what though, why don't you take the plastic off and remove the lid on those chocolates."

"They're for Ranger Whitman."

"I know that, but he's not receiving any gifts now. Please open the chocolates. I want to make sure it's not a bomb."

James Crow laughed and walked over to the chocolates ten feet away. He picked up his journal and put it back in his belt. He picked up the chocolates and took the plastic off the box. He put the wrapper in his pocket, and walked toward Ranger Divine with the box in his extended hands. Ranger Divine began to back up. "Hold it right there! Freeze, Federal Officer!" commanded Ranger Divine, as per his training at the Federal Law Enforcement Training Center.

James Crow laughed again, and stopped. He plucked the top off the box and threw it back to where the roses and card still lay on the floor. The nurse who stood tremulously on the fringe of the encounter jumped back against the wall. James Crow selected a sweet and popped it into his mouth. Now he advanced on the nurse who stood her ground, back against the wall. Crow smiled at her exposing chocolate covered incisors. "Want one, miss?"

"Well, maybe one," the nurse studied the assortment of sweets, making her choice. "I prefer the ones with nuts in the centers."

"I do too," said James cheerfully. "That's a chocolate covered almond there."

The ranger sensed that he was losing control of the scene. "I tell you what, leave the card here, but take the flowers, and candy, with you. We appreciate you coming by, but Ranger Whitman is not receiving presents." Ranger Divine wondered if he were repeating himself under the tension of the moment.

"I'll leave the flowers and candy with you, miss, if that's OK," said Crow, popping another chocolate into his mouth.

"Well, OK, I guess," said the nurse.

"No, take that stuff with you and please leave. Thanks for coming by though. By the way, Mr. Crow, could I please see some identification."

James Crow looked at his watch. "Uh, I don't have any I.D."

"Your drivers' license, please. You **did** drive here, didn't you?" the ranger persisted.

"Actually, I was driven. Usually I run everywhere or take the bus. I don't have a drivers' license and my only identification card is my tribal I.D. back in LaPush, and the people who know me, which seems to include Ranger Whitman."

"OK, then. Thanks for coming." James Crow checked his watch one more time. He collected the flowers, leaving the card on the floor. He pulled a rose from the bunch and offered it to the nurse along with proffering the box for her to select another sweet.

"Thank you, Mr. Crow," said the nurse taking another chocolate. James left the room and made his way out of the hospital.

"Nice guy," said the nurse smiling with chocolate on her teeth.

Crow passed a Forks Police Officer coming past the nurse's desk. Exiting the building, he walked around the front of the hospital to where the Valiant had been parked. He found that, as planned, the vehicle, and occupants were gone. Crow looked around to the northwest corner of the hospital. The heavy screen was cut free and had been removed from the window. James began the fifteen-mile run back to LaPush.

****

Officer Rice, of Forks P.D., walked over to where he found Ranger Divine shoving an envelope along the polished floor with a push broom. "Oh, hi John. Good, you're early. We've had a little excitement. A guy from LaPush came in here and tried to get to Whitman. He had flowers, candy and maybe another letter bomb." Ranger Divine pushed the envelope into a utility closet and shut the door. "I'm calling the FBI for instruction. I may be calling Fort Lewis bomb squad. If you don't mind, you can guard Ed and Gable while I make my notifications."

"Sure thing," responded the Forks officer. "Do you want me in here or outside where the Ascon guys are cleaning windows?"

"Who's cleaning windows?"

"Two guys from Ascon Glass Service were cleaning Gable's window when I drove in. I was wondering how they ever cleaned that glass with that screen over it."

"Nobody said anything to me about...," stress began to rise in his voice. "How were they cleaning the glass behind the screen?" he asked the cop, walking toward Gable's room. He put his key in the lock of the door.

"They have the screen off. It's OK. These guys were authentic 'vindow vashers.'"

Ranger Divine pushed on the heavy wooden door. It didn't budge. He looked at Officer Rice with panic in his face. The trace of humor was immediately bleached from the face of the cop. They both ran down the halls of the hospital and out the west-facing emergency entrance. When they got to the window, the screen was off. The glass was cut out of the largest pane and set behind the screen. To their horror, the patient/ prisoner was missing. The policeman's eyes bulged from their sockets. "They were polishing this piece of glass just five minutes ago!"

The ranger's exasperation eclipsed his sense of multi-agency diplomacy. He railed at the cop who was a full foot taller than himself, "You dumb shit! They

166

used the old trick of polishing air on you!"

Both men went for their portable radios and attempted to notify their respective agencies of the snafu (Situation Normal: All Fucked Up.) "I can't get Port Angeles," said the ranger. "Get a County Unit to patrol the LaPush Road and make sure they have a physical discription of Gable."

"I can't get Forks!" said the cop. He ran into the hospital and called his dispatcher to report the fleeing suspect. The dispatcher told him that both county and municipal radios were out. The town's radio station which broadcasted on the A.M. and F.M. bands was coming in loud and clear on the A.M., but was wiped clean on the frequency modulation spectrum. The dispatcher told Rice that it must be a sun spot.

"Why would anyone want to break Gable out of here, anyway?" marveled the ranger to the Forks cop. The ranger was calming down. "He wasn't much of a manslaughter suspect, since we couldn't put him behind the wheel of that Ford submarine. We brought that red devil back from the dead! What kind of gratitude is it to leave here without saying thanks?"

TWENTY-FOUR

Sparks' Basement, Second Beach Housing
July 6, 1992

*T*im had been given several full strength Valium the evening of his escape. Partly it was a carrot on a stick, to quiet him and assure his cooperation. Partly it was to ward off the delirium tremens associated with 'cold turkey' dissociation from drug dependence which were hard to manage even in a hospital setting. The Valium would serve to settle Gable in his new quarters of confinement. They hoped the drug might instill in him a sense of confidence in his new captors. When he woke up the next morning, he noticed with satisfaction that he was wearing his own robe and pajamas, but did not remember changing out of the hospital garment or the overcoat that was placed over him before he was conveyed out the hospital window to the receiving fork-lift arms of John Pinn. Jeff Sparks was dozing in a chair across the basement room. He woke up as Gable raised himself from the cot upon which he had slumbered.

"Good morning, Chief," called Sparks cheerfully.

"Yeah," replied Gable. "I've got to piss like a race horse." Gable reached the only door of the basement and puzzled at the resistance of the knob. It was locked from the outside.

"Sorry, Chief. You'll have to piss over there. You're a man on the lamb." Sparks pointed to a port-a-potty in the corner.

"How about some beer and a Valium to rough off the edges before breakfast?" Gable began to walk towards the toilet.

"I don't have anything to give you except some coffee and these muffins here in the basket." Gable stopped to accept the coffee, but his stomach did a little flip when he looked into the basket of dry, corn/raisin muffins. "Clarence Fourskins will be down to talk with you in about an hour. He's got Valium."

"Open the door. Let me talk to him," said Gable again walking toward the toilet. Something was strange here. He couldn't understand why he was locked in, and he had just discovered a strange necklace/collar around his neck. "What's this shit!" he shouted standing in front of the port-a-potty, his right hand still holding the steaming coffee.

"Don't fool with it. Oh yeah, Clarence Fourskins said he wants you to stop swearing. Take your hand away from it!" As Gable's fingers explored the collar, Sparks' big toe found an electric trigger in his right boot. The collar felt to Gable like something that a Saint Bernard should be wearing to charge into an avalanche. It had a small keg over his larynx and he was beginning to try to unbuckle the hasp behind his neck with his left hand when the shock hit him.

169

His coffee cup shattered on the floor and Gable pitched forward falling onto the port-a-potty; knocking it on its side. Gable lay on the floor whimpering through broken breaths. Whatever had hit him had caused him to piss his pants! "What the shit *was* that!"

Sparks talked in a low soothing voice. "Sorry, Chief. You can't be fooling with that collar. It's part of the program. Just leave it alone and you'll be OK. Did you piss yourself?"

"Fuck yes! I want this thing off me right now!" Gable quickly tried to get to the buckle, and a second shock racked his body and sent him into convulsions. When he returned to consciousness he found that a bowel movement had joined the company of the urine in his pajamas. Sparks, and this dude, Fourskins were pulling off his pajama bottoms. Next thing they were cleaning him with a wash rag. This was all a bit too personal for the spiritual leader of the Quileute Nation.

After he was cleaned, changed, and all but powdered and diapered by his new associates, Gable was face to face with Fourskins. He was not much liking what he saw. The big, stubborn Plains Indian kept looking him deep in the eyes. He was putting some kind of juju on Gable. Fourskins' determination and conviction intimated an incarceration that was more restrictive than these four concrete walls and solid oak door. Gable had asked again for sedatives and beer and this reasonable request had been denied. He was again told to be patient.

Gable had screamed into Fourskins' face, "*Be patient*? Hell, until last night I *was* a patient! I need drugs to live! They know that at the hospital. Get this shitty collar off of me! If you're not going to give me my drugs, take me back to where they will give me drugs!"

"Listen, Tim. You're not going back to the hospital. You're the spiritual leader of this village. Now the people need you. We're going to get you well and prepare you for the mission you were destined to fulfill. First I want to help you with your language and I'd like you to say a few words for me and then wipe them out of your vocabulary forever. Say the word 'S...H...I...T.'"

"What the fuck are you talking about! Get this shitty collar off me!"

Fourskins ignored Gable's order and called out to Sparks who had left the room, "Are you getting this, Jeff? Is the adjective OK or do you need the noun?"

"I need the noun! I got the object 'fuck', already," Sparks called back from the other side of the door.

This was really getting crazy thought Gable. His fingers began to move toward his neck, but paused on his chest with the remembrance of the two shocks.

"Say 'S...H...I...T.'" started Fourskins again.

"What?" asked Gable, as confused as before.

"Say the word 'shit.'"

"Shit."

"Thank you, Timothy."

"No big fucking...AHHHHH!" Gable was lifted off the cot and dropped on the floor by muscular reaction to the shock from the accursed collar. He lay still, on the floor, whimpering.

"I'm really sorry, Timothy. It's not a dignified way to treat a 'sachem,' but we don't have much time and there's so much that we have to do. The collar won't be on you for long. Just until we have you acting and talking like the chief that you are. There are four ways to trigger that collar. One way is by trying to take it off. The second is by using offensive language like 'fuck' and 'shit' - we just made a voice print of those words and Jeff has hooked up the trigger to a computer that listens for your voice on that microphone on the ceiling; The third way, which we'll set later is if you yell or scream - the collar is actually designed to stop dogs from barking. And, the fourth way, is if you just totally fail to cooperate with our program. We've gone through a lot of trouble to get you here and we feel that you must be with us in this. Do you understand what I've said?"

"Yes," said Tim Gable.

"Good. Let me help you back onto the cot. I'm sure that you won't be wanting to trigger the collar much more." Fourskins got Gable off the floor and back into a sitting position. He fetched some coffee for the prisoner and sat down at the edge of the cot to talk.

"We've got to talk about history. You must understand where the tribe is, in an historical perspective. Events and circumstance right now are not unlike a point in American history one hundred and thirty years ago, when President Lincoln faced the issue of state succession..."

"Lincoln freed the slaves, man." Gable sensed that things were expected out of him. He made this contribution in the hopes that the trigger on his collar could be lightened a hair. His statement, however, seemed to produce the opposite effect on Fourskins than what he had hoped.

"That may be true, but at what a price! You think the War Between the States was fought because of slavery?"

"Uh...yes."

171

"Well, it was the northern states that prevailed in the conflict, so, of course, they had to hang all kinds of ornamental causes on the most costly war in American history. Wars are fought over money, Timothy. That's what the War Between the States was about. The House of Congress in the United States is based on demographics. There were a lot more northerners living in 1861 than southerners and the anti-agrarian legislature was totally oriented to industry. Slavery was a small side issue. It was an institution that was dying on its own. It wouldn't have made it into the twentieth century regardless of Lincoln. In fact, Lincoln went on record as saying that he wouldn't prosecute the war on the basis of slavery. He allowed slavery to continue in a couple of border states until well into the war, at which point he was sending black regiments to the front to be cannon fodder. It was strictly an issue of succession. The same issues that were brought up by Thomas Jefferson in The War For Independence were articulated by the Confederate States, but, this time, the United States was the tyrant, so Lincoln threw "When in the course of human events..." and "Life, liberty and the pursuit of happiness..." out the window. Did you know that much of the language, and spirit of the U.S. Constitution, was borrowed from the Iroquois Confederacy?"

"No," said Gable in a small, tired voice.

"Well, that's part of a different discussion, anyway. Your hero, Abraham Lincoln, was a George Shrub in a stove-pipe hat. He was no great friend of Native America, in fact, he was an Indian fighter. Did you know that, Timothy?"

"Naw, I guess not. Say, Mr. Fourskins, I'm kind of shaky here. I don't need this coffee. What I need is a few Valium. You guys kidnap me from the hospital where they're taking care of me, and lock me in a stinking basement with only a port-a-potty for plumbing. You put this God damn collar around my fucking...Ahhhh!" Gable was back on the floor. He was whimpering and begging, "Take it off...get it off...please, take it off..."

Fourskins pulled him back up to the cot. "Did you get the 'G. D.' expletive, Jeff?" Fourskins yelled to the door.

"I got it," called out a voice from behind the door.

"Look it, Timothy. You've got to quit swearing. We've got a lot of ground to cover here, and we can't have you diving off the cot every five minutes, going into convulsions.

"As I was saying, Abraham Lincoln was an Indian fighter and in April of 1832, he had taken temporary leave of his store-clerk job in New Salem, Illinois to fight a brave and peaceful band of Sauk Indians led by a chief known as Black Hawk.' Do you know of this campaign?"

"No."

"The U.S. made the Louisiana Purchase in 1803 which included the heretofore French city of Saint Louis. The French had a good record of Native relations and understood the sale to include only the already settled and urbanized lands along the Mississippi. The U.S. has always demonstrated a disrespect and contempt for its Natives. Some of the Sauk Indians along the Missouri celebrated the changing of this guard by flying U.S. flags off the tails of their ponies. It provoked the local American authorities, who complained to Governor William Harrison - remember 'Tippecanoe and Tyler, too?'"

"Nope."

"Well, even in its infancy, the arrogance of the U.S. was beyond all reason and Harrison decided to acquire the land base of the Sauk Indians, who were showing disrespect for the new imperialist in the neighborhood. A Sauk warrior had been taken prisoner for resisting the trespass of Whites upon ancestral hunting grounds. When President Thomas Jefferson heard of the circumstances; he ordered the release of the Native. Five Sauk chiefs came to St. Louis to demand the release of their countryman. They were immediately given a tour of the grog and whore houses of St. Louis. Meanwhile the pardoned prisoner was shot in the head, supposedly trying to escape. When the chiefs sobered up with the news that the ward they had come to collect had been executed by the U.S. military, they were also told that they had sold title to their hunting grounds. *And* that they had spent the payment in the recreational pursuits which had left them with cannons in their heads, and puss on their penises."

"I've had a few mornings like that," offered Gable. "Say, how about a little firewater right now, while we're on the subject?"

"In 1812, another delegation of Sauk chiefs went to Washington, D.C., to meet with President James Madison. The U.S. was at war with England and trying to keep the peace with its Natives. The President promised that Natives along the Missouri would still receive provisions and ammunition in credit for the furs and game that they would bring to the forts as payment. However, when the Sauks went to Fort Madison to collect their necessities they were told that they had no credit and would be dealt no guns or ammunition. Returning to their village of Sukenuk on the Rock River, they were met by a British trader who had two boats of goods to trade and a keg of rum. Black Hawk and the warriors of Saukenuk went off to fight with Tecumseh in the Battle of Detroit. Perhaps you've heard about Tecumseh?"

"Sure, it's a lawn mower engine..."

"This is a different Injun. Tecumseh was the Shawnee chief who almost created a nation for Native America. But the Sauk warriors who joined his campaign had obligations to feed their families, which required a fall hunt. They returned to Saukenuk to find that the stay-at-homes had made major defections to the enemy side. In the absence of Black Hawk, the Sauks had appointed a tough-talking coward named 'Keokuk' as chief of the village.

"In 1813, Fort Madison, which had refused the Sauks credit, was burned to the ground. In 1814 war continued to rage along the Mississippi and the Sauks engaged, and were repelled, by naval reinforcements coming up the Wisconsin River at Prairie de Chien. A force of 430 American soldiers was sent out to annihilate the hostiles. The punitive expedition was led by a young major named 'Zachery Taylor.' Does 'Taylor' ring a bell for you?"

"The wine?"

"I don't think there's a connection. Anyway, Taylor did better in the Mexican War, because the Sauks and Brits kicked his butt. The Americans retreated to the site of Fort Madison, where they tried to rebuild the structure before giving up in retreat.

The Treaty of Ghent, was the cessation of hostilities between England and the U.S. In May of 1815, the English burned down their own fort at Prairie de Chien and isolated the Sauk resistance from all support. It took Black Hawk by surprise and he demanded an explanation from the British. He continued to fight, attacking Fort Howard, but was repulsed. He hurried back to Saukenuk where the Americans threatened to extirpate the village if Black Hawk did not sign a treaty. They were trying to reaffirm that 1804 treaty where the Sauk chiefs gave up rights to their ancestral hunting grounds to the east. Remember the hung over chiefs with cankers on their penises?"

"Yeah, say, could I have another one of those Valium?"

"So the Sauks were pushed into conflict with my Sioux ancestors when they came west on their fall hunts. Now the way a fall hunt works is that the whole village moves out after the bison. When they came back from the hunt, the Sauks found White settlers moved right into their village. The Whites fenced their cattle right into the Native's gardens. They were living in the Indian's lodges. There were incidents of white settlers beating Indian youths to death: once for eating some ears of corn from a White's garden; and another for leaving a gate open.

"Meanwhile, the Indian agent, Thomas Forsyth, was chumming up to that cowardly traitor, Keokuk, and showering him with gifts. This would be in 1831. The tribe divided with about 350 of the Sauks residing in Saukenuk. Black Hawk and the rest of the tribe followed the government's demand to surcease their ancestral village and follow Keokuk to a refugee camp on the Illinois River. General Edmund Gaines was dispatched with 700 troops - two soldiers for every man, woman and child hostile - and they were met in peace by Black Hawk's band. who were called 'the British band.' The Indians asked only to be able to 'lay their bones with those of their ancestors.' They returned to Saukenuk.

"White Cloud was a Winnebago prophet who came to Saukenuk to provide spiritual guidance. Whenever Whites see an Indian prophet, a flag goes up. General Gaines called for more troops. On June 25, he moved in and fired the village of Saukenuk. Black Hawk retreated with the British band, across the east side of the

174

river with no casualties. Black Hawk was forced to sign a treaty promising to never communicate with the British; acknowledge Keokuk's authority over the entire tribe; to never return to their homeland of Saukenuk; and to allow roads through their ancestral hunting grounds. For these concessions, they were allowed to live. They were promised corn in the amount that was burned at Saukenuk.

"But the Illinois militia wanted to kill Indians. Their marksmen practiced their sniping on the men, women and children of the British band. Only a token amount of corn arrived for the Sauks. When they constructed boats to facilitate hunting, the militia moved in and destroyed them. The Sauks faced starvation, as did some nearby tribes of Fox Natives who were being squeezed between the Menominee Indians, and the Illinois militia.

Meanwhile, the Potawatomis, Chippewas and Ottowas were exposed to similar treatment from the United States. These tribes were considering their options of fighting, starving or relocating. The British had assured 'White Cloud' that guns would be provided. They said if the Natives lost an armed rebellion, they could relocate along the Red River in Canada.

Black Hawk and his band returned to Saukenuk. Governor John Reynolds again called for troops sufficient to deal with the Native resistance. General Henry Atkinson was dispatched in April of 1832. In addition to all the government troops that were mobilized, the call went out for volunteers to fight Inidians. Along with the 1,700 other volunteers was a 23-year-old clerk from Denton Offut's store. His name was Abraham Lincoln. You've heard of him?"

"Who did you say?"

"Abraham Lincoln."

"Sure, we already talked about him...he freed the slaves. Say, about that Valium..."

"Keokuk wanted to join the fight to exterminate the British band that had reoccupied Saukenuk. However, he was refused entry into the sortie that was led by Governor Reynolds, himself. The heavy military pressure caused the promises of British weapons to evaporate. Zachary Taylor, now a colonel with his own command, joined the expedition with 1,500 cavalry troops. Major Isaiah Stillman begged for permission to chase the fleeing British band with 275 men. Black Hawk sent a surrender party of eight warriors, but the Whites fell on the Natives and began killing them. About 25 warriors charged the 275 regulars on a suicide mission to rescue the survivors of the surrender party. The brave soldiers saw more than twelve Indians and fled screaming into the wilderness.

"Governor Reynolds called for more volunteers. Major General Winfield Scott was ordered by President Andrew Jackson to march from Chicago with 800 regulars, six ranger companies, and about 3,000 volunteers. They picked up the trail of the British band, near Four Lakes, and followed them into the swamps along the

Wisconsin River. Black Hawk and his band were eating roots and tree bark.. They were heading back down the Wisconsin to the Mississippi. The sea of soldiers foundered in the marsh. Soon, they ran out of supplies. Governor Reynolds and Abraham Lincoln quit the campaign.

"Colonel Henry Dodge, with 500 cavalry, engaged the nonconforming Sauks as they were crossing the flood-swollen Wisconsin by lashing elm branches together. He was led to the Sauks by traitor Winnebagos. The warriors tried to hold off the soldiers, while the women and children crossed the river Many drowned or were shot. More of the band died of starvation as they headed down the Wisconsin. They arrived at the Mississippi, below Bad Axe, and discussed their predicament. Black Hawk wanted to go north to the Chippewas. Intimidated by the government, the Chippewas had refused the Sauks shelter before. The survivors voted to cross the Mississippi.

"On August 1, coming down the flooded Mississippi, the battle-steamship 'Warrior' came upon the pathetic tribe trying to cross the river with their lashed branch flotation. The Sauks raised a white flag and held up their hands. Winnebago interpreters aboard the Warrior explained that the Sauks wished to surrender. The Warrior opened up on the tribe, at point-blank range with a six-pound cannon, firing grape shot. They fired on the Sauks until they began to run out of fuelwood, and shot. They went down to Prairie de Chien to refuel and reload. Of the survivors, Black Hawk, White Cloud, and 50 other Sauks, headed north to join the Chippewas. The rest of the British band again attempted the river.

"Two days later, while Scott and his troops were tied down with cholera, Atkinson and 1,300 troops came on the Sauks trying again to cross the Mississippi. The soldiers were filled with hatred for having been embarrassed and inconvenienced by these hostiles. They clubbed the children. They hacked them to pieces with their long knives. They pushed the Indians into the flooded river. The Warrior reappeared and joined the melee. Its six pounder again rained death upon the Sauks, who swam for their lives. The Sauks had no weapons left for fighting. In eight hours, it was all over. Remarkably, a body count showed that 68 Sauks had made it to the west side of the Mississippi. They were killed, and scalped, by the Sioux that had been forewarned by the soldiers of this impending 'invasion' of their territory.

"A 100 dollar and twenty-horse reward was offered for the capture of the surviving hostiles who had fled north. Black Hawk surrendered to Zach Taylor, who turned over the prisoner party to his future son-in-law, Jefferson Davis. Does that name ring a bell?"

"Jefferson Taylor?"

"No, Jefferson Davis. He was President of the Confederate States of America."

"I thought you said he was some kind of Indian fighter. Please take this collar off of me. I really need some..."

"I'm almost done here, Timothy. Be patient, you'll get your medication after we're done with this history lesson. Black Hawk was taken to Washington, D.C., where he was made to understand there was no hope in resistance. He died, and his grave was robbed by Whites who put his skeleton in the Geological and Historical Society in Burlington, Iowa. There is a bronze bust of the great peace maker, Keokuk, in the Capitol Building in Washington."

"Now before I give you your Valium, a couple of questions to see if you understood what I've told you: Who was Keokuk and what part did he play in the Sauk rebellion?"

"Uh, I guess I missed that part."

"What part did Abraham Lincoln have in this campaign?"

"Uh, he freed the slaves...No, he was an Indian fighter and President of the Confederate States..."

"Before you get your medication, we'll have to go over it all again until you get it. In 1803 the United States came up with legislation it called the Louisiana Purchase. This clever bit of thievery included the Mississippi, all the way up into what is now Illinois. Among the Native American tribes affected by this transaction was a proud group of river Indians known as the Sauks..."

TWENTY-FIVE

Second Beach Housing
Wednesday, October 14, 1992

"*Y*ou've come a long way, Mr. Gable. I'm really pleased with the way our sessions have been going." Clarence Fourskins spoke with great earnestness.

"Well, it's been a lot more pleasant for me since you took that...," Timothy Gable paused searching for a inoffensive adjective. "...son of a dogging collar off of my neck."

"Before we review the ground we've been covering for the last two months, would you like one beer, or Valium before you turn in?"

"No thanks. It doesn't do much for me, anymore. I've been enjoying this *Arabian Nights* thing that you've been giving me on Native history. The beer just makes me get up in the night to...micturate."

"In that case, I would like to share something with you which may be of comfort...at least I hope it doesn't make you angry with us: We've never given you any beer that had any alcoholic content. Your dependence on alcohol was broken a couple days after you got here. The Valium have been decreasing in potency, so for the last week you've been taking vitamins dressed up like downers. You're free of your addictions, Mr. Gable! We'll leave the door unlocked from the outside from now on, so the only thing that keeps you here is your commitment to our operation...and that you're a fugitive from justice."

"This is my home. I want to see this thing through. I'm committed. Let's do the review and I'll get some rack. We've been at this for eighteen hours now."

"OK, Timothy, I'll give you a name, and you give me the encapsulated history. 'Oceola'..."

Gable sat straight upright, concentrating to pull the strings of fact from his newly acquired memory facility, "Leader of the resisting band of Seminoles in Florida. His Christian name was 'Powell'' - 'Billy Powell.' 'Oceola' means 'Black Drink Singer.' The Seminoles, who were displaced Northern Creeks, drank a strong dark colored emetic which caused projectile vomitus before going into battle. General Gaines attacked the Natives where they were living peacefully in an abandoned British Fort. That was the start of the First Seminole War. Andrew Jackson invaded Spanish Florida. He was made Governor of the Territory in 1819. At Camp Moultrie, the Natives were forbidden to settle any land within twenty miles of either coast, but guaranteed the Everglades and swamps in per... per... perpetua. The Seminoles were flim flammed at Paynes Landing by a crooked Indian Agent, Wiley Thompson, and a black interpreter called 'Abe.' By 1830, Jackson was President. He enacted the Removal Bill which was in total violation of existing treaties. The Second Seminole War involved several U.S. generals, eight-thousand troops, and a lot more volunteers, trying to subdue this handful of Seminole warriors. The army captured noncombatants and took them to Fort Mellon, near Tampa, where they were starved and left naked. Oceola desired peace and came to Fort Mellon to surrender his band of two thousand five hundred Natives. When he saw the people starving and dying of measles, he broke away with as many people as could still travel. War broke out again in eighteen thirty...thirty..."

"It was September, 1837, Mr. Gable."

"...eighteen thirty-seven and the Army and the plantation owner militia again captured some of the Seminole leadership. They poisoned their minds into thinking they had to give up their land, and move to Oklahoma. These men who were made to be traitors by the controlled suffering of their people, revealed the general location of Oceola. But it was Oceola that came to the militia. He held a white flag of truce, to discuss terms of peace. His white flag was taken from him and thrown into the dirt. Oceola was sent to Sullivan's Island where he died a few months later from starvation and infection from his wounds. The government said that the chief's care was consigned to a doctor, but the attending physician was the brother-in-law of Wily Thompson, the Indian Agent who betrayed the Seminoles. The doctor was so concerned about the death of his patient that he cut off Oceola's head and sent it to his home where it was hung on his child's bedpost. Three hundred Seminoles were pursued by Zachery Taylor into the Everglades where they lived for almost a hundred years until they were thrown out by the National Park Service. The rest of the nation was marched to Oklahoma where they starved, or died of disease."

"I'm really impressed at how you are retaining all this, Mr. Gable. Ready for another?" The rehabilitated Native nodded, drinking from a glass of water. "King Philip..."

"That's the Thanksgiving story, back in the Seventeenth Century. The Wampanoags were very accommodating to the English pilgrims, even though members of their tribes had been kidnapped and taken to be put on display in Europe, like circus animals. King Philip and his brother Alexander had been given Anglicized names so that the English would be comfortable pronouncing them. The first Native that came into Plymouth had learned two words He said, "Welcome, English, welcome." Governor Carver got the man drunk and had him sign a document that the Wampanoags would never strike against the colonists or King James, either. The other Natives returned with four deer, corn, and other provender. That November, the Wampanoags saved the colonists from their own incompetence in dealing with the American environment. The Plymouth colonists hadn't even wiped the gravy off their faces before they started pushing the Wampanoags, and taking their land. They enacted laws which prohibited hunting, fishing or work on Sunday. The Colonists put Natives in stockades for gathering the foods that had saved their own lives a few months previous. They put Alexander, Philip's brother, on trial. He died of humiliation, compounded by the inhumane treatment he received at their hands. By 1675, the Whites had proliferated to double the Native population. A Christianized Native was found murdered and three Indians were lynched. The authorities in Plymouth set out head bounties on Natives they suspected of Blue Law violations. They attacked villages, and took women and children into slavery. They introduced scalping to these Natives. The Wampanoags had disappeared into a swamp and camouflaged their village. A few years before, the Natives had given the Pilgrims Thanksgiving. Now, the Whites attacked Philip's village just before Christmas. The Pilgrims torched the village and beat the women and children back into the flames. This was the last Noel, as far as Philip was concerned. He worked relentlessly to confederate a Native resistance to the push of White civilization. In 1676 Philip took Plymouth by storm. His warriors burned part of the town. Of the ninety White settlements along the North Atlantic seaboard, fifty-two were attacked and twelve destroyed. The Natives could not feed their families, and fight the White man, too. Different tribes were taken into subjection. This began the White-man's technique of systematic starvation, to divide the Native's allegiance. In the end, it was Philip's sister-in-law who betrayed his position. He was in a renegade camp, continuing his fight, even though he was starving. The English ambushed Philip, shot him twice in the chest, cut off his head and put it on a stake in Plymouth where it hung for twenty-five years. If only the Natives had never rescued the starving colonist..."

"Do you remember the Pope revolt?"

"Yes, that's a chapter in history that shows that, united, Natives could expel the White intruder from the continent. The Pueblos and Apaches drove the Spanish right back to Mexico. The Conquistadors made their conquest throughout the Americas by remarkable feats of savagery, cutting off the arms of all Natives who resisted them. They butchered children before the horrified eyes of their parents. It made an impression. Natives of the southwest endured the cruel regime of the Spanish for many years rather than risk such vindictiveness. A map of the entire southwest was divided into hacienda fiefs and given, with the Natives as slaves, to the Spanish gentry. But during the droughts, and famines of 1660, a medicine man called 'Pope' encouraged other Natives to apostate from the Christianity that had been forced on them. He urged a return to the nature worship which had dominated their socio-religious culture. The Natives were severely persecuted for their religious expression. Pope and forty-six other priests were rounded up and flogged. Three of the men were hanged. They were thrown into jail and starved. Pope had a mystic vision. Gods gave him a date where 16,000 Native warriors would rise up against the 3,000 Spanish soldiers. The date for the revolt in 1680 was established by sending out strings with knots...count the knots to the days to revolution.

Suspected traitors were given strings with more knots. It worked. All outlying forts went over like dominos and Sante Fe was defended for three days of brutal fighting. Then the survivors beat a hasty retreat to Mexico. Two interesting aspects at the conclusion of this campaign were that the Apaches took the horses abandoned by the Spanish. Native America seized the power of the equine engine. The other surprising outcome was that Pope became a tyrant, and imposed his will upon the desires of his subjects with the same authority used by the Spanish..."

"Meet the old boss, Timothy. Same as the new boss. It happens all the time. You're really getting a handle on this material! I want to tell *you* a story. [2]

TWENTY-SIX

LaPush Village
August 1, 1992

*R*on Richland, the old, crusty radio technician hung out over LaPush village on the wooden mast of the antenna tower from his lineman's belt. He was too old to be climbing these towers - his bones too brittle and joints too stiff...and it was too damned hot. Next to the wooden mast, in front of the old Coast Guard Station, was a steel stairway to the platform upon which depended the video camera that fed the new inland 'Taco Bell' Coast Guard Station "real-time" intelligence. In the days of the previous station, that the Coasties used to gain the same data the old fashioned way: by looking out their windows.

Richland cut through a strand of 22-gauge wire and fumbled in his apron for his wire strippers. Not laying hands on the tool, he stripped both ends with his front teeth. He felt his dentures shift slightly forward on the roof of his mouth. He set the ammeter function on his multi-tester from his utility apron and bridged the two cut ends with the test leads of the instrument. The test signal was sending a full current of 500 milliamps from the base station to the antenna. There was no problem here. According to the Coast Guard, the station had gone down three times for half an hour or more in the last three weeks. The Coasties weren't the only radio users experiencing problems. Police, Park, HAM operators and other megacyclers had experienced interruptions. In the August heat, he half expected to see the insulation melted off the transmission wires and a dead short across the lines. The problem, however, remained more elusive. Maybe sun spots?

****

Dorothy Pinn and Wally walked toward the Woodrift trailer in the village. The county bus had dropped them off across from LaPush Ocean Park. As always, Wally felt immensely proud to be walking in public with Dorothy. She was the most beautiful woman alive and his best friend all in one package. Whatever genetic soup had combined to contribute to the upper body development of John Pinn, the same genes des jour had been served up to his daughter. Upon a body as curvaceous, provocative and dramatic as the skyline of James Island, rode a face of such innocence and purity as to confound the senses. At age seventeen, Dorothy was eight years into a world of sexual maturity. Though Wally was chronologically a year older than Dorothy, he was a pilgrim to this world. He found her physical presence reassuring, and uplifting to his ego. Beneath the fountain of his sexual maturity was a deep well of longing and unrest, which surged to the surface with artisan force with every stolen glance at her figure, or the smell of her hair, floating on the hot summer wind. These feelings in some ways enhanced, and in some ways detracted from what had been a young lifetime of friendship between the two cousins. Wally had just returned from two weeks of National Guard duty at Fort Lewis and it had been Dorothy who had met him on the county bus at Tillicum Park, in Forks, and accompanied him back to LaPush on the connecting bus. She would keep him company for the few hours before he went on duty for his evening shift as a Tribal Reserve Police Officer. Wally shifted the heavy duffel bag that he was carrying. He

183

moved from Dorothy's right side to her left. It allowed him to study her from a different profile, and he left his hand free to minister to her lovliness. In the heavy duffel were four <u>L</u>ight <u>A</u>rtillery <u>W</u>eapons, 100 electric blasting caps and ten pounds of C-4 explosive.

The geysering fountain of sexuality had laid dormant in Ron Richland for some time now. Occasional review of lusty pictorials presented in *Playboy* and *Penthouse* had served to stir the quiet waters, but such divination was usually motivated more out of a sense of inventory than out of an intent to prime the pump.

Something struck the old radio man as peculiar about the couple walking together. The skin headed young buck in camouflaged fatigues strutting beside Miss LaPush...in the heat, it was far more interesting than splicing 22-gauge wire together in sunlight that turned electrical tape to taffy. From twenty feet up the wooden mast, Richland squinted into the sun. He gazed down with genuine curiosity.

Even over the prickly sun, Wally felt the eyes burning onto Dorothy and himself. He looked up into Richland's face. He saw the man's face screwed up into a lewd leer. For the last two weeks, Wally had been training. He had been blowing up piles of rock, dirt and brick with charges of C-4 plastic explosive. A sense of protectiveness and propriety struck a match and ignited the short fuse of Wally's temper. "Something down here interest you, old man?" called up Wally, inviting the man to look away.

"You might say that." Richland was tired of young punks throwing their weight around. He had fought in World War II, setting up radio links across Europe in the wake of the advancing Allied Army. If this prepubescent skinhead was some kind of GI, then he owed Richland the respect due a veteran from a cherry. If he wasn't military, then fuck him for trying to look like he was.

"Better watch your mouth." The burning fuse was close to the blasting cap of Wally's temper.

"I'd rather watch your friend."

"Fuck you!" yelled Wally at the old lech.

"Fuck me with your friend and it's a deal!" The little shit. Who's he think he's talking to, anyway?

Wally knew that he was a reformed juvenile delinquent. He was a reserve peace officer with the LaPush Tribe. He was a private in the National Guard. He was a lieutenant in the army of the Confederation of Non-White America. The utterance of profanity, for him, was a profound event and the words echoed in his head like the explosion of a two-pound satchel of C-4.

Dorothy turned around and began running up the LaPush Road away from the village. She ran towards the Second Beach housing project where she lived.

Wally chased her for a few seconds, calling her name. She kept going like she intended to run the mile or so back to her house. He gave up trotting after her. He turned to run back to his family's trailer. He would get his uniform and ticket book and write this clown up for...well, he'd think of something to write him up for. Dorothy continued running up the road toward Quileute Heights housing project. She was crying. She was a little embarrassed that Wally had used such language in front of her. She was also partly mortified by what the White man had said. But mostly she was eager to get away from the clash of two male egos.

****

In the heat of August, the woods are closed to loggers. Though most of their saws and other equipment come with spark-arresting mufflers, few loggers are guilty of delicacy. There is a question about cigarette butts, oily rags, broken beer bottles - all of which can cause a wild fire in the bone-dry weather of August. John Pinn's crew had just been shut down by fiat of the DNR. They would be working a hoot-owl shift with big artificial lights for a few nights, but likely as not, by next week, he would be temporarily out of work. John Pinn was doubly impacted by such a layoff, because, unlike his co-workers, his sense of pride prohibited him from collecting state unemployment benefits. He drove home from Tillicum Park in his little pick-up, sweltering in the heat, and insecurity, of the afternoon. As he approached the right-hand turn to the housing project across from Second Beach parking, he saw his 17-year-old daughter running up the LaPush Road. Something was wrong. Her blouse was stained with sweat and her face looked wet with tears. He drove down to meet her. He opened the passenger side door for her. She didn't get in, but stood there struggling for breath; red faced from exertion.

"What is it, princess?" asked her father softly.

"He said...he wanted...to...do it with...me," blurted Dorothy.

"Wally said that!" John Pinn saw himself tearing the little skinhead, buttock from asshole.

"No...not Wally. Wally was speaking up for me...A man...an old man hanging from a telephone pole, down in the village."

"What exactly did this man say?" asked John Pinn sullenly.

"He said he wanted...to fuck me."

"He used *that* word!" bellowed the father.

"Yes. That's what he said."

John Pinn pulled the door closed and over-tached his little Datsun, racing down to the village.

185

The antenna mast next to the remote camera tower is about the first thing a person sees coming into LaPush Village. It was with no difficulty that John Pinn navigated himself to his quarry. Meanwhile, Ron Richland was congratulating himself on his manly handling of the insolent young skinhead, and Miss LaPush. He was redirecting his attention to the electrical matters at hand. Then this new distraction: an angry red ox bellowing something about did Richland say he wanted to fuck the ox's daughter. Twenty feet above the crazy red bastard, Richland felt a certain sense of security. "Yeah, I said I wanted to fuck her, but her skinhead friend wanted twenty-five cents, and she wasn't worth the price."

Richland immediately wished he hadn't spoken out when he saw the expression on the Indian's face. The crazy bastard pulled a big chain saw out of the bed of his pick-up and walked over to the pole directly beneath Richland. He drop started the saw and in fifteen seconds carved a wedge-shaped face in the pole, directly below the radio technician. Richland realized with horror that the red maniac was going to drop the pole so that it would land on top of him. He began working his way around the pole, but in another second, the Indian was making his back cut and the soft cedar was slicing like butter under the August sun.

Wally Woodrift pulled in behind John Pinn's pick-up with the Tribal Police rig. He immediately shifted his game plan from citing the radio technician to saving his life. He hit his emergency lights, and siren, to get John Pinn's attention, but there would be only seconds between his arrival and the toppling of the mast. He jumped out of the patrol rig and ran over to Pinn. He tried to pull Pinn off the saw, but it was like pulling the mountain off the valley. When Pinn did stand up he killed the saw engine and, in the wake of the saw noise, the cries and screaming of the radio tech seemed somewhat muted. The pole was going over. As it began its long arch to the ground, Woodrift looked up to see the old radio tech trying to jockey himself around to get to the uphill side of the falling pole. He would have made it, except his weight caused the pole to roll on the stump. His shoulder, arm, and knee were under the pole when it hit the pavement. The man's head slammed into the pavement and his dentures jumped out of his mouth. For a moment, Wally could hear nothing except the wail of his Smith and Wesson siren. Then the man began moaning. At least he was still alive, thought Woodrift with slight relief.

Wally watched with apprehension as Pinn returned from stowing his saw in the bed of the pick-up, and strode over to where the man was pinned under the pole. He picked up the dentures, and placed them, teeth down, in the hand of the trapped arm. John Pinn stepped over the pole and drove the dentures into the old man's hand with the heel of his calk boots. The man reacted to the pain by a muffled scream and Woodrift threw his arms around Pinn as if to restrain him. Pinn broke away from Wally and began walking back to his truck. The young tribal officer realized that he had an obligation to arrest Pinn. "Hold on, John," said Wally, running over to the side of Pinn's good ear, and taking out his handcuffs. John Pinn pushed Woodrift with one heave of his arm. Woodrift lifted off the ground and landed on his butt five feet away. The handcuffs skidded along the pavement. John Pinn got into the pick-up, and started the engine. Woodrift realized there was no stopping Pinn without shooting him, which was not in the game plan. He ran over to the driver's window as Pinn began to drive execute a U-turn. Woodrift pleaded, "At least loan me the saw, so I can cut the poor bastard free."

"Let him rot. I'll come down to the tribal police station after dinner to turn myself in." John Pinn drove off towards Quileute Heights, and his waiting supper.

Wally Woodrift ran over to his patrol rig and called the dispatcher at Forks Police Department on the Motorola radio in his vehicle. "Forks, this is Quileute 513."

"513," came the reply from the dispatcher.

"Send an ambulance to the old Coast Guard Station in LaPush village. Man down with multiple broken bones. There is an object impaled in his right hand. He's trapped under a large wooden pole. Send the rescue unit with the ambulance. 513."

"513, stand by." Wally knew the dispatcher was chattering with the hospital, the nurse was fumbling with the coded transmitter; which would activate the pages; which would bring the ambulance crew to the hospital; where they would receive their instructions; start up the ambulance; and bitch about how it's another taxi service run to LaPush; and maybe take a piss. Then they'd drink a cup of coffee, before poking along the 19 miles to LaPush, Code Green...

"513, Forks," the dispatcher broke in on Wally's ruminations.

"This is 513." Hospital notified, ambulance and rescue en-route, ETA is 20 minutes."

"Thanks, the patient needs help. 513."

"Forks P.D. 15:55."

It wasn't even four o'clock yet, realized Wally. He wouldn't come on duty for another two hours. He walked over to where the old man was pinned under the wooden mast. He kneeled beside the man's head. He spoke softly over the man's moaning. "It's gonna be all right. The ambulance will be here soon. Hang in there. You're gonna be OK." This guy is really fucked up, thought Wally. When's the meat wagon ever going to get here.

****

Forks Community Hospital
15:57 hours

The two EMT's stood outside the ambulance bay, waiting for the third team member to show up.

"I think we'd better call second-out crew to drive the rescue rig," said Greg Banter. "What if this patient is as fucked up as our last run to LaPush...the guy with bilateral hamburger?"

Bob Stork was still skeptical of overreaction. "Three of us can handle whatever there is in LaPush. Have Don drive the rescue rig. It's probably just a power pole blocking the road, and the tribe wants us to march out and get electrocuted to see if the lines are hot."

"The tribal cop who radioed this in said there's a patient under the pole with multiple broken bones and an impaled object in his hand..."

"He probably has wobbly knees, and the cop confused a beer can for the impaled object. What was that Crow woman's name, anyway. Was it May?"

"I told you! Her name was 'June.' Anyway, I'm going to have the nurse call second out."

"I'll do it. I have to take a piss, anyway."

TWENTY-SEVEN

Saturday, September 26, 1992

*O*ne day looks pretty much like the next at Whidbey Island Naval Air Station, with only a few of the base services closing for the weekend. If anything, operations were a little more intense this Saturday morning. Last week, an Israeli commercial jetliner had been hijacked from Tel Aviv and successfully diverted to Iranian soil. The hijackers were demanding reparations for Iranian civilians who perished when a second commercial airliner was confused for a hostile military target. Among the hostages were a dozen or so Americans and a handful of Canadians. The White House was snorting and growling threats of a retaliatory strike or at least a rescue mission - which most experts felt would rescue little more than the President's ego. Still, the military was following the Commander-in-Chief's vision of a topsy- turvy world stabilized by an armed American presence. All sectors were gearing up. The mobilization was costing the American taxpayers 220 million dollars a day. If the pattern of other mid-Eastern crises held, the duration of the mobilization would be measured in months or even years. In the Security Council of the United Nations, Canada and the U. S. were calling for economic and political sanctions against any country that traded or harbored Iran's commercial fleet. The President had promised that a handful of terrorists would not dictate the policies and economics of the world; but something like that seemed to be happening in this case.

Ensign Jack Jenson resented any reference to the above observation. The President was head of the freest, richest, and greatest country in the world. Jenson had graduated from the University of Washington in 1989, when radical scum were burning the American flag in front of the Federal Building in Seattle. It was this kind of behavior, and flawed thinking, that threatened the foundation of democracy. It set the stage for these piss-guzzling, oil-glutted, Iranians to do real damage to the Free World. It would be a pleasure to vote for George Shrub in the upcoming election.

Ensign Jenson's heart began to beat a little faster as he came into view of the row of A-6 Intruders. As he walked down the tarmac with his navigator, Ensign Ralph Powers, he felt immeasurable pride. He was happy in anticipation of the day's flight plan. At this morning's muster, Admiral Bingingham had been on hand to outline an exciting aspect of the general mobilization that would involve the participation of Jenson's squadron. The Landing Platform Dock, Alamo, would be moored at Bremerton awaiting dispatch to the Persian Gulf. The Admiral told the assembled pilots and navigators that immediately prior to disembarking for the Gulf, the Alamo would stage a rescue exercise off the coast of Washington. The ground forces would encounter dramatic and challenging beach landing, and land navigation problems. Federal Emergency Management Action would be invoked to legitimize low level flight through a maze of topographical features. The Admiral indicated that instant death would be the reward of any flight crews that washed out of this exercise. Better to die here in your backyard, explained Bingingham, than to embarrass your President and your country in another failed rescue mission like Carter's boondoggle twelve years ago. "I'm not taking any party stand here," said the Admiral, "But

189

another failed rescue could get you a Democrat for President. So, crashing into a seastack might not be so bad, after all."

Pulling on his nomex gloves, Ens. Jenson began his preflight checklist, the powerful jet engines roaring to half throttle. Ens. Powers and he would fly along the international boundary to the mouth of the Strait of Juan de Fuca. There they would turn south, and fly the Intruder along the north Washington Coast, which would involve about ten passes. They were to perform the patrols in radio silence with the exception of emergency messages. They would fly at an altitude of about 6,000 feet above Mean Sea Level at a speed of 250 knots. They were exempted from speed and altitude limitations for the purpose of achieving advantage in combat maneuvers. They were to engage other military aircraft they encountered in dogfight maneuvers to be terminated after five minutes. Five minutes was forever. Most real aerial combat was settled in the first 20 seconds of encounter, Admiral Bingingham had reminded them. Jenson and Powers rocketed down the runway and leapt into the clear, September sky of the Indian Summer.

****

" 'Indian Summer,' that's what White people call this kind of weather, Dottie." Wally held Dorothy Pinn's hand as they walked down to Second Beach along a trail that was wide enough to walk two abreast. "Like 'Indian Giver'....As if Native Americans are the ones to give things and then take them back. I've been learning a lot from Clarence Fourskins, and I know enough to say that it's the cruel White Winter which makes a lie out of the gentle, kind Indian Summer."

"Forget politics, Wally," said Dorothy. "Let's just enjoy each other. It's a beautiful day." Everything at LaPush was politics these days. Even her totally a-political father was stirred up about it. Political foment had a lot to do with her dad blowing his cork that day in July. For almost two months now, he had spent his weekends in the Forks jail for aggravated assault. As the investigating officer, there had been nothing Wally could do to prevent it. John Pinn did not enjoy the confines of jail. He missed his family. But Dorothy did not know her father's greatest humiliation upon the matter. Clarence Fourskins had told Pinn in quiet rage: one more screw up like this and Fourskins would be packing his bag and leaving LaPush to fend for itself. On the eve of his first incarceration, John Pinn had asked Dorothy not to have Wally over at their residence on weekends while Mrs. Pinn was working.

Dorothy had experienced some loneliness lately. There was the forced weekend absences of her dad, and Wally had been mostly occupied with this political thing that had washed over LaPush like a tsunami. She had suggested the walk this day as a way to honor her father's wishes regarding her not being alone at the house with Wally. She had been thinking a lot about her relationship with Wally. He had been like a brother to her for seventeen years. As surely as a woolly bear pupates and flies off as a moth, sexuality was encouraging the metamorphosis of their relationship. Wally and she had shared secret places all their lives. Given her choice, Dorothy would prefer to be the one to take him into the cocoon of carnal knowledge.

The trail led out of the Quileute Reservation and they came to the long, switch-backed cedar stairway leading down to the beach. It had been built by the National Park Service to keep 5,000 pairs of feet a year from defoliating the hillside. Climbing over the ubiquitous drift logs to gain the beach, the couple looked north at the surf-tortured rock finger which extended boldly into the Pacific, separating Second Beach from First Beach and LaPush village. Sometime back, in the course of the ocean's never ending dispute with land, a portion of the rock finger collapsed leaving an arched rock bridge. Though Second Beach, in main, was south of the trail, it was this bit of seascape that attracted the couple's interest as it had attracted the attention of professional photographers, as evidenced by its frequent appearance on calendars and postcards.

The low tide allowed Wally and Dorothy to round a rocky point on firm hard sand. There was a tiny bay between Second Beach, and the tunneled rock finger. From here they climbed up a steep slope of loose sedimentary rock to where they attained the rampart. They climbed through a low tunnel of salal vegetation until they came to the bridge leading to the rock parapet. Dorothy walked across this narrow rock gangplank, almost a hundred feet above the water. The view from here was quite remarkable. It was like being an ant on a chessboard. Seastacks and rock cliffs erupting from the land and ocean. Along with the view was a sensational sensation. Though it was low tide on a day of unremarkable surf activity, every swell impacting the rock buttress, carried the Pacific's power and long term plan for the land. The huge rock rocked with the punch of every wave.

"Imagine being up here in a storm," said Dorothy in a voice somewhat tremulous with the environment. "What these seastacks have to endure to remain standing!"

"On the scale of a million years, they fall down all the time," offered Wally. "See those flat-topped islands way out there? That used to be the mainland, but the ocean is advancing almost an inch a year. In a short 60-thousand years, the coast will be a mile that way." Wally pointed behind them to the east. "The first white man stole the title and now the ocean steals the real estate."

"Again with the politics," observed Dorothy, somewhat dejectedly. From this rock perch it was easy to view the world without being seen. It was a classical secret place: sitting on the warm rock, under the sun, with gulls crying on the fresh ocean breeze. A mile over their heads a warplane rocketed by, but the roar of the engine was soon lost to the crashing of the waves. "Too bad we didn't find this for one of our secret places when we were kids, Wally."

"Your dad would have busted my head down to my ass if I had brought you out here when you were young. How's John making out as a weekend jailbird, anyway? I checked with the Court Clerk; next weekend finishes your dad's twenty day sentence. I hope he never pulls a stunt like that again. That foul-mouthed, dirty-duck radio technician had that coming and worse, but Clarence Fourskins says we'll

191

never make any political headway if we get lost fighting petty racism. The real issues are more central to civil rights and human dignity."

Dorothy took Wally's hand in both of hers. She lay back, holding the young man's hand on her bare stomach. She looked up at the blue sky where the jet plane had been. "Wally, from up here we can make our own world. Look at this beautiful planet! Look at our friendship. The only way racism or politics is going to reach us here is if you drag it up on this rock like some stinking dead thing off the beach." Dorothy shifted. She moved Wally's hand closer to her breast.

"I can't just forget politics, Dottie! I'm scared. Our whole existence is on the threshold of big change. There will be sacrifices and losses. I have to look at everything in my life - working for the Tribal Police, my Guard duty, what I say to my family; what I say to you - in the context of how it serves the political interest of the tribe right now. There are only two things that I think of these days: one of them is politics... the other is you." Wally realized that his left hand was on Dottie's bosom and by whatever precognitive powers it had arrived there, Dottie was clutching it in place.

"Just be with me right now, Wally."

"I'm scared, Dot. There are real risks threatening my future. You know that I can't tell you what's happening with the tribe because you told Fourskins you didn't want to be involved, but there's a page of history about to be written in blood and you may not see my name in the next chapter."

"Don't do it, Wally! Whatever it is. No political achievement, or crazy coup is worth your harm. I was a happy kid because I had you as a friend. I don't want to lose your friendship to adulthood or politics. Just stay with me..."

"I can't pretend like this isn't happening! I wish I could just stay with you, Dottie. I want to be with you forever. I want to *marry* you. But for our relationship to survive we must have freedom for our people; we must be in control of our environment and our resources; we must manifest the spirit of our ancestors to show the world we are not second class citizens. I want you to have my children, Dottie. I have to start by carrying the burden that has been placed on my shoulders..." Dorothy started laughing. "What is it, Dottie, what's so funny here?"

"If you want me to have your children, the place to start isn't raiding the National Guard Armory, or hijacking Air Force One, or whatever the devil this big political egg is that you and Fourskins are sitting on...You want me to have your children! Did your parents ever explain to you how to go about it? Have you forgotten from our games as kids? I look different than you naked! You want me to have your kids, but you've got to write your Congressman for instructions? Come here ya big lug," Dorothy was still laughing warmly. "I'll show you the first step in making kids, and you can stuff my ballot box..."

****

Ensigns Jenson and Powers were making a low-altitude, high-speed transect of the coast. In the headphones of his Protective Flight Helmet, Jenson was listening to Powers rattle off figures from the dashboard, which Jenson could see himself, except his attention was absorbed by processing visual intelligence. Charging through seastacks at over 400 knots required more than a little concentration. Christ, he loved this! Every island or seastack they passed erupted into thousands of flying birds, shaken from their roosts. They were flying in the territorial boundary of Olympic National Park, and it was these dripping environmental douche bags that had put the kabash on reopening the Quillayute Airfield to the Naval air force for which it was built in World War II. Where did these eco-freaks come up with their sense of patriotism? Russia? It was bad enough driving by the official Navy sign on Whidbey Island: EXCUSE OUR NOISE / IT'S THE SOUND OF FREEDOM. The *sound of freedom* should require no apology. To Ensign Jenson, his presence at this speed and altitude among the seastacks was justified by the greater good of the country, and for his need to practice survival tactics.

Powers droned on, "Speed: Four one five. Altitude: Four nine. Heading: Zero zero four. Fuel: Eight zero six. Clean on the radar. Ooops, large islands ten clicks. It's LaPush. Nine clicks. Speed: Four one eight. Habitated area ahead. Better slow down and get back up. LaPush ahead. Six clicks. Five...four. Speed: Four two zero. Better slow down, Jack. Three clicks...two. Head up! Head up, Jack!..." Powers is interrupted by Ensign Jenson on the intercom.

"Holy cow, Ralph, check out the gazabas on this Indian bitch to starboard." The navigator and pilot's Military Anti-Shock Trousers inflated as Jenson pulled straight back on his joystick sending the A-6 into a vertical climb which spilled into a loop.

****

The Indian Summer has closed down logging again. I've jogged down the puncheon steps leading down to Second Beach and, after hopping over the pile of drift logs at the bottom of the trail, I see the rare opportunity to jog north from Second Beach. I run across the firm, flat sand left by the retreating tide into the small bay just north of Second Beach. I am going to jog out to the rock finger with the big sea tunnel and am just fifty feet from this objective when it sounds like the whole world is exploding. I think somehow the arch is collapsing and I go down on my knees with my arms covering my head. The roar blasts my ears and pushes my heart down into my stomach. I catch the movement in the periphery of my vision and follow the warplane's climb with my eyes, my arms now covering my ears. It must be an A-6 from Whidbey Island. The craft makes a full loop and I catch more movement as I stand with my arms still over my ears. Two young lovers are fumbling to put on their clothes, evidently disturbed by the intrusion of the Intruder. The young man is standing with his trousers in his hands. He is shaking his fist at the sky and you can see him yelling something at the plane though the jet engines cover all other sound. Then he pulls on his trousers. Our eyes lock with mutual recognition. It's Officer

193

Woodrift! I take my arms off my ears and turn to run back down the beach embarrassed.

****

Dottie had indeed plucked ripe Wally from the vines of his virginity. They lay entwined. Wally felt in himself a new level of total peace and safety. Dottie was right, this was a private place for just them and he could leave everything behind, if he so desired. For instance, what Dottie had said about him being sexually naive, made Wally uncomfortable about his lack of sexual experience. Dottie counted on him to be the older and more mature in their relationship and he did not feel compelled to drag the subject of his virginity to this secret place. After all, he had put on a pretty good show. Though Dottie must know that she was his only love she might never guess that she was his first sexual conquest.

Holding Wally's head against her bare bosom, Dorothy watched the ocean breeze tousle his black hair. She felt total joy and contentment. With only the sun to see them, Dorothy felt unembarrassed. She was at ease with their nakedness and their bodies. It was like when she was four, and he was five. There were no secrets between them. Well, there was still one secret. She was not a virgin. Not now and not half an hour ago. She had gone to a party over at Tim Gable's last year and drank beer, and smoked dope, out of a sense of adventure. One thing had led to another, and before the evening was through, so was her virginity. Her dad would have killed Gable for certain. She felt a sense of shame over the whole deal, so she kept the episode to herself and prayed that Gable would respect, or fear, her father enough to keep his mouth shut. Now, Gable was dead anyway, or so the rumor said, and her secret was safer. She had put on a pretty good show, anyway. Wally would never guess that he was not the first.

The explosion of sound made them both jump up and cover their heads. They shared a thought at that moment: that the ocean had won another inroad in its march, and that their parapet was collapsing into the sea. Military experience not withstanding, it was Dottie who first recognized the intrusion as a warplane and scrambled for her clothes. He removed his arms from his head and watched as the A-6 pulled into a vertical climb, rolled onto its back, and roller coasted down into a leveling dive to make a second pass at their secret place. Dottie tossed Wally his trousers. She was struggling to put on her bra over her beautiful breasts, when the A-6 came along side of them on its second pass. The navigator had come over into the pilot's seat, and both pilot and navigator had removed their flight helmets. They pushed their noses and tongues against the glass of the A-6's canopy. "We'll meet again, you lousy fuckwads," screamed Wally at the retreating Intruder; but in his aching ears, and in the aching ears of his lover, was only the explosive prop wash of the warplane's jet engines.

****

From his family's residence in the Park Service trailer at Mora, Ranger Ed Whitman dialed a telephone number from his rolodex: 206-257-2211. He touched the bandages covering his nose. He pulled up some gauze which drooped over the scars on his upper lip. His voice sounded like a cartoon character, owing to the multiple fractures of his sinus and the substantially restructured flesh around his nose. It embarrassed him, but he was really upset.

"Base Operations. How may I help you?"

"I wonna repurta violachun o' Owimpic Pahk's airshpace by wonna ya A-Shick's," began Ranger Whitman.

"Pardon me?" said the voice on the phone. Ranger Whitman sighed and took a breath. He began again.

"Thish ish Ranger Ed Whitchman. Dat's Whishkey - Hotel - Injia -Tanjo - No...No...Nowember..."

"I'm sorry. You're going to have to speak more clearly. I can't understand what you're saying. This is Naval Air Station Base Operations..."

****

Monday, September 28, 1992

In his Seattle office, Admiral Bingingham dialed the telephone number he found in his rolodex, on the unsecured phone reserved for non-critical communications with the civilian world. This would be just a routine notification, but he thought he might enjoy making it.

"Olympic National Park," answered the switchboard/dispatcher in Port Angeles.

"Give me Superintendent Donovan, please." Environmentalists claimed that the new superintendent was the first park steward in quite a while to have any balls. But, in the Admiral's office, the opinion was, that the only balls in the superintendent's office, were the broken testicles on the floor, left by the brave men he had sent to the park to arrange helicopter servicing of the Navy's Kalaloch repeater and the architects of the Quillayute Airfield retrofit - which the superintendent had nixed.

"Superintendent's Office." said the voice into the Admiral's ear.

"This is Admiral Bingingham, Commander of the Thirteenth Fleet. I want to talk to the Superintendent."

"This *is* Superintendent Donovan, sir. How can I be of service to you today?"

195

"I want to advise you of some critical Naval maneuvers that will occur within the territorial/maritime jurisdiction of the Park sometime in early November of this year. I've notified the boys at NOAA in charge of the Marine Sanctuary. I also notified Fish and Wildlife who administer the Island Refuge in the Park. So now I'm calling to notify the Park. We're coming."

The senior Naval officer smiled as he read the suspicion in the Park Servant's voice. "Admiral Bingingham, exactly what does the Navy plan for the Park this time?"

"Specifically, we intend to harbor the 700 Landing Platform Dock, Alamo, in the Marine Sanctuary. We're going to use A-6's from Whidbey Island to locate a couple of buoys released about ten miles out in the Sanctuary. The Intruders will call in the buoy's co-ordinates and we'll fire a few dummy rounds from the five-inch guns on the Alamo. I'll be on board to make sure that it's only a few rounds..."

The Superintendent was not impressed. "I can't imagine that the Marine Sanctuary will benefit from this war gaming in the midst of roosts and breeding grounds..."

"The NOAA personnel were *most* co-operative. But let me tell you about the Park's involvement. We will be landing on Rialto Beach with two large inflatable rafts carrying squads of U.S. Marines. The Marines will disappear into the woods. They will lay ambushes for a company of Navy seals, who will assault the beach with an L.C.P. - excuse me, a landing craft for personnel - and negotiate an evening, and night traverse, through the thick woods between Rialto Beach and the Quillayute Airfield...Oh, I almost forgot to tell you, we have permission from Governor Boot for our A-6's to make touch and go landings on the airfield. I suppose the bear and elk of the Park environs, will survive one day of our air traffic..."

"Admiral, C.F.R. - excuse me, Code of Federal Regulations - expressly forbids the carrying or use of weapons in the Park. Unless Congress has published some new law, of which I'm unaware, what you propose is illegal..."

"Excuse *me*, Superintendent. Did I *say* the men would be carrying weapons? They will only have war-gaming guns that discharge a blob of paint..."

"Admiral, excuse me. That's *still* defined as a weapon in C.F.R. In case you haven't been keeping up with current events, there is a boundary dispute with the Quileute Nation involving Rialto Beach. I can't imagine that the tribe will enjoy seeing a Naval assault force landing on a beach that they are claiming is theirs by treaty..."

"Excuse me, Superintendent Donovan, but in case *you* haven't been keeping up with current events, there is a hostage crisis in Iran. I'm not at liberty to discuss what the President may or may not have in mind in terms of rescuing these poor souls; but I can assure you that issues of National Security will always overshadow the interests of a few bird watchers or your imagined sensitivity of the handful of Indians there in LaPush."

"Admiral Bingingham, it's obvious that we will not come to agree on many of the issues here. There is only one relevant issue here. It revolves around the jurisdiction and authority of Olympic National Park. What you propose is within the boundaries of the Park. I am the premier authority within that jurisdiction. By the authority vested in me by Title Six of the Code of Federal Regulations, I prohibit your landing on Rialto Beach in motorized craft. I prohibit the carrying of any projectile throwing device. If your men plan to remain overnight in the woods, they will require an overnight permit, which they can get at the Mora Ranger Station at no charge to the Navy. The overnight group size is limited to twelve individuals including their leaders. Good day, Admiral Bingingham."

The Admiral was gloating. "Before you hang up, please let me get one thing clear, OK? I'm a little confused over the hierarchy in the civilian sector, because lines of authority are so clear in the Navy...but you answer to the Secretary of Interior, isn't that so?"

"Yes, I do."

"And the Secretary of Interior answers to the President of the United States. I believe that's how it works. Anyway, faxed to my office this morning was a copy of a memorandum from the White House to Secretary Luger, and there's some verbiage here that's relevant to our little discussion...oh yeah, here it is. Quote '*It is hereby, with an overbearing sense of duty to the imprisoned citizens in Iran, that I command you to co-operate to the fullest degree with Admiral Bingingham and other personnel of the Thirteenth Fleet, and make whatever administrative adjustments are required to accommodate the training needs of his branch of the Armed Services of the United States,*' end quote. This is signed by George Shrub. Does this have any bearing on our discussion? Am I getting through to you?"

"Yes, Admiral, I hear you."

"Then good day to you, Superintendent." The line in the Superintendent's Office clicked dead, while Admiral Bingingham laughed and congratulated himself in Seattle.

Superintendent Donovan threw the phone across the office and it slammed into the wall next to a large framed poster of the seastacks on the north end of Rialto Beach. The Superintendent slammed shut the office door for privacy from the receptionist/secretary who was standing up to investigate the ruckus. The Superintendent stood helplessly in the middle of the office. The stinging of her eyes predicted imminent precipitation. "Why can't they just leave the Park alone," blubbered Maureen Donovan. *"Why can't the Navy just leave us alone?"*

TWENTY-EIGHT

Sunday, October 25, 1992

*P*atricia Gillette loved the crisp, dry weather that preceded the November monsoons in Seattle. Standing in her small garden, in front of the Gillette's little suburban home, she scratched at the dirt with a hoe. She thought wistfully of her husband, the Navy Lieutenant, who had promised to call her this afternoon with news of when he would be coming home. The garden was her friend at times like this. When she lived on base with her father, the Captain, the Navy had not allowed her to indulge her horticulturist instincts. When she started the garden, her son was only two years old. Her father had called it a 'victory garden,' but Patricia referred to it as her 'peace garden.' The war games of her son, Brian, threatened the perimeter of the garden as he ambushed the neighbor's cat with his Uzi squirt gun, and pursued the fleeing feline into the green sanctuary.

"Brian, stay out of here..." the phone rang and Patricia threw down the hoe. "Just give the cat some peace." She hurried to catch the phone. She squirmed with excitement at the idea of her husband's impending arrival. Maybe he would be calling to have her pick him up...

"Gillette residence," she said breathlessly into the phone.

"Hi, honey. How are you and the little storm trooper?"

Hi, Richard. We...I was working in the peace garden...Are you coming home? Can I pick you up?"

"Um, we got some orders today..."

Patricia's heart took a nose dive. Orders never included the families of the orderee. "What...when..." she sputtered.

"We're going to be held off the Washington Coast for about ten days in a maneuver. I'll be coming home in two weeks, I hope, for..."

"Why...What will you be doing off the coast. Is it dangerous?"

"No, Patricia, it's safe. I promise. It's just a war game. I'd enjoy it if I weren't so lonely for you and Bri."

"Does this mean your company's going to the Persian Gulf?"

"Um, you know I can't divulge that sort of stuff, but...maybe."

"Richard, if you go to Iran, you might not come back alive. If you do come back alive, you might come back to find Brian and I are not waiting for you anymore. I'm really tired of all this waiting. I love you with all my heart, Richard, but I love a

199

man. Not a family picture in our living room or a voice on the phone. I want you, Richard. Is there something wrong with that? I don't even go along with this Iran thing. How the hell do they expect the American public to believe that the Navy can't recognize an air bus with all the equipment they have aboard those ships over there..."

"Patricia, honey, there could have been anything in those two air busses. They were flying over United States ships..."

"It's Iranian air space! I'm telling you, Richard, I'm not buying this. It's your personal and professional decision, about whether you buy it or not, but it's *my* personal decision about whether I'm going to continue putzing around in the garden while the U.S. Navy kills people in their attack on windmills clear on the other side of the globe..."

"Patricia, please. I've been with the Navy for twelve years. I was in the Navy when we got married. You're a Navy brat, for crying out loud! I haven't changed. Your dad hasn't changed. Just let me do what I was doing when you said 'I do', for another eight years. Eight years, and I'll do anything you want. With my pension, we can both work in your garden all day. Eight years is nothing! It was yesterday that Brian was born, and that was eight years ago..."

"Eight years is eight years, Richard! If I didn't love you so much, it would be easy. But I feel...so vulnerable. I just *want* the man I married..."

"Patricia, I'm sorry, but there's a line behind me. I've got to go..."

"Can I drive out with Brian to Bremerton before your ship leaves? I'd like to at least have lunch with you."

"I can't tell you where we're stationed. I've got to go. I love you, Patricia. Tell Brian 'hi.' (Click.)

Patricia put down the phone, opened the screen door and walked back into her little garden. She had trouble seeing the hoe through her tears and stepped on the blade. The handle popped up and slammed into her knee.

"What's wrong, Mommy?" young Brian's feline pacification program was interrupted by a security problem in the executive branch of his government. His mother was crying.

"It's OK Brian. Mommy just got whacked by the hoe."

****

200

Smith Field, Olympic National Park

In the crisp, dry October weather, Ranger Ed Whitman's feet made little crunching sounds on the fallen leaves under the trees along the Quillayute River. There had been a late summer and fall migration of Indians from all over the country to LaPush. The ninety to a hundred Natives gathered out in Smith Field with fifty dogs was the strangest sight that the Ranger had seen in almost 17 years of prowling the Park's boundary. It would smell fishy if there were any smell buds left in the ranger's reconstructed nose. The Indians appeared to be working the dogs on protection work. Little Cockerpoos and Peekamutts hanging off the padded arms of mock assailants like they were Rottweilers. Then the group went into formation and half of the Natives charged about fifty feed-bag manikins that were set up in a row. While the dogs pulled straw out of the ass end of the feed bags, the men removed two by fours, which might have been dummy weapons, from the grasp of the manikins. It was bizarre!

They gathered around a flip chart, as they had four months ago, and the tall Native who had then presided addressed the group.

At four hundred yards, Whitman could only guess what strange things were being said. The ranger held his binoculars to his eyes and moved between two alders for a better vantage.

Clarence Fourskins spoke to the assembled warriors, "These dogs are all that stand between many of you, and a bayonet in the throat. You've probably figured out the personal risk of what we're doing here. We will take casualties, and that's part of the plan. I believe that we can win a skirmish; and embarrass the hell out of the U.S. Army. But to keep the government from coming at us with every military resource at their command, and wiping LaPush off the map, we need to use the media to establish that the U.S. is the aggressor in this conflict. That's why there are so many rules about when and how you neutralize the enemy. The staging of the skirmish is more important than the military tactics that carry the battle. It's why we won't carry weapons into the skirmish. Any shooting at troops must be done with M-16's with government ammunition. Like our ancestors, our blood will soak the battlefield. But, unlike our forefathers, we have a strategy. We have a plan. We have a large network of allies. Take a hundred twigs and you can break them easily between your fingers, one at a time. Now take the same number of twigs in a bundle..."

As Ranger Whitman moved, looking at the world through the binoculars, he stepped on a small branch and it broke with a loud snap. This startled Whitman, but also a grouse within fifteen feet of the prowling ranger. The bird, in turn, took flight with a loud flutter and distracted the canine contingent of Fourskins' audience.

John Pinn spoke up over the barking mutts, "Something frightened the bird. Grouse are dumber and lazier than a southern Senator. They don't fly unless they're scared into it."

Fourskins turned to see the grouse fly out into the meadow. "Go check it out please, Lieutenant Pinn." The red behemoth lumbered off in the direction of the distressed grouse with a tiny yapping dog on the end of his leash. Pinn growled at the small dog. The canine immediately fell silent.

From behind the tree, Whitman tried to pick a course of action from the gloomy alternatives before him. Regardless of his authority and jurisdiction, direct confrontation seemed inadvisable given the mysterious, and sinister, appearance of what was going on in the field. Scratch that option; sniff out another. He could come out from behind the tree, pulling up his pants, like he had been taking a crap. He would pretend to be surprised and delighted to meet the red gorilla and his bimbo dog. Then he would get picked up, and carried back to main body of Indians, and probably replace one of the feed bags. Scratch that, as well. He could blow his cover and make for the canoe. That would make him look ridiculous, and perhaps a bounty would go out on his expensive and funny looking reconstructed nose. That might work. Or the default option: wait behind the tree hoping that King Kong and Trixie would give up the search.

John Pinn and the dog named 'Little Bighorn' advanced on Whitman's position on an unerring course. With a bounding crash, Ranger Whitman gave up on the concealment of the tree and revealed his retreat to the Indians. Pinn turned around for instruction. Clarence Fourskins made a cutting motion of his left wrist with his open right hand in an agreed upon message: *Release dog and give 'attack' command.* Pinn hit the quick release at the end of the leash, and gave the word to Little Bighorn. "Go!" commanded Pinn and the little dog streaked after Whitman like lightning chasing the mountain. "Go!" said forty-eight other dog handlers hitting quick releases. A growling, snarling tsunami washed across Smith Field toward the river where the Ranger struggled to launch his canoe.

The little hound of Pinn's hit the ranger in the right buttock as he bent over with his hands on either gunwale of the aluminum canoe. "Jesus Christ!" shrieked Whitman, standing up with the dog hanging off of him. The ranger tried pulling on the dog's dangling legs; but its jaws were set like a Pit-Bull's. Whitman pulled out his Mace, which he was told worked on dogs. He began trying to spray the dog's face which was buried in the ranger's pants. Above the dog's snarling, Whitman heard the din of the charging pack and began to panic. He considered trying to paddle back with Cujo chewing his ass, but what if he finished the main course and moved into Whitman's crotch for dessert? Whitman ran into the water carrying his Mace. He stood up to his waist for about two seconds before the dog paddled to the surface and tried to secure one of Whitman's arms for a second course. The ranger discharged the Mace directly in the dog's face and scrambled out of the water. He again tried to launch the canoe, but the little dog came out of the water right after him. This time he got hold of the ranger's ankle.

The ranger drew his service revolver. He tried to hold up his foot to shoot the dog off. As he squinted down the gun, his foot came dizzily in and out of the sight picture. Forty-eight dogs broke over the bank like a wave. The ranger again shrieked. He threw his service revolver into the canoe, and pushed off with the little dog hanging off his leg. He paddled for his life, ignoring his passenger who was chewing his way up the ranger's leg. The canine pack hit the water and continued the charge, dog paddling. They were gaining on the canoe. The little dog had worked his way up to the ranger's thigh, and the more fleet canines had caught up to the canoe. They were threatening to turn it over as they attempted to come aboard to join the attack.

John Pinn, stood on the bank next to Clarence Fourskins and Jeff Sparks as they watched the struggle. The Native flower child, James Crow, was shouting, "Call back the dogs! The ranger's hurt! Call it off!" Ninety-three other winded Natives stood in the trees along the shore and saw panic work against an agent of the United States government. Whitman recovered his service revolver. He pushed it into the flesh of the dog that seemed surgically attached to his thigh. He pulled the trigger. Finally, the dog let go. He picked up the twitching, snarling, dying, dog and threw it into the water. The bottom of the canoe was filling up with bloody water. Whitman realized that he had shot a hole through the bottom of the boat. A big dog was pulling down the upstream gunwale with his front paws; and trying to get his rear paw up to enter the canoe. Whitman broke his paddle on the dog's head. Whitman stood up in the sinking canoe to assess his situation, and almost fell out. He fired five more rounds at the canine piranhas, hitting nothing but water. He re-holstered an empty weapon, forgetting about the other twelve rounds on his equipment belt. The water was three inches from the gunwales. It would be over in a minute.

"Call off the dogs!" ordered Clarence Fourskins and forty-nine handlers began retrieving their canine minions. "Sand Creek, COME!" "Crazy Horse, COME!" "COME, Wounded Knee!" Somehow the dogs heard their new names. And the command and voice of their master...the only key that would turn off their attack instinct, besides a bullet in the head. The dogs came bounding out of the water, running to their respective masters, and shaking the river from their hair, as they were praised for their obedience. John Pinn was left alone on the shore, "Little Bighorn, COME! COME! Little Bighorn..."

"It's no use, John. Didn't you see what happened? It's too bad. You were really having success with that dog. It's too late to retrain another one." When Pinn finally turned away from the river, Fourskins was surprised to see tears on the big ape's cheeks.

Jeff Sparks came down to the river to join the two men. As they watched, Ranger Whitman disappeared into the cold, spring-fed slough that led to Mora. He swam like the devil was chasing him. "He'll go straight to the FBI with this," remarked Sparks dismally. Why didn't you let the dogs finish it?"

Clarence Fourskins spoke quietly. "The dogs wanted to do it. I have in mind the privilege going to someone who needs first blood more than that howling pack."

As Fourskins outlined a diabolical plan to Jeff Sparks, John Pinn walked away in disgust. He walked along the river looking for his wounded dog. As the big

Indian searched, the lifeless body of Little Bighorn rolled along the river bottom into the estuary leading to James Island.

****

Ranger Whitman dialed the phone number from his field notebook. He bent over exposing his naked and bleeding rear end to his wife's ministrations. Carol, unnerved by the site of blood, laughed nervously at his posture. His wife was saying, "I can't do anything but disinfect it honey. You need a bunch of stitches." Simultaneously, he was getting a recorded message from that twirpy little spook, Fred Prue, "You have reached 206-369-2468. There's no one in the office to take your call right now. If it's an emergency call 202..." Whitman slammed down the phone in disgust. '202' was the area code for Washington, D.C. Like someone there is going to want to know about a pack of man-eating dogs in LaPush!

Whitman tried to call his supervisor at home; but the phone just rung while the District Ranger enjoyed his day away from the intrusions of the Park staff. Ranger Whitman went to get a pillow off his side of the bed and went outside to put it on the driver's seat of the white Suburban with the light bar on top. His wife called out to him, "Let me drive you to the hospital, Ed. You'll just get yourself bleeding again."

"I'm OK and if I'm going to bleed, I'd rather do it in the government rig. Stitching up my ass is official business. I'm not using our gas to get to and from the emergency room. Call the hospital and let them know I'm coming." Whitman made an effort at humor. "They took tissue from my ass to build this nose. Tell them, they'll need to take skin back off my nose to rebuild my ass!" With that, Whitman drove off, without so much as a kiss to Carol or a goodbye to his kids.

****

James Crow had been somewhat confused after the training, when Jeff Sparks asked him to come along with him to the hospital to check on Ed Whitman. They drove to the hospital and found the ranger rig parked within easy limping distance to the emergency entrance. Jeff parked the Valiant where he had parked it for the rescue of Timothy Gable. Sparks did not get out of the vehicle to go into the hospital. He preoccupied himself with a Sign Wave Ratio meter testing his jamming gear. He was not communicative. James sat in silence, brooding about the ugly turn of events...all the injuries that were popping up. James was beginning to suspect that people close to him had been involved with sending Ranger Whitman the letter bomb that took his nose. He wondered if poor Mark's loss of his hands was the accident it seemed to be. With his own eyes, Crow had seen dogs, under the control of the Movement tear the Ranger's flesh; if they hadn't come to check on the condition of the victim, then what were they doing here? James also sat in silence.

In time, Ed Whitman exited the hospital's emergency entrance. He limped to his vehicle. He pulled out onto Bogachiel Way. He drove the half mile east to Highway 101. Instead of making a left, to return to Mora, the vehicle made a right and an immediate left, into the Pay 'n' Save parking lot. So, Ranger Whitman was going grocery shopping in an official government rig, observed Sparks. Strategically, this could work out really well! Sparks parked the Valiant on the north side of the grocery store. This was the entrance used by the distributors that brought the sprayed produce; processed, poisoned and over packaged frozen food; beer and wine fizz; animal carcasses; and other delectables. Sparks dialed up KLLM, the local country F.M. station. He threw a toggle switch at the bottom of his dashboard. The whining voice and twanging guitar were stripped from the carrier signal at 103,900,000 cycles per second. Sparks shut off the radio. He said to James Crow, "Let's go pay our respects to the Ranger." As they entered the service door, Sparks wrote a note about going to LaPush, on a cardboard box with a magic marker.

Ed Whitman was shopping for ice cream and a video for the kids. He picked up a couple of dish towels for his wife, because he was feeling a certain guilt. He had been gruff with her as she bent over tenderly to minister to his naked and bleeding buttocks. For himself, he searched for a six pack of ale - strictly for medicinal purposes. His ass was sore, but he was feeling the exhilaration of a man who has been kissed by danger, but returns faithfully to wife and home. As he examined the selection of ale, he was wondering how the stitches and soreness in his derriere would complicate his sex life. Whitman was pulled from his reverie by a conversation that he overheard from a man coming up the aisle behind him. The man said, "Have you seen Whitman's nose lately? It's got a hook to it just like a Chinook salmon. I tell ya, Scritch, next week we'll send him a jack-o-lantern with a bomb in it...just cut a hole in the top big enough for him to get his head in and, after it goes off, feed the leftovers to the dogs..."

"What did you call me? Don't talk so loud! There he is..."

Ed Whitman turned around to confront the men, who had painted the inside of the ranger station with his nose. It was Jeff Sparks - no surprise there - but, with him, was the runner, that goody two shoes, James Crow. He was some kind of chemist, so it all made sense! "Gentlemen! I would like to talk to you," said Whitman advancing on the pair.

"Good afternoon, Ranger Whitman," said Crow, holding out his hand as if he was greeting an old friend. "I saw what happened with the dogs earlier and I'm sorry..." Jeff Sparks was pulling him by the arm down the aisle and out of Whitman's sight.

The ranger abandoned the shopping cart and ran to the store's entrance by the coffee shop, where he expected to cut off the fugitives. He didn't quite have a plan, but anger was egging him on. His defensive equipment and radio were out in the Suburban. He couldn't exactly expect these two felons to cheerfully follow him to jail...though he almost thought Crow might. He needed backup. Without taking his eyes off the store's entrance he walked backwards across the parking lot to the Suburban. He opened the vehicle's door, started the engine and called to dispatch in Port Angeles. No answer there, so he tried to reach the Sheriff's office, who monitored the park frequency. No answer. He tried to call his wife at Mora. No answer. Hell, the wise guys who blew off his nose would get away. Whitman ran back into the store with his defensive gear on under his coat. He searched every aisle, but they were not in the store. He checked the side service entrance. Out where the delivery trucks park was a large cardboard box. It read, *Don't split your stitches, man, but Snatch and Scriff have split to LaPush.*

Ed Whitman limped, and ran, past the pay phone across from the coffee shop. He jumped into the Suburban. He winced in pain as his rear end landed on the hard bench seat. He activated his emergency lights and tore out of the parking lot, barely slowing down; hitting his siren, to run the only stop light in town. His tires squealed a mile north of town, as he made a sharp left turn onto the LaPush/Mora Road. He caught up with the Valiant at the Bogachiel Bridge, just beyond Three Rivers Resort. He was not sure what vehicle Sparks drove, but he saw James Crow turn around in the seat and wave at him. Whitman again hit his siren and motioned for the Valiant to pull over. The Ranger was motor mouthing on his microphone, transmitting into the ether, "Any receiving unit, this is Ranger Whitman in hot pursuit, two fleeing felons...driving a Valiant four door, Washington tag, Sierra Delta India Niner One One, please acknowledge..."

One hundred and twenty feet ahead of Whitman's Suburban, the two Natives argued in the Valiant. Crow sensed that things were getting out of hand. He had no idea what was going through Sparks' head, that he would deliberately subject the Ranger to verbal abuse, and invite this dangerous chase into LaPush. "He wants us to pull over," announced Crow to Jeff Sparks, who was driving down the middle of the bridge to keep Whitman from pulling abreast or ahead.

"Gee, is that so?" Sparks feigned astonishment. He picked up his CB microphone and broadcast on channel 40, "Rebel base, this is Johnny Ohm."

The CB answered, "This is Rebel base."

"I'm coming home with the bacon. E.T.A. is eight minutes. I should bring it right into the kitchen. In case I stumble with the bags, better send out a couple of boys to help deliver the groceries."

"Help is on the way. Look for a blue Datsun pick-up. Rebel base clear."

Everything was going Jeff Sparks' way except this blithering idiot, Crow, who wanted to stop and rap with the nice ranger. Also, it would be nice if Whitman would turn off his emergency lights and quit drawing such attention from any oncoming traffic they might pass. "Look it, James, Whitman thinks that you are the guy that blew off his nose. He wants to arrest you. We can't let him catch us here. Under your seat is kind of a ray gun that will screw up his electronics. Pull it out, plug it into the cigarette lighter, and after the strobe is charged, aim it at the front of his rig and pull the trigger."

"This won't hurt him will it?" asked Crow, complying with the instructions.

"Naw, , it'll just slow him down and turn off his lights. I swear. The high pitched whine stopped, and Crow pulled the trigger while sighting down the instrument. In the rear view mirror, Sparks saw the red and blues, and headlights of the Suburban dim. "Good shot, James!" Whitman hit his siren again. The Suburban's engine coughed, and the vehicle fell back. Whitman had had electrical problems before in his own vehicles. He knew how to read an idiot light. He put his foot to the floor with the accelerator and looked down to cut off the lights, the radio, the light bar. When he brought his eyes back on the road he was about to run into the back of the Valiant. Before he could get his foot to the brake he crashed onto the white sedan and the trunk flew open. "Christ, the crazy fuck rammed us!" Sparks saw a blue Datsun pick-up approaching, and pulled over to the right. He engaged his right turn signal and as he passed the oncoming blue pick-up Sparks stuck his arm out the window; signaling that he was pulling over.

Ranger Whitman was pretty worked up and approached the driver's side of the white Valiant with his service revolver in his hand. "Both of you stick your hands out of the vehicle where I can see them!"

"I don't think that will be necessary," came the soft spoken voice behind him accompanied by what he recognized, from his training and experience as a law enforcement officer, to be the muzzle of a large caliber carbine pressed into the back of his head. He froze as a large arm stretched out and removed the weapon from his grasp. He yielded as his arms were folded behind him; his wrists slapped into the cuffs removed from his own belt. Duct tape was placed over his mouth and eyes and some kind of giant picked him up, and threw him into the Valiant trunk. Ranger Whitman banged his head on some of the electrical equipment that shared the cramped space with him and a spare tire. For the next hour his was the nightmare of uncertainty. *I never even kissed the wife and kids goodbye.*

James Crow faced a different hideous nightmare. The Suburban and Valiant, along with its cargo, had been secreted in the garage identified by a small sign as *Sparks' Auto Body*. The grinders, body putty and paint were still on the counters to attest to the innocent purpose of this shop, while locked cupboards and hidden closets concealed the current function of the laboratory. As he stood outside the shop with Pinn and Fourskins, Sparks was explaining, "I'm really sorry it's come to this, James, but you have to take him out."

"There's no reason to harm him and **I'm no murderer!**"

"He's a liability," said Fourskins. "He just keeps intruding into our operations. There's no telling what he knows."

"He's just doing his job," argued James. "If anybody touches him, I'm going to the cops. This is supposed to be a bloodless revolution, remember?"

"James, I never said that it would be bloodless. I said that we would have to depend on cunning more than force to win our cause. This man strongly interferes with our artifice which means more people will have to die if he goes on unchecked."

207

"I'll do him," offers John Pinn. "It doesn't bother me one way or the other."

"Stay out of this, John," ordered Fourskins.

"Look, James. This *has* to be done," argued Sparks. "Here's the keys to the Valiant's trunk. Here's a knife. Cut from one side of the throat to the other. You should see the carotids spurt. Reach into his throat and pull out the tube in front, which is the trachea. Make sure that's cut, too. When there's no air moving back and forth, he's dead or close enough. Ranger Whitman is not leaving here alive. If you don't off him, we'll have to figure out a way to get both of you in the trunk."

A lie for a lie, a truth for a truth..., thought James Crow as he entered the garage. "I'LL DO THIS ALONE!" he roared at Sparks, chasing the man out of his own shop. He placed the knife and keys on the stainless steel table and prayed. After a few minutes of prayer and consideration, he knew he would have to spill blood to come out of this alive.

****

Fifteen minutes later, Fourskins and Sparks were talking about how to get rid of the Suburban. It would have to be disassembled and disposed of in multiple trips. Certainly the village would be crawling with FBI, trying to figure out the whereabouts of the missing federal employee. The security they lost by the FBI intrusion would be offset by having the nosy ranger out of the picture.

There were going to be some really unpleasant loose ends if Whitman had called anyone on the phone before initiating the chase. They would have to do some careful sanitizing of evidence. They were avoiding the conversation they both knew they should be having: what would they do if Crow would not submit to their orders? They were surprised to see the garage door go up. They saw the Valiant roll forward with James Crow at the wheel.

"Just a second," called Sparks. "Who gave you permission to drive my limousine? You don't even have a driver's license."

"The same Authority that made me take a life allows me to dispose of Whitman as I see fit."

"Getting rid of a stiff is a delicate thing, James. You'd better let us take care of it. Let's examine your work." Jeff Sparks held out his hands for the keys. Before surrendering the keys, James looked long and hard into Jeff's face, and into the stony face of Clarence Fourskins.

"We are no longer friends. We share no values or purpose. The voices that asked me to take Ranger Whitman's life cannot be heard by God." James Crow at last gave over the keys, remaining in the driver's seat. Sparks shrugged and went back to open the trunk. Fourskins nodded to John Pinn who stood by with a shotgun. Pinn leveled the weapon at the trunk. Sparks threw open the trunk, and got out of the line of fire.

"It's OK," called Fourskins. "James did his work." Sparks came back and saw that the Ranger was still handcuffed and taped. There was blood everywhere in the trunk. The visible and severed ends of the trachea protruded from the swollen and bloody cavity of Whitman's throat. There was no sound, or bubbles issuing from the puddled gore.

"OK!" said Sparks cheerfully, returning to congratulate Crow. "Move over, I'll drive."

"I said, 'The same *Authority* that ordered the taking of life allows me to dispose of Whitman.'" Crow would not move out of the driver's seat. Sparks began to think of the possibilities. If Whitman had been able to tip anyone off regarding the hot pursuit, they would be looking for the Valiant. Better to let the born-again executioner get caught alone with the corpis delecti.

"OK, killer. Good job. Take Whitman out and hide him so he won't be found. At least for a week. After that, it won't make any difference."

"I'll do that," said James Crow. "I swear to God Almighty, I will." He drove, lurchingly, out the LaPush Road, operating a motor vehicle for the first time in his life.

TWENTY-NINE

<u>**USS Alamo**</u>
<u>**Thursday, November 5, 1992, 14:25 hours**</u>

*L*ieutenant Richard Gillette's heart was flooded with anxiety and distress. As the gate valves opened at the stern of the Alamo, the <u>L</u>anding <u>C</u>raft <u>U</u>tility began to pitch around on the floor of the huge carrier. Usually a beach assault of this sort would be aboard a smaller <u>L</u>anding <u>C</u>raft <u>P</u>ersonnel; but the 22-foot swells and gale warnings dictated the larger, more stable craft. It seemed like one hell of a training stunt to risk the lives of a whole company. The LCU's inboard engine fired up. On either side of the steel craft, outboards were started from two 20-foot inflatable chase boats. The Marines aboard the inflatables hooted like wild Indians. They un-holstered their paint-pellet guns to wave them about in the manner of boys anticipating a backyard war game.

As the huge stern doors of the <u>L</u>anding <u>P</u>latform <u>D</u>ock, Alamo, swung open, the men instinctively pulled at the straps of their personal flotation devices. They checked the waterproof zippers of their gear bags and immersion suits. The ocean was Gillette's ally. In the course of his military career, Gillette had been up against so many dangers that it seemed strange that an impending war game, regardless of the accompanying environmental conditions, should awaken in him such a deep sense of foreboding. The three craft powered out of the huge L.P.D. They pitched wildly around in the tumultuous seas. Somehow, the pilots managed to control the crafts through the chop, while motor mouthing among themselves and the mother ship, on their citizen-band radios. Military protocol prohibited the use of their VHF units for the kind of banter and language attending such an excursion into twenty-foot swells.

"These swells don't have a break line so keep your compass at forty-five degrees. Or you'll get flushed down in the Pacific toilet bowl like the turds you are," Ensign Pierce, the LCU pilot advised the skippers of the two Zodiacs. "If you have to land north of Ellen Creek, stay away from those rocks around Hole-In-The-Wall or you'll end up with a hole in your ass...besides your sex window, I mean..."

"LCU One, this is Alamo," the VHF set interrupted the pilot in his admonishments to the marines. "How do you copy?"

The pilot picked up the Motorola microphone with his right hand, while he held the CB mike in his left. He steered the landing craft through the towering seas with his knees. "Alamo, you are <u>L</u>ima, <u>C</u>harley," which is how the military takes four syllables to express what could be said as "loud, clear."

"Roger, LCU One. We may lose you on radar, through the chop. Activate your <u>E</u>mergency <u>L</u>ocating <u>D</u>evice so that we can pin point your lo...." the VHF cut off in mid-sentence.

The pilot called over his shoulder, "Lieutenant, Alamo wants our E.L.T. on!" Gillette stood up and was steadied by his men as he threw the toggle on the orange box of electronics, which broadcast a signal of the craft's location. The pilot said over his VHF mike, "Alamo, LCU One. Willco ELT. You cut off. Repeat last." Nothing but a hum emanated from the short-wave set.

"Pierce, this is the Alamo. You copy on CB?" The pilot put up the Motorola mike and said into his CB mike, "Yeah. You're loud and clear as a fart in church."

"This is the Alamo radio room. We're experiencing radio and radar problems...must be a big sun spot. Check your Loran reading."

"It's zeroed out," reported the pilot. "Loran is down...wait! It just came back on. Reading is..."

****

From on top of James Island, Wally Woodrift, could not see his target. He stretched his gaze to the northwest, across the fog and spray of the roiling Pacific. A hundred feet below him, a raven flew north along Rialto Beach toward Ellen Creek. In the diffuse light of the stormy day, the sleek back of the bird turned from black to white and refracted light like the wings of an angel. He threw off the toggle switch which jammed all frequency modulated radio waves within a fifty-mile radius of LaPush. He briefly studied the picture on his laptop screen. He saw the big dot representing the LCU, and the two small dots which might be Zodiacs, or LCP's coming toward a diagonal line across the lower left quarter of the screen. The line represented the firing range of a LAW rocket. He pointed the launching stock of the LAW to which the traffic radar antenna was also attached to the horizon. He scanned watching the screen. He pressed the F-3 key on the laptop and watched a picture of the horizon on the screen. There was the low profile of a Zodiac, which disappeared behind the pitching surf on the screen. Woodrift scanned a little to the east and there was the LCU target! The target was big enough to hit, even with the big swells. He turned the jam back on. The target would be visible by the time it came into range.

****

In the five minutes that the radio was jammed three separate teams of Natives stormed the United States Coast Guard Station in LaPush. The point man of each five-man team carried a shotgun, while two or three carried assault rifles or M-16's. Unarmed Natives followed with duct tape. The guns were intended only as a compliance tool, since the Coast Guard weapons were all locked away in the magazine of the station. Clarence Fourskins came in the front door. He first secured the radio room. He pointed his shotgun at the Ensign's head, and yelled, "Everyone! Face down on the floor, palms up! Do it NOW!"

It took the Coasties just a minute to realize that the Natives with shotguns, and assault rifles were not trick or treating. Once the seriousness of the situation was perceived the men went onto their faces like corn through a combine. The unarmed Natives grabbed the down men by the wrists, binding their hands behind their backs with duct tape. The second team went through an emergency exit checking the dormitory rooms. The third team rounded up the officers in their offices. Five minutes after entry, the station was secured by the assault force. In the Communications Room, the radios came briefly to life with several commercial fishing boats complaining about the interruption to Loran, and FM radio traffic.

A citizen lay on the floor of the room wearing a plaster cast. He cursed his bad luck. The radio technician, Ron Richland, considered the irony of it: the crazy red bastard, John Pinn, had gotten out of jail, before Richland had gotten out of his cast. Now Pinn was some kind of deputy in a posse of crazy Comanches. Pinn straddled the civilian, and taped his good hand through his belt.

"Keep your teeth in your mouth, and your mouth shut, and no one will get bit," growled Pinn to Richland in a rare display of wit.

****

Only the choker-setters and riggers are working today. In the Pacific Northwest, the winds are what they are, when winter collides with and overruns summer. While the other bushlers watch reruns of "I Love Lucy" on TV, the winds of winter don a hard hat and dump trees throughout the forest. It's taken all day just to run out the back haul and skylines to pull out the one cedar that John Pinn felled yesterday. Two trees along the cut-line blew over this morning next to some of your co-workers, exciting the choker-setters, who narrowly avoided calamity. Before noon the main hydraulic pump on the logging tower blows out a seal. The logging show comes to a grinding halt. The VHF talkie-tooters are also on the fritz.

Rod has brought his .224 caliber carbine to work with the idea of doing a little deer hunting during lunch break. He is arguing with the driver of the crummy, who replaced Jimmy Shamuck, who had drowned in Lake Crescent. "You can't pull out just yet! I saw that five point this morning, and I know where he's bedding down. That's where he'll be laying out this storm. It'll only take a me half an hour, and I'll give you his pecker. Just half an hour..."

"Take all the time you want, Tarzan. We're leaving now. Save the deer's pecker for your wife. She'll know what to do with it." The new driver was getting the hang of things. " See you tomorrow."

The unhappy hunter climbs into the back of the crummy and pulls out the magazine from his carbine. "You insensitive fuck! I ought to leave the deer alone and cut off your pecker..." The two men exchange insults, as the crummy rolls down the mountainside.

I began to overhear strange conversation on the citizen band radio. It sounds like they're boats in trouble.

****

213

Trying to land in this surf was insanity! The three craft had been pushed too far to the north by the wind and current. They were in danger of running into the shoals around Hole-In-The-Wall. The VHF, Loran and E.L.T. were all down. Gillette had gotten on the CB to ask for verification of orders to attempt the landing under these conditions. The three craft had adjusted their heading to 85 degrees. The Zodiacs were pitching violently. Bravado had been replaced by fear in the voices of the two Marine pilots, who communicated their concern for the safety of their men to Ensign Pierce and Alamo Base. "We're wide open to these breakers on this heading!" came the distressed voice on the CB "If a wave breaks on us, we'll roll for sure! We need to change heading to two, two, two so we can face the breakers...Hold it! Hold on! Jesus, the wave got us...ruptured our starboard flotation. Mayday, Jesus, Mayday! We're going down..."

****

Wally Woodrift had turned off the jam at one point to study the weapon range finding of the Tank brain connected to the laptop. The three craft were skirting the beyond-range-line on the screen. Wally turned the radio jam back on. His screen went blank. In a few minutes, on their present heading, the craft would come into range. A wave broke on one of the Zodiacs. Clearly, it was swamped and in trouble. A second wave rolled the craft. In the distance, Woodrift could make out a dozen or so orange dots, with twinkling lights, surrounding the bobbing upside-down raft. Woodrift recognized the dots as men in immersion suits, struggling for their lives in the stormy surf. The flashing lights emanated from the salt-activated strobe lights on their life jackets. A wave of sympathy broke over Woodrift's conscience. His mouth was dry. He felt queasy as he toggled off the jam and again checked the F1 "chart" of the target. Only two dots were visible as the swamped Zodiac was not high enough in profile to reflect the radar beam. Both dots were within the range line. The small dot kept blinking as the giant waves obscured the surviving raft. On the screen, the blinking dot went out. Woodrift looked up from the screen and out across the turbulent expanse of tossing seas. The second raft had run amok. Twenty more fireflies bobbed in the surf.

Two out of three down, reflected Woodrift. There's almost no need for the high-tech attack. Just let the swimmers war it out with Nature.

Wally hit the F3 button and watched, through the cross hairs of a sight picture, the profile of the LCU pitched on the horizon. He counted the seconds between maximum wave shielding and total exposure of the target. He would have to place the round close to the water line to sink the large craft. He counted and he squeezed the trigger. The Light Artillery Weapon whooshed off.

****

The two crusty loggers stop arguing about deer and each others penises to give the interesting traffic on the CB their full attention. *"Alamo, this is Pierce! The other Zodiac got swamped! We'll idle down, keeping a heading of two, two, two and try to pick up swimmers...(GABOOOM!)...WE'RE HIT! An explosion and fire on board! We're going down! LCU is burning and going down. We have injured in the water..."* All I can think of is the naval carrier I saw at anchor yesterday across from LaPush.

"That's happening on Rialto Beach," I announce to the audience of the CB traffic.

The argument about deer hunting is put on hold. "Let's go down there, no shit!" yells Rod, ever willing to divert the homebound crummy to a field trip. "Maybe we can help those poor drowning sons of bitches and there'll be all kinds of juicy shit washing up on the beach! I mean it now. Let's go!"

****

Behind the glass of the wheelhouse of the Alamo, Admiral Bingingham looked grimly at the arch of blue smoke leading from James Island to where they had seen the explosion, and fire, before the LCU had sunk into the frothy brine of the Pacific. "Who the hell could have fired such a thing? It looked like a LAW rocket for Christ's sake!" The Admiral railed at the Captain. "Fire three phosphorous rounds from our five-inch gun at the top of the island to shake out the hostiles. Don't hit the Coast Guard fog horn facility if you can avoid it. If you can't get any of the VHF radios to work, bring up the Coast Guard on channel 9 on the CB, and have them dispatch a rescue ship from Ediz Hook. Get word to the Joint Chiefs that we've come under attack. Get one of our Hueys up on the flight deck and into the air to pick up our men on the beach or in the water. Go! Don't just stand there with your thumb up your ass, man..."

It would take an hour and a half to get the Navy's twin-engine Bell helicopter on the elevator and onto the flight deck of the L.P.D., to brief the crew, and get them in the air. A lot would change in that 90-some minutes.

****

Lieutenant Gillette and several other Seals were thrown from the LCU by the explosion. The first mouth full of icy cold, salt water revived his level of consciousness. He saw the rest of the men bailing off of the burning craft. What the hell had happened here? From the crest of the wave he could see a dozen to twenty Marines fighting to stay in position of their overturned, and partially deflated Zodiac. The best bet for him and his men would be to get to shore. He heard a crashing sound like the Devil's bowling alley. About 100 meters southeast of their position, Gillette saw a large collection of drift logs thundering together with the passing of every swell. The eddy fence created by Ellen Creek had collected this deadly wooden machine.

He swam over to his men to warn them of the danger. About a dozen of the 70 men in his company had tethered themselves together with leashes attached to their may west life jackets. Strobe lights twinkled everywhere. Gillette addressed a Seal at the end of the daisy chain. "I'm going for shore!" Gillette screamed over the roar of the surf and wind. "If I make it OK, follow me! Otherwise, hold back and wait for the helivac which will be here in less than an hour! Keep away from the driftwood, got it? **Keep away from that God damn driftwood!**" The seal gave the thumbs up to indicate that he understood. Gillette began to dog paddle, and breast stroke, towards the beach. From the crest of a breaker he could see about twenty civilians gathered on the beach. They all carried walking sticks. On the ride up on the next breaker he saw the welcoming committee more clearly. He realized the walking sticks were shotguns and assault rifles.

✳✳✳✳✳✳✳✳✳✳✳✳✳✳✳✳✳✳✳✳✳✳✳✳✳✳✳✳✳

After the five minutes it took to secure the personnel of the Coast Guard Station, a team of Natives moved through the prone men. The job and title of each man was determined in quick, quiet interviews. A boat pilot, and two crewmen, were garnered from the personnel and taken to the radio room which was being used as an interim command post. To the neck of one of the crewmen was taped the muzzle of an 820 Remington shotgun. A Native grasped the stock of the shotgun. He said, "OK, gentlemen. Please no tricks. Let's go down to the cutter. We're going to take a boat ride."

The crewman on the shotgun leash looked at his captor nervously. Amazement momentarily replaced his dread. He knew this Native and had partied down with him several times last summer before the local Native had supposedly perished from drowning in Lake Crescent. "Hello, Gable. I thought you were dead. Where are we going?"

"I was dead, Mike," said Tim Gable cryptically and with dignity. "But now I'm alive. I'd like for us all to stay that way. Please don't you or your friends cross me or your head will beat the rest of you to heaven. You're taking me to Victoria."

✳✳✳✳✳✳✳✳✳✳✳✳✳✳✳✳✳✳✳✳✳✳✳✳✳✳✳✳✳

Ranger Sid Divine arrived at the empty parking lot at Rialto Beach. He got out of the ranger vehicle holding a pair of binoculars. From on top of the driftwood, above the parking lot, he could see a sprinkling of strobe lights out in the surf across from Ellen Creek. Even the Navy Seals weren't crazy enough to be deliberately swimming in the killer surf! Through the binoculars he could see two huddles of men around overturned, and partially deflated Zodiacs. The largest group had no raft but were joined by tether with one another. A column of drift logs had piled up at Ellen Creek. The huge logs were pitching about wildly in the surf. The wind was pushing the logs through the outwashing of Ellen Creek. The swimmers had a greater percentage of their mass in the water. Divine studied the situation. He could perceive the distance narrowing between the killer drift logs, and the men in the water. Ranger Divine attempted to reach headquarters with his portable. Failing contact, he went back to his patrol rig to broadcast off the more powerful 50-watt mobile radio. Still, there was no answer. The radio was as dead as it had been the evening Tim Gable had disappeared from Forks Hospital.

216

Ranger Divine attempted to raise the Coast Guard on emergency channel 9 on his CB "Coast Guard, LaPush, this is Mora Park Service." There was no answer. He tried again and some citizens came on the channel.

"Hey, Park Ranger, this is Soleduck River Logging. We overheard some radio traffic that sounded like there is a Mayday down on Rialto Beach. If you're not too busy counting spotted owls you might want to mosey down there and see if any survivors wash up on the beach. We're heading there ourselves. You get that?"

"This is Mora Park Ranger, I copy." Ranger Divine required instructions from his superiors in how to deal with this curious turn of events. As he started up the engine of his vehicle and began driving out of the parking lot toward the phone at the ranger station, he thought he heard a gun blast. He rolled down his window. Firing any weapons besides their paint pistols, would be a violation of the military's special use permit, and the Superintendent would not like that! As he drove along the park road overlooking James Island and the Quillayute River estuary, he heard a jet engine approaching from the north. There were three enormous reports from the direction of the Alamo. Almost simultaneously, there were three explosions from the top of the island as the white phosphorous rounds impacted. Small trees, from on top of the island, sailed up through the cloud of smoke and fire. Dirt and shards of rock showered into the surf and back onto the island. *Holy shit!*" exclaimed Divine. Though James Island was outside the territorial jurisdiction of Olympic National Park, certainly headquarters would want to know about this strange behavior on the part of the permitee, the U.S. Navy...

****

Lieutenant Gillette rolled up onto the beach in the surf. As the wave pulled at his body on its retreat to sea, he gained his footing and trudged up the steep beach. A group of some twenty Natives stood on the beach hollering, and waving to the Seals still in the water. The Natives pointed to an advancing column of drift logs. Their concern for the safety of his men was a good sign. Three men broke away to accost Gillette. One carried a shotgun, which he trained at the Lieutenant's chest. That was not a good sign.

While the one Native covered the Lieutenant, the other two Natives advanced, flanking him. One of the Natives carried handcuffs; the other carried duct tape. Gillette began backing up, "Hold on. Stay back!" Gillette growled like an old dog with no teeth. He wondered if the men scattered out in the surf would be watching him, and judging his valor. "Freeze, you fuckers!" Gillette yelled, but the Natives continued to advance.

****

As Jeff Sparks covered the Seal with his weapon, he couldn't help but be amused by the man's pluck. He rolls out of a wave like a dead dog shark onto the beach and starts barking orders at three men and a shotgun. "Freeze, yourself, guy. We'll kill you if you don't," said Sparks as his compatriots came at the Seal from either side. Sparks wondered if the men bobbing out in the water could see over the breakers to witness the capture of their vanguard. One Native took the Seal by the wrist. It was like springing a trap. The Seal kicked low at the Native's legs. The man went down. Before the first Native hit the pebbly beach, the Seal had the second by the throat and was using him for cover. Sparks continued to train the shotgun at the target, finger on the trigger. Sparks was trying one last command, "Let go of him and put your hands behind your...," when the crazy Navy fuck shot him in the throat with his paint gun. It hurt like a son of a bitch and, reflexively, Spark's raised his left hand to his throat. He was distracted by the flash of the blood-red paint on his hand. The Seal was coming at him, all Bruce Lee and Chuck Norris. He kicked out wildly with his right foot and connected with the tip of the shotgun, deflecting it. Sparks continued to back up as the Seal spun around and prepared to deliver another round house with his left foot. The Seal's chest appeared for a fraction of a second above the bead of the shotgun sight and Sparks pulled the trigger. The shotgun kicked against his own shoulder, and the left arm and shoulder of the Seal jerked wildly. The Seal hit the beach, rolled and came back on his feet. Bright red blood spurted from his left shoulder. The wounded man clutched at his shredded shoulder and began to run up the beach to the driftwood. His left arm bounced spasmodically as if it were attached only by the rubber of his wet suit. Through the sight picture Sparks watched the Seal clamber up on the driftwood, making for the thicket of coastal forest.

"Shoot the bastard!" yelled the second Native rubbing his throat and helping the first up from the beach gravel.

"I already did," said Sparks. Out of the din of the surf was born a greater roar. The engines of the A-6 Intruder washed like a tidal wave of sound across Rialto Beach engulfing Sparks' words as he continued, "That jungle will swallow him." Sparks watched his two partners collecting themselves after their altercation with the Seal. The bellowing of the jet engines was deafening. The top of James Island erupted in smoke and fire. Instinctively, Sparks ducked as the low flying A-6 roared overhead. He knew the maniacs in the A-6 were flying in very limited visibility with no radar. He was astonished at the disregard they showed for their own safety.

THIRTY

*E*nsigns Jenson and Powers hurtled over Rialto Beach toward James Island in the A-6 Intruder. This was proving to be a very strange afternoon. Almost an hour ago, Powers had announced that their radar screen had gone dead while they were in zero visibility in the vicinity of the Quillayute Airfield. They had climbed to 12,000 feet above most of the clouds. They tried to radio Whidbey Island to announce their situation. There was no contact with Whidbey. They tried in vain to reach the L.P.D. Alamo and the other A-6 in the area. After half an hour of circling, Jenson had spiraled down to 500 feet on his altimeter, and headed east to land. He recognized Cape Flattery. East of here would be Whidbey Island.. But on the intercom, Powers agreed that they should fly south to check on the maneuvers of the Alamo assault force.

Hopping over Hole-in-the-Wall, they could see that all was not right. Two Zodiacs had overturned, and the men were clinging to the partially deflated crafts. The Seals had also lost their LCU. They were dangerously close to a deadly armada of drift logs. A bunch of citizens were on the beach, clutching sticks, and waving ridiculously at the swimming soldiers. One Seal had made it to shore and was clambering down from the drift logs. He was running into the woods...probably to take a crap. As Jenson again tried to radio the Alamo, to announce the distress of the assault force, he could see the muzzle blast and smoke from the five-inch guns on the LPD and two seconds later the top of James Island exploded. The whole summit caught fire in a blaze from the white phosphorous of the incoming signal rounds. "Holy shit!" Powers exclaimed over the intercom, "The Alamo is running berserk! They're a hundred and eighty degrees off in their target identification and they just blew up a friendly installation. There's a Coast Guard facility on top!"

"Unless they had some reason to fire on the target," reasoned Jenson. "Let's check it out." And they rocketed south to the phosphorous glare on top of the rocky cliffs. A citizen was running down the steps from the phosphorous holocaust to a waiting dugout canoe with an outboard. Jenson's view was somewhat challenged by the distance of 100 meters, and speed of 300 knots; but he put the starboard side down as he banked to orbit the burning island. The Native carried what might have been a folded laptop computer, a cordura camera bag, and what looked for all the world like a LAW rocket. The roar of the jet engines stopped the Native as he charged down the steps. He looked up at the Intruder as it came to its perigee with the steps. The pilot pushed up the visor of his helmet. His eyes momentarily locked with the citizen. "Ralph, it's the Indian lover from Second Beach! Remember that Indian bitch's tits?"

The navigator was preoccupied with something else. "Jack, here comes the other Intruder. Port side, coming three, five, zero up First Beach, about 600 feet AGL. They waggled their wings! They see us. Come on to a heading of three, four, zero and get up another 200 feet." The second intruder came along side of Ensign Powers who pointed in the direction of the Alamo. The second pilot, who Powers recognized as Lieutenant Harris, nodded and both A-6's roared off to see what the hell was going on with Admiral Bingingham, and the Alamo.

****

Wally Woodrift had watched in awe as the LCU exploded throwing a few Seals, and then caught fire. He removed the traffic radar antenna from the tube of the expended LAW. He threw the tube into the woods. He watched the twinkling of 70 more emergency strobe lights hitting salt water for a few minutes. The he began pulling wires and packaging up his apparatus. There were no more targets to strike from James Island and the second LAW would come in handy in the forthcoming conflict with the United States Armed Forces. He had come down about eighty of the three hundred steps when he heard the guns fire from the Alamo. The steps rocked and bucked as the phosphorous rounds impacted the island. He could feel the heat on his back as he ran down the steps. He reflected momentarily on the horror of death by fire. Then there was the roar of a low-flying jet plane, and he paused in his flight to watch the craft streak by barely above his head. He could see the aviator push up his visor as the plane banked to go around the island. In that instant, he recognized the pilot and tasted rage rising like bile in his throat. The Intruder continued its arch around the island; then Wally heard the roar of a second jet, rocking LaPush, as it flew north along First Beach. He climbed into the dugout, and fired up the little outboard. He motored back to LaPush. He was still tasting rage as he unloaded his gear onto the dock. From his vantage, he could only hear the jets as they swooped around the Alamo in their blind, deaf, dumb world of no radio/no radar. Burning in Wally's memory was the smirking faces of the A-6 pilot and the navigator, who had humiliated Dorothy and himself six weeks ago on Second Beach. On the next dock over, the 44-foot Coast Guard cutter was casting off. Wally could see Timothy Gable controlling the scene with a Coastie hostage to whom was taped a shotgun. As the cutter motored out of the estuary into the stormy Pacific, Woodrift stooped on the dock, attaching the radar antenna to the second LAW rocket. The jets would return and Wally would have his second target.

****

The Seals were swimming south to keep up with the Marines and stay ahead of the drift logs, both of which were being propelled by the wind. Forty-five Seals were tethered together and arguing about going to shore. Some had seen the Lieutenant shot down. They were disinclined to go up against a Native militia exercising their second amendment rights with shotguns. Some thought that the Seals could defeat the Natives; that the drift logs represented a graver danger; or that those who thought they had seen the Lieutenant shot down were mistaken about what they had seen. The Natives were clearly motioning them to come in, and were making threatening gestures with the weapons. It was a very confusing dilemma and the men hoped that the heli-rescue would get to them before the drift logs. Certainly the Alamo had gotten word of their distress, and the Intruder that had passed overhead a few minutes before would communicate the need to expedite.

****

Jeff Sparks was in charge of this part of the campaign, and things were not going on schedule. Two hundred feet of logging chain, and heavy nylon wiring straps, awaited the taking of an estimated hundred prisoners. But the Marines were hanging onto their popped rafts and the Seals were not coming ashore. In a few minutes the driftwood would be on them, and that would be a hell of a mess! A rescue ship or helicopter would be along soon and the phosphorous blaze from James Island indicated that there would be no more LAW rockets from that position. "Open up on the Seals with your shotguns on my command! That ought to soften up their resolution a bit. Listen up for the 'cease fire!'" Sparks was screaming to be heard over the surf by the twenty-some Natives who shouldered their shotguns. "Ready!" the Natives crouched on their foremost legs, bracing with their trailing legs. "Aim!" the Natives squinted through the grooves on the barrels, taking a bead on the faces of the various bobbing Seals. "Fi...!" and the cacophony of surf and shotgun blasts occluded all human voice on the beach.

****

Ensign Jake Smith has detached himself from the tethered daisy chain of swimmers. Having seen his friend, Richard Gillette, struggle with the Natives and take a shotgun blast at close range, Smith preferred to take his chances swimming. He could see that the driftwood was overtaking the group. He disconnected his tether from the main body of men. He was swimming aggressively toward Hole-in-the-Wall, when he glanced at the Native militia on the beach whom had formed a skirmish line and were shouldering their weapons. Their braced stance made it look like they meant business. All of a sudden smoke issued from the muzzles of the guns; the waves just in front of the Seals were cut by shotgun buck. Smith looked over his shoulder to yell a warning to the main body of his comrades. He saw some terrified faces streaming blood; and some heads falling forward in unconsciousness. The inflatable life vests were popping in the raking shotgun fire. With the flotation of the immersion suits and may wests there was no ducking under water. Smith began to remove the may west, but realized that he would be losing more than he would gain without it. He continued to swim south. But he started to swim back out to sea to try to get out of range. A round of #4 buck caught him in the shoulder, but he continued to swim earnestly, though the ache of the wound, and sting of the salt water in it, were unbearable.

Over the surf and the crashing thuds of the drift logs, he began to hear men screaming. He again looked over his shoulder and saw that the daisy chain had lost momentum by the dead weight of the dead and dying. The drift logs had overtaken them. With the passing of every wave the thundering logs crashed together killing all in their midst. In horror, Smith saw two logs slam together on a man's head. Brains and blood ejaculated four feet into the air. Men tried to climb onto the logs moments before other logs collided against their backs causing such intra-thoracic pressure that pieces of their lungs were expelled from their open mouths. Smith swam with even greater enthusiasm.

****

221

"Cease fire! Cease fire! God-damn-it, cease fire!" Sparks had been yelling at the Natives for several minutes, but everyone kept shooting. The drift logs were on most of the Seals, and if he couldn't get these clowns to stop shooting, there would be no survivors to carry that fucking logging chain back to LaPush. He walked down the line of shooting, and reloading, soldiers and gave each a jab in the kidneys with the butt of his own weapon. One by one, he turned off the shooters.

After the shooting stopped he yelled, "Motion them in!" The Natives again began waving their arms inward, inviting the surviving sailors to come ashore. The resistance was gone out of the Seals. All but the ones who had escaped the range of the shotguns swam for shore and rolled up on the beach. They were arrested and attached to the chain by duct tape and nylon straps. The Zodiacs had come victim to the pounding surf and the Marines washed ashore with less grace than the Seals who drilled regularly in beach assault. A dozen Marines were no longer breathing when they rolled up on the gravel beach. Several were gasping and clearly not ambulatory. Kicking and bludgeoning ministrations of their captors did not make them walk.

Sparks and his militia were behind schedule. Helicopters would be arriving soon. He gathered a total of sixty-two ambulatory prisoners, disarming them of their paint guns. The seriously wounded and dying were left on the beach or in the surf. Sparks began marching the chain of prisoners towards the Quillayute River, where they would use bolt cutters to cut the chain. They would ferry over the prisoners six at a time.

****

Ranger Divine had a hard time convincing the folks at headquarters that he was not either joking or mistaken about the firing on James Island, or the upset of the assault craft. The Chief Ranger had asked him to hold on the phone while he reviewed the terms of the permit, and the provisions for the various contingencies that surrounded such a maneuver. "The Navy insisted that they would remain outside the maritime jurisdiction to fire dummy rounds from the Alamo. The guns must have gone off by accident. If they have men in the water, they will be launching helicopters from the flight deck. They may need to land in the parking lot. If you're having radio problems there, maybe the Navy is, too. We'll call the Coast Guard and take care of the necessary notifications on this end. You'ld better get down there and block off the parking lot so the Navy can use the parking lot for an LZ If you see any of those clowns discharging anything besides a paint pistol, or line gun, get their names, ranks and serial numbers."

As Ranger Divine was putting up the barricades to close the parking lot, he could hear what sounded like several hundred shotgun blasts coming from Ellen Creek. The Navy was totally running amok. First they spill their assault crafts, and now they're using the park for a shotgun range. Damn the Superintendent for letting these monkeys into the park!

Ranger Divine was interrupted from his preoccupation, by the arrival of a crummy load of loggers who wanted to gawk at the spectacle of the Navy raping

Olympic National Park. "Sorry," Divine called to the loggers who disembarked from their vehicle. "We're closing the parking lot due to emergency operations!"

"Well, that's a fine how-do-you-do!" exclaimed one of the loggers who must have featured himself as the group's spokesman. "We report the shipwrecked sailors, and as a reward, we can't come into *our* Park! What's all the smoke and fire on the island?"

"Listen, guys...gentlemen, I don't have time for this. There are going to be helicopters landing in this parking lot and we don't need a bunch of tin hats blowing into the props. The parking lot's closed!"

"Can we park here and walk in?" piped up some long-haired dude. "What caused the fire on James Island?"

The Ranger ignored the latter. "The parking lot is closed. Period! You can't drive in, bike in, ride in on your horse, or roll your wheel chair in..."

"But you can come in by helicopter, right?..." the older one was starting in again on the beleaguered Ranger. Jet engines rumbled out over the Pacific. "...or jet?"

"Give me a break! It's an emergency. Cross this line and I'll put you under arrest. Got it?"

"We'll just wait here," said the hippie. "If you need any help, call on us." The Ranger glared at the long hair until the innocence of the young man's expression convinced him that there was no offense intended.

"Just don't cross the line!" The Ranger turned and strode across the parking lot.

Perched on the drift wood again with the binoculars; Ranger Divine saw a column of sailors in immersion suits marching south along the beach from Ellen Creek. Men with what looked like shotguns walked on either side of the column. Now there was no doubt that the Navy was illegally discharging weapons in the Park. Divine went back to his Suburban to get a tablet of paper to collect all the names and concomitant information that his employer would find necessary to process their complaint against the Navy.

"Getting some paper to go down to the beach and write mommy a letter?" jeered the logger who had previously abused Ranger Divine.

"Leave him be, Rod," said the hippie. "He's just doing his job."

The Ranger focussed on something he saw hung in the back window of the crummy. He pushed past the hippie. He came nose to nose with the logger called

223

'Rod.' "I notice a rifle in the gun rack in the back of the crummy. I'm going to examine it to make sure it's not loaded."

"Hell, no, it's not loaded. I know better than that," said Rod and the Ranger had identified the owner. The Ranger told Rod that weapons weren't allowed in the Park, loaded or not, and after some haggling the Ranger got hold of the .224, checked to see that it was unloaded, pulled out the action, and gave it back to Rod. Then the Ranger scurried back over the parking lot, and over the jumble of drift logs to confront the sailors marching up the beach.

The column of sailors was within easy calling distance. "Howdy," called the Ranger cheerfully. "Just a minute, I need to talk to you guys!" He advanced toward the sailor in the immersion suit at the head of the column, making eye contact with the man who wore a grim expression. "Watch it!" called out the sailor, which the Ranger took as a threat. Divine instinctively looked to the sailor's hands and was confused to see the entire column carrying their hands behind their backs. There was a long chain hanging on their right side. The Ranger shifted his gaze to the men on either side of the column. He saw that they were citizens - Natives, in fact - carrying the weapons. In his training and experience as a law enforcement officer, Ranger Divine perceived that something was terribly wrong here! Going for his sidearm he yelled, "Freeze! Police," as dictated by his training at the Federal Law Enforcement Training Center,. The shotgun exploded. Pellets tore into Ranger Divine's chest, stopping him in his forward progress. His Smith and Wesson flew from his grasp, as his hand continued upward. He fell straight back onto the beach. Two spurts of blood issued from his chest before his heart stopped.

Ranger Divine looked down at the mutilated chest of the uniformed man lying on the beach as if in a dream. He looked at the man's face as he drifted upwards and realized with a shock that it was his own face! He felt a Light coming for him as he continued to rise over the beach. He cast a last glance down upon the scene below him before turning into the light. As the column of sailors marched beside the fallen officer, sand was kicked into the bloody pulp between the Ranger's badge and name tag. "I'll have to change that shirt before coming to work tomorrow," thought the spirit of Ranger Divine. The spirit turned and faced an Entity so bright, an Expanse so dark, a Reality so wonderful and terrible, that neither pen nor imagination can follow.

****

I heard the nearby blast from the shotgun and risked arrest and citation. I ran beyond the barricades, across the parking lot, and gained the advantage offered by the drift logs. The ranger lay dead, on his back with his chest blown open. A parade of half a hundred men, in immersion suits shuffled by, bound by a chain. Natives with shotguns guarded the chain gang. The Native from whose shotgun still emanated smoke said to the Native next to him, "'Freeze, police!' did you catch that? The mother fucker must've thought he was Dirty Harry or some shit!" In my opinion and training as a choker-setter, I perceived that something was terribly wrong...like a high lead dragging a human arm. I jump back off the driftwood to the concealment of the parking lot.

****

The two A-6's circled the Alamo waggling their wings and watching the Huey being scrambled. A signal man with a Morse light stood on the deck giving the two Intruders a message in code. The message said, *"All f m out* (pause) *Hostiles sunk L C U* (pause) *Return to Whidbey* (pause) *Get orders and strike force* (pause) *We hear a m* (pause) *All F M out* (pause) *Hostiles sunk L C U..."* and so on. The crew aboard the A-6's shrugged. They held up their hands to the signal man in the universal sign of non-comprehension. Eventually, Admiral Bingingham had the men on the flight deck prepare two handwritten banners. The first read: *WE HEAR A M.* The Intruders waggled their wings enthusiastically to indicate that they understood. The second banner said: *RETURN TO WHIDBEY, DAMN IT!* The pilots waggled their wings again, less exuberantly. As the Huey began to lift off the deck, the two A-6's departed the area on a course that would carry them out to where the Seals and Marines were floundering a half hour earlier. Forty-five seconds later they were in the area of Ellen Creek. There were no signs of life, besides the dying. Ralph Powers pointed to a track on the beach that looked like a huge serpent had crawled its way north. Lieutenant Harris came alongside and put his thumb over his shoulder. The two A-6's charged north to investigate.

****

It had been almost a quarter century since the shoulder of John Pinn had embraced the firing stock of a Light Artillery Weapon. As he pointed the weapon at the bottom of the 50,000 gallon diesel bulk tank at the head of the LaPush Road he regretted what he must do. No doubt, the Soleduck River Shake Company and the historic Rosemond Lumber Mill would be kindling in the blaze. Fourskins was not ready to blow the Bogachiel Bridge, which would more effectively cut off LaPush from the outside world. Still, the Natives needed the seclusion and privacy that this mighty diversion tactic would offer their operation. With a whoosh, the LAW rocket took off for its target, and a gurgled **BLOOOOOM!** brought two men out of the office of the bulk fuel plant to find an eight-inch diameter hole in their main tank. Hundreds of gallons of diesel per second spewed across the parking lot. The owner stood in awe and horror, considering the liability of such an incident. The second employee ran in to call Forks Fire Department. The owner turned around; out on the road, he saw a big Indian standing next to a blue Datsun pick-up. The Native had what looked like a flare gun. He was pointing it in the direction of the spilling fuel.

"Jesus! Don't do it, PLEASE..." were the last words of Les LaPue, owner of the bulk plant. The orange flare flew into the spreading river of diesel.

THIRTY-ONE

*T*he A-6's found what appeared to be more than fifty survivors of the assault disaster on the jetty to James Island. It looked like they were chained together. It was hard to distinguish details at 150 knots - which is as slow as an Intruder can go without falling out of the sky. But the citizens with walking sticks appeared to be Indians with shotguns. Fuck! What a crazy afternoon! The Indians and prisoners were awaiting boat transport across the estuary. The Coast Guard Zodiac was being readied by a couple of Coasties on the dock, supervised by two gun-wielding Natives. The A-6's overshot LaPush and punched the throttle to climb vertically over First Beach, wing to wing, before sweeping down on the village in a hammerhead dive.

"The Coast Guard cutter is pushing north on a course to avoid the Alamo," observed Jenson out of the starboard side.

Powers voice answered on the intercom. "Did you see what that Indian lover had set up on the dock as we went past? It looked like a fucking LAW rocket. Maybe he shot up the LCU with a LAW!"

"It looked like a LAW to me on our pass thirty minutes ago, but you could never place a shot like that from a mile away in the pitching surf. We'll see what he's got on our next pass...Here we come..."

The two Intruders were coming onto the village again, flaps down for maximum drag and lift, noses flared up, both pilots and navigators all eyes at the mysterious events unfolding before them. From the starboard side, Jenson could see the Indian lover standing on the dock. He was pointing what damn well looked like a LAW at the sister Intruder just twenty meters off his wing. The Indian's weapon fired connecting a thin blue line of smoke to the port wing of the other Intruder. The A-6 fell like a rock out of the sky and skipped, like a stone, across the estuary breaking to pieces as it went. "Holy shit! He got Harris! Harris is down!"

Jenson did not seem preoccupied with the predicament of the sister ship. He was focussed on revenge.

The surviving Intruder raised its flaps and punched the throttle. Climbing straight up, Jenson was barking orders to his navigator. "Arm weapons! Weapons on!"

"Jack, all we have on board is tracers, and extra fuel on the wings."

"God-damn-it, we're going to frag that Indian fuck!" screamed Jenson. While his right hand controlled the joystick he lifted his left arm (which weighed about 25 pounds with the exertion of the G-force of their vertical climb), to flip up the switch guard and toggle on the weapon systems. A flashing red light came on his screen, *WEAPONS ARMED...WEAPONS ARMED...WEAPONS ARMED.* For just a split second, there was the butterfly sensation of zero gravity that reminds even the ace pilot of standing up on a roller-coaster ride on the crest of the big dip. The A-6 went over on its back. As the ground came back into view, Jenson controlled a defensive spin with the pedals of the A-6 as it plunged back to earth in a power dive. Through the glass of the forward cockpit, the pilot and navigator saw the wingless fuselage of the other A-6 sinking into the sheen of the kerosene covered estuary. There was no hope for the two men aboard. The prisoners and Indians, on the north side of the estuary had sought protection from the jet crash amid the rocks, and drift logs scattered along the jetty. The two Coasties on the docks had abandoned their duties with the Zodiac. They were fleeing back to the Coast Guard station with the armed Natives on their heels.

Through the spin, the pilot and navigator could see that the Indian fuck wad that had precipitated this incursion had abandoned his weapon system, and was fleeing the dock. The maggot was making for the concealment of a trailer about 150 meters north of the Coast Guard Station. Ensign Jenson pulled out of the spin and dove straight at the trailer. "Bombs away! Bombs away!" he yelled into the intercom.

"You want me to cut loose our auxiliary fuel tanks?" asked Powers incredulously.

"Yes, God-damn-it, DO IT!"

The navigator punched his orange button. "Fuel away! The tanks are away and above us, Jack!" The horizon came into view, and the bolus of excrement in Ralph Powers' large colon became a seven pound bomb. He almost shit his MAST pants with the G force and excitement. They were lighting up a civilian target in the United States of America!

****

Mary Wright just wanted the political hubbub to die down. LaPush had been inflamed ever since the arrival of Clarence Fourskins. As an unmarried, single parent, she was currently collecting benefits from Department of Social and Health Services. The influx of young, unemployed Natives to LaPush had stressed the welfare services, and doubled the time it took to file her claims. Once her baby was a year old, she promised herself, she would go back to work at LaPush Ocean Park. But a baby's first year was so important for bonding, and breast feeding...and the little rascal was always having his little colds, like he had right now.

Two hours ago, he had fallen asleep, at his mother's breast, making snuffling sounds as he fought for air while he fed. She had put him down for his afternoon nap, and then there had been a stupendous explosion on top of James Island, which startled both of them. She had gotten him back to sleep, and he'd slept through someone shooting off a shotgun across the river. Then two jets roared over the village waking up the poor little guy. As she walked him back and forth in the trailer trying to get him back to sleep, all hell broke loose in the estuary. She went to the door, babe in arms and opened it. A jet had crashed. She saw Wally Woodrift running for her little home as if his life depended on it. She assumed he was running to call 9-1-1 so she left the door open, and put her baby back in the crib. Wally didn't appear in her doorway so she went to see if he fell down. He was sprinting toward the Coast Guard Station. She ran out of her doorway and down the wooden steps and called to him, "You can use my phone, Wally..." Something plunged out of the sky. She was picked up off the ground by a flameless explosion, and thrown into a tree where she hit her head. She was knocked unconscious when she landed.

When she awoke, there were flames everywhere. A man held her while a Coastie sprayed her with a dry chemical extinguisher. Everything smelled of kerosene. The Coastie spraying her with the extinguisher was crying. That seemed strange...then she heard her baby screaming. She saw her trailer completely engulfed in the flames. She struggled like a mad woman trying to get free. But the two men held on tight saying, "It's too late, Mary! There's nothing anyone can do. It's too late." And, with the silence of her baby, came the eternal silencing of joy and happiness in her soul. As if her chest had been opened up and all hope surgically cut from her heart. Hope, discarded like a tumor, in the stainless steel can under the operating table...

****

Wally anticipated a retaliatory action from the surviving A-6. With all three LAW's expended, he didn't need the laptop or Tank brain. He left them on the dock. He needed a hiding spot. As the A-6 went into a power dive, he was running for the concealment of Mary Wright's trailer. When he was just a few hundred feet away, she opened the door, and the sight of her, babe in arms, awoke his sense of heroism. He couldn't bring wrath from the sky upon these innocents. He doubled back and was running toward the Coast Guard station, which would be a safe refuge, when the two 300-gallon tanks hit Mary's garden. They burst like water balloons fired from a cannon. The wash of kerosene jet fuel knocked him down and he slid along the road. He got up and started to run toward the Coast Guard Station, but there was no traction, and he fell down again. He was drenched in kerosene. He could hear the Intruder coming down again in a power dive. He wondered what strange torture they had planned for him.

He was still a couple hundred feet from the sanctuary of the brick station, when the A-6 opened up on him with tracers. It was like being inside of a firework. The slick surface upon which he tried to run was burning. Then his kerosene soaked clothing ignited. The pain of the melting polypropylene shirt surpassed any suffering he had ever known. Several Coasties were running out of the building with fire extinguishers. Wally guessed he would never make it to them in the hail of tracers. He veered to jump into the estuary. As he jumped, a tracer ripped through the flesh of his upper arm. He knew that the tracer had hit him because only one arm worked underwater. The tracers made a whining sound as they penetrated the surface of the estuary. Wally swam into several hot rounds as he pulled himself along under water like a one-armed frog. The whining stopped and Wally knew that the A-6 would be climbing for another dive. He broke the surface of the water. He gulped hot air. The fuel from the downed jet had spread across the estuary, and had caught fire from the burning village. Wally could feel the wall of heat, and see the carpet of flame rolling out across the water towards him. He could taste the kerosene covering the water, and hear the Intruder as it swooped down to spray more tracers. He plunged back under water. He pulled himself along slowly to the north. He could hear the whine of hundreds of tracers hitting the water. He could see that the surface of the estuary was aflame above him. He could hold his breath no more. As he swam up into the torrid water, he pulled a bandanna from his rear pocket. He surfaced into an inferno. With the bandanna clenched in his good hand, he pushed the burning fuel away from his face and then breathed the scorching air. He fought not to cough. He could hear the fat and cartilage of his outer ear burning. He could hear the hiss of extinguished flames as he pulled his head back under water to the refuge of cold salt water. He could not adequately ventilate his lungs for the exertion to which he was committed. He had to surface again, the burning kerosene adhering to his head like napalm as he came out of the water. The stubble of his hair was burned off, and each visit to the surface burned through another layer of skin.

As he pulled himself along he prayed, "Please, dear God, let me live. I'll suffer any pain, I'll conquer any wound or disfigurement. Please, please let me live..."

****

The Huey had set a Navy record for poor response time to a Search And Rescue. All the helicopters had been taken under deck because of the weather. A hydraulic pump had blown a seal, causing the helicopter to get stuck between decks. Another Huey had to be loaded onto another elevator; that had cost the response 40 minutes. *Then*, all personnel on deck were fooling around, playing charades with the A-6's, and holding up banners like it was someone's birthday. *Then* Admiral Bingingham wanted to ride along to see what was happening which meant probably one less survivor aboard, and five minutes to get the old boy squared away in an immersion suit and may west. It was 92 minutes after the Mayday received on CB channel 9, when the helicopter finally lifted off.

They were about a thousand meters from the mouth of Ellen Creek. They could see bodies in immersion suits on the beach. *Then* they saw the smoke and flames from LaPush. One of the A-6's went streaking by on its way to Cape Flattery, only about half an hour late in executing its orders. The Admiral had insisted that they go immediately to the scene of the fire to ascertain if the firing on James Island had resulted in the whole village going up, or if one of the Intruders had crashed and burned. At the mouth of the Quillayute River they found 60% of the estuary in a liquid-fuel fire, which told them that a jet had gone down. The crew aboard the Huey saw the Natives and men in immersion suits, hunkered down behind the rocks and drift logs. They were screening themselves from the heat. The helicopter put down on the jetty. The Admiral got out and started to walk toward the men. A corpsman, scanning the shore of the jetty for evidence of the jet crash, saw what he thought might be a small killer whale swimming for shore. The surface of the water broke. What drug itself onto shore gasping was not a whale. With such facial deformity, it took almost a second for the corpsman to realize that this was a human burn victim...maybe a survivor from the A-6. "Hey, we got a live crispy over here!" yelled the corpsman and four sailors went down the steep rocky bank to pull the victim out of the water and up the bank. The air and salt on the poor bastard's burns were causing him considerable discomfort.

Meanwhile, the prisoners were trying to wave off the Admiral, and one of the Natives was taking aim with a shotgun. "This is just a rescue ship," said Sparks. "Let's just get them out of here so they can get about their work."

"Hey, that's Admiral Bingingham!" cried one of the sailors, recognizing the advancing man in the immersion suit.

"Get him!" exclaimed Sparks, recognizing the hostage potential of this old gaffer. "Leave your shotguns." Two Natives stowed their weapons next to Sparks and took off to meet the Admiral like cats turning out to greet a mouse.

The Admiral was starting to pick up warning signs: a chain connecting the sailors; hands strapped behind backs; shotguns and assault rifles in the hands of civilians. Two Natives were coming at him with entirely too much enthusiasm for the kind of powwow he had in mind. The Admiral turned, and began to walk back to the helicopter. He looked over his shoulder and saw the two Natives break into a run to catch him before he reached the Huey. The Admiral ran to the helicopter and piled in on the port side as the crew was loading a burn victim into the back on the starboard. "Let's get the fuck out of here!" he yelled at his men, bumping into the medics loading the patient.

"Careful, sir!" said the ruffled medic who tore some of the patient's charred flesh when he was bumped. Two Natives jumped into the back of the Huey and grabbed the Admiral. They were pulling him out the door. His men were focussed on the crispy.

"Help!" croaked the Admiral. Two crewmen abandoned their efforts to cut away the remnants of a dark blue polypro undershirt, and joined the Admiral in his struggle to maintain purchase on the deck of helicopter. A brief tug-of-war developed over the senior officer. Just as the Admiral was being pulled back through the doors of the helicopter by the combined forces of the Navy crew, more Natives arrived.. Indians were winning the trophy. A crewman produced a .45 handgun and suddenly the Natives were looking at five drawn .45's. The Navy was staring at two shotguns. The pilot pulled back on the collective and three Natives jumped off the skids to stay on the ground. Jeff Sparks, who had just arrived to assist in the extraction of the Admiral said to the two men with shotguns, "Fuck it, you should have wasted the old man! A dead Admiral would make almost as big a splash as a live one for a hostage."

As the chopper lifted off, the Admiral rubbed his abraded wrists. He tried to collect his composure. "We should have taken some of them prisoners," he said through heavy breathing.

"You want to go back?" taunted the pilot.

"No," said the Admiral. "We have business north of here at the assault landing. The hostiles seem pretty entrenched. We'll come back later to get our men, and kick ass."

The helicopter landed on the beach near Ellen Creek and the crew began the grim business of triage, and separating the dead from the near dead. The medic had surveyed the crispy patient. Using the so-called "rule of nines" for burn assessment, the survival profile of the burn victim was not good. He was off loaded to make room for one of the many shotgun wounded, and/or near drowning victims, that would live to fight again.

"There's a county hospital in Forks," the Admiral was barking orders. "Take these men there. Have the hospital call Whidbey Island. Get every flight surgeon and nurse on base flown out to Forks right away. It's a small hospital so we may have to annex the nearest Federal building. If there is no Federal building, have the hospital annex a county building near the hospital with no steps..." The helicopter lifted off while the Admiral was still proselytizing his recipe for a MASH unit.

****

With a Ranger gunned down on the beach; troops from the Navy held prisoner; a jet crashed into the Quillayute River; and LaPush being dive bombed; strafed and burned by another jet aircraft; I deduce that something is askew. My feelings are that there is an obligation here to call authorities from the pay phone at Mora Ranger Station, but Rod and the others are disinclined to leave the show. A helicopter lands and the Natives try to take over the craft. A burned something or other is pulled out of the river. Thoughts begin to turn more toward personal safety and survival. The group finally agrees to depart the area. The phone lines are dead, and the power is evidently out, so our little group heads off to Forks, in the rain and failing light, to announce that Civil War has erupted in LaPush...or what's left of it. We can see the glow of the fires from LaPush, but a larger glow to the east defends against night in that part of the sky. We arrive at the scene of a conflagration fire at the end of the LaPush Road. The bulk oil plant has burned and, along with it, two large mills, five acres of woods, the Smoke House Restaurant, and a quarter mile of the LaPush Road. From what we can learn, a dozen people were killed. There are still people lost in the woods and trapped in collapsed buildings. The burned and wounded are being loaded into the two ambulances on scene. There is no way to drive through, so we fall in with the rescue workers. The fire seems to dominate everyones thinking and no one seems concerned about our reports of political violence in LaPush. A military helicopter flies by overhead, but doesn't land to assist. "Where's MAST when you need them?" says an ambulance worker, but I understand that the Navy has their own agenda this evening.

****

The crunching leaves startled the raven and his beak came out of his meal glistening with the vitreous fluid which had been contained in the sailor's right eye.

The bird hopped onto the man's forehead, over his nose, and jumped onto and off of his still chest, flexing to take flight. Mammals frequently survive traumatic amputation of a limb. The severed ends of veins and arteries constrict to arrest the escape of blood and the three-legged cat drags himself under the house to wait for the bleeding to stop. Lieutenant Gillette sustained a transverse severance of the brachial artery along with multiple perforations of the sub-clavian artery. He bled out as he ran from his enemies. He fell while crossing Ellen Creek. With the last of his energy, he pulled himself onto the bank where the crow found him looking vacantly up at the sky. A thin Native emerged from the trees, and stood brooding by the sailor's body.

Of the wonderful cosmic forces in the universe, gravity and atomic fission are the most profound. Gravity speaks of the loneliness of vast space: how two objects attract one another; how the planets encircle the sun in the necklace of their orbits; and how the earth pulls narcissistically at itself with such force that its core is molten magma from which extrude the great mountain ranges of this planet. It is the passive force of gravity that calls down the rain from the sky, washing the mountains out into the ocean, and it is gravity that pulls us to the ground. It swallows us in death. The enormous field of pull that our sun exerts upon itself creates the heat which sustains the atomic blast furnace. This radiates our solar system and powers every-thing we know on earth, radiation lifting up; gravity pulling down.

These two innocent and life-giving forces are corrupted by technology and given evil purpose. The atomic fission is packaged into a bomb so potent that it kills not only the target, but the whole planet. Peaceful gravity is enlisted in every delivery system developed for that bomb. The Native shakes his head sadly and sits beside the body of the sailor. There is not a god.

Somewhere out in the Pacific, photons beat down on the expanse of the ocean. The molecule of water is excited by the energy of the photon and moves faster. In phototropic excitement, the molecule jumps from the ocean where it is carried up into the stratosphere, following the prevailing wind currents, carried up by oriographic lifting over the Olympic Peninsula until it is condensed with a hundred million other molecules into a raindrop. The raindrop falls from the sky and spatters onto the surface of Ellen Creek where it articulates concentric circles on the pink brown confluence. The rain combines with the tannin of cedar and the blood of sailor and runs back out to the sea...another turn of the wheel and there is not a god.

The blood that runs to the ocean will find life and so will the vitreous fluid in the craw of the crow. As the forest quietly digests the physical remains of this man, the Native searches for a passage in the condensed New Testament which he carries, protected from the rain on his person...and there is not a god.

Look at that molecule of water for a second. Look at it for a nanosecond. Two hydrogen atoms dance in partnership with an oxygen atom. Freeze the dance and study the substance of the dancing partners. The subatomic particles are so insignificant that they stand on the threshold of reality. It is their motion that gives them substance, much like two blades of a prop articulate a circle. Without motion, matter is nothing...and there is not a god.

233

What matters of these men's death in the arena of infinity? Who will care one hundred years from now? Of what relevance are these lost human lives on the far side of the earth, much less the far side of the galaxy? Through the lenses of time and space nothing matters. Matter's nothing; nothing matters; and there is not a god.

The Native has put down the New Testament. He is studying a picture he has found in a flap of the sailor's immersion suit. The picture shows the sailor as he was in life. The sailor stands in dress whites with his left hand on the shoulder of his son who mischievously clutches an uzi squirt gun. In the picture, the sailor's right arm - the one that has been shot off - is around a pretty woman with green eyes and dark hair. The woman smiles at the camera with hope and security while the sailor grimaces for some reason known only to the family and photographer. The Native could feel the hope and security in the pretty woman's smile being dashed like a ship against the rocks. How she would call her husband's name and keen for his return. How she would watch her son grow and walk straight and unbent into the wind and rain...just like his father. When she would watch him doing jack knives off the high dive, swimming under water like a frog. She would look for the face of her lost husband on the young body that emerged from the water. The grief would rob her of her prettiness. It would weigh on her like the extra pounds of flesh that would visit her in the loneliness. She would cry from the ache and longing. There would be no relief.

A solution of NACL suspended in H2O ran down the Native's cheeks and spattered onto the photograph, dripping into the creek. The tears, blood, sweat and semen that testify to the trials and triumphs of our existence are only salt water borrowed from the sea, and there isn't a god.

Thus pondered James Crow: Ask the grain of silica in the middle of the beach, *Is there an ocean?* Ask the water molecule that pitches about in the murky depths of the ocean, *Is there a beach?* The lint studies the world through the louver of the belly button and wonders, *Is there a human?* There is an ocean, there is a beach, there is a human, but there is not a god. There is not a god.

THERE IS ONLY GOD! God and the Absence of God...and it is the Absence of God that walks this evening on Rialto Beach with shotguns. It is the Absence of God that leads men to war among themselves, and it is the Absence of God that steels them for the killing.

Dear God, give us peace! Give humanity peace and the rest will fall into place. Deliver us from Your Absence. Accept the soul of this unfortunate, comfort this poor widow, be with their son and let his generation find peace. Please, please, allow us to stop the killing. An explosion from the direction of LaPush rocked the forest.

And with this prayer, James Crow quit his vigil at Ellen Creek. He returned to the beach to check for survivors and aid the wounded. The rain increased in the waning light of a November evening. The gentle earth turned the wet cheeks of her northwestern hemisphere into the night and cried saltless tears.

There _is_ a God, but one's vision must be able to penetrate the Dark absence of same.

THIRTY-TWO

Thursday, November 5, 1992

*A*t her little cabin in Beaver, Washington, Frances Morganstern, the chief librarian from Forks, was disturbed that she was unable to receive the FM Canadian Broadcasting station which soothed her jangled nerves after a day of quelling spitball fights, and picking gum out from under the library tables. She had checked for other stations. Receiving none, she went out and jiggled her antenna. On a whim, she switched over to the AM band. Everything was business as usual there. She would endure the Forks country station only to get to the five o'clock news. At four thirty the station interrupted the lamenting and caterwauling to describe the holocaust fire at the head of the LaPush Road. The announcer was repeating the news bulletin with a greater reliance on superlatives and expletives when he broke in on this news with another announcement, "This just in! In an apparently unrelated event, several craft of the U. S. Navy were swamped and sunk by heavy seas just off Rialto Beach today. The Navy has been conducting maneuvers off the north Washington Coast for the last few days and was attempting a landing exercise. It is not known at this time if there were fatalities associated with the incident, but survivors have been flown by Navy helicopter to Forks Community Hospital which is already calling in all of its employees to deal with some thirty burn victims associated with the LaPush Road Fire..." The announcer is distracted by someone handing him another bulletin, "...What? No, the fire is by Highway 101...You're sure? Excuse me, ladies and gentlemen, another large fire is reported in the village of LaPush. No details are available at this time. We return to America's top country hits...."

The phone rang and Ms. Morganstern turned down the male banshee singing on the radio, "Good evening, this is Frances Morganstern."

"Frances, this is Edna LaBell, over by the Library," the LaBells had the flower shop, ice cream store, video arcade, dairy distribution and meat lockers between the library and high school. "You better get over to the library right away! They're bringing in injured sailors from some kind of boat wreck. They've taken over the library to work on them! They've been landing a Navy helicopter right in your parking lot..."

"What!" bellowed Frances. This sounded worse than spitballs and gum under the table.

"They've got thirty or forty vomiting and bleeding soldiers all over the floor of your library. They're stacking the dead in my meat locker. It's really a bad sight, Frances, and I am concerned upon the impact to the tourists who pass along Highway 101 right within sight of all this! When Jack does his butchering, he is very careful not to let any tourists see the carcasses..."

"I'm coming right over. Thanks, Edna."

"Frances, they say that this is a boating accident, but these men have been shot in the face and chest..."

237

"I'm on my way..."

"Just have them move everything over to the high school. There's more room, and it's not visible from the highway..."

Frances hung up the phone, ran out the door without a coat, jumped in her Tercel and sped off towards Forks.

****

The glass next to the back door had been broken out to gain entry to her library. Frances threw open the back door, to view a librarian's worst nightmare. Everywhere were the dead and dying...the groans, the suffering, the stink, the stained carpet...Two physicians ministered to some thirty patients that remained alive. Frances tripped on the legs of an obvious burn patient. His burned clothing had been cut away and there was a large puddle of blood under his buttocks and all over his naked groin. It looked like he had been shot through his left arm and he clutched a burnt bandanna in his right hand. Frances went into the CPR drill she had practiced with her co-workers. Lacking the supervision of the ambulance EMT's, she knelt in the blood and broken glass and gently tapped the poor man's burnt shoulder. His hair and ears were almost entirely burned away, but she recognized him as the young Native who came regularly to the library to check out books on criminal justice. "Are you OK?" Under the circumstances, it sounded ridiculous.

Amazingly, the man stirred slightly and made a muted sound through his mouth. Frances placed her ear next to the victim's mouth and burnt nose and heard a stirring of breath. She smelled the reek of the man's acidotic breath. *Check airway*, Frances went through the checklist from her practice. It looked like the patient's tongue was swollen up. No it wasn't a tongue. She gently pulled on the tissue and it came out of the man's mouth...

"Leave that one alone," said one of the physicians, who was also on his knees, working on a patient. "It's too late for him. I could use a hand over here, if you're not too busy. They're some latex gloves by the sink..."

The object came out of the man's mouth and he began to gasp and cough. She examined what she held in her bare hand and realized with horror that she held the man's testicles and scrotum. "Dear God, what have they done to you!"

The man answered, "P...pl...ease...h...help...me." Frances ran over to the kneeling physician with the testicles still in her hand.

"That man by the door needs your help right now! Someone's castrated him!"

"Everyone in this room needs our help right now, lady. Put down whatever it is in your hands, wash them and glove up..."

"Help that man immediately!"

"Lady, he's by the door because he's going to die. Didn't you see the burns to his face? His airway is shot..."

"So someone stuck his testicles in his mouth to help him breath?"

"I don't know how that happened. I don't care. I'm here to salvage the living and as far as I'm concerned, that man is already dead..."

"He's Native, is that it? Someone cut him because he's Native and you won't help him for the same reason!"

"Something's going on in LaPush, all right. It was Indians who shot up these men, but I don't give a shit. We're just a couple of Navy doctors here to save lives, while the nurses are out for a night on the town." The physician ripped the plastic protective cover off of a 1968 *Life* magazine and pressed it to the bared chest of his patient. "This is a sucking chest wound here! Just hold this plastic against the pellet hole or we'll have a tension pneumothorax. You wouldn't want that on your conscience."

The chief librarian would not be placated. "That young man was mutilated while you two doctors were in my library. It was a racist act! I don't care who did it, you're responsible..."

"Lady, this isn't about race, it's about saving lives. Either get with the program, or get your bleeding heart the hell out of *my* emergency room." Frances strode angrily away from the Navy doctor. "And take Hiawatha with you!" called the physician as he placed his mouth over the mouth of his patient to provide ventilations to check the seal of his plastic and adhesive tape dressing.

She stopped at the sink for a moment to compose herself and dropped the testicles into her clean coffee cup. *One lump, or two*...she reflected morbidly. She carried the cup out to the dashboard of her Tercel and started the engine. She left the passenger door opened; she went back into the library and blocked the heavy automatic door from closing; and clutched the Native under the armpits. "I'm going to help you. Hang in there. You're going to be all ri...all...you can live if you try..." Frances was pulling him through the door.

"Bye, now!" called the physician in mock cheerfulness.

****

239

Thursday, October 5, 1992, 21:40 E.S.T.,

The red phone on the bed stand rang in the Presidential bedroom suite of the White House in Washington, D.C. In the jubilation that had followed another landslide election victory for the Republicans, and a point of relaxation in the hostilities of the Cold War, the sobering effect of the so-called 'hotline' was instantaneous. The unannounced ringing of the red phone could herald the last few hours of human history. "George, it's the red phone!" said his wife, in bed, a note of hysteria creeping into her voice.

George Shrub dropped his toothbrush into the sink and hurried over to the night table to pick up the phone on it's third ring. "This is President Shrub," he said, offering nervously, "White House, Washington, D.C."

Mr. President, my name is Timothy Gable and I am the Interim President of the Confederacy of Non-White Americans. I'm speaking to you from Victoria, British Columbia, but our seat of power is LaPush, Washington..."

"What is this! How did you get on *this* telephone line..."

"Mr. President, we have gained much control over the communications structure of your country as will be revealed to you in the next few days. We are in a position to damage or destroy major components of the DEW, SAC and SDI systems..."

"Who are you! What do you want?"

"I already told you my name, but, once more, I am President Timothy Gable of the Confederation of Non-White Americans. Please listen. On October 12, we sent a Declaration of Independence to the Congress of the United States of America. We received no reply or acknowledgement of our sovereignty for our efforts. This was not acceptable to us. Today, a Naval assault force attempted to land on territory we claim as Indian Country and we took the gesture as an act of war. We took the men prisoner. Many of them were killed by drift logs because they foolishly disobeyed the instructions of our officers on the scene..."

President Shrub pushed the mute button on his handset and said, "Get Bob. Hurry," meaning, he wanted Bob Rucklesaus, his Chief of Staff, to confer on a matter of national security. His wife pulled on a robe and went out to find a Secret Service agent to fetch her husband's right-hand man. She was almost knocked over by the man, who was coming to the President's bedroom to confer on another matter.

"...We have also occupied the U.S. Coast Guard Station in LaPush and are holding the entire staff hostage..."

"If you read the newspaper or watched something on television besides Saturday morning cartoons, you would know that this Administration does not negotiate with terrorists! I don't think we have a lot to say to one another until you surrender to United States authorities whom I will dispatch to LaPush in the next few minutes. Furthermore, I'll be calling the Prime Minister of Canada to arrange your extradition for sedition..." The First Lady entered the room with the Chief of Staff.

The President looked up to make eye contact with his Chief of Staff. The Chief was impressed to see the President on the hotline. He said quietly, "We just lost a DEW down link over northwestern Washington. It gives us a blind spot. A bunch of retired satellites fell out of geosynchronous orbit. They are creating problems..." the President held up his finger and the Chief fell silent while George Shrub listened more intently to the queer message he was receiving on the phone.

"...already been in touch with the Prime Minister and have been given political asylum. With the Ottawa issue on his plate, the P.M. is playing sympathetic to separationists - which is what *we* are, Mr. President, in case you haven't been listening. And if the matter of Navy and Coast Guard hostages doesn't concern you, we knocked out the Early Warning satellite down link over Neah Bay to get your attention. You should be getting a phone call from your Chief of Staff momentarily with this information. We can destroy all space born defense systems in a day. We can map and publish the blind spots we create in Iran, Libya,...whomever. Please hold him on the line to discuss our demands. I'll be faxing you a formal copy of our demands, but, by way of courtesy, I'll tell them what they are right now."

The President pressed the mute button. "This guy says he represents a group of separationists...They took our Navy Seals landing on that Washington beach as hostages...They took over a Coast Guard station - or so he says. Bob, he says his group knocked down that satellite, and can screw up everything in space...Shit! Fuck! Excuse me, Barbara, I can't believe this is happening..." The first lady retreated to the bedroom.

"Excuse me, Mr. President. Get a hold of yourself. I understand that your Chief of Staff is there. I might as well explain to you, we take the message generated by your receiver and amplify it, so your mute button won't shield our ears from what you have to say. We're using a SAC down link to intrude onto the secure code of the hotline. Please put me on a speaker phone so we can involve your Chief of Staff."

The President covered the mouthpiece clumsily with his hand, "The crazy bast...the gentleman on the phone says that his group is commandeering a channel on the number fourteen SAC down link to break in on the hotline. They want to give us their demands so I'll put him on speaker phone." The President pushed a button and there was a click on the speaker. "OK, Mr. Cable, we're listening."

"That's G-A-B-L-E, sir, or you may call me 'Mr. President' if you prefer..."

"Just get on with it."

"Demand number one is recognition for, and non-aggression against, our government. 'When in the course of human events...' and all of that. The United

States has not successfully represented black and red Americans, the Confederation of Non-White Americans will..."

"So that I know what I am dealing with, Mr. Gable, what color are you?"

"I am a Native, Mr. President. You are presently dealing with a Native coalition, but this hinges on another demand, which is: that your government engage in no interference in the defection of non-white Americans to the Confederation."

"I don't see a problem there because, frankly, I don't think either Blacks or Natives will be busting down the door to join rank with your nonsense. No offense, President Gable."

"We will be asking you for guaranteed access to the U.S. Post Office to handle defection and census matters."

"Who will pay for the twenty-nine cent postage, or will this be part of your blackmail, Mr. Gable?"

"We will pay the stamps, sir, but finances of our fledgling government are certainly a part of our package. The fiscal year of 1992, budgets four point two billion dollars to the BIA. We want two hundred million in reparations. The balance of four billion we propose dividing per Native capita, and each new citizen to the Confederation brings with him that annuity for a period of twenty years. Twenty years down the line we will be saving your taxpayers four point two billion a year plus inflation..."

"And what do you propose we do with the Department of Interior employees who staff the B.I.A. and produce the greater part of that debit?"

"Fire them. That's seems obvious. The incompetence of the BIA is a good part of why you have a revolution on your hands. We also have a formula for dipping into the HUD coffer for each black defector; but that's incidental to this conversation..."

"Mr. Gable, this whole conversation seems incidental to reality. I've told you that we don't deal with terrorists. You can be sure that even if *I* would, the American people would not stand for it."

"We are prepared to take our case to the American people, sir. In fact I will be making a press release tomorrow. In considering your record for International Affairs, I certainly expect that you will consider violence as a way out of the hostage and defense crisis you face. Believe me, it will not work for you this time. The opinion of the American people will crush you if you resort to violence to settle this."

"So are we done with your demands, and now just wallowing in threats?"

"There are some more demands. We want a seat on the Security Council of the United Nations..."

"I don't have the *power* to create seats on the Security Council."

"We demand that you retire your selectee, and appoint a dual citizen of our choosing..."

"You can't be serious..."

"...for a period of one year, to assure our survival through this period of vulnerability."

"Well, is *that* all? Are you done?"

"No, sir. We demand a land base for our country. A continent was stolen from the rightful Natives of this land. Black men were violently removed from their homeland in Africa, and forcefully introduced to North America. Black men drift without anchor like flotsam across the nation without anchor. Now *we* demand land."

"How much land do you believe that you require, and where do you intend for us to find it? Or do the big thinkers of your terrorist's band dabble in such details?"

"Please leave out the sarcasm and hostility, Mr. President. We are just men here, looking for answers in a difficult situation. We require an acre for every new citizen...it's not much. We suggest you look for the land in the Department of Interior. But we will not accept arid, un-tillable land to satisfy this critical component of our demands. We are interested in lands held by the National Park Service. Parks like Badlands, Yosemite, and Nez Perce, represent an affront to Natives for the way the indigenous populations were removed and should be the first you hand over. We demand Rialto Beach, which is ours by treaty, anyway. Mr. President, we have some other incidental demands, and clarification of what I have just explained to you. Check your fax machine and you will find the copy I promised you. I am available to answer any questions you may have or suggestions you might want to make, about resolution of our demands...Mr. President?"

"I have no questions, Mr. Gable."

"Mr. Russelsaus, do you have any questions?"

"Yes, President Gable. What kind of timetable are we looking at here? What assurances do we have for the safety of the hostages..."

"We have no questions for you, Mr. Gable," interrupted the President of the United States. "Thank you for keeping us advised." He hung up the phone.

243

****

In the Oval Office, the President and Chief of Staff mulled over the hard copy of the terrorists insane demands. They discussed their next move. "Take my word, George," offered the subordinate. "These guys will hang themselves if you give them enough rope. The only demand I see here that amounts to anything is the two hundred mill up front. The rest will take care of itself in time."

"Time is what killed Carter in the same situation, Bob. The American public won't stand for an indecisive President, and I'm not one to put off a dirty job."

"Believe me, it will blow over. These guys aren't Thomas Jeffersons and Ben Franklins. They don't have what it takes to build a government. Can you imagine trying to put together a country with the social riff-raff they propose pulling together? Just give them the two hundred million in traceable currency in exchange for the hostages. Pretend to support the concept of a counter government for expatriated minorities...in some ways I like the idea myself. Imagine just being able to pass off all the treaty, and urban Black problems, to someone else! Of course, they'll never pull it off, but all the same..."

"You're ignoring the national security question here. These fuckers are threatening to pull down DEW, SAC and SDI in one whack. Can it be done?"

"I don't know, George. Maybe. We'll have to convene the Security Council and CIA. I'll make the calls..."

"Fuck that, Bob! Those high-tech bastards have their ears on every wire and radio wave going out of here! I want everything to be handled person to person." The President put his face close to the Chief of Staff and whispered. "I want a strike force put together and put on a jet for Whidbey Island in the next hour. We need to be ready to hit this place...LaPush, whatever... within twelve hours. I want an eye in the sky over the target - wherever that is - giving a map of every square inch of the city or town or reservation...or whatever LaPush is. We've got to knock out their threat to aerospace defense right now! The integrity of the Republican party depends on it for Christ's sake..."

"George, wait...We'd better not rush into this, or it could swallow us. We can just fall back and wait...take our time to draw out the targets..."

The President waved flamboyantly at a picture of Abraham Lincoln on the wall. "When *he* was in the same position did he sit around with his thumb up his butt. God-damn-it, I've got a duty to act here! I answer to the American people, and to the Republican Party. I'll tell you a story... in 1965, when I was the CIA division head for covert operations in Southeast Asia, the Johnson Administration was screwing up everything. The North Vietnamese were spilling down through Cambodia to the south like an overflowing toilet bowl. The Pentagon was doing what it could to stop them by bombing their supply routes and direct confrontation on the ground with Marines. This was back in the days when high-altitude fixed wings were the only 'eyes in the skies.' We were mapping the enemy movements with U-2's. Meanwhile, Johnson is telling the world that we're not in Cambodia, for-the-love-of-God! A U-2 is flying above some of the most intense fighting of that secret war. With all the shit flying around in the sky, the plane catches a round through the nose. The pilot rides the plane down for a soft landing in the rice paddies. So we've got a spy plane and five-hundred dead Marines in a Cambodian rice paddy where they're not supposed to be and I got sent over on damage control."

"Sounds like a messy situation."

"It *was* messy. Lockhead Aircraft had brought in a team of experts to rebuild the nose of the U-2, and design a runway through the rice to get the U-2 back in the air. We had several hundred American war dead stacked up in a bunker and the plane camouflaged, so it wouldn't be visible from the air. These big thinkers wanted to pave a *mile-long* runway through Cambodia, to get the plane back in the air. Don't you think that might have attracted a little attention?"

"So what did you do?" asked the Chief of Staff, genuinely interested.

"I put the U-2 in the bunker with KIA's, and used the earth-moving equipment to bury the whole mess!"

"Jesus, George! That accounts for ten percent of all the MIA's!"

"That's right." said President Shrub, in a whisper. "And just you and I and a few retired coneheads from Lockhead know about it. The MIA thing attached to the Johnson Administration like a dog turd to a shoe. I was promoted to Director of the CIA and now *I'm* President. I didn't get here by falling back and waiting for targets to reveal themselves."

"Look, George. The news this year is full of Native America. You hit these guys and it will be like taking a swing at the tar baby. You'll bring down the whole party! If you have to jump into it, use the Washington National Guard. You can level the target with tank attack. You need to insulate the Republican Party from political repercussions. What if this thing gets away from us or if the hostages get killed?"

"What about their threat to aerospace Defense? We need a team of experts to take care of that."

"How about we identify the antennas, generators, anything like that, with satellite surveillance. That should serve to draw out the target; we use a strike team from the Pentagon to neutralize that problem and move in with an armored unit of the National Guard to inflict punishment and take care of the hostage thing, one way or the other."

"That sounds acceptable, Bob. I'll call the Governor."

"Probably the hostages will get shaken loose at the first sight of the tanks. Better impress the Governor with the need for restraint once the hostages are freed."

"Fuck that! I'm telling him to flatten the target!"

✳✳✳✳✳✳✳✳✳✳✳✳✳✳✳✳✳✳✳✳✳✳✳✳✳✳✳✳✳

Friday, November 6, 199, 200:45 P.S.T.

The water in the estuary was still as warm as bath water when James Crow swam across in the dark to the smoldering village of his home. The fire had taken several homes, and the cannery, just west of the brick Coast Guard Station. The western walls of the station were scorched by the blaze, but the facility was in tact. James Crow strode angrily through the front door as a couple of guards saluted. The communication room, just to the right of the entrance, had been modified with multiple television screens, mixing equipment, video cassette recorders and telephone screening equipment. Crow found Fourskins and Sparks laughing. They were reviewing a taped conversation between Timothy Gable and President George Shrub.

Crow pushed the cassette deck off of the radio table and it crashed to the floor. Fourskins and Sparks stopped laughing and suppressed smirks as the 'spiritual founder' of their revolution ranted, "I resign from politics! This movement disgraces all that I stand for..." Crow picked up a chair and got in a whack, taking out a radar screen and some sophisticated dubbing gear.

"Jesus!" yelled Sparks, jumping up to subdue the man before he did any serious harm.

Clarence Fourskins stood up, "Colonel Crow, get a hold of yourself! This is behavior unbecoming to an officer!"

Crow struggled to get free of Sparks' grasp. "I'm not a colonel in your stinking army! I'm done with you! I stand for peace and brotherhood; you two stand for the same thing as President Shrub: Power!" Crow broke away and was making for the door.

"Stop him," said Fourskins quietly to two Natives who guarded the inside of the door with shotguns. The two men pointed their weapons at Crow's face as he advanced towards the door. Crow did not slow down, but pushed away the muzzle of one gun like he was shooing away a noisome fly. Crow was out the door and both men flexed with their fingers on the trigger, ready to fire. "Hold it!" called Fourskins. The two looked to their commander for orders. "Just follow him. If he tries to leave the village, then...do it." The men nodded. They followed Crow back to his shack. It was starting to rain. From where they stood guard, outside in the dark, they could hear James Crow weeping.

246

THIRTY-THREE

Second Beach Parking
Friday, November 6, 1992, 06:10 hours

A shotgun blast cuts through the early morning, and a chorus of Reservation dogs argue about what it all means. I wake up with a stiff neck in the back of the crummy in the Second Beach Parking lot. Everything in the crummy smells of smoke. There was no getting home last night with the road out. It would have been an easy walk, or I could have caught a ride, but the sense of danger and caution which had caused us to flee the scene yesterday transformed itself into an urgent curiosity. Nothing would do but to return to the conflict. Rod had been adamant about checking it out. If the Indians were being bombed back into the stone age - which is pretty much where they were anyway, according to Rod - it would be a thrill to eyewitness the blessed event. I had felt compelled to come along as a voice of reason and to keep my co-workers out of trouble. We were stopped by Natives with assault rifles at the barricade by Second Beach Parking. They told us to go home. We explained that this was impossible due to the road being out and Rod interjected, "What did you fucking featherheads do with the soldier prisoners you almost burned up I want to know GOD-DAMN-IT BOY I'M TALKING TO YOU SON DON'T WALK AWAY WHEN I'M TALKING TO YOUR SORRY MOTHER FUCKING FACE..." and two men put down their carbines and pulled Rod out of the truck sputtering, while two other Natives held shotguns trained on us and had everybody get out. They threw Rod against the crummy and patted him down for weapons. They made a hasty search of the floors and glove box of the vehicle for guns. Finding none, they threw Rod into the back seat of the vehicle.

"Move this vehicle out of the parking lot and we'll kill all of you redneck, White, honky, Hoquat, shitheads!"

"Gee, that was a fine bit of diplomacy there, Rod," I said. "Maybe if you get tired of setting chokers, there's a career waiting for you in the State Department." Rod had grumbled about how he ought to get his .224 out from behind the seat, where the Ranger had put it; ammunition from his lunch box, where Rod had left it; and start blowing away these crazy 'better-dead-than-Red's.' I had fallen asleep listening to how Rod would destroy the whole village armed only with his guile and .224.

After waking with the gunshot, I hear a helicopter put down to the west - probably on Second Beach. I stir uncomfortably. Rod's head has fallen over on my shoulder. He fell asleep chewing snoose as well as revenge. The brown juice of his chew, stains my right shoulder. I push at his head to get him away. He stirs, but goes back to sleep in the near dark. About twenty minutes go by as I look out the window in the growing light. I am astounded to see twenty commandos in camouflaged fatigues stealing across the road. They disappear into the woods between the Second Beach Housing project, and the LaPush Road. They carried enough weapons in their party to establish their own banana republic. "Look at that!" I exclaim, but my co-workers are still snoring. The shadows have disappeared by the time the weary

247

loggers open their peepers. They accuse me of hysteria, and counsel me to go back to sleep.

I can't sleep, and the full light reveals that the crummy is no longer under guard if ever it was. I get out of the back of the rig and approach the driver. "Let's get out of here," I say to him. "I'll drive." The sleepy head gets out and takes the spittoon seat beside Rod. Pulling out of the parking lot the CB roars to life startling everyone awake with an all points bulletin: *Attention all military, police and tribal personnel in the LaPush vicinity! A scientist in the employ of the Confederation has experienced a mental disorder and is fleeing the area carrying extremely dangerous chemical agents around his waist. The man is a Native of five foot, ten inches, with shoulder- length, dark hair and slight stature. He is believed to be travelling along the coastline in an attempt to smuggle out these dangerous chemicals. He has threatened to use the weapons on anyone who tries to stop him. He will lethally resist any attempts to incarcerate him. Consider him armed and extremely dangerous. We will broadcast more details as they become available.*

"Stop the rig! Stop the rig, God-damn-it!," Rod has opened his door and is threatening to jump out of the moving vehicle. I apply the brakes and stop the vehicle in the middle of the road. Rod is out of the pick-up and scrambling to get his .224 out from behind the seat.

I try to reason with him, "Let the Army or the Natives take care of it! There are all kinds of men with guns out there and they'll shoot your ass down if you go running around with a rifle. For crying out loud, Rod, listen to reason..." But Rod is taking off into the woods with my three other co-workers. "You'll get lost for sure!" I yell to the retreating men, the last man disappearing into the woods waves his hand without turning around. "It's illegal to have a gun in the Park!" I yell lamely. I drive another half mile and park in the Third Beach Parking Lot. I pull out the file of Metsker Maps in the glove box and find Teahwit Head on the map titled Township 27 north/Range 15 west. Unlike my co-workers, I carry a compass and map as I charge into the jungle.

****

LaPush
Friday, November 6, 1992, 05:30

The two Natives had tired of listening to the blubberings of James Crow. They had made a nest in a derelict school bus filled with trash. One stayed awake to monitor the front door of Crow's shack. Their subject had quieted sometime around two in the morning. At about six, one remained on guard, while the second went back to the Coast Guard Station to ask for further instructions. They wanted to shoot the traitor, and go to bed for a few hours.

At the Coast Guard Station, the second guard found Jeff Sparks in the communication room, briefing several of his staff in the use of portable camera units. He explained that the units were made up of little, transformerless inverters, powered by motorcycle batteries, which, in turn, drove video transmitters attached to eight-millimeter camcorders. "Now remember to keep your cameras off of any modern or sophisticated weapons we control. You want pictures of the U.S. forces shooting up our guys. The gorier, the better. The younger, and more pitiful, our warrior, the better..."

"I'm looking for General Fourskins." said the second guard, interrupting Sparks' dissertation

"He may be in the mess hall supervising the feeding of prisoners," said Sparks. The hostages had been unbound. They were enjoying a hot breakfast in the mess. The meal was being video taped and the display of weapons was kept in extremely low profile. The second guard did not see Fourskins here. He went to the muster room.

Here he found Fourskins, and Colonel Pinn excitedly planning the day's activity which, apparently, was war. Hard copy of a descrambled message from the President of the United States, to the Governor of Washington, had just been hand carried over from the up/down link station at Spark's residence. His house across from Second Beach Parking served as the headquarters for central intelligence. It was a request for military resources: a company of ten M-1 tanks, a battalion of 240 troops of the Washington National Guard, and six Hueys for medivac of casualties. It looked like a straight-on military assault, which played wonderfully into their plan. Sparks and Fourskins were trying to guess the travel time from Fort Lewis. They figured four hours to get the lowboys and deuce and a halves within striking distance of LaPush. The second gunman waited for a break in the conversation, which didn't happen. He considered going to the mess and eating with the prisoners.

A phone rang and Pinn snatched it up. The second guard saw that the phone was labled "*WOODRIFT.*" The second guard put together that the phone lines with the outside world were restored. The ringing had tumbled from the phone at Wally Woodrift's residence. The call had been routed over to the Coast Guard station by Colonel Sparks' high-tech lab boys.

"This is the Woodrift residence," lied Pinn to the person calling. There was hope in his voice thinking it might be the young Colonel himself calling in.

"No I'm sorry he's not in right now...No, I'm sorry I don't think I can reach him, but he should be back pretty soon...Oh! I *know* he would like to be involved...OK, zero seven hundred. I got it. I'll tell him as soon as he gets in...Thanks for calling...Goodbye." Pinn hung up the phone.

"General Fourskins, I've got to talk to you!" interjected the second Native.

"Just a second, Private. Who was that calling for Woodrift, Colonel?"

"It was Wally's Guard unit. They're the ones being activated. Dispatch time from Fort Lewis is seven o'clock."

"And I thought *you* were dumb!" said Fourskins almost hugging the big Indian.

"General Fourskins..." the second guard implored for the General's attention.

"Yes, Private."

"Remember, you asked us to guard Crow, which is what we did. He's been asleep for a couple of hours. Could we just get it over with him. Or get some relief, so we can grab a bite, and a few winks. It sounds like we'll need all the rest we can get for later in the day."

"Excuse me, Colonel Pinn, I've got a matter that I'd better deal with before morning." Fourskins followed the gunman down the halls and out to the front door of the station where he interrupted Jeff Sparks who was still briefing his media crew. "Excuse me Colonel Sparks, but there's a matter that needs both of our attention before morning." The three men walked back to Crow's shack. They couldn't find the first Native. The second gunman indicated the possibility that the first guard might be in the school bus, which is where the men found him sleeping. Fourskins was visibly angry and told the two men to wait outside the shack while Sparks, and he, went in to "talk" to the traitor. They came out a minute later.

"He's gone," Fourskins rumbled. "There was an open tide book in there, so we can assume he'll be travelling along the beach...He's got that God-forsaken journal and that could create some embarrassment in the wrong hands...Soldier don't hold your weapon that way!"

The first guard, who held his weapon by the muzzle with the stock and trigger over his shoulder, arranged the weapon in a diagonal 'present arms.' "Here let me show you!" said Sparks taking the weapon. He racked a round into the chamber and pointed the muzzle at the first gunman's chest.

"Wha..." said the first gunman as Sparks pulled the trigger. The explosion shattered the predawn silence. Dogs barked throughout the village as the man fell onto his back and died. The second guard was wide awake, and had lost his appetite for breakfast.

****

The devil's club, salmonberry, and vine maple, have become hungry man-eaters, pulling at my clothing and raking me across the face with their thorny appendages. What appeared on the map as a flat, half-mile push due west to the ocean, is becoming a Bataan Death March across a jungle of angry, persistent vegetative snipers, that never learned the war was over. I am wondering how Rod and the other maniacs are making out. I hope that the appetite of this hungry, rotting forest might be assuaged in digesting the members of that party. I hear helicopters behind me and guess that Third Beach is being used as some kind of staging area. Still, it's hard to get oriented in this environment. All of a sudden there is blanket-ripping sound of high rapid-fire weapons over my right shoulder. Quiet; then a pop. Quiet, quiet. And then a *BIG* explosion. I see a clearing ahead and push for it. At last! I stand on high palisades above a bay at the south end of Second Beach. On the hand like Teahwit Head, I figure myself to be between the ring and pinky finger. I am looking for a way down to the beach on the steep slopes...

****

The five Natives had been on guard all night. Two of them had been watching over a pick-up load of smart-ass loggers who had stumbled into their roadblock across from the Housing project. They had called over to the command post set up at the Coast Guard Station for orders to neutralize the intruders. It turned out that John Pinn knew these guys. He said to just leave them alone and fall back to guard central intelligence. The five men were cold and hungry. When the shotgun had gone off early that morning one of them remarked over the dog barking, "That would be James Crow going to his eternal reward, God bless him."

"Jesus will be happy to see him," offered one of the guards shuffling his feet to stay warm.

"Jesus and James will probably argue over who gets to sit at the Right Hand," said the first blowing into his own hands.

An hour after the gunshot, they'd heard the pick-up truck load of honkies start up and leave the Second Beach parking lot. Then, Colonel Sparks had driven up in a dark mood and told them that Crow wasn't dead: that he had escaped and was a loose cannon. Two of the security force had been ordered out to First Beach to try to intercept the defector and the three remained on guard, as Sparks went into the building to broadcast an all points bulletin and check on incoming intelligence. That had been 90 minutes ago and the three were cold. Damn cold! Cold, tired and bored...the ripping sound of high automatic weapons interrupted their cold, tired boredom and everything else. They fell to the pavement dead.

Inside, the unarmed employees of central intelligence dove to floor at the sound of the gun chatter. Sparks drew his .380 sidearm. He pushed over a table for concealment. How the hell could they be under attack already? Fort Lewis should still be two hours away; lumbering along on the highway. The tear gas grenade, crashing through the window, ended his speculation on the matter. He, and all the other intelligence personnel, made for the open door, choking and coughing. The sidearm was yanked from his hand and he was knocked flat down on the pavement. Nylon flexicuffs were cinched down on his wrists. These guys weren't fucking around. The dozen technicians were shucked of their lab jackets like corn cobs. They were searched for weapons. They were lashed together in a hostage circle around five commandos from the Delta Force - or whatever the fuck this was - and pushed out of the Housing project area toward Second Beach Parking with bayonets inside the circle. One of the other fifteen of the strike force, threw a cordura bag into the central intelligence headquarters. Sparks' residence blew sky high leveling the satellite dishes outside of the structure. Debris rained down on Sparks and the other men as they were pushed along from the housing project. At Second Beach Parking, the strike force set up a perimeter with Claymore mines, infrared motion detectors and high automatic weapons, that squirt bullets like the spray from a shaken up Champagne bottle. An old World War Two deuce and a half, with a big steel cab in back, drove down the LaPush Road toward the parking lot. The commandos opened the perimeter to receive the truck. The back of the truck was labeled *Clallam County Search and Rescue*. Sparks and the other technicians were cut off their nylon tethers, and pushed into the back of the windowless cab. "Some Search and Rescue," grumbled Sparks as he was pushed through the door.

****

The blast broke out the glass in the Pinn house and Dorothy instinctively dove for the floor. A minute before, at the chatter of automatic weapon fire, her cousin, Judy, had run to the crib of her four-month-old son which she instinctively sheltered with her body. Judy's sister, Mary Wright, just sat on the couch looking straight ahead like the zombie she had become since the loss of her baby the day before. Streaks of blood from the shattered glass mingled with the dirty tears and burns that discolored her cheeks. After the fire in the village, Judy had moved to the relative safety of the housing project, with her infant. Before driving out to the diesel bulk plant, John Pinn had collected his grief-stricken niece, Mary, and brought her back to the house, as well. He called his wife at the Outreach Office in Forks and told her not to try to get home to LaPush. Now Dorothy looked out the blown-out window to see what trouble might be coming at them next. She saw the hostages being pushed out of the housing area toward the LaPush Road.

About twenty minutes later, her father and Clarence Fourskins arrived at the crater where Sparks' residence had stood. Their arrival on the scene was delayed by the circuitous course they had taken through the woods, to avoid the military presence at Second Beach Parking. They studied the rubble which had been their intelligence command, and tried to formulate the next move. "There goes our ability to bring down satellites," said John Pinn glumly.

"We can set up other uplinks in the village," said Fourskins. The important thing is the software which we still have and our staff - which aren't lying around here in bits and pieces, anyway. We can assume that Sparks and all of them were taken as prisoners, in one piece."

"Jeff got me into radios when I was a kid. I still have the short wave and CB base stations we used to play with. Let's go to my house, check on my daughter and nieces and see if we can raise that ghost force on the CB We can threaten to start killing hostages, or arrange a trade, or something."

"Actually, I have other plans for the hostages, but it's worth a try. Those workers are very important to our movement..."

The two men entered the Pinn residence and Dorothy was recalcitrant upon seeing her father. Her cynicism for the movement was spilling over into suspicion of the nature of her father's involvement. It did not help that all he cared about, at the moment, was a report on who had been taken prisoner, how many soldiers had comprised the unit, what kind of weapons they carried and so forth. Then the two men went into the basement and set up the old CB base station.

"U.S. military personnel trespassing on Second Beach Parking, this is General Fourskins, Confederate Commander, do you copy?"

"This is Captain Warren, C.O. of Operation LaPush Thunder, I hear you."

"Uh, Captain Warren, what's going on?"

"We bring greetings from Washington, D.C. to President Gable. In case you don't understand the message so far, I'll give it to you as we got it directly from President Shrub: The United States of America does not negotiate with terrorists."

"Is the United States of America forgetting that we have one hundred and fifteen hostages lying on the floor of the Coast Guard Station down in the village."

"No, sir, we have not forgotten the hostages. But it is our assumption, that as loyal Americans and representatives of the Armed Forces, they would choose to die, rather than have their country betrayed. I know that you can only hear my voice, but read my lips, *the U.S.A. does not negotiate with terrorists!*"

****

Friday, November 6, 1992, 08:45

The northernmost finger of Teahwit Head - the 'pinky,' if you will - lies like a bony, phalangeal skeleton, upon which seastars, anemones, algae and other living proof of the intertidal zone cling. The skeletal finger points to an island which has been remarkably excavated by wave action. The constant drilling of the surf has formed a sepulchral tunnel, offering a window of the Pacific. From the vantage of this finger, I pull devil's club prickers out of my forearm. A runner approaches along the wide, sandy expanse, dubbed 'Second Beach' by not so poetic White cartographers. Even half a mile away, I recognize the stride of James Crow and realize that this is the run-amok scientist. I feel no desire to return up the steep slopes to the savage vegetation I have fled, and stand fast on the barnacles and mussel shell watching the man fly over the sands of low tide. The splashing of a wave through the tunnel, signals that the ocean has changed direction and is chasing the moon back up across the beach. At this distance, I can see a strange nylon equipment belt about the man's waist, which appears to be a bandoleer of test tubes. However, the approaching man awakes in me no fear. I stand my ground and wait serenely for him to reach my location.

When Jim Crow is only 150 feet from my spot on the rock, I hear Rod Hill yelling from the headland. "Get out of the way, Hippie!' he orders. "Give me room; I'm going to waste him! He could blow sky high!"

The first shot from the .224 rings out and barnacles, two inches from James Crow's foot, explode in a shower of organic shrapnel.

"NOOOOO!" I scream louder and with more desperation than I have ever felt in my life.

****

James Crow was almost feeling good as he began the two mile stretch of his run along Second Beach. He had gathered a few chemicals that would assure his survival for the twenty-one mile journey from LaPush to the mouth of the Hoh: white phosphorous for light, rounding headlands; and sulfur, potassium chlorate, and modeling clay to make his own C-4, in case he needed a warming fire. He carried his loose-leaf journal, which chronicled the last three years of his existence - the other twenty years worth of writing was kept in a bedroom chest in his deceased parents' trailer. He had waited for the guards placed on him to get tired; one went to seek relief, the other went to seek sleep. In this interlude, James escaped to seek asylum with his Great Aunt. The old woman shared his enthusiasm for God and cynicism for violence. As he ran, he felt like a bird released from a cage, returning to its peaceful nest in the woods. He felt fleet like an osprey or eagle.

It was with these feelings that he approached Teahwit Head. He saw the lone figure that stood between him and the overland route to Third Beach. The silhouette carried no visible weapon; from a distance, James could see the long brown hair and hickory shirt. He knew that this was not a LaPush Native sent out to bring him down. The man's body telegraphed non-aggression, and James continued running towards him, jumping up on the rocky finger, hearing the crunch of the mussel shell...someone yelling something on the cliffs above. The man in front of him was screaming "No!." He had a horrified look on his face.

James heard the shot of the near miss and felt the sting of barnacles as the tiny pieces cut into his leg. He tried to cut an evasive maneuver to his right, running even harder, but a second shot cut through his left calf and penetrated his right ankle. James went down hard on the knife like barnacles and tried to push himself up on his lacerated and bleeding hands. His legs would not support him and he attempted to drag himself into the shelter of the sea tunnel. A third shot pierced the back of his chest and exploded out the lower right front of his rib cage. Then the brown-haired stranger was picking him up and dragging him under the cover of the stone sepulchre. Even through the pain, James still had the feeling of the uncaged bird coming home to its nest. As he lay on his back, with his head in the lap of this stranger, the pain receded like an outgoing tide. A bright Light was emerging from behind the clouds of suffering. It was coming for James...coming to illuminate the way to his peaceful nest.

And as the Light burned off the shadows of anxiety, and radiated joy and infinite peace upon the dying man, he began to surrender all that was left of himself on earth to fly away with this Light. Two items remained on the earthly agenda. James swooped back to earth to utter a dying confession to the stranger that visited with him before he disembarked. It was hard to make his tongue work and there was only a little air in his lungs.

"I ha...have...killed. Ste...Steven Holl...oway an...and a...tur...turkey." The long-haired man was confused. He was entirely agitated by the peaceful Light which came to take James Crow.

"What turkey? Did you kill Ed Whitman? Is that the turkey you killed? Where is the body? You're going to be OK! Just breathe in and out. Hang in there!..."

James held up his shredded and bleeding hands to silence the stranger. He came out of the peaceful Light. He committed his last earthly energy to return to the shadows of his suffering and free the journal from his belt. The brown-haired man received the journal with fear and wondering. He began again to say banally, "Hang in there! You'll be OK..."

James tried to give the stranger important instructions that might benefit him in understanding the purpose for which he had given the man the journal. "St...st...stop..." The Light was everywhere. The heavens were glowing with hues of love, eternal peace and brotherhood... James was carried up in the Warmth. "Wa...wa...war..." As the spirit of James Crow ascended, he was unsure if he had communicated his dying declaration. The brown-haired man was so frightened...and it's hard to articulate words when your spirit is leaving your body.

****

I am still screaming 'no' when the maniac, Rod, begins cutting the poor red man to pieces. Rod stops firing when I get to the victim, but the man is shot right through the back and is trying to claw his way to the cover of the sea tunnel. I drag him into the sepulchre and when I turn him over, I see the exit wound of the .224 slug. It's sucking air and I am trying desperately... as I cover the wound with my hand... to remember from my Industrial First Aid...*frothy blood, spurting between my fingers*...do you let go on inspiration?...*sucking and gurgling*... or expiration? This is really serious!

His trachea is being pushed over to the left side of his throat and bright, bloody sputum is coming out of his mouth as he tries to talk. A wave breaks over me and the dying man, momentarily washing the blood away. The poor bastard is trying to confess himself to me and says that he's killed people. He mumbles the name *Steve Holloway. My* memory is pricked of some long ago amusing front page article I read in college. Then he's talking about killing 'a turkey.' It's got to be what happened to Ranger Ed Whitman. Somehow it doesn't make any sense. I can't understand how this gentle looking man could be driven to violence. Then he wants me to take his journal. He's got all these chemicals around his waist like some kind of human bomb. He struggles to talk while drowning in his own blood. The tide will have us both in a few minutes...maybe with the next wave.

"*Stop war.*" Those are the peculiar, last, dying instructions from a self-confessed killer. He stops breathing. I try giving a few rescue breaths but the air passes from the holes in his chest to the environment as uninhibited and noisily as a bathtub fart. I sit with the body a minute, considering what he has said. I glance through the journal which appears to be the political, religious and social ruminations of a man bent on peace...not a killer. I lay his head down on the sharp gash of the barnacles and give the body to the tide. As I tread along the rock causeway leading to the tunneled island, a Navy helicopter puts down on the flat, sandy beach, fifty meters from the rock finger and several figures disembark with M-16's. I tuck the journal into the back of my underpants and continue to walk toward the waiting soldiers.

"Hold it right there!" calls a shrill voice. Damn, the volunteer Navy sure robs the cradle!

"This isn't the guy, Captain Scott." Says one of the soldiers to the leader. "We're looking for a thin Native, not a hippie."

"What are you doing out here, sir?" calls out the Captain, and through the Nomex and flight helmet, I realize that I am being addressed by a woman.

"You tell me what you're doing, Captain Scott, and I'll tell you what I'm doing." What the hell. The worse they can do to me is take away the journal.

The woman Captain calls out as the party advances on me, "We're looking for a Native American who is carrying dangerous chemicals. Have you seen him? He's of slender build, dark hair and about five foot six inches. Is that blood all over your pants? Are *you* injured."

"Yes, I've seen the mad Native. Yes, it's blood and, no, I'm not injured." The four soldiers converge on me.

"Search him," says the Captain. Two soldiers pat down your belt and arm pits, looking for obvious weapons. They miss the journal. "Where's the subject?"

"The man you're looking for is James Crow, from LaPush. This is his blood. He's dead and back there," I point to the rock tunnel.

"How do you know he's dead," asks one of the soldiers. "Did you kill him?"

"No, I didn't kill him and I know he's dead because I was with him when he died..."

256

"Did you palpate a carotid pulse for at least ten seconds?" asked the woman Captain.

"No, I didn't *palpate a carotid pulse for ten seconds*. The man is dead, OK? He died..."

"You two stay here with the witness and we'll go check it out," ordered the Captain.

"You don't have to go, Captain," said one of the men protectively.

"Of course I have to go!" said the Captain. "I'm the Flight Surgeon." The woman Captain and two soldiers headed out toward the sea tunnel which is now breathing waves and I begin walking back toward the helicopter with the two soldiers.

"Be careful. He *does* have chemicals on his belt!" I turn around to holler. They proceed about two hundred feet towards the sea tunnel when a large swell breaks and races into the tunnel with the sound of a belly flop. The concussion evidently shatters the vials attached to the waist of James Crow and the tube of the sea cave explodes like a cannon throwing salt water, blood, bone and tissue fragments all over the Captain and two nearer most soldiers. They all go down. My escort breaks away to run to the assistance of the three and I jog past the helicopter and begin climbing the slopes back to my receptive and concealing friends: the devil's club, salmonberry and vine maple. Half way up the slope I turn around and can see all five soldiers together. The three have gotten up and have sorted out their own body parts from the atomized body of James Crow. They would find no body in the sepulchre. "HEY!" I yell out to the Flight Surgeon as loud as I can. "If you find his head, don't forget to check for a carotid pulse!"

****

Friday, November 6, 1992 08:55

Ranger Ed Whitman's legs were wobbly as he came out of the tiny shack next to the Bogachiel Bridge on the LaPush Road. He had virtually fulfilled his promise to James Crow to wait until late morning. Now he would go home. James had explained that he was still pressing for nonviolence but that the leaders had momentum in a more deadly direction.. He would desert on the morning of November 6, in any case. Crow's survival depended on Whitman staying put. Then Whitman had seen Indians rigging the bridge with what appeared to be homemade explosives. The Ranger had worried that the bridge might be blown before the 24 hours elapsed and that Whitman would be killed, anyway. Whitman had heard the thunder of battle from LaPush the previous day. Last night, the sky was lit up as if Forks were burning. Whitman worried for his family. But Crow had risked everything for him and Whitman would never betray the man. If there's one thing the Park Servant knew, it was loyalty.

The Ranger got down to the river. He splashed cold water on his face. There were still pieces of flesh colored bondo, and spatters of turkey blood on his face and neck. While the Ranger had trembled in fear for his life, James Crow had escaped through a high shop window, and returned with a turkey. He butchered the turkey over Whitman. He cut off the neck and molded it into the cavity of his throat with car-body putty. Crow had even thought to quarter the turkey carcass and smuggle it out of the shop in the hubcaps of the Valiant. Whitman had fed hungrily on the turkey meat for the duration of his voluntary incarceration. Crow had jogged over yesterday, in the wind and rain, and told Whitman to abide 24 hours longer. Having fulfilled this promise, and revived from cold water, the Ranger turned from the river to begin the five mile hike back to his home at Mora. He was suddenly overcome by thoughts of his family which he had driven from his mind from the time he was pushed into the trunk of the Valiant. His eyes burned with tears. Then he heard a runner on the bridge. Maybe it would be James Crow coming to say goodbye.

****

As I run across the bridge, I know I am taking a chance. While I waited for Captain Scott to clear out of Third Beach Parking with her helicopter dawn patrol, I skimmed the last twenty pages of the journal surrendered to me by the dying Native on Second Beach. I had learned many things in those pages, not the least of which was that the bridge I ran across was wired with 300 pounds of diesel impregnated horse shit awaiting radio-controlled detonation. I had learned that Ranger Ed Whitman was not dead, but hiding in a squatter's shack beside the bridge. I had learned that James Crow had spoken of his drive for peace in every page of the journal and the circumstances of Steve Holloway's passing had been shaken out of my tenuous memory. My eyes stung with tears as I reflected upon the man who had written these pages: A spiritual being, who aspired for peace and justice...whose own movement had turned against him. Tears streak my face as I jog down to see if Whitman is still at the squatter's shack. We surprise one another. He is loping up towards the bridge.

"Hello Chiggers!" says the Ranger. Strangely, tears streak his wet face as well. "What are *you* doing here?"

"Hi, Ed. I came to make sure you weren't waiting here in the cabin. This bridge is wired with horse shit and might blow at any moment!"

"Do you know anything about James Crow!"

"Well, yes. I was with him on Second Beach a few hours ago."

The Ranger's countenance lightened. "How *is* James?" He asked with some relief.

"Well, really, he *isn't*. Let's get out of here before this bridge blows and I'll explain."

258

As we run together, I give the ranger the news of his friend James Crow. Ed Whitman is visibly shaken by the news. I am extending condolences and approaching Three Rivers Resort, where we will part company, when the ground heaves and there is a tremendous blast from behind us. We turn around and the sky several hundred feet above the horizon is dirty with the Bogachiel Bridge. There is no doubting the potency of horse shit. The ranger drags me off the road where we take shelter under the canopy of a large spruce from the deadly rock fly which lasts for fifteen seconds. We shake hands and the ranger runs in the direction of Mora, nervously skirting the road, while I head out to Forks jogging straight down the pavement.

Eight miles further, as I approach the outskirts of the fire which took the bulk diesel plant and two mills, I come on the two M-1 tanks of the National Guard's strike force. I try to hail the tanks but they roll by me. I find the main column near the intersection with Highway 101, unloading the tanks from lowboy trailers and engaging the troop carriers in all wheel drive to cross the cratered section of burned-out road. I approach an officer and say, "You'll never get to LaPush. They blew the Bogachiel Bridge. You might as well turn around."

The C.O. laughed in my face. "There's a fucking ocean between us and Iran, but that won't stop us either. We'll manage, but thanks for the report."

"Is it too late for peace?" I ask in remembrance of someone who would want the question raised.

"Jesus, what are you...some kind of a nut? Stand aside!"

THIRTY-FOUR

*F*rom 1898 until 1907, Olaf E. Erickson was a County Commissioner and de facto mayor of the small Scandinavian village of Mora, Washington. The village sat on banks overlooking the Dickey River, near where it flowed into the Quillayute Estuary. Olaf was much interested in the goings-on in the Native village of LaPush across the water. In particular, his fascination was drawn to the cloud-shrouded rock monolith of James Island, which served as the ancestral burial grounds as well as for purposes of civil defense. He pled with the villagers to escort him to the lofty palisades atop the island; but was consistently rebuffed by the Natives for this was a sacred place, off limits to Hoquats. Finally, by a generous bribe of tobacco, he was able to persuade the local shaman to permit the trespass and guide him on the difficult climb to the top of the island. The treatment of the deceased, which he beheld atop the island graveyard , staggered his imagination. He stammered to his Native guide, "My God, man! The climb up here, dragging the dead and those heavy dugout canoes is, in itself an unbelievable feat! But, how in the world do you manage the impossible task of raising the canoes into the trees with their dead cargo!"

"It's easy," said the old shaman, blowing smoke and spitting. "We make the women do it."

****

Second Beach Housing
Friday, November 6, 1992, 08:15 hours

It was the desperation of the moment that caused John Pinn to go along with Fourskins' wild scheme. The intelligence personnel were critical to the long term goals of the Confederation. Obviously, human hostages would provide little leverage to an Administration that chose not to "negotiate with terrorists." Pinn and Fourskins assumed that the strike team which had divested them of their central intelligence was waiting for a helicopter transfer of the prisoners. An unidentified explosion from the direction of Second Beach gave some hope that there had been a helicopter crash or some other military misadventure to delay the movement of the prisoners. He called down to the village for four ounces of the C-4 Wally had brought back from Guard Camp. He asked the runner to bring a small thirty-minute firing delay, hundreds of which had been mailed around the country for the Columbus Day demonstration. While they waited for the runner, Fourskins went out to fetch the best looking lab coat from under the debris by the blown-up building.

"I've got an idea for getting back the prisoners, but I don't think anyone under this roof is going to like it. It will work, and, believe me, it's safe..." Fourskins was interrupted by the arrival of the runner with the C-4 and detonator delay. Fourskins placed the explosives on newspaper and excused himself to go to the bathroom. When he came out of the bathroom it was pretty obvious to everyone that he had flipped out. In his left hand he carried one of his turds! He placed the excrement on the newspaper, armed the C-4 with the detonator and asked Dorothy if she had a count-down feature on her watch. She did. "Mark!" said Fourskins arming

261

the detonator and beginning the countdown. He pushed the C-4 into the turd. He laughed and said, "Usually I wear gloves when I do this, but we're kind of in a hurry here." He walked over to where the infant was just getting back to sleep in his cradle. That's when the arguing, screaming, and fighting started.

Fifteen minutes later, on Dorothy Pinn's chronograph, she clutched her cousin Judy's baby and walked toward the Search and Rescue vehicle. *Her father had made her do it!* Of course, the whole time that demon Fourskins had promised that it was safe and that no harm would befall her or the baby. He'd explained how she could always just throw the diaper into the woods - which is pretty much how diapers were managed on the Reservation, anyway - or confess the turd bombs presence to the soldiers...But Fourskins had made a strong case that the prisoners must be recovered, and that lives would be saved by this subterfuge. John Pinn's was among those lives.

There was no time for a vote. John Pinn was following orders. Although Judy physically resisted the "loan" of her baby, John Pinn enforced the will of the Confederacy. The infant was armed with the turd bomb in a bulging diaper. Dorothy was hastily briefed, dressed in the lab coat and pushed out the door. Thirteen minutes and fifty two seconds would reveal the plan as a success or failure..., fifty, forty-nine.

"Halt! Put the baby on the ground. Step back five paces!" Dorothy did as she was told.

"You've got my husband," she offered Fourskins' lie. "We want to stay together."

Two soldiers were on her in a second. They weren't mean but they weren't gentle. They pulled off her lab coat and threw it on the ground. The pushed their hands into places even Wally hadn't explored. They pulled all her pockets inside out; took off her shoes; bound her hands in front with flexicuffs.

Then they went to consider the baby. "I'll need the cloth diaper, please. You can clean it," said Dorothy as per her instructions.

After looking into the diaper and confirming what his nose and the crying baby were already telling him; the soldier refastened the safety pin. He placed the diapered baby in the cradle of Dorothy's bound arms and said, "Sorry, lady, we're not a diaper service out here."

They pushed her towards the back of the Search and Rescue vehicle. Two men stood by with shotguns pointed at the locked door. "Just a second," said the soldier in charge. "Get her watch." As they unstrapped the device, she looked longingly at the face which read, *09:23:(blur)*. They opened the door and pushed her and the baby into the steel shell. "Happy reunion," the soldier said. The door slammed and locked behind her.

Dorothy focussed on keeping track of how long it took her to whisper to Sparks, "There's a bomb in the baby's diaper; mark: eight forty-five, forty-four, forty-three..." as Dorothy counted, she handed the infant to a female intelligence worker. She pulled off her nylon webbed belt, which fortunately the soldiers had missed. She sawed the belt across the flexicuffs behind Sparks' back and, amazingly, the belt cut through the nylon, as she was told it would.. In two minutes, the nylon band broke and fell to the floor. "... three, two, one, six minutes, fifty-nine, fifty-eight..." As Dorothy counted she sawed on the next team member's cuffs with her belt. Sparks found the C-4 in the turd and was impressed with the generosity of the charge.

"This is really going to make a boom!" he said molding the putty into a cone and pressing the self-adhesive C-4 against the door just behind the locking mechanism. "We have to get all our hands free and over our ears, or this device will destroy our hearing. It would be a hell of a deal to have a deaf intelligence agency." Sparks had picked up the flexicuffs that had fallen on the floor. "These work just as well," he said, sawing on the cuffs of one of his co-workers.

"...two, one, four minutes, fifty-nine..." the nylon bands fell to the floor from the woman cradling the baby. Dorothy took back the crying, naked baby and nestled the infant to the warmth and shelter of her bosom. She heard the engine of the vehicle start. The prisoners worked frantically to saw away their nylon restraints as the vehicle began to move.

****

Captain Warren was pissed about the delay. The use of the Clallam County rig, from Port Angeles, was Admiral Bingingham's big idea to avoid any more aerial targets like yesterday's A-6 crash. In the deaf/dumb world that had engulfed the Alamo since yesterday, the parade of this campaign was passing by Admiral Bingingham. Nonetheless, helicopters from the LPD were needed to clean up the casualties. Captain Scott, who was leading the medivac, was drafted into prisoner transport. She had been outfitted with a sophisticated a.m. transceiver and ordered to stand by at the staging area at Third Beach Parking. As soon as the prisoners were taken, they were supposed to be moved to Third Beach Parking for helicopter pick-up and transporting to a debriefing facility. Captain Warren had called on schedule to announce the securing of the prisoners. Captain Scott had not responded. Rather than retreat up the road, opening the way for enemy pursuit, his men dug in at Second Beach Parking and waited for Captain Scott to finish polishing her nails, or whatever she was up to besides monitoring the radio. An enemy intelligence worker with a baby and huge tits had surrendered to them while they waited. It almost made Captain Warren wish he was the prisoner husband inside the steel shell. Then the errant Captain's voice came on the radio. "Warren, Scott."

"This is Warren at Control Point One. We have the package and are ready to move. Where the hell were you, Captain?"

"Sorry, Warren. There was a chemical warfare threat that we had to investigate. The subject blew himself up. You may have heard the explosion. There was another subject that got away dressed up like a hippie logger. There's a yellow pick-up at Third Beach Parking which may belong to him. He'll probably turn up on the LaPush Road if you could pick him up."

Captain Warren had seen the brown-haired subject in the same pick-up parked at Control Point One, but did not want to get distracted by this business incidental to his mission. "We're proceeding to Control Point Two with the package and four," said Captain Warren, meaning that Jeff Sparks and other hostile intelligence workers were in custody. They were being transported in the custody of four Army Rangers to Scott. "The rest of us will maintain C P Two until school begins." School for the LaPush students, would commence with the arrival of a large detachment of the Washington National Guard. Warren doubted that the students would sleep through the class. His orders were to secure the package, hold the road and fade, allowing the Guard to level the target. He made a horizontal spiraling with his finger, indicating for the driver to start the old Red Diamond engine of the deuce and half. A soldier climbed aboard the running boards on either side with automatic weapons. On the bench seat in front were two soldiers: the driver and the other riding shotgun with a shotgun. The package, plus four, pulled out of Second Beach Parking and drove south with the smoldering top of James Island shining in the mirrors of the old deuce and a half.

****

Fourskins had lied to Dorothy about saving her father. He had put the Native in command of a grim little suicide band that would provide distraction to these hot-shot Rambos, while the intelligence personnel scattered into the woods. Out in streets of the Second Beach Housing project, the Natives checked their weapons while Fourskins counted down, "...two...one...five minutes...fifty-nine...fifty-eight..."

John Pinn had pulled one of the Confederation's heavier ordinance, which was a full acetylene tank with a 30-pound potassium percolate/lead azide warhead. They had put together about thirty of these weapons to fire out of well-casing launchers at tanks or armored carriers. It wouldn't penetrate the heavy tank armor, but it damn well would blow it off track skids and immobilize the target. It would also make a crater out of the Second Beach Parking Lot and everything in it. This would have to wait until his daughter and the other prisoners had exited the exploded back door and made it into the woods. They would give their lives to provide that window of opportunity. Some of the men held the multi-barrel, mini rocket launchers they had practiced with out in Smith Field. They wore eye protection, but Pinn's guess was that they would only have use of their eyes for a few seconds after discharging weapons, immediately after which, they would be shot dead. If only the deuce and a half would move away from the soldiers. Several chase vehicles stood by, at the ready, for this contingency. As if answering a prayer, the engine of the old war wagon roared to life.

"Four minutes! Colonel Pinn! Forward with ten men! When you engage the target, we'll fire the missile. You, five men, into the foremost chase car. If the missile is fired, the deuce and a half is heading south on the LaPush Road. Follow them and engage the enemy." Pinn's forces were already into the trees. They had to wait only a few seconds before the deuce and a half pulled out with a gunman on each running board and two shotguns up with the driver. Pinn waited for the vehicle to get two hundred feet south along the road. He motioned the men down. From his training and experiences in southeast Asia, he recognized a well-defended perimeter. If the missile could do most of the work, there was a chance to get out of this alive. He got down behind a stump, held the M-16 over his head toggled on to automatic and pulled the trigger. A split second later fifteen Claymore mines exploded and peppered the large stump that covered the hulk of John Pinn. Every alder sapling that screened the housing project from the LaPush Road was cut down. The roar was deafening. The Rambos opened up with high automatic fire that cut even the larger trees to pieces and, a second later, there was the whoosh of their homemade missile, a deafening roar and then scattered plops and thuds as pieces of the Second Beach Parking lot rained down from the sky. A boot with a foot in it landed next to John Pinn and he shook behind the stump as memories a quarter century old clawed their way back into his conscience.

The chase rig pulled out of the Housing project with a great squealing of tires and then all Pinn's men were up themselves, jumping over the debris and offal from the explosion, running towards the deuce and a half which had come to a stop, the four soldiers forming a skirmish line between the Native onslaught and their prisoners. The soldier on the right fired a LAW right into the engine of the chase vehicle as the Natives attempted to get out with their weapons. The engine block exploded like a grenade, taking down all five men with shrapnel. John Pinn realized his ragamuffin squad was no match for this team. Just then the steel back door blew off the back of the armored wagon, knocking down all four soldiers. Two were down for the count; but the other two scrambled on the ground to get their weapons. The freed prisoners streamed out of the back , making it impossible to fire on the soldiers. "Hold your fire!" screamed Pinn, fearing someone would waste his daughter. The two dizzy soldiers had regained their weapons and began dizzily spraying the charging Natives. Indians fell in the charge, unable to shoot back.

****

Inside of the steel cab, Dorothy had known that they were not going to get all the nylon bands off in time. The vehicle had been moving for a full minute when she said, "Two minutes! We're not going to make it. We need some cotton to stuff in our ears!" There were still four Natives with their hands secured behind their backs.

Jeff Sparks approached Dorothy and said softly. "I really do appreciate you coming after us like this and...excuse me!" He ripped the buttons apart on her blouse, poked his fingers into her cleavage, and ripped off her bra. He shredded the material in his teeth and pushed fluffy plugs of polyester into the ear canals of the four men who were still bound. He was inserting the last of the eight plugs he'd made. As

Dorothy was trying to recover her composure enough to pick up on the count down, the vehicle shook with an explosion. The door was still in place, so it wasn't the C-4. Sparks was pushing everyone to the front of the cab and piling them on top of the four with the cotton/polyester ear-plugs. There was a second explosion outside and a few seconds later the chatter of automatic weapon fire just outside the door. Sparks was yelling, "Cover your ears! Open your mouth! Close your eyes!" Dorothy jumped on top of the huddle. She opened her mouth and closed her eyes. She cupped her hands over both the baby's ears and held him to her naked bosom. The explosion inside the cab, knocked her out.

When she stirred through the shooting stars and stabbing colors of returning consciousness, all was silence. There wasn't even a ringing. Everyone was gone and with a start she jumped up to find the baby which was somehow still under her. She could feel it crying and see its little mouth open in fear and distress. She made comforting sounds that only the baby could hear, as she carried it to the fresh air of the open door. She had to get them away from the stench of the smoke. She stood at the open door of the armored cab, clutching the baby to her breast and issued a scream that escaped from her soul, fled her throat and flew from her mouth where it was taken prisoner by her deafness. The open road leading to the turn off to her home at Second Beach housing was strewn with dead bodies. Ten feet away, her father stomped a soldier's brains into the pavement of the LaPush Road with his logging boots.

****

Friday, November 6, 1992, 13:20 E.S.T.,

In the White House the President sat in front of some four different cameras. The three network cameras sat inert, while the only red light, indicated that he was connected by closed circuit with the Chief of Staff and Secretary of Defense. The signal followed fiber optic cable directly to the Pentagon where the two men waited through this military crisis. Network professionals worked over the President's face with camel hair brush, and flesh-colored powder. He looked fresh and energetic as he spoke, "My fellow Americans, our country faces another threat to freedom and it is with a heavy heart that I report to you an atrocity against military personnel of the Armed Forces of the United States of America..."

"No, no, Mr. President," cut in the Chief of Staff. "Just say 'the U.S. Armed Forces.' Most of your audience is going to be housewives who were watching *As the World Turns*. Your audience is in a hurry to get back to their scheduled viewing. Don't antagonize them. Just read the teleprompter and don't adlib..."

"God damn it, Bob, I don't give a shit! We're scheduled to go on in ten minutes and we still don't have a report on the destruction of that pirate uplink station. How are these poor viewers going to get back to *As the World Turns* if the world gets blown off its axis because of some crazy, power hungry, Apaches disrupting the balance of world powers..."

266

"Mr. President, calm down. Get in the proper mood to make this address: You are heart sore that a military action must be taken; you discussed the situation with Governor Boot, who begged you to allow him to use the National Guard; you have asked the Governor for assurances that no civilians in the area of the target will be harmed; you regret terribly this violent turn of events in a country that treasures peace above everything but freedom...read the teleprompter, but put some feeling in it Mr. President."

The make-up specialist finished with the President's face. She fell back to consider her work as the man spoke, "I might choke on the part about the civilians. That whole village is hostile. The sooner we go public on that, the sooner the American people will understand the casualty figures - which we'll have to release in the next forty-eight hours..."

****

Friday, November 6, 1992, 10:27 P.S.T.

Meanwhile, on a pirated signal, being received at the Com Center at the U.S. Coast Guard Station in LaPush, two Native studio technicians studied their monitor. They watched as the make-up specialist finished making up President Shrub's face. The President was discussing his intentions for the citizens of the LaPush. "We ought to be broadcasting what he's saying. It's incredibly damaging!"

"We'll give it to the networks, along with the videos of the prisoners eating, for the eleven o'clock news. That gives us the biggest audience and the publicity we need. Anyway, we don't want to put our cards on the table just yet. Keep the video recording this channel, but bring the screen around to the Victoria, CNN station.

The screen revealed Timothy Gable, who sat alone at a table studying a pile of notes. He looked up and saw the red light.

"Hello." He said into the camera.

A speaker next to Tim came to life. "Hello, Tim," there was the squeal of feedback. "Use the ear piece, Tim. Turn off the speaker." The President of the Confederation of Non-White Americans turned off the speaker and listened into the earphone.

"We're about ten minutes from going on the air, Tim. General Fourskins wants to talk to you. Gable's make up felt like morning-after puke crusted on his face. He was nervous and he felt a fleeting desire for the illusionary relaxation afforded by his previous overindulgence. He looked into the monitor. It was the countdown to a satellite patch, "...four, three, two, one..." The face of his mentor, Clarence Fourskins, came on the screen.

"Hello, President Gable. You look really regal on my screen here at the Com Center. How are you feeling?"

"Frankly, Mr. Fourskins, I hate to admit it to *you*, of all people...but I could sure use a drink."

"You know that's all behind you, sir. Remember? We get high on justice!"

"Well, right now it feels like someone's been watering down my justice..."

"You'll be fine, Tim. President Shrub is coming on about the same time you go on. That will make for the most impact. Most of what you say will just appear on the screen as closed captions. I recruited the stenographer from the Tripp County Superior Court to transfer your speech to the caption format we will probably use.

"Let's see. To keep you posted on recent developments: There was an attack on our central intelligence. We lost the building, but recovered the personnel that were taken prisoners. The intelligence workers had set up collateral communication links here in the village, so our broadcast is still possible. But they will be working around the clock to restore our influence upon aerospace defense. I'll risk a breach in security by telling you that the main strike will be from the National Guard from Fort Lewis. Their attack has been locked in by President Shrub regardless of whether or not we return the package. We blew the bridge about an hour ago to slow things down a bit. The tanks, I'm sure, will just snorkel across the river downstream of the bridge; but the infantry will have to walk five miles, which gives us a real advantage. We're dug in and waiting. Just take your time and interact with what's on the screen. We'll want you to talk directly to President Shrub at some point during the broadcast. He should be quite surprised. We'll catch him off guard, giving you a strong advantage. I appreciate you sticking with the program."

"Mr. Fourskins, I know a lot of you will be dead in a few hours. I just want to say that I appreciate what you've done for our cause and for me personally. I'll do my best to honor the sacrifices being made today."

THIRTY-FIVE

Friday, November 6, 1992, 10:05 P.S.T.

Special Agent Frederick Prue was not having a good day as he rode out to Mora with the Park Service District Ranger in a four-wheel-drive pick-up. They had needed four-wheel-drive to get across the burned out section of the LaPush Road. The National Guard had set up a road block; the pimply-faced punk soldiers would not let them pass. Prue's investigation of the Whitman case had focussed on two principal suspects: his old punching bag, Clarence Fourskins; and some 'born again' by the name of James Crow. Investigation revealed that Whitman had definitely left the hospital. Witnesses had seen a man, resembling Whitman, running back and forth, behaving strangely in the Pay 'n' Save grocery store. An unattended shopping cart had been discovered by store personnel and Whitman's wife, Carol, identified the video as one that her kids had wanted to see; the empty ice cream carton, as the flavor preferred by Whitman's children; and some wash towels as being typical of the kind of gift that would follow any act of discourtesy on Whitman's part. Carol remembered the way Whitman snarked at her as he left for the hospital.

Prue had not much probable cause when he went to the circuit judge in Seattle for a search warrant to ransack the Crow and Fourskins residences. The judge had grudgingly signed the warrants, but told Prue, "in the future, get your fishing licenses at a sports store." The warrant had been specific to the government Suburban Whitman had been driving, which would be hard to hide, or articles of Whitman's clothing, which got Prue into places smaller than a garage.

He executed the search warrant on Crow Thursday morning. He had found all kinds of mysterious chemicals and several bottles of Valium without a prescription , which he seized. Crow, who was on scene, laughed and told the agent he had better do a field test on the pills, which turned out to be some kind of placebo. A search of the mobile home on the property turned up a stack of loose-leaf notes going back to 1968 in a bedroom dresser. It was Crow's personal journal. The Fourth Amendment presented an obstacle in reading or removing these notes from the Crow residence.

Up at Second Beach Housing, the Special Agent had searched the Fourskins' residence without luck. Fred Prue was well aware that something political was coming down in this sleepy reservation town. But there was no evidence at Fourskins' residence. Without Mark White as an informant, Prue could only wait and see what developed in the village. The LaPushans were no help and no one knew nothin'. On October 12, Fourskins group had sent out a Declaration of Independence - for Christ's sake, and if that's all this was about, the FBI was wasting his time here in LaPush. The G-man was beginning to believe that Whitman had maybe slipped off to some little senhorita in old Mehico and that the whole political thing was hot air.

That was yesterday morning. Today, there was a crisis. Big time! And no one had told him shit! There was a news black-out of everything but the Navy's boating disaster, and the bulk-plant fire. These were headlines. However, they were not the concern of the FBI Prue had opened up his Seattle office that morning, and there were no messages or dispatches from anyone. He headed out to the Peninsula to carry on his overtime-filled weekend investigations. He stopped at the Park's West District Office to touch bases. The more the District Ranger told him, the angrier the Special Agent became: a Park Ranger gunned down on the beach; a Navy jet crashed; and boat disaster under mysterious circumstances; the Navy apparently firing on the village; the Coast Guard station non-responsive, and apparently overrun by hostiles; a whole company of Seals shot, drowned or taken prisoner; owners of Three Rivers Resort calling out on their phones to report that the Bogachiel Bridge was just blown up; ...a few developments, to say the least! The reports alone would take the rest of the Special Agent's career.

"Why in the hell didn't someone call me!" bellowed Prue. He seized the Park Servant's telephone. He called his home office: Quantico, Virginia. Supervisory Agent Shortbrand was temporarily out of the office, but there was a total blackout on this event. The FBI in Quantico knew nothing. They wanted Prue to keep *them* informed.

The Park man said he was personally going out to Mora to evacuate Ed Whitman's family. He offered to take Prue, since he would need four-wheel-drive transport, anyway. Whatever Ed's condition might be, the Whitman investigation was dead - particularly in light of recent developments. Agent Prue could give Carol Whitman the standard line about how the FBI would leave 'no stone unturned' and would 'pull tenaciously at every thread of evidence.' Then could pitch the whole investigation into the file cabinet.

After being turned back by the Guard, the park man turned down a logging road a half mile east of the LaPush Road. He took Prue on the back road to the Quillayute Prairie, and then onto Mora. The mobile radio in the pick-up came out with an announcement that the President would make an important televised message at 13:30 relating to National Security. "Your radio tells you more than I get from the FBI, Howard," said the G-man trying to make up for his outburst in the Park office an half hour earlier.

"The radio's been off and on for the last day or so," said the District Ranger.

****

10:20 P.S.T.

At the Whitman mobile home, Carol and her two kids were moping about. They'd packed some clothing, a few special toys, heirlooms, and photos for the retreat. Barricades closed the whole Park area. All other personnel had left. Special Agent Prue stood next to the television set, delivering his spiel about the aggressive investigation, and the search for her husband that would proceed in spite of all this. Prue waved at the door in the direction of LaPush. As he pointed, there was the sound of footsteps on the porch; the door opened; and Fred Prue's outstretched hand pointed at Ranger Ed Whitman, himself. He lost his audience.

10:25 P.S.T., Coast Guard Station LaPush

Clarence Fourskins addressed the collection of government hostages which had been accumulated in the last 24 hours. The Coasties, Marines, and Seals listened nervously. They stood in orderly rows. They could not believe that there wasn't a catch to the instructions they were being given.

"It's in our interest to see that you are all returned unharmed to your friends and families. Some of you may bear grievance against us from which you will never relent. But all of you should agree that we have treated you decently. In exchange for your release, we expect you to give this message to the American people: contrary to how your government will portray us; we are soldiers that treat a vanquished enemy with respect.

"We are not releasing you to avoid a fight, which is what some of you believe. On the contrary. Vicious fighting will break out immediately, subsequent to your return to your lines, so keep moving. We are heavily armed and expect to inflict devastating casualty to those who attack us. Once you reach your lines, move as fast as you can to safe cover. If you fall out of line before you reach your point of release, you will be shot. Those are just the rules of war. Remember, you were treated humanely and with respect."

Fourskins ran his eyes over his audience. The Coasties were buying it; but the Marines, and Seals, were still unhappy about their units being peppered with shotguns and ground up by drift logs. Hey, that's war. There was no time now to dwell upon it. "Take the prisoners to the line!" The column moved out the doors.

Fourskins walked into the Com Center and checked the Coast Guard's closed circuit camera, set up to offer views of First Beach, James Island, the estuary, and LaPush Road coming into the village. The first two tanks, still wet from crossing the Bogachiel River, had arrived and were taking a position just in front of the sewer main. The Natives had turned off the main and flooded it with ether two hours ago. Luckily Crow had given them the location of a buried 55-gallon drum of ether in Springfield, Oregon before becoming hostile to the Command himself. The ether-charged sewer pipe was just one little surprise that was coming out of the 55-gallon drum.

Fourskins checked the open camera from the CNN news room in Victoria. He saw Timothy Gable nervously reviewing some his notes. The monitor showed the SATCOM 1 satellite transmission of a daily soap opera reaching conclusion of another sob-filled, love-shocked episode. "Cut into the commercial stations with our 'stand by,'" Fourskins gave one of the ten studio technicians a cue to display a message on the teleprompter. The words, *NATIONAL EMERGENCY\STAND BY FOR MESSAGE* interrupted the kissing on the screen. "That will get the housewives on the phones to their husbands. They'll think nuclear war is a few hours away.

They'll tell hubby to watch the news and pick up a few extra TV dinners on his way home."

Fourskins talked into his the control desk mike and Tim Gable looked up at the screen. "No use for any cramming, you're on in ten seconds. Just relax and do your best. We're counting on you." Gable addressed his senior production manager and said, "Screen one, five seconds...Mark."

****

13:24 E.S.T.

In the control room of Radio City, New York, headquarters of the National Broadcasting Company; and home of the Rockettes, half a dozen technicians laconically watched the renown fabulist, President George Shrub, preparing another great fiction on the issue of 'National Security.' All the networks would carry the President's message, so there was no competitive edge in the studio room. One studio man watched the tangle of arms, legs, and lips, that marked the conclusion of 'Another Spin of the Globe' and prepared to launch a deodorant commercial. Suddenly, his screen went blank and a message appeared, "*NATIONAL EMERGENCY/STAND BY FOR MESSAGE.*" The technicians watching the President's five minute curtain call were spilling coffee and dropping doughnuts as they threw switches and tried to figure out what was interrupting their signal. "This signal is coming from Westar 5, from the west coast...wait! We were just patched to the CNN uplink in Victoria. What the hell is this! The President comes on in three minutes!"

The screen flashed...five, four, three, two... and a middle aged Native American looked up from a pile of papers on the desk behind which he sat. He addressed the camera clearly and gravely...

Ladies and gentlemen, I am Timothy Gable, President of the Confederation of Non-White Americans. Twenty-five days ago, my countrymen in LaPush brought forth upon territory, heretofore claimed by the United States, a new nation. Born out of more than 200 years of repression our tiny country is dedicated to the concept that we are - all of us - equal in the eyes of God...

****

"He's feeding us the Gettysburg Address, for crying out loud!" roared Clarence Fourskins in the Control Room. He watched ten different monitor screens feeding in from Sparks' crew. They were out with portable cameras, with the prisoners who were marching as a column. The guard soldiers had put flowers in the muzzles of their assault rifles. Fourskins expected it would be interpreted as an expression of non-aggression, as it had in the '60's. He had locked the Coast Guard Camera in on the LaPush Road. Three more tanks had arrived. They were positioned within 20 meters of the sewer line. Close enough. But there wasn't enough time for this Fourth of July fanfare that Gable was spouting.

This was stuff that Sparks was supposed to handle. Sparks was still having trouble hearing well. H was completely overwhelmed with having to find solutions to countless computer problems. His greatest priority was setting up an entirely new uplink for the failsafe to compromise the United States aerospace defense. Fourskins watched the column of prisoners passing one of the camera men. "Cut in with Remote Four...Mark, five, four, three, two, one, now..."

****

CNN Newsroom, Victoria, B.C.

"We were met on the battlefield of Rialto Beach...," As he delivered what he hoped would be the speech of his life, the tiny voice of Clarence Fourskins interrupted in the hidden earphone he wore, "Watch your monitor, Timothy." Gable looked down. To his relief, he saw that he was not on the screen. He was watching the release of prisoners as they were marched out of the village. Some of the hostages laughed, and gave the 'v' sign with their fingers to the camera. The guards had flowers in the muzzles of their carbines...A small clock in the upper-right corner of his screen read: *President Shrub- 92...91...90.* Gable had a lot of explaining to do in a minute and a half. *"....where a handful of our countrymen disarmed an entire company of Navy Seals. They stood by to render assistance when the reckless Seals were endangered by drift logs pitching in the surf. After rescuing the Navy personnel, we filed a protest with the President of the United State. George Shrub has consistently ignored our sovereignty and threatened our security..."*

****

Mora Housing Area

Special Agent Prue was a non-sentimental cynic. The joyful crying, passionate embracing, and slobbering utterances threatened the custody of the Special Agent's brunch sandwich. To proceed with his investigation, he had tried to separate the family bread that had enveloped the lunchmeat of Ranger Whitman. The District Ranger had said, "Give them a few minutes, Fred."

Not to miss the President's address, Prue had turned on the family's TV. He was watching the same brain-numbing, time-wasting, kissypoo, that NBC broadcast everyday at this time. He repaired to the bathroom of the mobile home to escape the joyous delirium and to find a constructive use for the few minutes before the President's speech. When he returned, the reunified family was a tight knot in front of the TV with the District Ranger pressing forward for a view. Whitman and his superior were exchanging remarks like, "So *that's* where he disappeared to!" and "Golly, he sure looks sober!" From Prue's vantage of the screen, he could see a long column of prisoners being led out of, what he recognized as LaPush Village. Some of the prisoners wore Coast Guard uniforms, and smiled at the camera giving the 'v' sign. "Jesus!" said Prue recoiling like a vampire from garlic. As he listened to the narration with the picture he became more agitated...

"...We return these prisoners freely now as a gesture of our good will to their families and to the people of the United States, but we cannot ignore the grave

273

threats that have been made by your President, which have necessitated our engagement of a high-tech program to exercise influence over the aerospace defense capabilities of the United States. This morning as most of you slept, the U.S. Armed Forces again struck, trying to destroy our only influence over your country, in the absence of U.S. conscience and reasonability. We successfully defended our installation..."

"Who's this talking?" Agent Prue wanted to know. But the picture on the screen changed, and what he saw hit him like a baseball bat in the groin. "Jesus God NO!" Prue screamed. "NO! It can't be!" A close up picture revealed Jeff Sparks, also known as Johnny Ohm, putting the finishing touches on a satellite dish that he was converting as an uplink. The screen revealed an array of low-noise amplifiers, computer-enhanced tuners, frequency scanners, and other high-tech components to tell the informed viewer that this was a real system assembled by one of the foremost authorities on the subject. "No, please, no, no no..." Prue was saying, as the screen changed to show the LaPush Road, as it comes into the village. Seven tanks had drawn up in close formation. Foot soldiers were gathering behind the tanks. "Please no, please no, please no..."

****

White House, Washington D.C.

In the final few minutes before the President's speech, the network and press personalities in the conference room became aware of the unfolding of perhaps the strangest media event that had ever transpired across the radio waves of the United States. The three monitors showing the picture being sent to their respective employers showed the President practicing his opening lines; but one of the newsmen had a small liquid crystal display pocket TV which was receiving quite a different signal than '*Another Spin of the Globe*' programming which was being transmitted on NBC "Look at this, will you." A small tangle of newsmen looked incredulously at the tiny screen. Several of them had beepers go off and hurried to the bank of telephones which facilitated their communication of news from the lips of their President. The three network representatives called in. They were told that it appeared that radio pirates had taken over air waves, and were declaring succession from the United States. They could report the situation to the President himself, and tell The Man to stand by and edit his speech accordingly.

One thing newsmen really hate is a press release in which they are not given copy beforehand. Such practice requires the journalists to furiously take notes, which is demeaning to their station in life. It forces the members of the press community into spontaneity, in digesting Presidential verbiage, and regurgitating their analysis to a public that is hungry for such interpretation. The three had been aggravated by the White House's insistence that there would be no leak of the content of the President's speech. The three network men got together to discuss the right thing to do and two of the three remembered being left out in the rain of the West Lawn for two hours just three days earlier; waiting for the smug George Shrub to make his victory speech. The third had not been invited to the victory buffet given by the taxpayers for the press the following day. Though it was not discussed, none of the three had voted for the President.

One thing that all newsmen love is a good joke. The press all went back to their seats, and silently prayed that they would get to see the arrogant senior executive step on his dick. George Shrub left the lectern. The White House Press Secretary, who somehow remained oblivious to what was going on, said, "Ladies and Gentlemen, the President of the United States." Shrub returned to the lectern, as if just arriving, and the journalists smirked as they passed around the little TV, which showed a tiny split screen with the President on one side, and a long line of what appeared to be prisoners, smiling, waving and giving the 'v' sign to the camera. They were guarded by Native soldiers who had flowers coming out of the muzzles of their guns.

"My fellow Americans," intoned the President. "Our country faces another threat to freedom. It is with a heavy heart that I report to you an atrocity against military personnel of the Armed Forces of the United States of America..."

"This is *really* going to be good!" said the CBS man to the NBC man, passing him the little TV.

****

Coast Guard Station, LaPush, 10:35 P.S.T.

In the Communications Room of the Coast Guard Station, Fourskins and the half-a-dozen production technicians were joined by Jeff Sparks. "Good of you to honor us with your company, Colonel," said Fourskins. "Things will get pretty busy here in a few minutes. I may have better things to do than supervise this media production."

"Excuse me?" Sparks was still having trouble hearing. "Sorry, I'm late, but getting the aerospace failsafe back on line was a bitch. I just now got the fiber-optic interceptor functioning so we can eavesdrop, or break in on the White House phone lines.

The voice of President Shrub droned on about how there had been an unwarranted slaughter of Navy personnel involved in military maneuvers; the Confederation's President was arguing silently with closed captions. It wasn't the best media technique, but it would have to do, thought Sparks assessing the situation.

Then the split-screen signal, going out to the world, showed President Shrub on one side of the screen, with a fully-developed skirmish line on the other. The column of prisoners was about 300 meters away from the tanks and Guardsmen. Falling in behind the guarded column of prisoners was John Pinn leading a company of young Natives. None of them carried rifles, though each man, besides Pinn,

275

paraded a dog on a leash. John Pinn carried a loud speaker attached to an A M receiver.

A green colored phone rang on the control console. Fourskins got right in Sparks' face to point at the green phone and ask, "That's incoming *to* the White House, correct?" Sparks nodded emphatically.

"White House reception," said Fourskins, pushing a button to put the call on speaker phone. "How may I help you."

"This is Bob Rucklesaus over at the Pentagon. Listen, something wild is happening with the President's speech. Those insane devils in LaPush are interfacing his speech with the attack. Go to the press room immediately. Have him terminate his speech. Get up close to him and draw your finger across your throat. He'll know what that means. When the other cameras go off, have him turn on his closed circuit monitor and **talk to me**."

The Natives in the Communication Room were choking back their laughter. "I'll see that he gets the message, Chief. Don't worry."

"Do it right away, and who am I speaking to?"

"This is Clarence Fourskins. I'm Commander in Chief of the Confederation of Non-Whites. But, I'll see that he gets the message..." the line had gone dead. For several seconds the men in the Communications Room were incapacitated by laughter.

****

Mora Housing

Special Agent Prue stared into the TV screen watching his career, reputation and credibility destroyed. How had anything this big happened right under his nose! There were closed captions appearing at the bottom of the screen, purportedly the words of fugitive-from-justice, turned President: Timothy Clark Gable. A long streaming sentence, listed the injustices and intrusions endured by Native Americans at the hands of White men since the time of Governor Stevens. Stevens had promised the Natives Rialto Beach; but instead of keeping that promise, the United States had sold it through the General Land Office. The rabble said that the only three things that White people had given the Native population of this continent that they didn't have already were disease, alcoholism, and ecotastrophy.

It looked like the President might follow Prue down the toilet. The President said that the hostiles had refused to let go of the prisoners; they were being cut free right in front of the screen. He said that the insurgents had developed and threatened to use high-tech weapons against commercial and government aerospace targets, which had been neutralized by a lightning attack this morning. Guess again, Mr. President. He was going on about how the United States valued peace above all things except freedom, while the screen showed ten tanks and a whole battalion of highly-armed soldiers going up against what looked like 80 Natives with their dogs. (Ranger Whitman had yelped when he saw the mutts.)

Even to Special Agent Prue, something seemed out of synch with the President's words and what he saw on the screen. "I need to get over there," said Prue. "Do you have a boat?" Prue was grabbing at straws. If he could get over there, and come back with a few heads for trophies, he might save his pension.

****

John Pinn set down the loud speaker on his deaf side so that his good ear would not have to cope with the 120-decibel blare of Timothy Gable ordering the United States out of the territory claimed by the Confederation. That Pinn's blood would spill along with that of most of his men, he had no doubt. It was a suicide mission designed to stop the immediate threat and discredit the Administration. John Pinn boiled inside. He wanted to die. He wanted desperately to escape the guilt he felt for the threat and injury which he had allowed to befall his precious daughter. The speaker sprang to life.

*Gentlemen of the National Guard! This is Timothy Gable, President of the Confederation of Non-White Americans. We have peacefully turned over prisoners who trespassed against our territorial boundaries. We invite you...***NO***, we command you to go in peace. Leave the way you came in, immediately, or suffer the consequences. The men that you see opposing you are not carrying weapons, but they are determined to expel you from our country. Also, you will see cameramen throughout the area. Your actions are being filmed. The world is your audience! Go in peace before you disgrace yourselves and your country!*

THIRTY-SIX

Coast Guard Station, LaPush
10:45 P.S.T.,

*I*n the Com Center, Fourskins lingered a few minutes watching the reaction to Gable's proclamation. As the camera panned the scene, a few of the Guardsmen got in goofy smiles, and waves to the folks back at home. "No! Keep that off the air! We want these guys to look evil, not like the poor dorks they are. Keep on Remote Three with all the tanks. Now get a long shot of the whole shooting match squaring off against our canine unit. We need the Guardsmen in masks, so detonate number four chlorine grenade at my signal...Wait! Here comes the Guard Lieutenant Colonel with a megaphone to ask us to surrender...live feed from Camera Two which is on the Lieutenant Colonel. Can it into a fifteen second delay; play it if they make threatening statements..." Fourskins picked up the last of the remaining cameras. He went out to see if he could capture some video trophies in the last few minutes available to him. He intended to follow John Pinn into the gathering storm. Fourskins knew that if his kids, Nauto and Toobe, would ever see him again, it would only be through the camera's eye, as video feed captured his image being thrust into the bayonets of the enemy. It would be his grand finale.

Fourskins could hear the tinny voice of the Lieutenant Colonel of the National Guard. He was saber rattling over the megaphone, "...put down your weapons and surrender immediately or suffer the consequences. We have orders from the President of the United States to dismantle this hostile infrastructure by whatever force necessary. I repeat, put down your weapons immediately or suffer the consequences!"

Some of the Natives in Pinn's group were hooting and calling back, "We don't have any weapons to put down! We're still going to tear your butts off!" Guard troops were still arriving from the rear. The released prisoners were milling about amidst the armed soldiers. If they were going to serve their intended purpose, things would have to move along. As if reading his mind, Sparks remotely detonated a chlorine bomb near the head of the Guard's skirmish line and the soldiers immediately donned their gas masks. The released prisoners began moving back, away from the impending fight.

****

In the Com Center, Sparks watched John Pinn, his childhood friend, lead *the charge of the light brigade.* Some 150 Guardsmen had formed up on the line. The balance of the battalion was scattered between LaPush, and the blown up Bogachiel Bridge. The Guardsmen wondered what would come next. They lowered their bayonets to the ready position. The command resisted firing upon this strange assemblage because they saw no display of weapons. They felt compelled to demonstrate restraint for the benefit of the cameras and avoid another Kent State fiasco. Standing shoulder to shoulder, they placed confidence in the solid wall of bayonets. "Hold your fire!" the Lieutenant Colonel yelled to his men, through his gas mask.

279

John Pinn moved forward. "Halt or we'll shoot!" the Lieutenant Colonel yelled at the menacing Native. Pinn made a chopping motion with his right hand upon his left wrist. At once, the Natives hit quick releases on the dog's leashes. A wave of canine fury swept over the National Guard .

The dogs came in low, beneath the bayonets, as they had been trained. Most of the dogs sought targets below the waist. A few of the larger dogs found soft flesh below the gas masks.

****

Mora Housing Compound

As the District Ranger helped Special Agent Prue launch the inflatable raft into the slough of the Quillayute River, he pled with the man to reconsider. "There's a war going on down there, Fred. They'll shoot you and our Zodiac." The District Ranger could see that he wasn't getting through. The Special Agent stared across the river with crazed eyes. He pull-started the outboard. Prue withdrew his 40-caliber side arm from his shoulder holster, and put it on the seat beside him. He sped down river in the direction of the gunfire. The District Ranger went back into the Whitman residence to watch the war in his own backyard unfolding on television.

Ranger Whitman had flushed into a sweat when he saw the dogs break through the Guard's line. The Natives followed the canine soldiers through the broken perimeter, and fierce hand to hand fighting broke out. A Guardsman swung around, flailing wildly with a small dog hanging on one buttock while another was burying its snout in the man's crotch. Ranger Whitman was crying, "God, oh no. That poor man! Oh God!"

****

Coast Guard Com Center

On five of the monitors in the Coast Guard's Com Center, were gory scenes of soldiers being stabbed to death by their own weapons. John Pinn and his men were encouraged to kill with the M-16's. When the final casualty counts were made, it would appear that these men were killed by their compatriots. Pinn had secured an M-16 early in the game. He was using it like the professional he had once been, to cut down the Guardsmen surrounding him. All the smoke made it hard to see what was happening with Pinn and the other soldiers.

"Stay off of Camera Number Six with Pinn," directed Sparks. "Pinn's too deadly out there with the M-16. If he loses his weapon or gets shot, go to Six. Who is the camera man on Six, anyway?"

The cameraman on Pinn followed his every move and was catching scenes of heroism. Pinn's M-16 ran dry. He impaled a Guardsman who was laying out a deadly spray of bullets at a huddle of unarmed Natives. Pinn thrust so violently that the bayonet twisted off its lock, and fell to the ground with the impaled Guardsman.

"Now! Come in on Six!" said Sparks excitedly. He appeared to be enjoying himself. "This is great stuff. We'll send still frames of this to the wire service!" John Pinn was swinging the M-16 like a baseball bat. Whap! Down went a guardsman. Whap! Whap! Down went two more. Whap! Then there was a Guardsman attacking from the front with a bayonet while two more behind Pinn brought their weapons up to shoot. Pop! The Guardsman in front fell to the ground. Pinn was waving an old .22 revolver - a relic from his Viet Nam campaign. He swung around and, pop, pop, shot both Guardsmen behind him in the face.

"Oh no! Pinn's pulled a gun!" lamented Sparks. "He's not supposed to be carrying a gun! Get the camera off him. Go to Two!" Before the camera was averted it caught the live action of Pinn taking two rounds in his arm, and dropping the .22. A Guardsman drove a bayonet into him from behind and Pinn ignored the assault trying to bend over to pick up his .22. The Guardsman came off the ground hanging onto his weapon. "Stay on Six! Stay on Six!" Sparks was yelling in the Com Center as his friend received another bayonet thrust from the back and as perforations tore through his chest spattering the pavement with blood. Sparks could see that one of the two pickadors had found his way to the trigger. "Give me slowmo-. Slowmo- for this shot!" Pinn stood up for just a moment and was hit by a third bayonet thrust and he went over in slow motion.

A huge tree falling in a forest of saplings...crashing to the ground to which it has been rooted for so many years. "Yes! Yes! That was wonderful!" cried Sparks exhilarated and his staff in the Communication Room began to plumb the depths of the man's depravity.

President Shrub's voice provided the commentary to this horrific backdrop, "...why we have become known to the world as a kind, gentle nation. "But we will not shirk our duty..."

White House Press Room, 13:45 E.S.T.

"But we will not shirk our duty when the United States is threatened at home or abroad...or when American lives are placed on the board as bargaining chips..."

The Chief of Staff broke into the room. He ran to the front of the room standing ten feet from the face of the President making violent slashes across his throat. President Shrub nodded that he understood, and continued, ad-libbing double talk now. "For the United States will always be the first in peace, but the last to surrender; the last to intervene in the affairs of other nations, but the first to share freedom; the first to speak in truth for the full scrutiny of the media, and the last to cover up whatever mistakes a well meaning government may make along the way..." It was annoying and distracting to the President the way his Chief of Staff persisted in drawing his finger across his throat. The President was just getting the press where he wanted them. They were smiling, and nodding at every nuance. George Shrub had never seen the press enjoying one of his speeches so much. He was finally getting through to these lug-heads...

****

The hand to hand fighting was starting to die down. The dead and dying were everywhere. Through the smoke and chlorine gas and piles of bodies, it was hard for Fourskins to make out who was losing. The dogs were still having a pretty good time of it. Then, as it became increasingly evident to the National Guard that they were up against more than a handful of rock-throwing student radicals; the tanks opened up on targets behind the melee with their 50-caliber machine guns. There were a couple of thunderous booms. Ground-shaking explosions followed as they fired ordinance at buildings in the village. Sparks would be firing the ether mines. The Native warriors began fighting their way back towards the village to get away from ground zero. Fourskins maintained his position next to the fallen warrior John Pinn. The firing of the tanks had also panicked the released hostages, as was planned. They were now running from the front, knocking into the armed soldiers that were trying to advance to the front. Fourskins continued with his camera, catching the picture of armed soldiers trying to get into the fight being knocked over by soldiers trying to get away from it.

Then the sewer line exploded, knocking Fourskins to his knees where upon he lay down with his hands over his head, facing the reservation. Before the rock fly even began to impact the ground, there were five secondary explosions from ether charged 55-gallon drums. The Natives had buried the mines beside the road, with radio-activated igniters. As the deadly rain of broken pavement, helmets, bayonets, and other soldier parts fell from the sky around him, Fourskins looked through the loose mesh of his arms. He could see the garage doors opening, and mobile-home walls swinging up on their electric hinges. The jury-rigged rocket launchers and other instruments designed for tank warfare were ready to fire. Things were about to really heat up.

While the lips may profess that it is a good day to die, when death appears at the door and begs an appointment, the body will invariably pursue a different agenda. It was with this reflexive action that Fourskins drug himself behind the largest cover he could find, which, in this case, was the prostrate body of John Pinn. Fourskins pushed his head into the cave of the dead man's armpit. The acetylene rockets and solid-fuel missiles flew from their launchers. They punched into the earth's viscera with such violence as to affect projectile vomitus of tons of soil. Tank parts and rocks rained from the sky. Old car bodies, road-kill skeletons, disposable diapers, beer cans, and the other detritus, evidencing a small planet's diet proximal to a reservation, fell from heaven. The explosions came closer together in interval until it was almost a constant roar. The body of John Pinn shook spasmodically. His arms slapped against the pavement as if the man lived. Cedar chips, and sawdust danced on his clothing. In death the mighty logger smelled like a hamster cage.

The falling rock and detritus fell upon Pinn which Fourskins used for a helmet. Then there was silence...more silence and, the conclia of his inner ear became re-perfused with oxygenated blood, which had been driven away by the awful noise. Sound began to return like someone adjusting the fader knob on the speakers of hearing. As he faced the demolished front line of the National Guard, he could see no standing soldiers. He heard the moaning and screams of the wounded, which over the ringing in his ears, sounded like the keening of gulls on the beach. Then, as the smoke cleared, he could see the great army retreating ...the men in the rear, dragging what casualties they could; other wounded, limping, and dragging broken limbs...a sea retreating with the tide of defeat. All but three of the tanks had thrown their tracks. Hatch doors were thrust open as crews abandoned their steel fortresses to join the rout.

There was a commotion behind him. A flood of Natives tore by Fourskins in pursuit of the vanquished. They were mostly women and children. They carried chlorine grenades to battle with the still operable tanks. Fourskins picked up his camera and saw that it still worked. These villagers had been excluded from the training. Fourskins had never authorized the conscription of such combatants. But there was historical precedent and it made great footage.

Fourskins held the camera on a ten-year-old child who bent to pick up a .22 pistol that Colonel Pinn had dropped in the combat. The child stuffed the weapon into his belt. Fourskins felt stirrings of his responsibility to these people. "You shouldn't be out here. Go back to your home. Now!"

The child spoke into the eye of the camera. The number of viewers which had begun with bored housewives watching *Another Spin of the Globe,* had grown proportionally with the drama depicted on the screen. The boy addressed the largest audience in the history of the human race. With eyes red and wet from chlorine and perhaps the moment of the circumstances, he said, "My father was in this fight. He's out here somewhere." *Great sound bite!*, thought Fourskins.

After speaking, the child pulled out a pair of kitchen shears, and began cutting the ears off the dead and dying soldiers. Fourskins watched, in horror, through the view finder of his camera, at the compromised media bite. He knew such atrocity followed the heels of war, much the way corruption follows power. Still, he felt like he was being crushed under the weight of a huge turning wheel. As the dead and the dying were squashed under the roaring retreat of the three mighty M-1 tanks, Fourskins felt the ponderous gravity of human wretchedness. He could no longer see through the view finder because of his tears.

****

"Get off Six! Get off Six! That kid is swiping ears! Go to the Coastie high remote. Bring back Shrub's voice..." Sparks was stressing out in the Control Room. The camera from on top of the antenna tower showed three tanks retreating. Soldiers dove out of the way to avoid being overrun. At the bottom of the screen appeared the trilling Natives who pursued the hapless soldiers. Some Natives had given up on the chase. Some were helping the wounded, most of whom were Guardsmen. When everything was tallied, it hadn't been a very successful day for the United States military, in spite of what George Shrub was saying. "Wait a minute, Shrub is bailing out of his speech," monitored Sparks. "Stand by to go to Victoria. Stand by...five, four, three, two, one..."

****

"Mr. President. Mr. President. **MR. PRESIDENT!**" George Shrub was extremely irritated by his Chief of Staff, who was now verbally interrupting his speech. There was nothing to do, but give up the last ten minutes of his stirring speech, and see what his subordinate thought was so important.

"...so it is my promise to the American people to report on the events transpiring on the northwestern tip of our country, immediately, as news becomes available to me. I again repeat the assurances given to me by Governor Boot, that the National Guard will use restraint; but will not relent until the hostages are free. Until I report back to you, pray for the safety of the Americans who defend our country against terrorists. Good afternoon." The President watched the red lights on the three network cameras wink out until only the closed circuit camera was left on. He changed his tone to deal with the rain on his parade. "What do you mean interrupting me! You pull a stunt like that again, and you'll be jumping naked out of a cake at the Democratic National Convention..."

"Mr. President!" the Chief of Staff spoke in a hushed urgent voice. "There's been a terrible upset in LaPush. The strike team was sacrificed after taking out the target. The enemy cloned the target. While you were giving your speech, there was radio piracy. The element in LaPush televised the whole battle which lasted less than fifteen minutes. They surrendered the hostages *before* the fight. Someone told me as I came in here, the Guard was badly defeated. Both prongs of our program failed..."

"I don't believe it!" the veins stood out in the President's neck.

Meanwhile, the press, which have developed remarkable clarity of hearing - such that they can hear Scotch being poured into a glass across a crowded room - were straining to hear the conversation from which they were being deliberately excluded. The situation appeared to them, in varying degrees of hilarity, depending, in part on their political orientation; and, in main, on what callousness they possessed for the extinguishing of human life. "It's true, Mr. President," said the owner of the pocket TV. "The National Guard was defeated, and they are fleeing the insurgents."

President Shrub pushed his angry red face close to the closed circuit monitor for a private conversation with his Secretary of Defense and about 105 million Americans. "Mr. Secretary, I want that target sanitized; I want it done in a hurry; I don't care how many woman or children get between us and the target. The Alamo is within spitting distance, for Christ's sake I don't care if you personally have to swim out there with ordinance. Arm that boat, God-damn-it, and launch a strike..."

"Mr. President," interrupted the press man who had confirmed the Chief of Staff's outrageous report, "if your discussion is intended to be discreet with the Secretary of Defense, perhaps you should know that you are being broadcast. We can see and hear you on this little TV."

"May I see that please," asked the President. He was starting to feel a little wobbly behind the lectern as the press man brought him the miniature TV. He looked into the screen. He winced when he saw himself on the right hand side of the picture and a middle-aged Native American on the left side.

"Hello President Shrub," the small voice said from the pocket TV. "I am glad to be meeting you face to face before the American people..." All in all, it hadn't been a good day for the President or militia of the United States.

****

11:15 P.S.T.

Fourskins had walked dejectedly back to the Com Center. The memory of the child engaged in mutilating war dead weighed heavily upon his mood. He experienced none of the jubilation he should have been feeling at such a political juncture. The satisfaction in seeing the expression on President Shrub's face, which looked more like apoplexy than surprise, had cheered up Fourskins a bit. But it was not armor enough against a sorrow that stabbed like a bayonet in the heart. He had expected to lie among the war-dead heroes of this campaign. He felt strangely out of place to be among the living.

The high remote Coastie camera continued to pirouette revealing Navy helicopters coming to dust off military casualties; James Island still smoldering; the jetty leading to Rialto Beach; the estuary, from which a thick fog rose from the warm water; an inflatable raft coming down the Quillayute River; the Coast Guard Station; the village proper with fires caused by the previous incoming tank ordinance; the helicopters landed and a field of medics triaging more than a hundred wounded... "Any idea who would be coming down the river in an inflatable?" Fourskins asked..

Sparks gave him a curt answer, "You can stop the camera and zoom in with those controls over there, General. Come in on Remote Three for a close up of those Native women helping to carry the stretcher to the helo. Get those still shots wired to AP for evening editions..." On one side of the split screen, President Gable had come up the stairs of the CNN building and was meeting six different ambassadors. The international party had been on a tour of the Provincial Parliament when the news of the move for revolutionary independence was circulated through the government seat. As the men shook hands, the staff in the Com Room were trying to co-ordinate with their CNN contact on the phone to place appropriate titles under the representatives from Paraguay, Columbia, Honduras and Brazil.

Fourskins stopped the camera on the incoming raft. The auto focus adjusted from blur to a clear image. Fourskins was looking into the face of the man who had sent him to prison twenty-three years ago. "Colonel Sparks, could you look at this a minute."

"I'm kind of busy, General!"

"It's Agent Prue, he's coming into the village in a Zodiac."

Jeff Sparks walked over to the monitor and studied the face for a minute. "I'll take care of this personally," said Sparks picking up a shotgun from under the console. "Just when I thought the day couldn't get any better..."

"No, Colonel Sparks! I'll take care of it. You're needed here. Just keep the camera on us in case Prue pulls something."

"You bet!" agreed Sparks, returning to his directing. Fourskins left the Coast Guard Station. He went to meet his old nemesis.

****

Special Agent Prue stepped out of the Zodiac clutching his .40 caliber. It was too late for the niceties of warrants and "stop and frisk." He needed a head on a stake for his career to survive.

"Hello, Fred, I've been expecting you," Clarence Fourskins stepped from behind a power pole and the jumpy Agent almost shot him on sight.

"I came for you, Fourskins. You've gone too far this time...way too far. I'm taking you with me. There's been enough killing today, so why don't you just come along peaceful like..."

Fourskins was backing away from the Agent with his hands up. He kept backing behind the power pole, where Fred Prue followed him and as soon as Fourskins and the FBI man were *en defilade* to the camera, Fourskins' empty right hand snaked out as if he were throwing something at the Agent's face. Prue ducked even though he hadn't seen anything in Fourskins' open hand the moment before.

Fourskins took two steps forward, holding his hands up, and came again into view of the camera. Special Agent Prue began his battery of banter to encourage acquiescence in the subject that 22 years earlier had surrendered without a fight. But Fourskins continued to advance with his hands in the air. Prue's foot swung out cracking into Fourskins' left knee. On his way down, Prue pistol-whipped the back of Fourskins' head - a bad way to treat a semiautomatic weapon, but what the hey! Fourskins went down. Prue watched his hands the whole way down. Fourskins kept holding up his empty hands like he wanted his fortune read. Fourskins was on the ground. Prue couldn't resist kicking him in the head while he was down. He was kneeling on Fourskins, reaching for his handcuffs. Fourskins rolled away and came up with his right hand in his pocket...a dangerous situation.

286

"Fourskins, take your hand out of your pocket right now, very, very slowly...or I swear you're a dead man."

The Native glared at him from beneath a gash in his forehead. Blood washed down over his brow and streamed down his cheeks like war paint. He appeared to look west beyond the arresting officer, toward the Coast guard camera tower...*the oldest trick in the book: feint that someone's behind you.* But then his eyes came back to lock on Special Agent Prue's smirk and the FBI man felt fear steal into his own soul. The muzzle of the .40 caliber began to tremble when Fourskins hissed, "Fred, you sent me to Federal prison where I had years to practice this move. That's all we did in the jug: we practiced drawing a gun made out of soap from our pockets, there was no way to defend against it. I've got you just where I want you, so to make it fair, I'll make my move in five seconds. I promise I'll destroy you with the weapon in my hand. Ready?"

"No, Fourskins, don't...No one has to get hurt."

"Five, four, three..."

****

Quantico, VA 14:30 E.S.T.

Division Chief Shortbrand returned from his work-out on the cross country course, sweating, even in the cool November air. He felt refreshed and exhilarated from his exercise. He would take a long, hot shower; and try calling Special Agent Prue again at his Seattle office. From the message he left earlier on the answering machine, he sounded pretty flipped out. A group of his co-workers were bunched around a TV screen watching some news story break. "What's up, guys. Anything big?"

"Not really," said another administrator standing in the back of the huddle. "A little Indian Reservation seceded from the United States; they killed, oh maybe a hundred soldiers and blew up seven or eight tanks; they say they can touch a button and bring down our whole aerospace defense program; they took over all the network communications and made President Shrub look kind of silly and, oh!, this will interest you...your agent Fred Prue is on TV right now kicking the shit out of the rebels' Commander and Chief. They put titles right on the screen, so there's no mistaking it's Prue and this Indian, Fourskins..."

Shortbrand was pushing his way toward the TV screen and there was his subordinate, Agent Prue, drawn down on a bleeding, helpless Native who appeared to be pleading for his life. "He's really been working over this poor featherhead. The subject doesn't appear to be armed, but it looks like Prue is going to waste him. I wonder if he knows that he's on National TV.."

Shortbrand was praying to the screen, "Please don't, Fred. Please, please, don't, please..." Fourskins suddenly pulled his empty hand out of his pocket. The subject, labeled on the screen, 'FBI Special Agent Fred Prue,' fired his automatic into the chest of the man identified as "General Clarence Fourskins."

****

Tripp County, South Dakota 13:33 R.M.T.

"Dad! NO, DADDY!" screamed Nauto.

"...ohhhhhhh!" wailed her brother Toobe.

Their mother walked across the tiny living room. She turned off the TV. Angry tears clouded her vision. She had seen her husband's gaze: the spell he had cast on the unfortunate Federal Agent who'd killed him. She was one of the few human beings alive, including Fred Prue, who understood that the Special Agent had been manipulated. Her husband had laid down his life for another public relations coup in a media extravaganza. She was all alone in the world with her two adolescent children.

THIRTY-SEVEN

Peninsula Apartments, Forks
Tuesday, November 10, 1992, 17:25 hours

I turn on the new TV in my dingy little apartment and sit down on the tired hide-a-bed that serves as a living room couch. From within the bowels of the hide-an-atrocity, I hear the resident tribe of mice complaining about the intrusion and cramped space occasioned by my bottom's application to the furniture. Somehow, it reminds me of LaPush, from whence I just returned. I was challenged at the Customs and Immigration barrier gate just south of the newly replaced bridge. I waited in a line of a hundred and fifty pilgrims, coming from the inner cities to da lan' o' milk and honey. Black and red faces passed the gate with no problem, but a pale face like mine required birth certificate and proof of non-White lineage. Word in the line is that if alcohol is found in your possessions or in your system, you are turned around. After inspection I had been shuttled down to Smith Field in an old World War Two deuce-and-a-half with Clallam County Search and Rescue emblems on the sides. It was missing the rear door and the inside looked like it had been used as an industrial laboratory for igniting farts. Smith Field was a metropolis of 3,000 immigrants who brought to the once pristine meadow, the squalor of the inner city. Like most cities, the adjacent river served both as sewer and water supply. Looking into the cloudy water along the litter strewn bank of the Quillayute, I saw a human body pushing along in the current.

I walked back to the village and searched for the shack and mobile home of James Crow. A dozen squatters had moved into the mobile home and a cloud of marijuana smoke emanated from the windows and front door. "Who's there?" answered my knock.

"Confederation Police!" I joked. One of the squatters opened the door. If they believed I *was* the police, they made no attempt to hide the pot they were smoking. I decided to carry on with the sham. "We're looking for documents prepared by the former resident of these premises, a James Crow..."

"He wants all that notebook paper from the bedroom!" called back the Native from the front door to the tribe that lounged about the mobile home. "We didn't know it was important. We used some of it for fire starter..." A resident brought the collection of the neatly bundled loose-leaves, accounting for two decades of a man's effort to commit his life to paper.

"Do you have a bag I could put this into?" I asked the young woman presenting me with the small arm load of documentation. I followed her into the kitchen where she takes a large plastic bag of dry leafy material. She pours it out onto newspaper on the kitchen table. She put the papers in the plastic bag, and handed it to me without comment or apology. What kind of relationship does this new society have with the police, that they open doors to warrantless search and seizure, and divulge the possession of felonious drug caches without the slightest embarrassment!

289

I returned to the Smith Field immigration camp on foot. To avoid questions by either CNA or USA personnel, I swam across the cold river with the bag over my head. On the way home I stopped at the Express Lane food store at the north side of Forks, advertising "Last Beer Stop Before Confederation." I picked up *News Week, Time* and *U.S. News.*

Now, waiting for the six o'clock news, I peruse the covers. One shows my old co-worker, John Pinn, impaled from behind with a bayonet and a man hanging off the weapon as the giant bends over. The caption reads *A Kinder, More Gentle America?* The second magazine shows a child with tears streaming down a war grimed face. He stands amid a sea of bodies and the caption reads, *My Father is Out Here.* Even a bias for sensationalism from the conservative publication, *U.S. News;* the cover showed a split television screen with President Gable on the left aspect with President Shrub, saucer eyed and dazed, on the right. *I'm Pleased to Meet You...*read the caption.

I set the magazines aside, and make some notes on research details of the book I feel compelled to write. I'm taking a sabbatical. Somehow logs are still finding their way up steep slopes and into log truck bunkers, without the benefit of my expert choker setting. I check the list I am compiling:

---

1. *Interview Woodrift*
2. *See if Pinn's daughter will talk*
3. ~~*Call Quantico and see if you can talk to Special Agent Prue*~~
4. *Interview National Guard C.O. or survivors of conflict*
5. *Call Navy in Seattle and see if you can arrange to talk to C.O. of Rialto assault*

I cross out #3 because I had called the FBI earlier in the day before going to LaPush, and had reached Special Agent Prue himself! He had talked to me with the frank openness of a government employee that had been awarded a termination date and stripped of everything he had to lose. The conversation had been most informative, detailing everything from his recruitment in 1968 to his impending termination from Special Agent in charge of Indian Affairs.

I glance at my watch and with five minutes until news time, I call the number given to me as the Seattle office of the Thirteenth Fleet.

"U.S. Navy," says a communications technician on the phone. "May I direct your call?"

"Yeah, good evening, I'm Chiggers Stokes and I'm preparing a story on the Navy's mishap last week on Rialto Beach..."

290

"Admiral Bingingham is personally handling the media contacts for that tragedy. Just a moment..."

"This is Admiral Bingingham, Thirteenth Fleet."

"Good evening, Admiral," I say, a little surprised to be talking to the Commander of the Thirteenth Fleet. He was still answering calls an hour after office hours. "My name is Chiggers Stokes and I'm preparing a story about the Navy's upset last week..."

"Who did you say you were with , Mr. Stokes?"

It wouldn't do to tell him that I am with Soleduck River logging. "Well, actually I lack affiliation and am doing the story free lance. I wonder if you could arrange for me to talk to the commanding officer that lead the maneuver that resulted in the deaths..."

"Yes, you can talk to Lieutenant Gillette who was in charge of the beach assault this Thursday at one thirty. He'll be at a funeral at the south lawn of the Ridgecrest Funeral Hall where the Navy has been spending quite a bit of time in the last ten days. You can talk to him all you want. I'm sure he won't mind a bit."

I am tremendously impressed by the senior officer's professional courtesy and helpfulness to an unknown correspondent. "I really appreciate this, Admiral. I know I'll learn a lot from Lieutenant Gillette..."

"I wouldn't count on it, Mr. Stokes. It's *his* funeral. I've been answering calls from the media all day and my other line is ringing. Good evening, Mr. Stokes."

I slam down the phone. *What a jerk! What a Naval button hole!* My search for an explicative, suitable for the occasion, is interrupted by the six o'clock news...

"...news continues to be dominated by events surrounding the extraordinary bid for independence made by a handful of Natives known as the Quileute Nation, carrying with them what was assessed today as two million, three hundred and twenty-five Afro and Indian Americans. The flood of petitions for citizenship in the infant nation are being processed around the clock at the temporary National Capital which has been set up in LaPush at a previous coastal resort called 'LaPush Ocean Park.' Jane..." the male announcer deferred the next story to his female partner.

"Where to place the new citizens has become a problem for both the United States, and the country which calls itself the Confederation of Non-White Americans. The Department of Interior has pledged two million acres of land, which combined with other reservation lands being assimilated into

291

the new sovereign, come to total of some six million acres of land. Spokes-persons within the Interior Department say that more land will follow, but will not disclose how much. Harry..."

"Other developments in the Department of Interior include the announcement today of a massive reduction in force within the Bureau of Indian Affairs. Approximately five thousand employees were served termination notices today, and further lay-offs are anticipated.

"BIA employees were not the only ones to get sacked today. Dr. Alex Newhall, United States representative to the Security Council of the United Nations was replaced today by Ellen Rainwater, a dual citizen of the US of A and C of NA. From the White House, President Shrub stated in a five-minute press conference that his Administration was committed to affording every opportunity of survival to the struggling young nation. He went on, quote, Ms. Rainwater's expertise in political science and Native American history were critical factors in her selection to the post, unquote. The U.S. President ignored questions fired at him by the press concerning what promises had been made to leaders of the CNA. The US President was asked whether or not his Administration still contemplated a vindictive strike against CNA leadership, for casualties inflicted against US Armed Forces personnel two weeks ago. President Shrub answered, quote, We will not let the irresponsible actions of a few hot-headed terrorists interfere with our meaningful dialogue with the, by and large, responsible leadership of this fledgling nation, unquote. Jane..."

"President Shrub also ignored questions which relate to his own job security. Impeachment hearings were again underway in the House of Representatives with Congressmen watching video recordings of the President's press release two weeks ago which apparently conflicts dramatically with events which were broadcast simultaneously with the President's speech. Harry..."

"Interim President of the C of NA, Timothy Gable, announced today that his country would have an entirely different approach to drug enforcement than the United States. Citing a lack of law-enforcement resources to wage a war on drugs, and the traditional use of such hallucinogens as peyote and psilocybe mushrooms by Native American cultures, President Gable proclaimed the legality of many substances held as contraband in the United States. President Gable pledged to maintain his administration's prohibition against all forms of alcoholic beverage, saying that, quote: alcohol and not drugs have been the source of societal upheaval in Native America, unquote. Officials in the United States Justice Department expressed outrage over the decision and claim that Columbia and Panama, which have already established embassies in the town of LaPush, intend to use the coastal village as a pipeline for drugs coming into the United States. Jane..."

292

"Joining Dr. Newhall and five-thousand employees of the B.I.A. in the unemployment lines will be an estimated fifteen-thousand workers nationwide, who were fired from their jobs today for unauthorized participation in what has become the largest international peace demonstration of all time. An hour long pray-in for peace occurred today at eleven o'clock eastern standard time. An international organization calling itself **'Stop War,'** organized the event. The pray-in, according to its organizers, demonstrates world opinion against a rumored vindictive strike on the part of the US against the C of NA, and calls for a cessation of military conflict everywhere. Organizers are saying that this pray-in represents the largest collective prayer in the history of mankind. Spokespersons for **Stop War** criticize the employers of the fifteen-thousand who were terminated from their jobs when they refused to work through the event. Good news for golfers and housewives: How the power of prayer can influence the weather and even your weight, after these messages from our network..."

Twenty two thousand, three hundred miles above the equator at 139 degrees longitude, the communications satellite SATCOM beams down commercial messages of vital interest to fifteen million of its network viewers, the western third of which are engrossed in the six o'clock news. The first message will describe new scientific advancements in the arena of suppressing the perspiration function of glandular zones found in the human arm pit. While the world holds its breath, waiting to see if the United States will stamp its mighty military foot down upon the tiny Confederation; on a planet where one out of four stomachs is aching with hunger; in a political climate where the switch of nuclear holocaust can be thrown accidentally by some President, in the dark, on his way to the bathroom; from a satellite that sees a globe, suffocating and putrefying from the pollution of its human inhabitants...comes GOOD NEWS for perspiration sufferers...and then another important para-health bulletin for the female component of the audience here on earth: Forget the embarrassment of running to the bathroom with your purse or changing your sanitary napkin as frequently as some politicians change platforms. This product offers total confidence to homo sapiens of the female persuasion from the torturous repercussions of their fecundity. 'Sanakins' offer a whole new meaning to 'light days'...

The announcer, rescues me from the commercial bombardment from space. "Today, disturbances occurred in weather and gravitational pull as reflected by real tidal flow and scaled measurement of absolute weights. NASA and NOAA officials are calling it a coincidence growing out of heavy sun spot activity. Leaders of the major international pray-in, which occurred today in major cities across the world, claim a direct correlation between precipitation, unaccounted for neap tides, and low gravity with participation in the peace prayer activity. Clerical organizations in the United States point to the crowd of some seven hundred thousand that defied unseasonable rain, and governmental edict to march for peace in the streets of the Iranian capital of Teheran. United Nations officials in the city reported a 1.26 per cent relaxation of the gravitational field. A housewife weighing 200 pounds at the

U.S. Bureau of Standards in Gaithersburg, Maryland would weigh only a one hundred and ninety-eight pounds eight ounces this afternoon in Teheran...

"It offers a whole new meaning to 'light days...'" offered the anchor man.

Jane continues, ..."This map of North America prepared by our studio weather man shows lines of infra-red gravitational pull, while the map beside it shows lines drawn by reported participation in the 'Stop War' pray-in. Government agencies refute any relation."

'**Stop War!**' It echoes in my conscience. I look at two identical maps on the TV screen. "Do you see any resemblance, Harry?"

"Only if I look at the maps with my eyes open..." I turn off the TV.

"Stop war," I say to myself, holding the head of a dying man on the lap of my memory. "Stop war..."

THIRTY-EIGHT

08:10 Thursday, November 19, 1992

*A*s the phone rang in the Mora Ranger Station, Ed Whitman was outside collecting the high/low temperatures and daily precipitation. This information was sent off to NOAA every month to be archived with the tomes of other bureaucratic data collected by the government. A week had passed since he returned from his self-imposed captivity. Without major difficulty; he was falling into the automatic routine of his office work. There was nothing too stressful about preparing monthly public use reports; posting the tides and daily weather forecast for the visitors; putting out the park maps; and the other details of a ranger station. He had attended a "critical incident debriefing" with the District Ranger and several other park employees whose lives had been touched by the LaPush hostilities. In addition to the debriefing, Ranger Whitman had been required to seek counseling from the Forks Outreach Services. Ironically, a husband of one of the Native American counselors had been killed in the incident. One member of the staff listened to Whitman tell the story about being stuffed into the trunk of the Valiant with a turkey neck sticking out of his throat. On the other side of a paper-thin wall another member of the staff dealt with Julie Pinn's crying and keening over the death of her husband.

"Mora Ranger Station, Ranger Whitman here." The Park Servant caught the phone on its fourth ring.

"Uh, hi Ed," said the voice of the District Ranger. "How are things going? Say, one thing we forgot to cover the other day at the debriefing is that your law enforcement commission is suspended until the park can convene an inquiry as to why you didn't report the hostilities when you had a chance. Lock your defensive equipment in a safe place. I'll pick it up in a couple of days if we haven't already cleared things up."

"Fine, it's already locked up," said Whitman looking across the office room to where his side arm, mace, and retractable baton were locked in the closet.

"Have you been following the news of the Administration's concessions made to the Confederacy?"

"Not really, sir." What Whitman could see across the river was depressing enough. He was avoiding watching it being rehashed and analyzed on late-night news.

"This morning they announced that they would be giving both Yosemite, and Everglades back to the Indians. The truth is that they're dumping those two parks because they are environmental hot potatoes. But they're saying that: because Everglades is land that was given to the Seminoles by un-abrogated treaty; and that Yosemite was seized from the Indians without legitimizing legislation; that they are the first Parks to be put on the sacrificial altar."

"Yosemite was established by the Presidential Proclamation of Abraham Lincoln," recalled Ranger Whitman from his Orientation to Park Operation Indoctrination. "It was the first Federal land set aside for a park in the world. The President has always had the power to create National Monuments..."

"It's the old question of title to the land. The first white men to see Yosemite Valley were Indian fighters. The Natives of the valley under Chief Tenaya were totally passive and submissive to the soldiers that burned their lodges and relocated them to the same reservation as their Indian enemies. The question that's being addressed here is *by what authority did the soldiers evict the Natives and how do you proclaim park out of land that's already got an indigenous population.* That's why the U.S. Attorney's Office has been poring over treaties for the last two weeks. There may be another military strike against LaPush, which could topple their government, and change things quite a bit. But for now..."

"How does Olympic stand up under the test?" asks Ranger Whitman.

"Not very well, really. There's the Point No Point Treaty which gives Natives in this area hunting and fishing rights on all 'unclaimed' Federal lands and then there's an Executive Directive from F.D.R. assuring the LaPush Indians unrestrained use of their Native and accustomed lands...It's the reason I'm calling, Ed. The Federal Government is giving the coastal strip of the Park to the Confederacy. You're finally going to get your transfer. If the military does launch a strike, they'll be supported by Air and Naval forces. They won't need a bunch of Park Rangers running around on the beach, popping off cap guns. All of us on the west end will be transferring."

"Where are they going to find work for the combined staffs of Yosemite, Everglades, and half of Olympic National Park?"

"Actually, that's not a problem. Besides the erosion to our land base, the Park Service is coming out on top in this deal. Congress is pumping a lot of money into the system to re-inculcate the public with a sense of national pride and purpose. We're doubling the staffs at most of the historic sites. The sites that touch the events of Native America - the ones that don't get turned over to the Confederacy - will do really well. History, as you've probably figured out for yourself, isn't the recording of events, but the reconciling of a nation's conscience."

Ranger Whitman began to sift through the implications of this news. "I don't want to be transferred back east. I don't want to move my family. I don't like that whole 'Cannon Ball Circuit' back there."

"None of us have much choice, Ed. You in particular. Just be glad that you still have a job. There are people at headquarters that are saying that you could have prevented a lot of bloodshed if you had just come back to Mora when you had your first chance. Some of the folks in Forks are calling you a **traitor**..." the word struck Ranger Whitman like a slap in the face. "My other line is ringing, Ed. I'll talk to you again in a few days. I'm coming to pick up your defensive equipment. Please, put it in a safe place...and take down the American flag in front of the station. No point in pissing off the Indians at this stage. Bye now."

"Traitor". The word stuck, stinking in Ranger Whitman's consciousness like wet bullshit on a barn wall.

****

Since 'the Revolution,' life for Wally Woodrift and Dorothy Pinn had become a waking nightmare, mostly spent in the hospital. Daily, the bandages were removed from Woodrift's face and chest and a surgical cheese cutter drawn across the skin of his thigh and buttocks. This spread was laid out on the cracker-like crust of Pinn's upper body, where the skin wept plasma and struggled for life against infection. It itched like round worms up a dog's butt and he wanted to drag his whole body across the carpet. Woodrift felt a deeper and more scorching burn in his spirit. He felt that he had been used, and betrayed by some power-seeking mob. In the week of the new nation's existence, he could perceive no profound shift toward human rights; no overall improvement of Native America. He was largely alone in his cynicism. Now many black ghetto lords infused the hierarchy of the Confederacy of Non-White America. The political climate of LaPush seemed more like children playing a game of 'king of the mountain,' than of founding fathers forging a new course in human events. More and more, Woodrift was being squeezed out of the directorate along with the underlying goals of the movement. The smoke-filled rooms of the Ocean Park Capitol; the power mongering; the old guard parading around in new costumes; it all combined with the intense physical discomfort of the young Native in a bad dream interrupted only sometimes by sleep. Meet the new boss - same as the old boss! Though Woodrift's testicles were still anesthetic, he carried an ache in his chest which was palpable.

Locked in the large and ornate chest of Dorothy Pinn's bosom was folded unutterable grief for her father. Her despair was all the more unspeakable because of the underlying anger she felt. The explosion of politically motivated violence had taken her father and left her lover a eunuch. The total hearing loss sustained by Dorothy in the hostilities, contributed to her mute reluctance to air her inner feelings. Her mother Julie, continued to spill out her heart to all her cronies at work, but didn't appear much improved for the emotional outpourings. Julie was a wreck. Family and friends were amazed at Dorothy's stolid demeanor in the wake of such catastrophic loss. Inside Dorothy's heart, the tears rained inward. The tear-soaked, folded blanket of grief lay putrefying at the bottom of a chest, closed and locked by anger.

Much of the physical trauma body had sustained in the last week had been inflicted in exploratory surgery. Many times, mechanical hearing loss, unlike sensorial hearing loss, can be reversed in surgery. They had kept Dorothy awake for the operation, at Swedish Hospital, in Seattle because they needed to know when, and if, she perceived sound. Dorothy neither heard nor felt anything as the conchas of her ear were cut away and her ear drum was pierced by the scalpel, much like the *medicine* prescribed to General George Custer by the angry squaws on the battlefield of Little Bighorn. The inventory of the damage to the middle ear was made with notes on reconstruction. Then fiber optics intruded into the semicircular canals of the inner ear. Bilateral rupture of the canal walls were discovered. There was general destruction of the capillary beds of the sensorial cilia. A message was scribbled onto a whiteboard with a greased pencil which the surgeon used to communicate with Dorothy. It was held by a nurse in front of Dorothy's face. The message read, *Sorry. It doesn't look good.* With bloody craters intruding to within five centimeters of her brain, on both sides of her head, if she were given a mirror instead of grease board, it wouldn't have looked good to Dorothy, either. The surgeon repaired the ruptures of the semicircular canals with microscopic thread and closed the ear drum over the un-restored middle ear to keep water out. The conchas of the ear were sewn back onto her head for cosmetic reasons. Dorothy would never hear the surgeon's bill for the two-hour operation.

As profound as the total hearing disability, was the disruption to balance and chronic motion sickness which attended the injury. They had given her a wheel chair at the hospital. They said that she might experience some relief from the vertigo and motion sickness in a few months. Dorothy experienced extreme vertigo in standing up. The mere perception of motion could make her vomit. It was hard for her to watch anything presenting motion for more than a minute without becoming nauseous. Even TV ...

Yesterday, she had watched television in tacit, burgeoning disgust as Wally appeared as a guest on the Phil Donacue show. Some program director got it in his head that it would be a real showstopper to get survivors of the hostilities together for some warmed over reminisces. Wally had seen the offer as an opportunity to discuss problems with the Confederation's Administration, and to make a plea for conciliation to ward off the threatened retaliatory strike.

He had gone to the KVAC/KLLM station yesterday morning, where he would discuss his points via satellite link up with Donacue, and with other survivors. Woodrift was assured they would want to talk about the critical issues facing both nations. Dressed up like a mummy, with his left arm in a sling, and the bristles of the sutures that held on his scrotum prickling his crotch, Woodrift sat patiently in front of the camera, and screen. He was introduced by Donacue as "the young man who started it all, and fired the first shot." Donacue discussed only the burn and tracer wounds Wally received in LaPush, which were the only injuries appropriate to the focus of a day-time talk show. Wally squinted into the camera through the matrix of his gauze bandages. He talked about his disillusionment with the Movement. He expressed his regret for the injuries incurred by all parties. He reiterated his hope that there would be no retaliatory strike, but peace and dialogue from the United States. Several burn victims from the mills at the head of the LaPush Road came on and talked about the horrible fatalities which had occurred at the mills, and the economic damage to the community by the loss of the two industrial sites. The widow of the owner of the bulk fuel depot was on. She talked about how her husband's insurance policy would not cover acts of insurrection; how their family business had been destroyed and how the loss of the fuel depot would impact the timber trucking business. Then there was a National Guardsman who escaped being torn up by buckshot or cut down by M-16's by lying down and playing dead. He had taken on a dose of chlorine gas. He was breathing through a nasal cannula attached to an O2 bottle. He made the point that the Confederates had used the media to dupe the American public and that the American press was excluded from the Capitol City, except for whatever naturalized Native agents the U.S. media could field.

"Our next guest is one of the many wounded casualties that washed up on Rialto Beach a week ago on that fateful, stormy November afternoon. Ensign Jake Smith was thrown into the water when his so-called 'LCP'craft was hit by the Light Artillery Weapon, fired from James Island by Colonel Woodrift. Once in the water he and the men around him were strafed by shotgun blasts from Natives firing on them from the beach. The Seals were unarmed and carried no defensive gear of any kind. Tell us about the nightmare, Jake." Then, to Wally's amazement and horror, upon the screen appeared the man who held him to the floor of the Forks Memorial Library, while another used a survival knife to cut away the skin and vans deferens that connected Woodrift to his testicles. Wally immediately began to sputter and articulate words that eluded his tongue. Dorothy sat in living room of her deceased father, and grieving mother, trying to make sense out of the closed captions that appeared at the bottom of her new television, "But, but...BUT! He...He's the one...HIM!"

"Excuse me, Colonel Woodrift. Wally, here in New York we're not understanding what you're trying to say. Please speak more clearly." The words appeared on Dorothy's screen under Donacue's paternal face.

Woodrift's mind tried to engage the words to describe the atrocity, while his tongue continued to double clutch, "He's...that man...in the Navy dress whites...he's the one who emasculated me!"

"We all feel emasculated by war, Wally...soldiers and citizens alike. Haven't you heard what these other men have been saying on your monitor? You weren't the only one hurt in this campaign that was started by you firing at and sinking vessels of the United States Navy..."

Behind the screen of bandaging, Dorothy could not see the tears on her lover's face, nor could she read the suppressed sobs, and catching of breath on the closed captions: "Mr. Donacue, put that man in the Navy uniform back on the screen so I can see him. Put me on his screen." Dorothy's screen split to show her the mummy that was Wally, and the stranger in dress whites. His face was so red, she wondered about the color adjustment of the new television which gave her the closed captions. Under the mummy's image came a rehash of a message from the Christian Bible: "For five centuries White civilization has interfered with, dominated and persecuted Native America. A continent was taken forcibly from us. In opposing the U.S. Armed Forces we hoped to achieve an Indian Free State, a political refuge for the oppressed non-Whites that are caged in ghettos and reservations across a land to which they had been forcefully introduced or, from which, forcefully removed. We achieved that goal. But the government of man is flawed, and I find little sanctuary in the new State, which was created in this resistance.

"This man in uniform took something precious from me. My blood... and the blood of my people is on his knife. I forgive him. Let's fight no more. There is nothing in fighting, but more sorrow and loss. I appeal to the people of the United States to put down their weapons and deep-seated hostilities against Blacks and Indians. I appeal to the government of the Confederation to pray for deliverance from the corruption and hate that have already infected this infant State. I forgive everyone, everything. I ask only for peace and tolerance to get on with the healing. I pray to God for the manifestation of His will..."

"This little man dares to talk about God!" interrupted the man wearing the Smith name tag. As she read the captions, she realized that the color in the man's face was adjusted upwards by his burning rage. "The United States Navy came to Rialto Beach in peace, to practice life-saving techniques that we might employ to rescue distressed innocents in a far away land. We were ambushed while on that mission of peace. That little viper that just talked brags about firing the LAW rocket that blew us all out of the boat. My best friend swam to shore and was killed with a shotgun at point-blank range. I saw that with my own eyes! Then the attackers turned on us in the water with their shotguns. They used living breathing human beings for target practice; took over and shut down the Coast Guard Station, leaving fishermen and other boaters to shift for themselves; they disrupted components of the United States strategic security, inviting nuclear holocaust; they held innocent hostages prisoner and constantly threatened to murder us; they committed extortion upon the President and the whole government of the United States; and the little man dares to talk about God...*God doesn't hear Confederates, you little weasel!* The fighting men of this country will be given a chance to avenge the atrocities that have been carried out against soldiers and civilians of the US of A. Your day will come, little man, your day will come."

On Wally's side of the split screen, a mummy stood up to retire from the program, "I hear God and God hears me, Ensign Smith. Peace be with all of us." Dorothy turned off the television and trundled toward the bathroom in her wheel chair. She vomited on the floor before she got there.

****

Today, in the few hours between other appointments, Dorothy and Wally had planned to go the Rialto Beach. Wally had been wakened this morning by some black man claiming to be the press liaison officer to the interim President of the C of NA. "We can't have you shooting your mouth off about the Confederacy on television. It don't bode well, bro'. Keep a lid on, cool?"

After breakfast, and before his hospital appointment at eleven, Wally walked over to Dorothy's to pick up the little Datsun truck and drive them to their outing. The handicapped access to Rialto would allow him to wheel her right out to the driftwood fence of the beach. He could carry her from there. On this day, that could do anything weather-wise, Wally wore a full length, beige colored trench coat, which, besides his face, covered his bandaging. Dorothy wore a burgundy rain slicker. If it didn't rain, it could always puke, she thought morbidly. They were driving down the Mora road, Dorothy with her eyes closed and Wally squinting through the bandaging. "I'm sorry it didn't work out better for you on the Donacue Show yesterday," commiserated Dorothy.

"Thanks, Dot. It scares me to think that the homicidal maniac in dress whites might be speaking for more than himself. How do you break the arrow or smoke the peace pipe with guys like him running around in jackets that don't secure their arms behind their backs?"

"He's not alone in his anger, Wally. There's so much anger... it's like it feeds on itself. It's like the Antichrist," said Dorothy. Her eyes were shut to avoid seeing motion.

"Peace. Love and brotherhood, that's our only defense. We have to keep up the hope...Just a minute! Hold on here!"

Driving by the Mora Ranger Station toward the beach, Woodrift saw Ed Whitman, taking down the American flag. He pulled the vehicle into the parking lot. "I'm going to stop the car for a few minutes to talk to Ranger Whitman...if you want to open your eyes." Wally climbed out of the Datsun and called out, "Good morning, Ranger Whitman. Can I help you fold the flag?"

"Woodrift, I'm in no mood for fooling around this morning... especially, not with you. This ranger station will be yours soon enough. Just give us the time and privacy to clean out our stuff."

Wally walked over to Ed Whitman with his right hand on his slung left arm. He waited for him to finish folding the flag into a triangle, and held out his right hand to shake Whitman's.

Ed ignored the proffered hand. "Look, Woodrift, just leave us alone. You've done enough harm in this country. Remember your friend, James Crow? I got close to him. It may have been White men who pulled the trigger, but it was your Confederacy that sold him down the river..."

"I just want the hostilities to end, Ed. We **all** lost something in the fighting."

"Someone told me that you got your nuts shot off."

"Something like that, but, for what it's worth, I'm still wearing them."

Anger at the sight of his old enemy, at the uncertainty of his future, at how he had been impugned by the District Ranger: these things combined into a tempest in the *rolling boil of the roiling bowl* of Whitman's heart. A strong westerly wind from the ocean blew clouds, and tree tops and, as Dorothy stared out the windshield, it invoked a spasm of nausea in her and she gagged. She opened the door in front of Woodrift and Whitman, and spit pathetically on the ground.

301

"Getting any?" Ranger Whitman said sadistically to Woodrift. "Your girlfriend could get old just waiting for you to take off all those bandages."

"I get it, Ed. You're feeling like a victim! You're still sore about your nose, which, incidentally, is looking a lot better. You have to find a new place to work...I already admitted, we all lost something in the fight. I had my testicles cut off and stuffed in my mouth! I'm not getting any, Ed. I may never get any. I haven't exactly had the time lately to sit around and concentrate on getting an erection...maybe I'll never get an erection. I'm pretty sure I'll never have kids of my own. Is this all pretty hilarious to you?"

Ranger Whitman had stopped smirking. He was listening to what his old enemy had to say. "No, the subject of your sex life is not that amusing to me. So did you stop to cry on my shoulder or jack me around or *just what are you getting at?*"

"I'm trying to defend what's left of my life with the only tools in which I've come to trust: love and brotherhood. Peace, Ed."

"Give me a break, Woodrift!"

"That's what I stopped for: Peace between us. And that starts with forgiveness. And forgiveness starts with honesty, so I'm here to level with you. I guess you know about the cars I hit at Third Beach over the years...well, anything since 1981 wasn't me. Maybe you already figured out that I had something to do with blowing off your nose and that's correct, Ed, I helped put together that Snatch and Scriff card that took off your schnoz..."

"You little son of a bitch! I'll break your good arm and pour lighter fluid on your stinking bandages!" Whitman advanced on the Native and with his hands out as if to make good his threat. Woodrift held his ground holding open his right hand in a gesture of surrender.

"Do it if it makes you feel better, Ed. I'm beyond caring about physical pain. If we could just start over before all the violence began. If we could just turn back the clock...You've got to find forgiveness in your heart, Ed. We all do..." Wally's voice petered out into silence. Whitman paused with his hands a few inches from Woodrift's throat and he began to shake profoundly. Simultaneous to his encounter with Wally Woodrift, Wilbur Ed Whitman was receiving a visit from an old childhood friend: the God of the Quakers.

For a moment, all Whitman was aware of was the silence. In what he would later modestly describe as "a spontaneous and isolated petite mal convulsive episode," something strange was happening to the Ranger's perception. Like the Friend in his heart that sat with Whitman in Quaker Meeting when he was a boy, something was stealing into his heart from out of the silence. The wind had blown a hole in the clouds letting down a shaft of light which was shining down on the upper body of Wally Woodrift. A strange auroral glow was coming off of the exposed

302

fingers of Woodrift's right hand and as the intensity of Whitman's shaking increased, so did the illumination. Light was pouring out from behind the facial bandages and the trench coat was turning white. The figure in front of Whitman was metamorphosing before his beleaguered eyes.

An angel of peace, all in heavenly white was standing before Ranger Whitman! It was more vivid than anything Ed Whitman had seen in the astral-plane called 'reality.' It's left wing was folded in front of its body and its right hand was held up in a gesture of supplication. Ed Whitman felt the angel as much as seeing it, and what he felt, through the shaking that racked his body, was the most wonderful feeling he had experienced in his lifetime. From the glow of the angel emanated the Love of God and the Brotherhood of mankind. There, before Ed Whitman, stood the Promise of Peace for his children and their children. The power of what he saw and felt, put Ed Whitman quaking on his knees.

And, lo, the angel spoke. It was the voice of neither a man, nor a woman. "Are you OK, Ed?"

Whitman fought for control of his voice over the convulsive twitching. "No, I've been an asshole...excuse me. I've been selfish and belligerent. I just want peace and a better world for my kids...for *all* the kids, everywhere." The angel had lowered its right hand; its arm reaching out in the tremulous light. The passive force of gravity is perhaps the most powerful, all encompassing agent in the tool chest of Natural Law. It was gravity which lifted Whitman off his knees and propelled him into the open arm of the angel. Whitman fell into the angel's bosom and pressed himself against the chest and folded wing of Love, Peace and Brotherhood. The angel spake again, saying "I just asked you for forgiveness. I didn't ask you to marry me!" Though the angel seemed to Ed sexless, it was reminding Whitman of what he had learned in the Bible studies of his youth: that angels were constrained from conjugal relationship with mankind. But the angel was laughing and, like Ed, exulting in the warmth and the light. "Peace, brother," said the angel in parting, leaving Ed's embrace and climbing into - of all things! - the Datsun pick-up which Wally Woodrift had driven minutes before!

Looking in the window, Ed Whitman's wondrous eyes beheld yet another angel! This angel was shimmering in a burgundy robe and spoke to the angel that had come to Whitman, "It looks like you finally made a convert!" The angels drove off. In the silence, Ed looked around at his world with new eyes. He laughed. Crumpled and forgotten on the ground was the flag of the United States of America.

THIRTY-NINE

Ridgecrest Cemetery
13:30 Thursday, November 19, 1992

In her garden of grief grow many weeds, flowers, and a strangely bittersweet harvest. In the spring of grief, the weather is tempestuous with convulsive sobs and torrential tears. The low hanging clouds and mist are so thick that the grieving gardener cannot see from one end of the plot to the other. In the summer of grief, the garden begins to sprout unwelcome foliage: financial insecurity, behavioral change, family distress, anger and irritability. The gardener toils under a hot, dry sun of loneliness and celibacy to keep the weeds from overrunning the ripening fruit of tender remembrances. The fall harvest of grief finds the gardener clutching a family photograph to her breast, trying to fill the aching emptiness that lies therein; returning to a closet to feel and smell the clothes of her lost love for the ten thousandth time; looking deep into the folds and recesses of the recliner chair, trying once again to hang flesh on the spirit abiding there. In the stillness of winter, the garden plot of grief looks much like the neighboring plot of joy...but for the seeds in the ground.

****

"To every thing there is a season, and a time to every purpose under heaven: I read from the book of <u>Ecclesiastes,</u> the third chapter." This was the tenth funeral in the last two weeks over which the Navy Chaplain had presided. Unlike the other ceremonies, this one hadn't been as easy as planting corn. *"A time to be born, and a time to die; a time to plant, and a time to pluck up that which is planted..."* Of the twenty Navy Seals who had been killed in the LaPush hostilities, ten bodies had come to this cemetery. *"A time to kill, and a time to heal..."* Lieutenant Richard Gillette had been a late comer because his body had not been on the beach, but out in the woods. Animals had fed on the Lieutenant's body. *"A time to weep, and a time to laugh; a time to mourn, and a time to dance..."* Then the wife freaked out because she wanted a burial at sea, which was against regs; and then she didn't want her husband embalmed, which was also against regs...The chaplain had seen the body and it *really* needed some freshening up. They reattached what was left of the Lieutenant's arm, closed the empty eye sockets... *"A time to rend, and a time to sew; a time to keep silence, and a time to speak..."*

Mrs. Patricia Gillette made the chaplain nervous: the way she sat on the edge of her chair, like she was about to jump up and interrupt. She wasn't dressed in black. She was wearing some kind of pants suit instead of a dress. When the color guard took the flag off the Lieutenant's coffin, and passed it to the widow, it looked for a moment as if she would not accept it. She was a woman on the edge of more than her seat... *"A time of love, and a time of hate; a time of war, and a time..."*

"Excuse me, chaplain, may I say a few words?" the widow spoke, interrupting the chaplain and striding towards the microphone holding the folded flag as if she were going to throw it at the chaplain. "Excuse me," she said again in front of the mike. "I've had so much trouble trying to sleep. Last night I stayed awake with the TV until two in the morning. When the station went off the air, I was left alone with ...with my grief. The last thing was the station playing the National Anthem of the United States of America. A woman sung the lyrics while the camera panned across images of our armed forces. Our ships, tanks, guns and you fighting men. For the first time in my life I listened to the words that we have sung since we were children. It is a song about war...Words by Francis Scott Key, that don't even rhyme, put to the melody of an old English beer hall song...How patriotic.

"The men and wives of my husband's company have come to me in the last two weeks. They've promised that there will be a vindictive raid on LaPush to avenge the death of...Richard...and the other soldiers. They want to punish the killers. But it was not the finger on the trigger, or the Indian on the finger, that tore my husband's flesh. It was shotgun buck...Weapons killed Richard. The same weapons that paraded across my TV screen this morning, with a chauvinistic wave of this flag, took my husband forever! I want no vindictive strike on LaPush. I want peace for my son... I want my husband back...

"My father, who grieves with me here this afternoon, was a sky pilot in Viet Nam. My older sister was a war protester in the '60's. Janet would argue with my father that Ho Chi Min had been our ally in World War Two against the Japanese; that the Viet Cong fought for reunification of their country which had been artificially divided by the imperialistic French; and that the puppet government of South Viet Nam opposed the will of the people of the country. She was right.

"My father argued that the V. C. went into "Vietnamesed" communities and cut the heads off the village leaders. They left the heads on stakes as a warning to the citizens. He argued that the Soviets were supplying North Viet Nam, and the Viet Cong in the South, with weapons. He said, if the United States didn't stop the Communist in Viet Nam, one by one, the governments of south-east Asia would topple like dominos. He was right.

"The error in war is not in the perception of our enemy as evil. They torture, sabotage, terrorize, maim and kill like Satan walking on the earth. The mistake lies not in realizing the enemy is evil...the error is in thinking that we are in any way different from those we fight.

"My dad would spend his 'r and r' from Nam, arguing with my sister and carefully inventorying the spoils of war with me. 'Freedom is never won without a cost,' he would tell me. My father said without George Washington, and the Revolutionary War, we would still be living under English subjugation. Without Abraham Lincoln, and the Civil War, slavery would still be a black mark on the complexion of the United States. Without General Patton, and World War Two, Adolf Hitler would rule the world, and Jews everywhere would be in gas chambers. 'Something like the Third Reich could never happen in a free society like ours,' explained my dad, 'and that is why we must oppose the King Georges, Adolf Hitlers and Ho Chi Mins of the world with force.

"But I look just a little further north to Canada, and I see a people who live in freedom, and equality with Great Britain. They never fought a war for succession, though they had to fight the United States to protect their southern boundary. I look around the world, and in no corner of the globe do I see blacks being held by Whites as outright slaves. Did Lincoln free the slaves of South Africa or did world opinion and economic sanctions kill Apartheid? The Nazis wanted the Jews money and power and they took it. The United States wanted land. How can we stand in the middle of a continent, taken by force, deceit, corruption, and genocide and say, 'It cannot happen here.' It already has happened.

"There was World War One - the war to end all wars, and then World War Two, the Korean Conflict, Viet Nam, and now we sharpen our swords and count our bullets to engage the people of Iran in war. Every enemy we fight or vanquish is replaced by a new enemy. And to get at that enemy we commit our husbands, sons and national resources to fight a people that bleed, cry, and hunger for peace and freedom just like ourselves. We fight people, while the real tyrant walks alive and healthy across the field of time and space...The real enemy took my husband. *It* will be back for my son. The real Enemy has a face and a name. In English, it's name is *'War'* and I want it stopped before it comes again to my door.

"Let me inventory the spoils of war given to me by my husband's willingness to engage weapons toward the political aims of the United States. My father said that, if the Communist took over the United States, I could no longer worship in the church of my choice. It was not Communism, but Agnosticism, that separated me from church. What special freedom do I now enjoy? I have the freedom *not to* cook, *not to* clean the house, or *not to* diet because I no longer have a husband to please. I can cry as hard and as long as I want to...I can snap at my son for no reason at all. Richard is not there to equilibrate my moods or reassure him. I have the freedom to lie awake, night after night, without my husband to hold me; the freedom to sleep into the morning, and afternoon, tormented by nightmares about how Richard...died. The freedom to give up forever being a wife; to neglect being a mother...the freedom of being nothing more than a ...frightened ...little girl. I...can't...stop crying," sobbed Patricia Gillette. "And I believe that my tears are not only for my own loss and for the death of the other Seals and National Guard. I cry for the Indian casualties, and for war dead everywhere.

"I would work in the salt mines of Siberia joyfully every day for the rest of my life, if I could work beside Richard. I would pay any tax, and worship God only in the privacy of my soul...I would salute any flag, if I could only have him back...I would do anything, but rise up in war to deprive some other innocent the *freedom* to live out her life with her husband."

Patricia Gillette took the folded American Flag and bent over to place it on the ground next to where she stood. Twenty-one soldiers stood by at attention waiting to discharge the blank cartridge in their carbines. "But why should I wave the flag that took Richard from me? My grief does not need a twenty-one gun salute. My heart needs...peace." Patricia's puffy, bloodshot eyes explored the audience. She found the eyes of the soldiers and the soldiers' wives exploring the dress shine of their boots and the minute fissures of the concrete upon which their chairs depended. Her eyes caught and were held by a long, brown-haired stranger.

"Peace...peace for my son, and myself and my country, and my world. *Peace*. The freedom that my father talked about seems so empty and lonely. Freedom from war seems the only cause worth arguing about and...I will give what's left of my life to that argument. I leave you now to the desecration of my husband's body."

Patricia Gillette stormed from the stage in front of the casket. She strode over to where her son, Brian, sat next to his grandparents. She took his hand and led him from his seat and out the aisle. Her father called, "Patricia, wait!" and followed her. The long-haired stranger followed them across the cemetery to a black limousine.

****

I stand awkwardly next to the limousine as the uniformed grandfather fights for temporary custody of his grandson. The driver, also in military dress whites stands at attention holding the back door open for whomever will climb aboard. "Patricia, for Christ's sake don't do this! Come back now! Everyone is waiting. What do you mean shooting your mouth off like that in front of Brian?"

Patricia climbs into the back seat dragging her son with her. The grandfather beseeches his daughter, "OK, leave then. But, Patricia by the love and respect I've given you all your life, honor this one request: Give me Brian so that he won't remember running away from his father's funeral for the rest of his life."

I bump into the grandfather's back trying to get close enough to the limousine to say a word to Patricia Gillette. The gentleman turns and his red face explodes in mine, "**Who the hell are you!**"

This is awkward. I grasp for words, "Um, my name is Chiggers Stokes and I'm writing an antiwar book."

"Well get your flag-burning, muck-raking, chicken-manured butt the hell out of here before I kick it back to the commune you escaped from..."

"No, wait!" Patricia pushes her son from the back seat. The grandfather unclenches his fists to accept the ward of his grandson. "Keep him tonight and have him back to me in time for school tomorrow. Is that what you want?"

"Yes, princess. You won't be sorry." Returning to the funeral, the captain bumps my shoulder as he passes with his crying grandson. "Beat it, God damn it!" he hisses under his breath.

"Can you get in, please?" asks Patricia in a small voice from the bowels of the black limousine. I climb into the posh back seat beside the grieving widow and leave the door open. "How can I help you write your book?"

I am at a loss as to what to say. "I was with a man who died in the hostilities two weeks ago. He was a Native named James Crow. He was with your husband when he died." I go on clumsily, "Well, maybe your husband was already dead when James came on him, but I believe their spirits touched..."

"Could you shut the door, please," Patricia snuffled, "And come with me a while?" And as the limousine moves out into the congested no-man's-land of I-5, I tell her what I know of the circumstances of her husband's death from reading Crow's journal. I tell her what I've learned about Crow and about his remarkable last words. I finish with this information as the limousine leaves the traffic-choked free-for-all-way, and finds the small, suburban Gillette chateau. There is a postage sized flower garden with a few drying vegetable stalks protruding from the ground. The driver sits awaiting instruction in a silence that becomes contagious. The awkward seconds conspire into minutes and finally Patricia asks, "Can you come in?"

"Sure. For just a while."

"Would you like for me to wait for the gentleman?" asks the sailor/driver.

"That's OK," answers the widow. "We'll call a cab. Please go back to the funeral and drive my...family back to their home... afterwards."

Inside the small home, the obligatory snacks have been arranged for the post funeral bash. To most vertical surfaces have been tacked or taped the colored art work of eight-year-old Brian Gillette. Brian's hand depicted several family portraits, showing a father in dress whites towering over wife and son. A small house was in the background. The hands and heads, of the people portrayed, were disproportionately large. "Have something to eat, if you like," offered Patricia. "The others will be along shortly, get it while it's...it's...there." She was fumbling for words.

I continue to walk around studying the art work, and the family photographs. "Brian makes a heavy association with his father, and the military," I say studying five pictures in a row of the large man in dress whites on a ship, in combat, in a parade, in a helicopter, piloting a war plane. I stop in front of another combat picture. The sailors in dress whites are firing carbines at Indians who return the complement with bow and arrows.

"That's the one that really frightens me," says Patricia. "Brian drew that up before the hostilities at LaPush. How do kids get this stuff in their heads. It's like Brian knew before we did that there was a problem brewing in Native America. Please sit down," said Patricia from the couch/hide-a-bed.

I briefly consider the recliner chair, but decide against it, for fear of sitting on a ghost. That leaves me sitting beside Patricia, both of us sitting rigid, and in awkward silence. "Really, eat something if you like."

"No, that's all right. I'm not hungry." More silence. "Do you believe in God? I couldn't tell by what you said in the cemetery, except you said you were Agnostic."

"It's organized religion that makes me Agnostic. I can accept God, but not the church. Like the chaplain at the service. Our society thinks that a prostitute - a woman who sells her body - is the lowest rung on the ladder. What about a man who sells his soul?"

"I don't think I get what you're talking about," I say to this widow. From her proximity I can feel the warmth radiating from her skin and smell her shampoo.

"The fifth commandment, *Thou shall not kill*. How does a man dress up like that chaplain - as if he represents God - and lead the soldiers in prayer to vanquish the enemy. Where in Christianity do we find license to make war and ignore the fifth commandment? He's paid by the Department of Defense to keep the soldiers in a state of spiritual fight readiness, and he does it in the name of God. Who will our Creator judge more harshly, the chaplain or the prostitute?"

"It's not for us to guess," I venture.

"I believe in God. It's a small silver lining in losing Richard in that I've begun to pray again. I've prayed a lot. It's kind of like making up with somebody when you've been estranged for a long time. I didn't know how to talk to God, how to reveal myself, what to call God in my heart...Have you ever owned a puppy?"

I'm trying hard to follow the widow's train of thought along a skipping and divergent track. "Yeah, sure." My memory scans back to a little Golden Retriever given to me by my grandparents on my mother's side - Native Americans, themselves.

"What did you call the dog?" Patricia asks.

"Her name was 'Woodsie.'" There is a small tug at my heart as I remember the loss of this close canine friend. I try to translate that sense of loss to what it must be like to lose a spouse.

"How did you arrive at that name?" asks Patricia.

I remember sitting in the family's living room about five miles and twenty years from here. As I sat in the chair, the pup sat before me, intent on my every word. I experimented with different names: "Tasha!" I said, and the dog sat. "Fido!" and the dog sat still, waiting. "Woody!" I said and the dog began to wag her tail.

"Woodsie!" and the dog jumped into my lap, licking my face, wagging her tail and urinating on my pants.

"I guess Woodsie kind of helped pick her own name. What's that got to do with anything here?"

"Well, what is God's name? I've done a lot of praying in the last two weeks and I've experimented with the names of *Yahweh, Jehovah, Allah, Jesus, Heavenly Father* and such. I'm not saying that these are not God's names, but the words that get my tired heart racing are *Love, Brotherhood, Peace...*" There was a knock at the door. "Excuse me," said Patricia, going to the front door.

"Hello," the widow speaks to two couples at her front door. The two men wear military dress. "Thanks for coming. Cindy and Marcia, could I talk to you for a moment inside. Just wait here a moment, please," she closes the door on the two men.

"Chiggers, this is Cindy and this is Marcia. Their husbands outside are Richard's best friends. I mean were Richard's...," Patricia is fumbling for words again. "Chiggers brings an eyewitness account of Richard's death."

Cindy falls on the news like a vulture on a splattered road kill. "Bring in Jake and Larry and we'll get names and physical descriptions. The Navy will kick ass..."

"It's nothing like that, Cindy," Patricia intones. "Listen, sit down. Have something to eat." Marcia sits in the recliner.

Marcia sits down, but Cindy stands nervously awaiting an explanation of why Richard's best friends are parked on the other side of the door. "Pat, what's going on here? Let's bring in Jake and Larry."

"The problem is that I don't want any uniforms in this house. I'm all done with soldiering. I'm not a good little Navy wife anymore and I don't want Brian growing up in the Navy tradition of kill and be killed. Tell Larry and Jake, I'd love for them to come in, but they'll have to take off their blouses..."

Cindy recoils, "They can't do that. They can't walk around in their under shirts wearing their dress pants!"

"That's what they *can* do in this house. What they *can't* do is come through the door with their campaign ribbons, and insignias on their shirts. Please tell them that."

Cindy strides toward the door. Marcia reaches over and smears some cheese on a cracker. "Marcia, come here!" calls Cindy, like she was fetching a dog.

311

Marcia stands up, and puts the cracker with a bite taken out of it on the table. "I'm really sorry about Rich. If only they'd had live ammunition when they landed on the beach..."

"Marcia!" Cindy again pulls on the social leash that attached Marcia to her companion. The two women leave the house, closing the door behind them. In a few moments there is a knock at the door and Cindy sticks just her head in to announce, "Like I said, they can't take off their dress blouses, so if you want to throw out Rich's best friends, that's up to you..."

Marcia's head pops across the threshhold above Cindy's head, "Thanks for the food, Pat. The crackers were terrific..." Cindy pulls the door shut on Marcia's culinary review of the transpiring events. Some of Marcia's hair is caught in the door. Another knock at the door and it opens just a crack. Marcia's cheerful voice, "Bye now!"

I sit in silence for a few minutes and then ask, "Are you going to hold the line on everyone who shows up in uniform or were you just trying to get rid of Cindy and Marcia?"

"It has nothing to do with those two. Actually, I need all the friends I can get now. I don't want uniforms in this house anymore. That's all."

A few more minutes in silence and I say, "I didn't understand what you were saying earlier. Are you saying that God's like a puppy and you've got to pin a name on Him?"

"I didn't say that. Where do you get off calling God 'Him?' Does God have testicles and a beard..."

There's knocks at the door. Patricia goes forth and defends her doorstep from a uniformed detachment from the funeral. They go. She comes back and sits down.

I say, "It says in the Bible that God created us in *His* own image. That's in Genesis. It uses the word 'His.' And it says that God has a name and His name is 'Jehovah.'"

"The word given originally in the Red Sea Scrolls was 'Yaweh,' but it was considered profane in those times to utter God's name. John One One gives God as 'the Word'...just 'the Word.' Kind of like you fill in the blank..." More knocks at the door; more couples with uniformed sailors being turned away. Patricia comes back toward where I'm sitting and the door pounds on its hinges. She turns around and opens the door to her father. He fills the doorway in his dress whites.

"Just what in God's name is going on here!" bellows the Captain. He pauses for only a moment before pushing past his daughter into the small living room. "What's *he* doing here?" the father roars pointing at me like he had discovered a dog turd on the carpet. "What do you mean by throwing all of Richard's friends out of your life? Young lady, you need all the real friends you can get right now and your actions don't deserve friendship. Who is this turkey?" the captain's finger still waggles at me.

"Father, this is Chiggers. He brought me an account of Richard's death. Where is Brian..."

"Half the sailors you threw out of here this afternoon were there on the beach when Richard got killed. They were taken prisoner by the Indian scum that killed him..." the Captain strides right over to me and I come to attention and hold out my hand which he ignores. He puts his face so close to mine that I can smell the Dentucream when he growls: "This is a military family; a Christian family, God damn it! There's nothing for you here. You've no business with my daughter. Please leave us to our grief." The captain does an about face and strides to the door.

"Brian's out in the car with his grandmother. He's not coming back until you straighten out your life."

"Please have him back in time for school tomorrow. Dad..." she calls out to the angry white cloud storming across the walkway away from her little home. "Dad...DAD!" There is no response from her father. A car door slams. A car engine starts up. "Dad, I'm sorry," says Patricia in a voice so small that I hardly hear it.

"I had better be going now," I say, standing as Patricia again approaches.

"Please stay," she says sitting down. "I understand your discomfort at being here, but...if you have the time, please stay a while longer." And I sit beside Patricia and spend the afternoon talking about God...about pacifism...about the things I read in the journal of one, James Crow.

And it is past eleven o'clock, when I start to wonder how I'll get back to my car: no money for cab fare, no flashlight and about a ten mile walk in the dark. "I'd better be going." I begin to stand up, but Patricia restrains me by placing her left hand on my thigh. "Please stay," she says softly, leaving her hand perched like a bird on a power line. The bird clutches innocently to the wire, innocent and unaware of the power that surges through the line. We both look down at Patricia's left hand on my thigh...the small golden band on the ring finger. "Please stay," she repeats removing her hand and pulling off the ring. Placing it lightly beside Marcia's cracker with the bite taken out of it.

****

To some, life is predictable, while, to others it is laden with surprise. The parent may see accident before the child fumbles. The dear, patient reader may anticipate the outcome of a chapter before it even occurs to the writer. But it is with genuine surprise that my lips taste the light salt crust on Patricia's face from her tears. It is with surprise that I am led away from the crackers, cheese spread and spoiling

313

shrimp dip, down a hall and to a closed door. Patricia opens the door and, it is with surprise, that I see the unmade bed and watch as she removes the *TV Guide* and remote control unit from the foot of the bed. It's like a dream as Patricia turns from me and begins undressing and I shut the door for privacy from the crackers, shrimp dip and family photographs in the living room...

****

"Wake up, Chiggers. It's 6:30." Next to me, in the bed, Patricia is lying with the sheets pulled up around her neck with only her bare wrist and left hand extruding from the bed covers. Her hand clutches the sheet. "I'm sorry, but my father's an early riser and he could be bringing Brian home any time now." Her green eyes are puffy and bloodshot as she concentrates on the ceiling. Her black hair sticks to her briny cheeks. She was crying while I was sleeping. Body language is everything and there will be no warmed leftovers of the passion from last night. "Are you really writing an antiwar book, Chiggers?"

"Yeah, I am." I climb out of bed and begin the search for my underwear. I feel totally naked beyond my lack of clothes as I say, "It's a story of this whole LaPush thing. Well, I haven't really started to write, I'm just putting the story together."

"Is that what you were doing with me last night? Getting material together..." her voice trails off. "Chiggers, are you going to write about what happened between us last night. My father would disown me if something like that were published."

"I don't even know if it will be published. I said I was writing a book...that's all." I'm wearing underwear and a shirt and am feeling less naked as I say, "Do you think that what happened last night is part of the story?"

Patricia still studies the ceiling through her red and green eyes. The pillow upon which her head depends, is wet with tears. "I'm afraid it is. If you write a book about war, it has to discuss the victims...not just the ones that get killed, but the ones that have to go on with life. Chiggers, make it a good book because it will destroy what's left of me." She is sobbing as I leave the room.

I walk down the hall. It's not hard to imagine this handsome woman being ruined by her grief. I can picture her sitting in this living room with everything dead inside of her. The TV will babble on while she sits in its flashing light; ingesting stale crackers and cheese; sipping water from a cloudy glass; letting her hair go gray. I walk past the family photos and Brian's art work. The ghost in the recliner chair watches me pass. I open the door and step outside into the crisp November morning to begin my ten mile hike back to the cemetery. To my horror, Patricia's father is helping Brian out of the front seat of his vehicle. The captain sees me on the porch step and shortcuts across the lawn, charging through the little garden. He is knocking down flowers as he comes at me dragging his crying grandson by the hand. I close

314

the front door softly on a strange, bittersweet chapter of my life to which I know there will be no return.

FORTY

Monday, November 30, 1992

I pull into the parking lot of the Mora Ranger Station. One look at the surviving ranger, tells me that he has flipped his flat hat. Ed Whitman is outside the station burying something. He works a neat hole that he has dug about fifteen feet from the flag pole. He is wearing his green dress tie as a head dress with the knot tied off to the side, the running ends of the tie spilling over the Park Service patch on his left shoulder. It's evident from a distance, that it's been a week or so since a razor visited the ranger's chin. The man turns towards me as I get out of my vehicle. I see that his badge has been wrapped in black electricians' tape.

"Hi, Chiggers," he calls out cheerfully. "I've been expecting you. Did you finally find something to write about?"

As I approach the ranger, I get an uneasy feeling about what's in the hole. Beside an empty briefcase is a policeman's equipment belt. Missing, are the service revolver, speed loaders, mace and baton, used by peace officers to enforce the 'peace.'

"Yeah, I kind of got hit in the head by this LaPush thing. I just need a keyboard to put it into writing. Are you stashing some weapons for when the Natives come to claim the ranger station?"

Ed Whitman is tamping fresh dirt onto the mounded refilled hole. "I was visited by an angel from God last week at this exact spot," announced this stranger ranger, confirming my suspicions regarding his sanity. "Now I'm applying what I learned."

"Do I have it straight that you've buried your service revolver in that hole. Don't you have to answer to someone about what you do with a gun?"

"Sure I do! To God, that's Who!" the ranger was laughing and seemed genuinely happy with his new perspective.

"But what will you tell your employer?"

"I'll tell them that I lost my defensive equipment while I was outside the ranger station wrestling with my conscience. Let me tell you about how this angel came to me...Well, I had a petite mal convulsion, was part of it. Remember Wally Woodrift, that Indian kid-cop you saw at Third Beach Parking? One second he was in my face talking some love/peace/flowers crap and, the next thing, he's gone and I'm talking to the angel. It was the coolest thing that's ever happened to me! And, you know what? A lot of the flower-child jive that Wally was laying on me makes sense...He drove by a minute ago with his girl friend in the Pinn's pick-up on his way to the beach. The weirdest thing is the angels...did I tell you there was another angel...they drove off in that same pick-up last week!"

317

"Have you seen any counselors in the two weeks since you were taken hostage? It seems like you must have had a lot of stress in your life lately."

"Sure, I had the routine government critical incident debriefing. I've been going to Forks Outreach for counseling. I was in this morning telling them about the angels. They called the District Ranger and that reminded him that he was supposed to pick up my defensive equipment. That's what got me thinking that it would be better off buried for good..."

"Say, Ed, I need to take a little jog to clear my head. If Wally and Dorothy Pinn are down at the beach, I'd kind of like to talk to them about how things are going. I heard they both got badly wounded in the fighting two weeks ago. When I get back, can I talk to you a little about James Crow and what happened to you? Can I use your station's computer a little when I get back? I want to start writing my book?"

"The government doesn't allow the private use of official equipment. I guess I know you're writing about LaPush. What are you saying about Woodrift and the Indians that started it? What are you saying about violence and war?"

"It started long before Woodrift and these other Confederates. I'm sympathetic to their long list of grievances, but I don't think their new government's going to make it. The equality and justice that they are looking for can only be found in peace. I just want to write about truth...and truth cries out for peace."

"You can use the station's computer."

EPILOGUE

I jog into the parking lot of Rialto Beach and I see Dorothy Pinn and a mummy that must be Wally. They walk arm and arm, from the beach to the waiting Datsun. Dorothy appears to be balancing on Wally's arm and he is pushing an empty wheel chair. The young woman is speaking in a loud voice, given her proximity, to Wally and she is unaware of my footfalls. The wind carries her every word to me and it is what she says that causes me to lap the parking lot to give the couple their privacy.

"I wanted to tell you this back on the beach, Wally, but those waves were making me sick again. Not all my nausea is motion sickness, though. Remember that afternoon six weeks ago on the rock at Second Beach?" Wally nods affirmative and stops walking. "When you stuffed the ballot box, you brought another voter into the precinct. I'm going to have your baby. They confirmed it at the hospital!" I am close enough to see tears on Dorothy's cheeks. The news is received as either real good, or real bad, by Wally. He is hugging and kissing the mother-to-be so hard that he is starting to bleed through the bandages. He is sobbing.

318

As I finish the second loop of the parking lot, with the couple embracing, there are some big booms from across the river. The citizens of the new nation carry on like Ewoks in the last scene from *Return of the Jedi*. A big white limousine drives into the mostly abandoned parking lot and pulls in beside the grasping couple. A black man and a Native get out. "Howdy, Wally...Ms. Pinn," the black man says respectfully. "They need to talk to you over in LaPush about discussing matters of State with the media."

"We don't have anything to say to them," says Wally a note of concern and surprise in his voice. I begin to jog over to see if I can help out the couple.

"You're just going to have to come with us," says the Native folding up the wheel chair and putting it in the back seat. The Native firmly pushes Dorothy into the back seat and, after her, Wally abandons resistance and climbs into the back seat. I reach the Cadillac as it begins to pull out.

"Wait!" I order the vehicle, which rolls as inexorably away from the beach as the tide.

****

I sit in silence by the computer trying to collect my thoughts. In the distance, I hear another boom, as match is applied to fuse in another display of LaPush's pyrotechnic exuberance. On the keyboard my callused fingers tremble with anticipation like ten race horses at the starting gate, but the course for the horses is hidden in a haze. I can't recognize the starting or finishing line. Where to begin this story and how to end it? Do I begin with nomadic Asian tribes pushing across an ice choked Bering Straight in the hazy predawn of history? Does this story end with prominent war heroes of a revolution being rounded up as political prisoners and pushed into the back of a big white limousine? How can I compose a story line that will carry a reader's interest from point 'A' to point 'Z'? In truth, isn't point 'A' preceded by another point 'Z' in some big carousel of human events? I aspire to write history from the truth and circumstances that have become revealed to me. Does history follow a line, or is it an avalanche of events, crashing down the slope of time, briefly igniting sparks of a reader's interest, as fact impacts fact Or is "history" just a cover up? Are the peaks of truth and reality of the past obscured in clouds of human bias?

Does a line exist in nature? The upper edge of the sea presents a straight line as it grasps for the lower edge of the sky. Light particles, I am told, travel in a straight line. But, from space, the interface of sea, land and stratosphere is a circle. And the universe, said Albert Einstein, comes back upon itself.

A school bus full of kids from LaPush rolls by the ranger station on a field trip. They have come to inspect the young nation's heritage along Rialto Beach. They are singing as one voice about taking down bottles of beer and passing them around. My hands come off the keyboard and push fists into my eye sockets. Little colored circles dance in my brain. I try so hard to concentrate. The government clock

319

over the computer ticks and another minute is pulled from the present and falls into the past... another minute is plucked from the future. In the theory of relativity, spatial limitations are placed upon the universe. Time and space are inextricably connected. Are there a limited number of minutes left on the wall, to be taken down and passed around? Does time also come back upon itself. Certainly the history of Native America has repeated itself time and time and time and time again.

The clock ticks again, the big hand pulling the little hand inexorably along the path of a circle. The tick marking 1/1,440 of the earth's rotation in space/time: one half-millionth of the earth's orbit around the sun. These are circles, pushing and pulling circles, but no story line. Ranger Whitman comes into the room. "You'd better get rolling on that story, unless you want the tribe to write it for you."

"I'm just trying to arrange the story line," I plea, but Whitman's attention is given to the task of hand shredding a file he has kept for over ten years of observations and intelligence on several LaPushan's. The American flag remains folded in the corner of the station, the naked pole out front awaiting a new standard.

Where to begin and where to end? The story line writhes and recoils as I attempt to caress it. The story lies in coils before me, its head ready to strike and its tail beating a tatoo as I drum my fingers on the desk. I keep seeing circles. Maybe there is no story line, but only a story circle.

You, dear reader, sit at the banquet of life, hungry for knowledge and fact. But just as you develop a taste or tolerance for what you've eaten from the plate of experience, the stern hostess of reality spins the lazy-susan from which you sup. You must again adjust your palate to the exotic or mundane dishes of fortune. So, if my story is to follow the events of reality, it must spin, and needs no beginning or end.

A serpent slithers across the wide plateau of techno-stasis. A pebble is dislodged and rolls from the garden. Outside the cave, the Neanderthal pushes a rock-fall away from the entrance and ponders as the rocks crash down slope. Millennia later, Egyptians drag huge stone blocks along log rollers to build gargantuan pyramids that thrust into the skyline. In the circle of the coliseum, the Romans watch the spinning, gilded chariot wheels as civilization rolls along, gaining momentum. While on the North American continent, a Native ties the first stick travois to the family dog and scratches the first minute arcs of technology upon this hemisphere. In Europe, Galileo drops globes from leaning towers and is inquisitioned for the first lensatic exploration of the heavens. On the same day of Galileo's death in Italy, a woman in England bears down in the pain of labor and delivers to the world another cosmic giant. Isaac Newton bounces balls, one against another. The circle of civilization articulates a spiral as it spins forward. Gunpowder and internal combustion, causing civilization to make minor hops along its ever-quickening course, until Mr. Einstein successfully challenges the ultimate globe of the atom. The cushion of man's limitations and capability is removed from the rolling circle of events. Mankind can do anything...except end war, stop starvation, and control greed. Like the Neanderthal's crashing boulder, civilization rolls uncontrolled down ever steepening walls of time, disappearing out of sight into the chasm where certainly it must beat itself into rubble with its velocity and momentum.

The Native studies the scratches of the dog-driven travois upon the face of his world and somehow sees the pieces of an enormous hoop. In the same millennia, the precious canine turns over garbage cans for scraps of food in the reservation, while satellites mock the sacred hoop by hanging over the planet or circumnavigating it several times in the course of a day.

A circle: the sacred hoop of Native America. The story must follow a circle. Around and around and around she goes, and where she stops...A cyclone of events, occurrences and remembrances whirl across my consciousness and push my fingers into the staccato of computer writing, like a gale beating on a rain hat, emotions blowing like wind across the rocky jetty of my memory - the eroding connection between my past and my awareness. I begin:

The Native American stooped over, holding the gunwales of the dugout as he stepped out of the boat and onto the wet, rocky jetty leading to James Island. A salty, wet wind whipped over the jetty lifting the man's rain hat...

Appendix 1
Historical commentary of Clarence Fourskins excerpted from story by popular demand
(continued from page 179)

"Some White historians try to pass off this chapter of Native America as some warmed over Pontiac Rebellion. There are geographic and demographic similarities. But, to Natives, it's one of the most impressive displays of nationalism and courage in the history of civilization. It's the story of a great patriot named Tecumseh, a Shawnee from a territory called *Indiana*...So named, because it was supposed to belong to Indians.

"A lot of Americans try to white-out the economic factors which drove the colonies to secede from England. The biggest factor was not the price of tax for tea. The colonists had as much representation in the House of Commons as the lower middle class in the motherland. They enjoyed the same degree of freedom as their old-world counterparts. But Great Britain had already gone up against Native Americans such as the blood drinking, liver eating, tattooed Ottowan named Pontiac. Flying the English flag, Captain Cook had visited disease, culture shock and thievery upon aborigines around the globe. To the Brit's credit they realized that military might did not settle the moral dilemma of displacing an indigenous population out of convenience and greed. By royal order, the Appalachian crest was defined as the western limits of American intrusion upon the continent. The Iroquois Confederacy realized the significance of this executive order. They fought with the British and Shawnees in the War for Independence, even though much of their ancestral ground laid within the lands targeted by the English for settlement. The proclamation made worthless large tracts of land in Ohio 'owned' by a Virginian developer by the name of George Washington. The French and English wanted the Native's fur and natural resources. The Americans wanted their land. Natives turned to England as an ally at every opportunity.

" 'Tecumseh' means 'panther lying in wait.' The man was born along the Mad River in Ohio. As White settlers invaded their valley, the Shawnees resisted their displacement. When he was a child, 'Cornstalk', the Chief of his tribe engaged a unified front of settlers, and militia, in the Lord Dunmore War. By standing and fighting, they were given a treaty which guaranteed no White settlements north of the Ohio. Then the Whites poured north of Ohio and 'Cornstalk' was murdered by settlers. The Shawnees moved against the settlers, and took twenty eight prisoners including a Kentuckian named Daniel Boone. They treated the prisoners with respect, and released them unharmed.

"In 1780 Tecumseh fought his first battle shoulder to shoulder with his step father. In the furious fighting, his step father began to spring bloody leaks and Tecumseh ran in fear. He vowed, he would never again cow from an enemy and he never did. In 1790 he joined forces with another Shawnee called 'Little Turtle' and successfully repelled fourteen hundred American troops. On November 4, 1791, up the Miami River, Tecumseh's band defeated General St. Clair's army of two thousand troops. It was the largest military defeat in American history of conflict with us good guys. In August of 1794, in the Battle of Fallen Timbers, Tecumseh and his band went up against Major General Wayne's army of 3,600 regulars. They were overpowered by the well armed and fully supplied men. The action on Tecumseh's rifle jammed and he continued to fight using his gun for a club. The Shawnees retreated to a British fort on the lower Maumee. The Brits would not let them in to treat the walking wounded.

"General Anthony Wayne built a fort at Greenville. He named it after himself. He convened a thousand Indians to Fort Wayne and insisted on the Native's surrendering two thirds of Ohio for twenty thousand dollars worth of trading supplies. Tecumseh was not there. He had retreated to Indiana country, which he vowed to defend with his life. At age twenty-seven, he was the dominant Native leader of the region.

"He married an older Native and she gave him a son. The relationship did not endure, for whatever reason, and about 1800, Tecumseh met Rebecca Galloway, the daughter of a White settler. He fell desperately in love. There was a tender courtship, and Tecumseh asked Rebecca to marry him. She consented on the basis of Tecumseh recanting his Native heritage and dressing like a White man. Tecumseh departed Rebecca and remained a single warrior for the rest of his life.

"Tecumseh had lost brothers in his fighting with American troops, but he lost his youngest brother to the bottle. The young Indian had lost an eye in brawling and, like other survivors of the white tide, lived from one drink to the next. In 1806, the young Native sat in bored, disinterest, as Tecumseh lectured him on the evils of alcohol. The Master of Life imposed a message upon the youngest brother and "Tenskwatawan" – 'the Open Door'- was born out of the young alcoholic. Tenskwatan never stopped preaching, and filled the ears of all around him with the imperative need to maintain religious culture; to refrain from drink; and to keep a reverence for land. He espoused much prophecy and in 1806 Territorial Governor Harrison said scoffingly, "Let just one miracle come true..." The Prophet called together all Natives who would hear his voice on June 16 and boldly predicted that the Master of Life would temporarily remove the sun from the sky. The crowd laughed at him. A full solar eclipse chased the amusement from the terrified and awed Natives. Soon after, the Prophet and his brother, Tecumseh, built a religious camp on the west bank of the Tippecanoe.

"In 1809, Tecumseh was in Florida with his distant relatives, the Seminoles, that you talked about a while ago. This was at a time in history where you didn't just hop on a Greyhound bus to ride to the far corners of the country and Tecumseh had tirelessly traversed half the continent, which was now settled with hostile Whites, to bring the message to his cousins. The message was: *We must stand together. We must not sell our land. A strike against one Native is a strike against all Natives...*

"Meanwhile, Governor Harrison convened seven thousand Natives again at Fort Wayne. This time three million acres deep in the Indian Country of Indiana was sold for seven thousand dollars and enough grog to intoxicate seven thousand men.

323

When Tecumseh arrived back from his pilgrimage to Florida, he was of course, not very happy with how things had gone in his absence.

"Because of their popularity, and the nature of their doctrine, Governor Harrison had to deal with the Prophet and with Tecumseh. The Governor had seen other Native chiefs changed by trips to Washington D.C., where they met the 'White Father' and saw the endless sea of civilization from which spilled the tides of settlement upon the frontier. He asked Tecumseh and the Prophet to come to the Governor's mansion in Vincennes three miles south of Fort Knox to propose this excursion. All did not go well. This is what Tecumseh said to Governor Harrison: *You killed your Prophet by nailing Him to a cross and thought He was dead. Now you scoff at Shakers. If you want peace, truly, go back east yourself, from where you came. Selling land is like selling the sea, clouds or air..."* The Governor interrupted, to point out that Shawnees, like the Seminoles, were originally from Georgia and that Tecumseh was out of his jurisdiction in Indiana. The United States has always been fair with Indians, claimed the Governor. Evidently Tecumseh, didn't take the Governor's view on this issue. A shout out occurred where both men drew their ceremonial swords and threatened one another. There would be no trip to visit the Great White Father for this crazy Injun!

"In 1811 the young United States was busting its britches, listening to the incantations of Kentuckians and Georgians, that wanted Indian removal from their frontiers without British interference. War with Britain again loomed on the horizon and whatever school children are taught about 1812, it was fought because the United States wanted Natives and Britain out of Indiana, Florida and Canada. Tecumseh knew that this would be the last chance to side with a world power in demanding an Indian Free State. He set out to Florida, again with this message, and like Pope's knots on a string, he distributed an advent calendar for a consolidated uprising. These were bundles of red sticks. Knowing that Tecumseh was out of the region, Governor Harrison waited for the first opportunity for a surprise attack. Three Potowatomis killed some White men in Illinois, in July, and Harrison personally led an attack on Tippecanoe. He sustained about two hundred casualties in the attack, while 25 to 40 Natives were killed. Governor Harrison described the campaign for the press claiming "the Indians have never sustained so severe a defeat since their acquaintance with White people." The lie would have twenty-nine years to mature and enlarge before winning William Harrison the Presidency of the United States.

"Returning again to Tippecanoe, Tecumseh found all the winter provisions burned by Harrison's attack. The warrior went to Fort Wayne, where Harrison was trying to honey tongue a large gathering of Natives into moving against Britain in the impending conflict. Tecumseh picked up the peace pipe offered by the Governor and addressed the braves. "Here is a chance as will never come again - for Indians of North America to form ourselves into one great combination and cast our lot with the British!" Tecumseh broke the peace pipe and marched to British Fort Malden with Kickapoos, Potowamis, Delawares and his own Shawnees.

"Not waiting for provocation, the United States invaded to Canada under the leadership of General William Hull. Tecumseh cut the American's supply lines.

The Americans retreated to Fort Detroit on the River Raisin, where they promptly found themselves under siege. Tecumseh approached the British commander, Major General Isaac Brock, with a plan. They allowed the capture of a British soldier, who, under interrogation, broke down and told them that no less than five thousand Chippewa braves were arriving to storm the fort and eat the livers of the Americans. Five thousand savages! Then Tecumseh took his several hundred braves to a little clearing which was visible from the fort. He marched them single file in a big circle through the woods that came out in clearing. All day the lonely Americans watched this huge Indian army arriving to eat their livers. They argued how to best preserve their organs. That evening, the white flag flew over the fort, Hull surrendered to Tecumseh and the American fort fell without a shot fired. The American prisoners were treated as guests by the victors.

"The treatment of prisoners was always an issue with Tecumseh. When his friend and ally Brock was killed in action, the British sent Colonel Henry Proctor as replacement. Proctor had allowed the torture and slaughter of eight hundred and fifty Kentuckians that had fought at River Raisin. Henry, the Governor's brother, marched with eleven hundred more Kentuckians to avenge the massacre and built a fort near Fallen Timbers where Tecumseh had been defeated eighteen years earlier. One hundred and fifty Kentuckians were captured by Tecumseh, and turned over to Colonel Proctor. Natives under Proctor's command began murdering these Kentuckians as well, and Tecumseh galloped to the British camp. As one Native was eviscerating a prisoner he was clubbed down by Tecumseh. Another Native that was scalping a dead prisoner. He was picked up by the throat by an enraged Tecumseh who roared, "Are there no men here!" He confronted Proctor and stormed, "I conquer to save, and you to murder!" The romance between the English and Natives was over. Proctor pulled out and the siege at Fallen Timber was broken. Commodore Oliver Perry took back Fort Detroit by navy assault. Proctor's supply lines were cut. Proctor retreated. Tecumseh begged for the English weapons to continue resistance. Proctor promised to withdraw only as far as the River Thames. The Natives covered the rear of the English retreat to this point, where Tecumseh demanded Proctor dig in and fight. They formed a skirmish line with the Natives in the swamp and the British on the highway, so they could have an unobstructed retreat. Tecumseh addressed the Natives. "Brother warriors, we are about to enter an engagement from which I will not return. My body will remain in the field of battle. Our lives are in the hands of the Great Spirit. He gave our ancestors the lands which we possess. If it is His Will, our bones will whiten on them...but we will never give up our land." Tecumseh went along the skirmish line shaking hands with each man, smiling and holding up his clenched fist.

"The spearhead of the attacking American was a column of thirty five hundred war frenzied Kentuckians screaming "Remember River Raisin!" Proctor fled in a carriage at the sight of them. The British surrendered at the first shot. The Natives fought all day receiving heavy casualties. Tecumseh was seen throughout the day fighting in increasing stages of dismemberment. He was, in my opinion, the greatest warrior of all history." Clarence finished talking and drank from his glass of water.

About the Author...

Chiggers Stokes was born in Rio de Janeiro on March 21, 1950, the first day of fall in the southern hemisphere. A contrarious thread connects the events of his life and imbues his writing. Raised in the woods of Langley, Virginia, the construction of the CIA and the National Park Service's George Washington Memorial Parkway, were the first obstacles in the author's childhood explorations of the natural world. During the course of the author's formative years, suburban sprawl would digest the undeveloped fields and forests which typified the Potomac Valley in the '50's and early '60's.

The author was influenced by the Society of Friends, marching with Dr. Martin Luther King in August of 1963, being eyewitness to the civil rights leader's speech, "I have a dream..." Later, in the 60's the author read the names of Viet Nam war dead in front of the U.S. Capitol building and participated in "pray ins" in front of the White House.

In the later '60's, the author studied journalism at the University of Miami, Florida and New York University, Washington Square campus. He reported on large and sometimes violent demonstrations through college radio stations and politically oriented newspaper. In April of 1970, the Ohio National Guard opened fire on students of Kent State, killing four. Universities across the United States closed down for the political climate to settle, and so ended the author's formal education.

Chiggers Stokes was hired by the National Park Service as a Resource Educator and worked at the Chesapeake and Ohio National Historic Park for several years before becoming a River Safety Technician on the Potomac River. He transferred to Olympic National Park in 1977 where he worked as a protection ranger until retiring on April 1, 2000.

Since 1978, the author has lived on a portion of the "Flying S " homestead, settled by German immigrant, Otto Siegfried, before the turn of the twentieth century. In 1982, he electrified the property by a micro-hydroelectric scheme on Hemp Hill Creek and writes by the lights and power from this alternative energy project.

Nineteen Hundred and Ninety-Two is the author's first novel, which was written in 1991. Between Forks and Alpha Centauri is his second novel, written in 1997.

Ordering your books...

Books from Flying S. Press make unforgettable gifts. Seasonally, they are great turkey* and stocking+ stuffers!

*At about 300 pages each, Nineteen Hundred and Ninety –Two or Between Forks and Alpha Centauri can absorb a lot of fat. Though the author has been a vegetarian for forty years, he has seen countless turkeys in the meat section of Forks Outfitters and has received several hours of ornithology training as a Resource Educator for the National Park Service. "Your modern turkey is an eating/defecating machine," remarks the author. "A huge hole is made when the digestive system is removed in preparation of you eating the thing. Stuffing your bird with copies of my books offers a low cal alternative to bread. For particularly large or juicy fowl, you may want to order several copies of each title. And, a tip: If you're planning on reading the book after the turkey is done, you may want to keep it in the refrigerator."

+ Flying S books make great stocking stuffers! Says Chiggers Stokes, the author and sole proprietor of Flying S. Press, "If your foot is less than a size 6 and your shoe is over a size 10, you may want to order a couple of copies for each foot. Unequal foot sizes? No prob! Put 19&92 in the shoe with the smaller foot and Between Forks in with the fatter foot.

"You'll want several copies of each book in your earthquake preparedness kit," remarks the CEO of Flying S Press. "They have wonderful insulation value and are very effective, when ignited by a match, in giving you fire. Plus, either title is (by weight) **four thousand times** less expensive than any prescription sleep remedy." Fill out the form below, tear it out and mail it to:

Flying S Press
2674 Dowans Creek Road
Forks, WA 98331
Chiggers@olypen.com
Fax: 360-374-9251

Order your copies today!

I want to support the arts. But instead I'm buying _____ (total number of ...) books from Flying S Press at $12.95 a piece. I include a check or money order for _____ # of books x $14.95 ($2 for shipping and handling)
 WA residents add $1.00 sales tax.
+ Add $0.50 if you don't want your copies signed by author.

Please send _____ (number of copies of Nineteen Hundred and Ninety-Two)
Please send _____ (number of copies of Between Forks and Alpha Centauri)

Send my books to: _____
_____

Phone number or email: _____

Don't forget to order a copy to replace the book you just ruined filling out this form !